To René'marc,

Hidden Wishes

Books 1 - 3

May all your wishes come true.

by

Tao Wong

TWong '24

Copyright

This is a work of fiction. Names, characters, businesses, places, events and incidents are either the products of the author's imagination or used in a fictitious manner. Any resemblance to actual persons, living or dead, or actual events is purely coincidental.

This book is licensed for your personal enjoyment only. This book may not be re-sold or given away to other people. If you would like to share this book with another person, please purchase an additional copy for each recipient. If you're reading this book and did not purchase it, or it was not purchased for your use only, then please return to your favorite book retailer and purchase your own copy. Thank you for respecting the hard work of this author.

Hidden Wishes Books 1-3.

Copyright © 2020 Tao Wong. All rights reserved.

Copyright © 2020 Sarah Anderson Cover Designer

A Starlit Publishing Book

Published by Tao Wong

69 Teslin Rd

Whitehorse, YT

Y1A 3M5

Canada

www.starlitpublishing.com

Ebook ISBN: 9781989458433

Paperback ISBN: 9781989458624

Hardcover ISBN: 9781989458839

Books in the Hidden Wishes series

A Gamer's Wish

A Squire's Wish

A Jinn's Wish

Contents

Book 1: A Gamer's Wish 9

    Chapter 1 11

    Chapter 2 23

    Chapter 3 37

    Chapter 4 49

    Chapter 5 57

    Chapter 6 65

    Chapter 7 79

    Chapter 8 85

    Chapter 9 93

    Chapter 10 113

    Chapter 11 125

    Chapter 12 137

    Chapter 13 153

    Chapter 14 167

    Chapter 15 187

    Chapter 16 199

    Chapter 17 207

    Chapter 18 217

    Chapter 19 227

Book 2: A Squire's Wish ... 233

Chapter 1 ... 235
Chapter 2 ... 243
Chapter 3 ... 249
Chapter 4 ... 261
Chapter 5 ... 273
Chapter 6 ... 287
Chapter 7 ... 295
Chapter 8 ... 307
Chapter 9 ... 315
Chapter 10 ... 331
Chapter 11 ... 343
Chapter 12 ... 361
Chapter 13 ... 371
Chapter 14 ... 387
Chapter 15 ... 403
Chapter 16 ... 415
Chapter 17 ... 421
Chapter 18 ... 429
Chapter 19 ... 447
Epilogue ... 453

- Book 3: A Jinn's Wish 455
  - Chapter 1 457
  - Chapter 2 467
  - Chapter 3 481
  - Chapter 4 493
  - Chapter 5 499
  - Chapter 6 505
  - Chapter 7 515
  - Chapter 8 527
  - Chapter 9 541
  - Chapter 10 555
  - Chapter 11 563
  - Chapter 12 579
  - Chapter 13 587
  - Chapter 14 595
  - Chapter 15 605
  - Chapter 16 615
  - Chapter 17 625
  - Chapter 18 637
  - Chapter 19 653
  - Epilogue 659

Author's Note 663

About the Author 665

About the Publisher 666

Book 1

A Gamer's Wish

Chapter 1

Simple curiosity. That was all it took to change my world.

My life changed with a black briefcase one spring evening. It had a 1960s design, a perfect rectangle made of black leather with a number-combination lock, still in pristine condition. It was the fifth and last piece of luggage I had purchased earlier that day at the lost luggage auction—and the most expensive piece. Unless I was really lucky, I might make enough for a week's groceries from all this. At some point, I knew that I had to find a new job, but lucky for me, retail jobs were a dime a dozen right now. If you were willing to take late-night shifts at least. Still, that was a concern for future me.

Luggage like this always left me wondering about its story. The smell of the leather, the faintest hint as I held it to my nose, told me it was probably genuine. Maybe it was a hipster throwback, a handmade piece for people with more money than sense, but something told me it was the real deal. A genuine 1960s briefcase. That raised a number of questions: Was it an old purchase, set aside and never used till recently? Perhaps given to a new graduate, a present to commemorate their graduation? Did someone buy it at a thrift store, a discarded piece of luggage that wasn't wanted or needed till it was unceremoniously lost and abandoned again? That was, after all, how it had come into my possession. The airport auctioned off uncollected lost luggage every sixty days after it entered the system.

I sat silently for a time as I ran my hands along the briefcase and made up stories about its former owner, the briefcase, and what I might find within. Small stories, daydreams of the kinds of things I'd find inside—a laptop, a journal, maybe a calculator for an accountant. Business cards, of course. It was a briefcase. I took my time because this was half the fun of buying lost luggage—the stories I got to make up before the inevitable disappointment of reality. And while I thought, I ran my fingers along the numerical lock and attempted to open the case.

Click.

Four-six-seven. I idly noted the number that worked before I continued my attempts on the opposite side. It took another two minutes, an impatient two minutes as I found myself suddenly anxious to see what I had bought. When the click came, I held my breath for a second before I finally opened the briefcase to see my prize.

A leather journal, a single, expensive-looking fountain pen, and a capped bottle of ink snuggly fit into an inkwell dominated one side of the briefcase. On the other side, a series of nine small boxes with carved runes on top of them sat in what had to be a custom-made enclosure. I frowned as I traced the runes, never having seen anything like them before. Not that I was any expert, mind you, but they sure were pretty. On the underside of the top of the briefcase was a simple, silver-lined mirror that reflected my image to me.

Wavy brown hair that was about two weeks overdue for a haircut, slanted brown eyes that I had been told were my best feature and thin lips reflected back at me. I rubbed my chin, realizing I had forgotten to shave again and grown a sparse, stubbly goatee. It was a bad habit, but shaving was never a priority when you only had to do it every few weeks. Just another gift of being ethnically southern Chinese. At twenty-eight, I was glad I'd finally gotten out of the "baby face" period of my life, even if I was still occasionally mocked for looking like I was in my early twenties. That was okay, considering some of those same mockers were already losing their hair.

Initial perusal over, I began the process of stripping the briefcase. I started with the book first and found, to my surprise, it was empty. Nothing was on the front page or any of the succeeding pages. It had very nice binding though and high-quality leather. I'd probably make a few dollars selling it online. The fountain pen was an old dip-and-write type, might have been worth something to a collector. I capped the pen and put it away carefully. The ink I pulled out and set aside with the rest of the junk. No money in reselling used ink.

Lastly, I started opening the boxes. And that's when things started getting weird. The first box held scales; the second, a series of dead beetles; the third, feathers from a single type of bird; and the fourth, old, dark earth. After the second box, I grabbed the garbage and started tossing contents into it immediately. Perhaps this had been owned by a taxidermist? Or a naturalist?

"Oww!" I howled and shook my hand. When I had touched the fifth box, what must have been the accumulated static charge of living in a basement apartment had shocked me. It had never been that bad before, but I made a mental note to get a humidifier… when I had the money.

Gingerly, I touched the box and, finding the charge gone, I opened it, ready to toss its contents away. Instead, I found a simple signet ring made of a dark metal. Or alloy of metals. I frowned as I plucked the ring out and rubbed at it to clean it up, curious to see what it was made of.

As I said, curiosity changed my life.

***

"Are you done yet?" the blond woman, who had formed in my apartment from smoke, asked me. Clad in a pink bra, tiny vest, and billowy sheer pants, she reminded me of an actress from an old, cheesy TV show, almost uncannily so. Seriously, the blond genie that stood in front of me with her sardonic smile would have sent copyright lawyers salivating at the fees they'd earn. If they could have seen her. And if she hadn't wished them away.

"You… you're a genie! But that was a ring, not a lamp!" I spluttered, the ring that the smoke had streamed from still clutched in my hand in a death grip.

"Jinn! And yes, I am. What may I do for you, Master?" the genie said. Turning her head, she looked around my bachelor suite with a flicker of distaste. "Maybe a bigger residence?"

"You're a genie…" I stared at the blonde, my mind caught in a circular trap as it struggled with the insanity in front of it. After all, genies didn't exist. But there, in front of me, was a genie.

"Oh, hell. I really can't wait for this entire 'enlightenment' period to be over," the genie said with a roll of her eyes after I just continued to stare at her blankly. She turned away from me and walked around the room before she stopped at my micro-kitchen to open the fridge. Bent over, she fished inside before extracting day-old fried rice and popping a bite into her mouth. A conjured spoon later, she was digging into last night's dinner and prodding my stove, flat-screen TV, and laptop. "What is this?"

"Fried rice."

"I know what fried rice is. And this isn't bad," she complimented me, ignoring my mumbled thanks while she pointed at the TV screen and then laptop. "This. And this."

"TV and laptop."

"Huh." She returned to the TV before she prodded at it a few more times and inevitably adjusted its angle. "That's amazing. I guess your science actually does have some use. Well, outside of indoor plumbing. That isn't as good."

My brain finally stopped going in circles after I decided to stop trying to actually understand what was going on. If I had a genie in my house, I had a genie. "So, your name isn't Jeannie, is it?"

"Do I look like a Jeannie to you?"

"Well…"

"The Seven Seals!" The genie flickered, and the previously blonde creature transformed into a black-haired, hawk-nosed Middle-Eastern woman…with

14

considerably less clothing than before, which should have been a challenge. "Call me Lily. What's yours?"

"Uhh…"

"Aaargh!" Lily stared at her clothing and then stared at me for a moment. A second later, she was clad in a T-shirt that said "I Aim to Misbehave" and a pair of jeans. I would admit I found the new clothing options even more distracting, especially since they were an exact replica of what I was wearing.

"I'm Henry. And what was that about?"

"Nothing. Nothing at all," Lily snapped at me and waved her spoon at my laptop. "What is a 'laptop'?"

"A portable computer," I explained.

"No, I've seen a computer before. They take up rooms three times the size of your… residence," Lily said, prodding my laptop.

"Computers haven't been that big since the fifties. Okay, maybe sixties. And I guess there are supercomputers that are that big these days," I blathered on. "But most people don't really need a supercomputer. I mean, all I do with mine is play some games and get on the Internet."

"Internet?" Lily raised her spoon. "Wait. Stop. Two things: what year is this, and do you have more food?"

"Twenty eighteen, and there's some pizza in the freezer," I said. "What year did you think this was?"

"That explains why the enchantments have faded," Lily said as she finished raiding my fridge. She stared at the pizza and then looked at me imploringly. I sighed and helped her add it to the microwave, which I then had to explain to her. That certainly dated her further, putting her at least into the 1960s, which was around the same time as the briefcase. Once the pizza was ready and the genie was eating, I got back to the important questions.

"What enchantments?"

"All of them, of course. They really should have closed off the runes between the concealment and defensive enchantments. If they'd asked me, I could have told them. But of course, they never do," Lily said, shaking her head. "Once the enchantment wasn't being regularly recharged, the concealment rune started draining the rest. Took it about fifty years or so, at a guess. Good thing for you they were sloppy; otherwise, you'd be dead."

"Dead?"

"Oh, yes. Heart attack when you failed the third time on opening the briefcase," Lily said. "Always a good defensive spell—few creatures can survive without a heart. Well, except the undead, but they wouldn't be able to even touch the briefcase with the wards against them."

"I could have died," I said weakly as I stumbled to my bed and sat down with a thud.

"Blazing suns." Lily sat down across from me. "You humans are always so damn sensitive about your mortality."

I sat there in silence and stared at the far wall, my brain refusing to work any further at this new revelation. Genies. Magic. My death. There is a certain point in an individual's day when one just can't go on, and I'd hit that point. Without speaking, I flopped onto my bed, grabbed my comforter, and rolled into a ball.

***

When I woke hours later, the sun had set, and my basement apartment was shrouded in darkness. I exhaled in relief, grateful but slightly disappointed that the blond/brunette genie had been but a weird dream. Paper rustled, and I twisted my head to the side to spot a pair of glowing red eyes bent over a book.

"Well, that was a very manly scream," Lily said, hiding a smirk.

"You... what are you doing?" I gulped, clutching my comforter to my body after I finally managed to turn on my bedside light. The additional illumination drove the fire from her eyes, making them look human again. I recalled the flames that lit her face from within, doubting I'd ever forget them. Not demonic though... at least, they didn't feel demonic. Just otherworldly.

"Hmmm? Reading. You have quite a selection here." Lily nodded to the bookcases that lined the walls of my apartment. I will admit books are one of my indulgences. The books are wide ranging, covering everything from history to fiction. Really, I just grabbed whatever seemed interesting when I hit a garage sale.

"It wasn't a dream," I muttered to myself and put my head between my knees.

"Yes, yes. Are you going to have a breakdown again, or are we finally getting to the part where you make a wish?" Lily said, bored. "If you want to wait, I've still got two books in this series to finish."

"Don't bother. The author's still not done book six after six years. So magic really is real?" I said, my voice muffled by the comforter. "And you're a genie. Like, 'rub the lamp and get three wishes' kind of genie."

"Yes, and I'm a jinn, not a genie, and sort of," Lily said absently as she continued to read.

"Sort of?" I latched on to the wishy-washy word.

"I'm not actually bound to fulfill all three wishes since what I can do is limited by the ring and my powers," Lily said and then, when I said nothing, looked up and explained further. "If you wished for the sun to go out, I wouldn't be able to do it, and you'd have wasted my power in trying. And annoyed like a hundred gods at the same time. I am also bound to the ring, not a lamp, unlike what Antoinne might have written."

"Antoinne?" I shook my head. No. I was not going to get distracted. It was hard enough keeping my head on straight. "Magic is real." I could not keep the wonder from my voice as I said that. In a world of mediocrity and the mundane, magic was real.

"Always has been."

"But how did I not know of it?"

"Your world of science and rational thought blinded you to the arcane. What cannot be explained was relegated to hidden corners of the world, and rare as the gift is, it is no wonder humanity forgot. Magic is still practiced in back alleys and small towns. The supernatural world still exists, but it is more than happy to be forgotten. After all, humanity has never been kind to what it considers others."

"You've given that speech before," I said, and Lily nodded. "All right then, so magic is real, and you're a ge—" At her pointed stare, I corrected myself. "Jinn, and I have three wishes. Is there anything I shouldn't wish for?"

"Life. Death. The fate of countries. Time travel. I can alter the minds and physical reactions of others but not their souls; I cannot make someone love you or stop hating you, just lust for you or perhaps temper their physical reactions to your presence," Lily answered promptly. As I nodded along, she opened her mouth and then shut it.

"You were going to say something."

"I was."

"What was it?"

"It doesn't matter."

"Why not?" I leaned forward in my chair. I wished the light shone better on her face. At least then I would have a better view of it. There was something in her voice.

Lily stayed silent for a time, obviously fighting something internally. In the end, her lips twisted wryly, and she waved a hand in front of my bookcases, causing them to glow slightly. "Because you won't listen."

"That's a bit insulting. You don't know me," I said, and she laughed, her laughter brittle and high.

"I know you. I've known a hundred thousand like you. My masters never listen," Lily said with a smile. "So tell me your wish."

I almost snapped back that I wished she would tell me what she was going to say. Almost. But annoyed or not, I was not going to waste my chance at real magic, at a real chance to change my world. "You don't know me, and I don't know you. So why don't you tell me, and maybe, maybe we'll come to know one another."

Lily stared at me for a long time, her eyes glowing red before she finally spoke, her voice weary. "I am bound by the ring to fulfill your wishes, but I am not omniscient. I can only change what I understand, and I am not responsible for the consequences of any changes. Not that it'll stop you from blaming me."

I stared at Lily for a time, then slowly nodded. "You're saying if I made a wish, you'd be forced to make it happen even if it was a silly wish. Like, if I wished for a million dollars right this second, you'd be forced to make it appear right in this room. Maybe as bills, maybe as dollar coins, which probably would suck."

"I am not malicious, no matter what you people might say," Lily said. "But most wishes for wealth are not well thought out. I once gave a goatherder a mountain of gold, and he and his family were killed for it. A hundred years ago, a gentleman asked for a million pounds. Of course, I had never seen the kind of notes they used, so I made the bank notes for him, a million dollars' worth, all exactly the same. He was unhappy about that."

I slowly nodded, staring at her. "You're not all-powerful and all-knowing, just powerful. Like a giant hammer wielded by toddlers."

"Yes!" Lily said, excited for a second.

I grunted, closing my eyes. The worse part was that I was the damn toddler. But still… magic was real.

I had not realized I had spoken that thought aloud till that whisper echoed through the basement. Into the silence, she slowly spoke. "Do you desire magic then?"

"With every fiber of my being," I answered honestly. "But I can see a million, billion ways it could go wrong. Wish for magic, and I might get the ability without the knowledge to wield it. Wish for knowledge and ability, and you'd stick it all in my head and maybe make me go crazy while doing it. Wish for a mentor, and, well, it might be a black mage who comes in."

"You did listen." Lily's lips twisted into a wry smile. "Though, again, not directly malicious. If you wished for the knowledge to wield magic, and that alone, I'd probably only insert enough that you would not be driven mad."

"You can do that?" I blinked, having rattled off my words without thought. I hadn't actually expected her to know how to inject information into my head.

"Of course. I'm a jinn who has been in the service of some of the greatest mages this world has ever known. I am no dotard myself," Lily boasted. "Adding knowledge direct would be no different than creating a magical book of learning. In fact, it would be simpler without the preservation and containment spells."

"Huh," I said, rubbing my chin and staring at the girl. "So, it's not the amount of knowledge but the speed."

"Close enough," she said, and I grunted.

"I guess I'd have to level up first."

"Level up?" Lily asked, and I waved my hand toward my bookshelf where my RPG books were neatly stacked from D&D's first editions to more recent RPGs, indie and mainstream publishers. "One second." She muttered that word and then shimmered for a brief moment, a second at most, and suddenly all the books were stacked neatly around her. "How interesting. Entire universes written and governed by rules and dice."

"Did you just read all of them with super speed?" I asked.

"Not super speed. That's always more trouble than its worth. You have to deal with friction and air resistance and heat. I prefer to slow time," Lily said nonchalantly. "I do see what you mean. These 'levels' characters have limit their growth, giving them knowledge and strength as they pass each milestone."

"You're saying it's possible? For me to wield magic if we put it in a game system?" I said excitedly, fallen hopes rising again like a rocket at her words.

"Of course. Who do you think you're talking to?" Lily asked.

"Perfect!" I paused, frowning as I worked out the implications. Perhaps I had found a way to cheat the system. "All right. One last question - how do I know everything you've said is true?"

At those words, even in the dim light, I saw Lily's face twist with quickly concealed hurt. She looked away for a second and then back at me. "Well, that's the rub, isn't it? You can't."

That was the rub. It wasn't as if I could look this up on Snopes or jump on Quora, seeking expert advice. The stories I did know of, they conflicted. The original stories of jinn said they were like us, neither good nor evil, creatures of free will like humanity itself. Since then, they'd been both friend and foe in a myriad of stories. Of course, it wasn't as if I knew how to tell which were true or fake.

In the end, it came down to trust. Could I, should I, trust Lily? Did it matter though? By her own admission, anything I wished for needed her interpretation. Of course that too could have been a lie. But for a chance at magic, however slim it might be, I would take it.

With that thought, I smiled and leaned forward. "All right, so here's what I was thinking."

Chapter 2

-Hours later and—at Lily's insistence—a bunch of Thai takeout later, we'd gone back and forth on the game system we might implement. Crouched over pad thai, red curry, and pineapple fried rice, I argued with a raven-haired jinn about the merits of game systems.

"We should skip character creation entirely," Lily said, waving a pair of chopsticks at me with an egg roll still held in them. "You don't want to go through the most equitable way of doing so—"

"I'm not letting you roll for my attributes. I am not going to risk getting a three on intelligence," I interrupted.

Lily continued without pausing at my interruption. "We should just avoid it altogether. Unintended consequences, remember?"

"But a base ten stat option and a number of points with the ability to increase and decrease the attributes would give me more ability to customize myself," I argued back.

"Yes, yes. Not only do we risk angering the gods if we do it that way, there's the actual work involved. I still have to physically alter you to make it happen. If you doubled your existing strength, I'd have to balance various muscles, tendons, and ligaments to make sure you don't tear yourself apart the moment you move. And strength's the easiest. I mean, constitution? What is that? Your immune system?" Lily asked. "And don't even get me started on wisdom."

"You've said. And of course, willpower is the soul, which you can't touch," I muttered. "So I guess no altering attributes when I level up either? Fine. We'll skip character creation and direct changes to my body, just pure knowledge."

"Well, one change - I've got to open your magical pathways," Lily corrected, a finger held up.

"Ah. Right…" I frowned, eyebrows drawn together as I stared at her. "How complicated is that?"

Lily held her hand up horizontal and waggled it sideways, then snagged the last piece of chicken from the curry. Seeing my flat stare, she said, "It depends on how innately gifted you are. The more gifted, the harder it's going to be."

"Isn't it the other way around?" I frowned, and she shook her head.

"No. Because if you're already gifted, you should be using magic already. If you aren't, you've simply got a blockage that I'll need to remove," Lily explained.

"That's going to hurt, isn't it?"

"Yup!" Lily said, way too cheerfully, as she poured curry on her rice. "We should order more."

"What is it with you and food? Can't you just conjure it?" I asked.

"Conjured food never tastes right. There's always something missing. Now, I saw a menu for Greek?"

For an all-powerful jinn who was about to change my world, she certainly seemed to be costing me more than she earned. As I walked toward the fridge to grab the takeout menu, I pulled out my wallet and stared at the last few dollars I had. Well, it would be worth it.

"This is a computer game?" Lily asked, poking at my screen.

I smacked her finger away, growling. "Stop that. You're going to leave prints."

"One, owww!" Lily waved her hand. "Two, I don't leave prints. This body isn't exactly corporeal like yours."

"Still. Don't touch the screen. And yes, this is a computer version of the games we've been talking about. This is a single-player game where you control a party. It's a bit dated these days, but it's quite fun," I explained. "This is my saved game, which lets me start from where I left off. Character creation is done, and this is my inventory…"

***

"No skills?"

"Too complicated. I'd have to either give you all or nothing. What would we use as a basis? All these systems are too broad; unless you want to end up forgetting how to swim simply because your athletics are zero. I mean, who designs these things? Swimming, gymnastics, hurdling, and sprinting all under the same skill?" Lily clicked around my computer screen.

"Can't you just give me a low rating for a bunch of skills I should know?"

"No. You can't handle it." Lily waved her hands, fluttering her fingers apart. "A point in, say, science might do that. Or we could get granular and then realize we forgot some important skill like typing. You wouldn't be able to use this computer of yours because you'll automatically fail every attempt."

"Ugh… okay."

***

"Perks?"

"My ring might consider that cheating." Lily rubbed her chin. "I could do weaknesses."

"Hard no."

Lily giggled at my reaction, flipping to the next page in the book while she stabbed a portion of tiramisu. "Equipment's out, same as perks."

"Well, shit." I rubbed my temples, staring into space. "Way I see this, all I'm getting is the ability to use magic at a gradated level."

"All?"

"Fine, fine. It's a lot," I said, waving my hands at her. I knew it was a lot. It was more than I'd had a day ago. And yet, I felt cheated. My eyes burned, and my heart ached, exhaustion finally kicking my doors down.

"Damn right it's a lot. If we do this right, you might be the first archmagi I've ever been able to create with my wishes," Lily said. "You need to rest."

"Yeah… yeah." I glanced at the single bed in the apartment. "Do you… I mean, well…"

"I'll rest in my ring if I need to," Lily said, waving me to bed.

I nodded numbly, lying back down. As I drifted off to sleep, I wondered if leaving an unbound magical being—that some might consider evil—to run around unchecked and alone was a good idea. As I rolled onto my side, I stared blearily at the raven-haired jinn who was idly chewing on a strand of hair, brows furrowed in concentration as she clicked away on her mouse, killing cows and picking up loot.

***

Light streamed in from the single basement window when I slowly woke up. The continuous *click, click, click* of a mouse, the occasional stab of a keyboard key, and a repetitive fantasy soundtrack punctuated the silence, making me think I was back in my college dorm with Wynn. That man had been obsessed with his 4X games. I rolled over to tell him to lower the damn volume, and I spotted discarded food containers, a pair of unwashed glasses with the last of my orange juice in them, and a stack of books. However, instead of an overweight gamer with bad hygiene, I saw a toned and very feminine body hunched over my laptop with a face that could have graced a celebrity magazine.

"Have you been up all night?" I muttered as I swung my feet over the edge of the bed. Daylight hit my eyes, and I automatically twitched my head to the side—hiding in the shadows—and corrected myself. "Day."

"Yes. I'm level forty-seven now. Just took the portal back to town. My inventory's full—"

"You know, you were supposed to be doing research."

"This is research. And you need a bath," Lily said, sniffing.

"Me? You—" Well, if she didn't leave fingerprints, who said she sweated or had any of the other grody side effects of having a physical body? Surreptitiously, I sniffed myself and wrinkled my nose. Well, she had a point.

A quick shower later, I was standing over my coffee pot as I contemplated the remnants of my kitchen. What should have lasted me a week had been consumed overnight, leaving me with two slices of bread and the jam to go with it. As I made my meager breakfast, I said, "Did you learn anything?"

"A lot. I like these computer games better than your tabletop ones. No skills, character creation is simplified, no need to create backstory or hooks for your GM... experience is received from quests that are clearly defined, and development of abilities is clear," Lily said, never looking up. "I think we can work with this. I can even give you all these bars, but they'd be estimations. So, something like health wouldn't be reality. You could still die from smacking your head too hard."

"Really? Do you think we're ready?" I sat next to her and placed my sandwich on the table beside me. Without even looking away from the computer, she snagged half of my sandwich.

"Sure. Sure... hey, how do you pass into the level forty-seven boss chamber?"

"Ah..." I squinted, staring at the game and racking my brain. "Eh... check the Internet for a guide."

"Guide," Lily said, slowly and carefully.

I reached over and paused her game, then tabbed over to a browser. In a few seconds, I had a guide open. Before I could even scroll down, the laptop was snatched back, and Lily perused the level.

"Ooh… I missed this portion entirely."

I coughed into my hand, dragging her attention back to me. "My wish?"

"Sure, sure. No character creation, no skills, magic and knowledge that's gradated by levels, and level-appropriate quests so you don't die fighting a dragon on your first day," Lily said distractedly as she chewed on her hair. "I wonder what I missed earlier…"

Oh, hell. She was a completist. I rubbed my eyes. "And the ability to add patches if we realize we missed something."

"Patches. Right. Right. Sure. That your wish?"

"Yes, I just—"

"Great!" Her hand raised and waved at me before I could finish my sentence… and then pain.

My nerves felt like molten fire had been poured along them, my entire body gone rigid as muscles locked. I tasted blood after I accidentally bit my tongue, its copper taste and blueberry jam mixing in my mouth. A moment later, an ice pick slammed into my brain, and the world shimmered and distorted in my vision. Light shifted and broke apart, and through my screams, I heard a bell chiming before a new wave of pain hit me. My existence became the pain, the twisting in my bones and nerves before I finally fell and passed out.

***

When I woke up, I found the raven-haired jinn leaning over me. She was dabbing at my face with a wet cloth that was speckled with blood. My head felt like someone had decided to use it as a punching bag, but at least the pain in my body had fallen away to a dull but constant thrum, reminiscent of a deep muscular ache. As my eyes opened, Lily offered me a pair of pills, which I gratefully took and washed down with the cup of water she proffered.

It was only after I had swallowed them that I thought to check. "What was that?"

"Pain killers. It says take one, but I figured you'd need two," Lily said, offering me a chance to look at the bottle of naproxen. I sighed in relief, grateful for clear pharmaceutical labeling. After all, I did not want her to be grabbing my Imodium instead. "How are you doing?"

"Hurts," I said, being careful to move ever so slowly as I peered at her. "What was all that about?"

"I made your wish come true," Lily said, looking ever-so-slightly guilty.

"But I—" I felt a rush of anger push aside part of my pain. "I wasn't ready…"

"Yeah, sorry about that," Lily said.

"Sorry?! You could have killed me. And we haven't even discussed experience and leveling and quests and—"

"I know. I know!" Lily shouted, the loud noise making me wince. She stood up and threw her hands up toward the sky. She blushed with guilt before she calmed and squatted beside me. "I'm sorry. I… got distracted."

"Distracted? You got obsessed," I growled, and she nodded. I slumped backward with my eyes closed and forced myself to draw another deep breath. "Tell me about what you did."

"What we said we were going to do. I opened your arcane pathways and inserted the basics of magic into your mind. I have my own spells that will record your progress, and when you're ready, I'll level you up, and you'll get your next dose of knowledge."

"About that."

"What?"

"Leveling up. How do I get experience?" I frowned as I slowly sat up. "I mean, I don't want to go out killing things if I don't have to, and—"

"Leveling is just an abstraction of your growth and development as a mage. You gain experience by practicing your magic or studying. Though…" At my pointed stare, Lily continued. "High-stress situations are extremely strong methods of acquiring knowledge. It's not just about sitting in your tower all day, reading books. The way we've set it up, you'd likely learn more this way too."

I grunted. "So, questing."

"Definitely," Lily said. "Don't worry though. I'll make sure they're level appropriate."

"There's a lot of you in this conversation," I said suspiciously, and Lily flashed me an innocent smile, even going so far as to flutter her eyelashes at me. "Lily…"

"Well, someone has to be your class trainer and GM," Lily said.

I stared at the raven-haired beauty for a time as a thought worked its way through my throbbing head. "What normally happens when a wish is granted? Or all three wishes?"

"Well… ummm…" Lily looked aside and then sighed. "Fine. I normally get banished into the ring whenever I'm not needed."

"But being my GM, you're always going to be needed," I said, completing the thought that had wormed its way in. "So even if I make my other two wishes, you'll still be free."

"Not free. Just out of the ring," Lily said seriously, pointing to the ring I had slipped onto the middle finger of my left hand. "I'm still bound to not use my powers in any meaningful way."

I mulled the thought over for some time, Lily's admission and the way she'd managed to get something out of this. I would have felt betrayed, but if I'd been trapped in a ring for fifty years, maybe I would have been as manipulative. In the end, it came down to trust… and the fact that she only stayed out for as long as I was alive.

"Henry?" Lily said, and I looked up to see her sitting nervously, waiting for me to speak. I frowned at that, at why an indescribably ancient being with the power to change reality was nervous. What could she have experienced in that time to create that level of fear?

"It's fine," I said finally. In either case, I had better things to focus on. "I can do magic now, right? How?"

"Just think about it," Lily said unhelpfully.

Instead of chiding her, I fell silent and focused. At first, my thoughts were distracted and jumbled as I thought about thinking about magic, but eventually, they settled down. It was at that point I realized I didn't need to think about it as an abstract concept; it was more like moving a muscle I hadn't used in a while. All I had to do was want to use it.

"Light!" I muttered to myself and found my hand shifting, making the arcane signs needed.

Light Ball Cast
42% Synchronicity

The ball of light that flowed out of my palm was weak and cast a pale, fitful yellow light not even as strong as a sixty-watt bulb. On the other hand, it was mine.

"What was that?" I stared at where the words had been in the corner of my vision, gone now.

"The user interface I built in. It'll give you information about your magic and how you're doing," Lily said, smirking.

"And synchronicity?" Even as I asked, the answer was popping into mind.

Still, Lily felt the need to answer me. "As you know, magic can be cast in many ways, just like a painting can be painted with different colors. The one you've learned is older, more direct. At its earliest stages, it requires a mental and physical component—"

"The closer I synchronize both mental and physical actions, the more powerful the spell," I said, finishing for her. "And at later stages, I won't even need the physical actions."

"Correct." Lily smiled at me even as I began to add to the single floating ball. Each time a new ball was conjured, the same message would appear, telling me of my progress. After my initial cast, most sat around the 60 percent region, bouncing higher and lower as I practiced.

When nearly two dozen light balls had appeared, the first one finally flickered and died. As I reached toward the sky to cast the spell again, a blue bar appeared in the top of my vision, already mostly empty. "Is that my mana bar?"

"Close enough," Lily said before she put a hand on my arm. It was the first time we had actually touched, and I found her flesh smooth and surprisingly warm. Warm like a roll of bread freshly drawn from the oven, a comforting heat that traveled down my arm. "You should stop now. Mana, the arcane energy you wield, should never be fully depleted. The arcane powers you, your life force, and soul. Always make sure to leave a little behind."

Even as she finished, I realized my headache and the fire in my nerves had returned. In my excitement and focus, I had not noticed the growing pain. As I sat back onto the bed, Lily walked away and returned with some water for me to drink. I considered the implication of what she said and marveled at my first spell. As my head throbbed, I made a few attempts to bring my character sheet up. Status. Status screen. Character. In the end, I realized that like my magic, I just needed to actually want it with focus.

Class: Mage

Level 1 (4% Experience)

Known Spells: Light Ball, Force Bolt, Warmth, Chill, Chime, Breeze

It was strange, having the system and the knowledge in my mind. On one hand, these spells were hard-coded, distinct artifacts I could conjure with a thought. On the other hand, the knowledge imparted to me actually explained how they were all manifestations of a few alterations of the same formula. Light, Warmth, Chill, Chime, and Breeze were all about the alteration of energy, a conjuring and displacement of physical energy. It was like a punch— you could throw a jab, hook, uppercut, haymaker, and more, but in the end, they were mostly the same muscles used in different ways, broken up into distinct ideas for ease of use.

In time, with more building blocks, I could probably even make my own spells. However, I needed a lot more blocks before I could even think about that. The only real disparity in my spells was Force Bolt, my only offensive spell and also my most advanced. Even thinking about the various parts that made up the spell made my head hurt—figuratively. At a guess, I'd need more practice before I understood it. On the other hand, my rental was not the place to throw around destructive magic.

In time, the silence brought on by my thoughts—punctuated only by the clicking of the laptop after Lily returned to the computer—was broken by my stomach rumbling.

"I wasn't going to say anything, but your kitchen's empty," Lily said from behind the computer screen. "We should order more takeout."

"Har. Not happening." I shook my head and stood, the pain having receded as my mana bar filled. "We blew my budget for the week already. I'm going to have to sell some of the stuff from the auction if we want to eat. Maybe that book—"

"Your spell book? I wouldn't recommend that," Lily said.

I looked at where the book had been discarded, the book no longer mundane but glowing with a faint blue light. I picked it up and noticed the pages were filled with words and diagrams, all written in a tight cursive script that hadn't been there before.

"This... where did this come from?" I muttered.

"It's always been there. You just weren't able to see it with your arcane sight inactive."

"I have arcane sight?"

"Yes. The hidden world will be open to you now. Look at the briefcase."

Faded runes crisscrossed the briefcase, covering every inch of the leather. Strangely enough, I understood some of the runes now—unearned knowledge of individual parts of an alphabet—even if I did not understand the words themselves. I popped the briefcase open and stared at its contents, the wooden boxes that had been neatly replaced, the words that I now knew.

"Were these spell components?" I pointed to the empty boxes, the ones whose contents I had thrown into the garbage.

"Yes. You know, we could sell some of those for good money. The squid eggs themselves would be worth a lot to the right alchemist," Lily said.

"Won't they have dried out?" I frowned and then stopped as knowledge of the runes flowed into my mind. "Preservation runes. But won't I need them?"

"Not at all. Those are for hedge mages. They need the components to jumpstart their spells. The magic you know bypasses that."

"Huh. Cool," I said as I put the book and the rest of the boxes away. Well, I didn't know any alchemists, so selling the spell components was pointless. Instead, I pushed the briefcase aside and proceeded to bundle a bunch of clothing together before I tossed it into a garbage bag. "Okay, time to go."

"Where are we going?" Lily said, suddenly looking excited.

"Nora's. Now, come on."

Chapter 3

I squinted slightly as I walked into the sunlight, my eyes adjusting to the brightness. Midsummer, we had a ton of time before the sun set, but not so much before Nora's was closed. Beside me, Lily looked around with wide eyes as she took in the city. In the distance, skyscrapers reached for space, metal fingers stabbing into the bottom of the blue sky. Cars drove past, sharing space with bicycles and motorcycles, the constant rumble of the city assaulting our ears. As I moved to step forward, Lily grabbed my arm, holding me back as she continued to take in the changed world.

"Sorry. Just a lot to take in," Lily muttered, and I nodded.

The same for me as well. I realized the world had changed a little since I had last come outside. A small apartment building glowed with arcane runes, and farther down the road, gargoyles that were once decorative moved as they looked at us. As a pedestrian strode pass me, my jaw dropped when I realized she was a lizardwoman, scales running along her face and along her wide body. Down the street, a humanoid dog creature scurried down the street followed by its larger, fur-covered handler. "What is all this?"

"The hidden world," Lily said. "Your sight is letting you see what was there before, hidden by glamours and spells."

"How do I turn it off?" I muttered, shaking my head. "I mean, how do I know what they're trying to show me?"

"Let your eyes unfocus a bit, look slightly away from them. Use your peripheral vision," Lily coached, and I focused on the dog creature and his handler. I struggled for a few seconds before I learned the trick, unfocusing my eyes to see the glamour. For a second, I saw what they were showing the world—a child and his father—rather than what they were.

"Huh," I said. I turned to Lily, but the raven-haired jinn looked the same no matter how I squinted, unfocused my eyes, or looked away. I only stopped when I realized that passersby were giving me strange looks and starting to walk wide around us.

"Don't bother. You can't break through my glamor yet, though you'll get better with practice and higher levels," Lily explained.

I turned away from her then to practice further. Lily nudged me, and I turned away from the eight-foot-tall giant I had been staring at and started the thirty-minute walk to Nora's, my bag slung over my shoulder.

***

The walk to Nora's took longer than normal, and I had to switch the bag in my hand a couple of times. Both Lily and I stared about us as we walked, the jinn asking questions about the modern world and I about the hidden. Smartphones, elves, earbuds, and alchemical potions—all were queried and explained. At the end of the walk, I wasn't sure who was more awe-filled.

I stood outside the used consignment shop and noticed a series of runic carvings along the door, glowing with the light blue that I'd come to recognize as an active enchantment, that curled around the simple sign saying "Nora's." I unfocused my eyes for a moment and saw the plain old store I had visited dozens of times. For a moment, I hesitated, but in the end, I stepped in. I needed the money.

"El?" I called as I stepped in, the bell ringing as the door swung open.

"Hey, Henry…" El's voice trailed off as a person looked at me, her eyes wide.

A second later, as Lily stepped into the store and passed the runes, the entire room glowed red. The shop woman's eyes narrowed, focused on the raven-haired jinn.

"Who are you?" I stared at the person who had El's voice. Gone was the friendly five-foot, black-haired, and slightly dumpy shopkeeper, and instead, a slim, flame-red-haired beauty with long, pointed ears stood in her place. As I unfocused my eyes, I realized that this was El, as she truly was. "El…?"

"You became a wizard," El said, her tone disappointed. "Did you use her to do it? Did you make a deal with one of them?"

"What are you?" I said, shaking my head and ignoring her questions.

"Pixie. She's a pixie," Lily said, sauntering to the counter and leaning on it. The jinn let her gaze wander around the shop, eyeing the runic enchantments that lined the walls and the glowing glass cases that were always locked. "And this is not just a used clothing store."

"What do you want, demon?" El's hand came out from under the counter, carrying a wand. Even inexperienced as I was, I could guess it wasn't for turning pumpkins into coaches. Though she might try turning Lily into a rat.

"Nothing. I'm just along for the ride," Lily said, and El growled as she lifted the wand.

"Not that kind of ride!" I hastily added and stepped forward. "And Lily's no demon. She's a jinn. And I didn't make a deal. I made a wish."

"Toe-may-toe, toh-mah-toh," El said. Still, the words I'd said seemed to calm El down slightly, her gaze straying to my hand, where the ring rested. "Wishes with a jinn never go well."

"El, all I'm looking for is to sell some clothes. I didn't expect…" I waved my hands to encompass everything.

"Henry, you're a nice boy. So, here's a piece of advice. If you've got a wish left, wish for things to go back to the way they were before," El said.

"Actually, that's a horrible wish," Lily cut in, shaking her head. "Altering time is impossible, so I'd have to take away your gifts without taking away all the knowledge you have."

El frowned as she stared at Lily while I dropped the clothing bag on the counter. I coughed and drew her attention back to me. "Look, El, I really need your help. Ms. Never-Ending Stomach here ate through all my food and blew my budget. She even found my three-year-old cans of Spam."

"How long have you been living with her?" El said, her head tilted to the side.

"Ummm… a day and a half?" I sighed. "Come on, El, you know I don't bring junk."

"Henry," El sighed and waved at the clothes. "Have you ever looked at the prices I sell the clothes you bring me?"

"Noooo."

"I barely make any money on the clothing I sell. The entire used clothing side is a sham, a front," El said and waved a hand to the glass cases. "That's where I make my money."

"Okay. That's fine, but…" I pointed to the clothing. "Can't you take it as usual?"

"No. Because you're in my world now," El insisted, and I grunted, deflating.

"Fine." I started packing the bag again. Second Chance was a bus ride away and would probably only take a third of my inventory, but at least we'd have enough for dinner. "What do you sell anyway?"

"Spell and runic components," El said.

I choked, staring at the diminutive pixie. As casually as I could, I added, "And do you buy those too?"

El laughed, nodding her head. "Of course. But the careful sorting and care for spell components is a skill. Capturing the first breath of sunlight, containing the sap of a necrotic beetle, it's not something you can just do."

Lily beside me just grinned, and I finished stuffing the clothes away.

"Right. Right. Thank you, El. See you soon."

Outside the door, I turned to Lily, who chuckled quietly beside me. After a few yards, Lily asked, "Isn't the basement the other way?"

"Yes. But I've still got a bag of clothing to get rid of," I replied, hefting it.

"You do know that a single spell component is worth more than ten of those bags of used clothing?" Lily said.

"How would you know?" I shot back. "You've been stuck in a ring."

"I was looking at the clothing," Lily said. "And even at full price, a spell component is worth ten bags. At least."

"Whatever. I still have to get rid of this." I hefted the bag. "Waste not, want not."

***

It was nearly late evening before we found ourselves back at El's door. The titular Nora was, of course, not around, but El was still inside, finishing up for the day. I frowned—tempted to not knock—but decided to do so anyway. It had been a long, long day already, and I just wanted this done. Beside me, Lily was eating a shawarma, her foot tapping on the ground impatiently.

"We really should be home," Lily said. "You're not really ready for nighttime yet."

"Yeah, yeah," I muttered and knocked again.

El finally opened the door, glaring at the pair of us. "What do you want?"

"I might have something you want," I said.

"Henry—"

I shook my head. "Not clothes," I replied immediately. I quickly glanced around, then reached into my jacket and pulled out one of the rune-covered boxes. "A spell component."

"Where did you—?" El clamped her mouth shut. "Fine. Come in."

A few minutes later, we were hunched over a table in the back of the shop, in a room I had never seen before. In the center of the table, the opened enchanted box dominated our conversation, El lifting and placing aside small green crystals with a tweezer, inspecting each piece as it came out.

"Where did you get this?" El muttered, shaking her head. "I haven't seen quality like this in years."

"So, you can give us a good price?" I said, almost bouncing with anticipation.

"Definitely," El said and then clamped her lips shut, a look of frustration flickering on her face. "Damn it, Henry. I've been buying clothing from you too much."

I chuckled and sat back while she carefully stored them away in a glass container of her own. Once she had finished, she weighed the container before turning back to me. "Would you sell the box too?"

Out of the corner of my eyes, I saw Lily shake her head no, but I did not require her advice on that. I had no intention of selling the boxes and told El as much. The pixie ran a hand through her red hair before she pushed the pad forward, showing me her offer.

"Whoa…" My jaw dropped a bit, staring at the price. Ten times what I had earned this was not. Obviously, Lily's time in the ring had seen more changes than the jinn had expected.

"I take it this is agreeable," El said with a smirk, and I could only nod dumbly.

***

Outside Nora's, lighter one spell component and a newly counted wad of cash stuffed in my pocket, I turned and started the walk back to my basement apartment. Lily fell in beside me, eyeing shops with interest and muttering about supper. It was no surprise I never saw the hand that reached out of the alleyway and yanked me in, dazed by the new hidden world and my newfound wealth.

A large, green, and rough hand gripped me and dragged me deep into the alleyway, holding me by my jacket as I scrabbled at it, trying to make it release me. In the dark, my attacker slammed me into the wall once and then again, sending stars dancing in my eyes while a second hand pinned my right hand to the wall.

"Give me what you bought, Wizard," snarled the green, tusked face inches from mine. To punctuate his words, the orc squeezed my neck, making me choke.

I slapped at his hand ineffectually with my left hand, stars still dancing in my eyes. The repeated blows and lack of oxygen made my eyes unfocus, and for a moment, I saw the hulking skinhead that he showed the rest of the world.

"You know, he can't answer you if he can't breathe," Lily said.

The orc blinked, turning to stare at the jinn who was standing and watching us indifferently. Beside her, a pair of his associates floated in the air, their limbs failing to find purchase.

"You're a wizard too!" the orc growled, yellow eyes narrowing.

He reached a hand backward but stopped when Lily tsked.

"No, no. I'm not your target. He is," Lily said, pointing to me. "Now, this is a decent random encounter but not level appropriate with all three of you, so I'm taking your friends out of the equation. You, Henry will have to deal with. Isn't that right, Henry?"

I didn't get in fights as a matter of course. That being said, it didn't mean I hadn't been in fights before. One of the main rules: don't get distracted, and if your opponent does, capitalize. A raggedly drawn breath gave me enough clarity to focus and cast my only offensive spell with my free hand. I swirled my hand, fingers dancing, before I jabbed it into his chest, the glowing ball of force smashing into my mugger's short ribs.

Force Bolt Cast
Synchronicity 41%

Force Bolt does 9 damage to Orc Mugger.

The surprise attack cracked bone and forced the orc to exhale a surprisingly minty breath into my face, and he reflexively released my neck. Now on my knees, I tackled the orc even though he was clearly heavier than me, my shoulder striking his broken ribs and driving the monster back. Reflexive motion made him hunch over, which gave me the perfect setup for an elbow to his chin. I pushed away from him, giving myself space as I shook my arm out, elbow aching from the strike.

"You know, you're a mage now," Lily said casually. "No experience for slugging it out."

I growled in response and then coughed, choking from the newly formed bruises on my neck. The orc stood up, rubbing his chin, a glimmer of respect in his eyes.

"A wizard with some physical skill," the orc said, his voice a low growl. He flicked a glance to Lily, who waved her hand for him to continue. "This might just be interesting."

"Yeah... no," I said, my right hand darting and twisting as I formed another Force Bolt. Before I could finish, the orc charged me, which forced me to dance backward and interrupt the spell. I twisted and turned as my mugger refused to give me time to finish it. Again and again, I would start the spell before I found it interrupted.

"You're going to have to learn to cast under pressure," Lily coached from the sidelines. A thrown knife from one of the other orcs hung suspended in midair, stopped the moment it had been released from his hand, its target Lily. "Don't let his attacks distract you. The spell is the most important thing."

A fist glanced off my jaw and sent me sprawling to the ground. The orc dashed forward, but I raised my feet high, holding the creature off with my feet. As the monster tried to get to me, I started casting Force Bolt again even as my head throbbed. Two seconds was all the time I would need. Even as the orc finally pushed my legs aside, I finally completed the spell and sent it hammering into the monster.

Force Bolt Cast
Synchronicity 53%

Force Bolt does 10 damage to Orc Mugger.

On my back, feet up in the air, I formed the next spell, which the mugger dodged. Two more spells followed, cast from my back, only one of which hit. My head continued to throb. The pain grew, and I spared a glance upward to note that my mana was nearly gone. All those failed attempts had required mana even if I hadn't completed them.

The orc, arm clutched where it had taken the blunt of the last spell, growled at me. I had heard the crack of another broken bone, but he was still on his feet. Still, the mugger did not attempt to rush me anymore, and I slowly stood up, keeping a distance from it.

"We done?" I asked, trying to keep my voice confident.

"Wizard, I am disappointed. You have some skill. Why do you refuse to fight honorably?" The orc growled and eyed me warily.

"Got to level up."

"You speak strangely even for a wizard."

"Yeah, yeah. We continuing this, or are we done?" I growled, my hand raised as I bluffed the monster.

"We are done if you will have it so, Wizard."

"Go."

"I am Ulrik of the Yellow Eyes," the orc said. "You shall not be as fortunate in our next encounter."

I waved Ulrik away, and Lily let the pair of orcs drop. The trio scrambled off as they eyed the jinn warily. In moments, Lily and I were alone in the alleyway.

"Thanks for all the help," I grumbled at her.

"You need to level up. I made sure it was level appropriate," Lily said unapologetically. "That technique was less than orthodox. Effective though."

"So, did I get experience for that, or did I need to kill him?" I asked as I leaned against the wall and held my hand to my throbbing head.

"What did I say about experience? It's about learning and growing your magical strength, not your ability to kill monsters. Look at your sheet."

Class: Mage

Level 1 (48% Experience)

Known Spells: Light Ball, Force Bolt, Warmth, Chill, Chime, Breeze

"All that from one fight?" I said as I stared at the updated sheet.

"No. You gained some experience while walking around with your arcane sight today. But a lot of it did come from the fight."

I slowly nodded, somewhat mollified. Although I was bruised, headache or not, the random encounter had been worth it. "Fine."

"So, I've got an important question," Lily said, smiling as she walked forward. "Is that Ethiopian restaurant any good?"

Chapter 4

The answer to that important question was no. Very much no. That did not stop Lily from finishing it all while she hogged my computer. Funnily enough, I did not mind it as much as I spent my time poring over the spell book I had acquired. Most of it was unintelligible, series of arcane words and concepts that I had no basis of understanding, but some of it made sense. It was like reading a post-graduate textbook on physics and only having a grade-school education. Still, I persisted.

As I sat reading, I realized my mana was recharging, albeit slowly. Too slowly for my liking. "Lily, is there a way to recharge mana faster?"

"Of course. Certain tonics, foods, and alchemical potions are the most common. Staying in ley lines or nodes will help," Lily said, not bothering to look up. "Meditating, of course."

I nodded slowly and closed the book. Well, okay then. We might not have given me any skills, but grade-school lessons on mindfulness might still help. As I crossed my legs on the bed, I slowed my breathing and tried to clear my mind. Not surprisingly, it was a lot harder than the last few times I had done this. The last days had been somewhat hectic—a jinn, magic, a hidden world, and an old friend not being who I'd thought she was. And then, the first fight I'd been part of for years.

In time, I found my thoughts slowing, relaxing. My eyes closed, my breathing slowed, and then darkness came.

***

"Morning," Lily greeted, along with the enticing smell of fried bacon, tomatoes, scrambled eggs, and the nectar of the gods—coffee. The jinn stood over the stove as she finished plating the meal. Hair left unbound, the raven-haired jinn was bent over in a pink blouse, a flowered vest, and a pair of tight blue jeans that looked uncannily familiar. Doing mundane tasks like this, I could almost think of the jinn as just another gorgeous woman and not a powerful supernatural creature.

"Breakfast?" I swung my feet off the bed and wandered over to snag a plate from the counter. Used plates piled high reminded me that I really needed to do the dishes. "Are those clothes from El's store?"

"I copied some of them for use. Your wardrobe is less than fashionable," Lily said, shaking her head. "Really? A dozen shirts about this *Firefly* thing?"

"Don't knock it till you've seen it," I muttered around a mouthful of food. "So, what now? I wander around the city looking for trouble?"

"No. I've got a quest for you." Lily waved her fork at my desk. It took me a few minutes of searching through the scattered papers before I found the right one. On it, circled in red ink, was "Quest One."

"Rats?" I poked at the paper as I walked to get more coffee.

"Rats. It's tradition."

"You are kidding me," I grumbled and sipped my coffee. "Also, what did you do to the coffee? It's really smooth."

"Cold brew," Lily said. "Your coffee maker is pitiful. And I'm not. Devil Rats should be perfect for your first quest. Level appropriate."

"How do you know these are Devil Rats though? The news report just talks of an increase in disappearances of pets in the neighborhood," I said. "Might be coyotes."

Lily shook her head. "GM. I expanded a bit of my power to check our surroundings. Now, off you go to kill some rats. Though maybe a shower first?"

I growled softly before I walked to the bathroom. Now, the real question was, what do you wear when you go hunting supernatural rats in the sewer?

***

It took a bit of hunting, but I found a pair of rubber boots, wool socks, and workout pants along with one of my faded shirts. A simple polyester rain jacket to keep the cold and wet out and I was ready to go. Or as ready as I could be considering I had no idea what I was getting into.

An underground train ride and a bus ride later, I found myself in the Devil Rat-plagued suburban neighborhood. I never understood how people could live out in these cookie-cutter houses with their carefully manicured lawns and nosy neighbors. Every time I came out here, I was reminded how stale and artificial it all felt, a residence made by design rather than need, a place to rest and hide away from the world.

As I walked away from the bus stop, I eyed the ground, searching for a manhole cover. It was only when I found one in a deserted cul-de-sac and attempted to pull it open that I realized one flaw with my plan—my lack of upper-arm strength and leverage. A few minutes of futile gripping and straining later, I sat down beside the manhole cover and applied some brainpower to the problem. Perhaps…

I held my hand over the manhole cover, focusing not on my hand but slightly past it. I focused deep within and cast the spell, altering the flows slightly so that instead of forming right at my hand and shooting outward, the spell would form beneath the cover. Three failed attempts later, the spell finally formed, and the Force Bolt crashed into the underside of the obstruction, tossing it into the air by a few inches.

"Owwww," I muttered as I carefully levered the manhole off my foot, which I had shoved into the opening. That was going to leave a bruise. Right. Crowbars. Definitely adding a crowbar to my adventuring kit.

I left the manhole propped mostly open and climbed down to the sewers, finally ready to complete my quest. At least the hard part was over. How hard could rats be?

***

"Force Bolt in your face, Mickey!" I snarled as my spell finished forming and smashed the Devil Rat aside. Crushed under the blue bolt of arcane energy, the splattered remains of my attacker left a red smear against the grey walls of the sewer tunnel. Above me, a floating light orb—that I had figured how to tether to my body—gave off fitful light, casting shadows all around. Thankfully, the sewer system that was connected to this suburban zone was actually part of the flood water preparations, so the sewer itself was tall and wide to accommodate a large amount of water. It meant that I could, for the most part, stand upright while hunting around.

I slumped against the wall and dug into my backpack, searching for the bandages I had thoughtfully brought along. A dose of iodine later, I wrapped my injured calf tightly and hoped Devil Rats were not as plague-ridden as their mundane counterparts. Somehow, I had a feeling that was wishful thinking.

"Good thing Lily isn't here to see this," I said to myself. I imagined the jinn smirking while I struggled to fight Devil Rats in the dark. In truth, I wasn't sure what I had expected for this quest. She'd said this was level appropriate, and my previous life as a retail store worker and part-time bargain hunter had done little to ready me for monster hunting. I looked sideways, eyeing my mana bar, which stood a quarter full. Enough for one more fight.

With quick motions, I put away my first aid kit and stood, testing my foot and finding it sound enough. That it had to be same foot I'd bruised earlier made walking even harder than before, but not impossible. As I rounded the next corner of the damp, noxious sewers, I made sure not to think about what I was walking in. Thankfully, years of babysitting for uncles and aunts for extra money had inured me to the concept of feces as a whole, even if wading through the sewers tested the limits of my attitude.

Another mangled body greeted me as I stepped around a corner, a poodle with its innards scattered, and a Devil Rat poked its head out from within. The fellow in front of me was typical for the Devil Rats I had encountered—the size of a housecat with glowing red eyes and an aggressive temperament. As it arched its back in defense of its meal, I finished my spell and pointed my fingers at it, the bolt catching the monster in the center of its body and crushing its heart.

Force Bolt Cast
Synchronicity 67%

Force Bolt does 11 damage to Devil Rat.

Slumping down to the corpse, I exhaled in relief and tried to get the adrenaline spike under control again. Thankfully, this time, I'd been the one to catch the rat by surprise. The monsters had a tendency to attack from hiding, crawling from dark corners to set upon me. Still, with my mana bar nearly empty, the headache had returned, and so I settled in to wait and rest.

This was not going to be easy.

***

I stood up after a bit, meditating having slowly driven my mana bar to half full. I would have stayed longer, but there were limits to my ability to ignore how disgusting all this was even if my nose had long ago shut off. A low squeaking had taken me down a side corridor, and I was forced to hunch over as I scrabbled forward. A small worm of worry crawled along my guts, the noises before me growing louder and more numerous than I had heard before.

"Oh, shit," I muttered softly as my light finally illuminated the nest before me. Curled up in a pile of bones, rat droppings, and shed fur, a mother rat twice the size of any I'd seen before was nursing a group of Devil Rat pups, each the size of my fist. Crouched near them was another Devil Rat, gnawing on a pale bone. As my light drew their attention, the mischief of rats turned and regarded me with their hellish red eyes. Taking the better part of valor, I started to slowly back away as I readied a Force Bolt.

At first, the rats just regarded my slow retreat without moving. As my light pulled away, the rats started squeaking louder and louder, the noise echoing through the cramped quarters. Mouth dry, I could sense the monsters getting ready to attack as I sloshed backward. Fear clutched at my stomach, knowing I had insufficient mana to kill them all. I needed to make sure when they charged, I had time to do something.

Inspiration struck as I stepped backward. I snapped and twisted my fingers, then pointed down, sending arcane energy into the water as I chilled it in front of me and backed away. Within seconds, a light crust of ice formed on the water, spreading faster and faster as the arcane energy drew heat from the already chilly water. As if my magic was the signal, there was a sudden silence as the rats barreled forward.

I scrambled backward as I poured mana into the water, creating a slick surface that the first Devil Rat hit without warning. Front claws dug into the slick, wet ice, sending it spinning and twisting to slam into the wall. The rat shook its head to clear it while the pups, unsteady on their feet, skidded and scattered on my impromptu ice rink.

54

As a spike of pain erupted in my head, I stopped the spell, unable to continue, and backed away as fast as I could. Once out of the small tunnel, I turned and ran, the sounds of the larger mother rat crashing into and crushing my ice echoing through the tunnel.

I never looked back, running as fast as I could to the nearest ladder and climbing as quickly as possible. I hit the manhole cover with my shoulder, adrenaline and better leverage allowing me to push it upward. Outside, the feel of sunlight on my face and the smell of blooming flowers carried on the wind blew away some of my fear, some of the nightmare-inducing madness below. As I replaced the manhole cover, I flashed a smile at a child playing on the sidewalk, grateful to have survived my first quest.

Chapter 5

Extra clothing. That was what I'd forgotten to bring with me. That was clear as I sat in my own smelly sphere on the ride back. I kept my face down in embarrassment as other passengers threw disgusted looks at me, even those from the hidden world. By the time I made my way back, that lesson had been deeply ingrained into my soul. Always bring extra clothing.

Lily was crouched in front of my laptop when I came back, clicking away and killing virtual monsters the entire time I had been dealing with real ones. Rather than speak with my titular GM, I stalked into the bathroom to shower and clean up as best I could. Leaden silence carried through the air as I walked out in a fresh set of clothing and began to cook dinner.

It was only when dinner was served that I spoke, my voice tight and controlled. "So, I killed some Devil Rats."

"I'd hope so," Lily said, taking the plate of pork chop, gravy, mashed potatoes, and brussels sprouts from me. "Did you kill the ten rats?"

"No," I said as I stabbed my pork chop and sawed at the piece. "There was a mother rat, about the size of a medium-sized dog, in there."

"Ugly little creature, isn't she?" Lily said, already having walked back to the laptop.

"She nearly killed me. They nearly killed me!" I shouted and then drew a deep breath, forcing myself to calm down. Last night, the orc had been scary, but it had just been a mugging. I'd been mugged before, and while it was never fun, muggers were never really there to kill you. Rough you up a bit, maybe hurt you, but not kill. Not unless things got out of hand. At least, the ones who weren't on drugs. The rats though, the rats didn't care about legal consequences or moral imperatives to not kill. To them, I was just food.

"Of course. You were trying to kill them, weren't you?" Lily sighed and put her cutlery down before she stared at me, my shaking fingers, and my shallow breathing. For a moment, I saw a flash of sympathy before Lily continued. "This is what questing and combat is. High-stress situations that require you to learn and explore your abilities."

I gulped as I stared at my hands that wouldn't stop shaking, at my body that refused to stop shivering. I could not stop thinking about the fact that I had nearly been eaten alive. Of the pain of being bitten and the sharp needlelike teeth.

"It's your choice, Henry. We can continue doing quests like this, or you can stay home, casting spells and learning slowly. You can level up however you want," Lily said softly, but I could barely hear her as I contemplated my mortality.

For the first time, I had an inkling that perhaps learning and wielding magic wasn't just about having a cool trick. There were real consequences here.

***

When I woke the next morning, my wounds had miraculously healed, and there was new, lightly-scarred skin where they had been. I exhaled a sigh of relief, glad we'd managed to get that sorted. Of course, the healing had left me ravenously hungry since all it did was speed the healing process, but I'd take a higher grocery bill over limping for days.

Surprisingly, I found that Lily was not at the laptop when I woke. A very brief check showed the jinn was not in the apartment, which left me staring at the ring. Of course, she could have left the flat entirely. I briefly contemplated rubbing the ring to bring her to me before I shook my head and discarded the idea. Instead, I reveled in the fact that I had my apartment back to myself.

Living as a bachelor for years now, I had forgotten what it was like to have a roommate, the constant presence that intruded on my daily routines. I could lounge about in my underwear. I could watch schlocky TV or just play on my computer. And I did all that, a bowl of instant noodles in hand.

Yet, every few minutes, I found my gaze traveling back to the rubber boots I had so carefully cleaned off last night. Distractions that used to carry me away from my life for hours, even days, on end barely held my attention for minutes now. Even casting a spell felt hollow, an exercise that had no point.

No point... that was the thing, wasn't it? There was no point to this, to my life. It was a malaise I had felt before, that had left me fired from retail jobs when I simply stopped caring. There was no point to this, to TV shows that had no end, computer games that had no challenge, and jobs that had no future. But magic and that quest? At least there I was doing something. I was progressing, making myself better. I had dreamed of having magic all my life, and now I had it. Even if all I was doing was questing and killing monsters, I was progressing.

I stared at my rubber boots sitting accusingly by the door, and finally, I sighed and stood up.

"Fine. Let's do this."

***

Of course, it wasn't that easy. First, I had to find more disposable clothing. At this rate, I'd become a customer of Nora's. A sealed plastic bag contained a second set of clothing while sandwiches and water, a crowbar, a hammer, and an old hunting knife ended up in my bag for later. An extra flashlight and some light sticks were added along with a new roll of bandages. I frowned, trying to decide if I had missed anything, and realized I was just killing time, avoiding the next step.

As I was about to walk out the door, my phone rang. I frowned, fishing it out and staring at the glowing caller ID. I drew a deep breath, feeling my stomach clench even as I answered it.

"Mommy," I greeted.

"When were you going to call?" immediately on the attack, my mother's familiar voice resounded through the phone. I felt my shoulders hunch, my entire body shrinking down slightly at the accusation. Justified. I hadn't spoken with her or my dad in months.

"Soon. Sorry, things have been busy," I answered apologetically.

"You found a new job?" Hope was in her voice even after all these years.

"No. Yes. Sort of," I said, unsure of how and whether to explain things. Actually, no. I knew better than to explain.

"Oh." Disappointment now. I wince, knowing once again, I've let her down. As usual—the black sheep of the family, the useless one, especially compared to my doctor sister and accountant brother.

"It's a part-time thing," I clarified, figuring that was true enough at least. "Anyway... I was just about to head out…"

"I wanted to ask, are you coming back for your father's birthday? You know he'd like it."

"I don't know," I answered truthfully. I really didn't want to go back, to travel hundreds of miles to be subjected to passive-aggressive stares and the constant looks of disappointment. It was why I had left Vancouver after all.

"Do you need money? I can send you some."

"I can pay for it. It's just a new job…" I explained hurriedly and then glanced at the door again. "I really need to get going…"

"Fine. Just remember to call and tell us."

"I will. It's not for months yet!" I said. "Bye!" I hurriedly finished the exchange of pleasantries before I finally ended the call, my stomach aching with phantom pain. Stupid family. Pushing aside the never-ending drama, I left the apartment.

A train and bus ride later, I was back at the suburb. I checked my phone and its GPS tracking of where I'd been—which, by the way, was sort of creepy—and I was at the manhole cover I had crawled out of the previous day. Unlike the first one I'd entered, this manhole cover was in the middle of the street, but at this point, I was more than done with being circumspect. A crowbar and an almost-strained back later, I was back in the nightmare-inducing darkness.

"Light," I muttered as I cast my spell. A vocal component was not required, but one aspect that I knew of this magic was that "required" did not equal "not important." I wasn't entirely sure if it was the addition of a vocal rhythm or the addition of a vocal aspect itself, but the results certainly showed up.

Light Ball Cast
93% Synchronicity

As an added precaution, I popped a glow stick and zip-tied it to the ladder. Nose scrunched from the smell, I stood at the ladder and listened, trying to discern if I had a greeting party. Hearing nothing, I slowly approached the corridor that I had exited so ignobly a day ago.

As I walked, I wiped sweaty palms against my sweatpants and swallowed around the copper taste of adrenaline in my mouth. In my left hand, I hefted my crowbar, ready to ward off a Devil Rat while my right readied itself to cast a Force Bolt. At the mouth of the corridor, I raised my hand and cast another Light Ball, this time in silence, and directed it to the edges of my current illuminated area. Again and again, I did so, lighting the entire corridor till the excited squeals of Devil Rats alerted to my presence reached my ears.

The first adult Devil Rat exploded from the shadows and rushed me, closely followed by another. Right behind, the pups raced to catch their larger, faster brethren. From my hand, a Force Bolt flew out to strike the lead Devil Rat. The Force Bolt crushed the monster's front legs, causing it to fall and mewl pitifully. No longer a threat, I turned to the next adult rat.

Seconds had passed, and the monster was already halfway to me, the pups only a short distance behind. I snarled as my second Force Bolt passed by uselessly, the third injuring but not killing the monster. Too close for a follow-up spell, I instead swung the crowbar and battered the attacker away, blood and brain matter spattering around me at my successful strike.

And then it was the rats' turn as the pups swarmed me. The next few seconds were a blur as I swung, punched, kicked, and stomped at the tiny monsters that crawled, bit, and tore at me. I had no time for spells, no time but the dance for survival. But monsters or not, they were only the size of normal rats. One after another, the monsters fell before my weapon and stomping feet before a searing pain ripped into my calf.

I fell to the ground, the mother rat clamped onto my ankle and refusing to let go. Each movement tore the wound open wider. In pain, I raised my crowbar to swing at it, but a last pup bit into the edges of my triceps. My hand spasmed open, and I screamed again.

The mother rat twisted its head one last time and tore my calf open before it backed off and lunged toward my torso. Its teeth clamped onto my hip, sharp teeth tearing into the tender flesh. I thrashed on the ground, a wild swing batting away the last pup and driving the mom aside.

"Die!" I scowled as I tried to scurry away and twisted, my injured foot swinging at the monster.

Teeth clamped onto my boot, sharp teeth unable to penetrate the rubber immediately. My hand twisted and pointed, and a Force Bolt flew forward at the enraged monster.

"Aaarggh!" I screamed, the spell tearing the mother Devil Rat away as the bolt impacted my foot and the rat. Bones cracked under the impact of the spell, pain making my eyes widen. The mother rat, its teeth missing from when it was ripped away and its mouth bloody, rushed me once more. I shoved my hand forward, fingers dancing faster than ever, and I sent the spell into its open mouth as it lunged for my neck.

The Force Bolt tore down its throat and tore it apart as it threw her back. Blood sprayed and aerosoled as the creature fell to the ground, dead but still twitching. I coughed, throat sore and dry from screaming as blood dripped from my wounds.

Blood, so much blood. I grunted, struggling to pull my bag out from under me. Its contents were soaked by sewer water, but thankfully, the first aid bag was waterproof. As my fingers shook, I slowly pulled my first aid gear from my bag and began the long and painful process of cleaning my wounds.

***

The trip back this time was less of a social issue as wet wipes and a new set of clothing made me look and smell less like a hobo. It didn't hide the way I moved or the pain that flashed across my face, but no one bothered me at least. The lack of public embarrassment unfortunately left me more time to consider the waves of pain that rose and fell with each bump and step on the journey home.

Two blocks from the train station to my house, and for some reason, I was drawing looks again. I smiled and nodded, too tired to answer queries about my health as the world begin to shimmer before my eyes.

"I see you. And I got a Force Bolt for you if needed," I said to the gargoyle who shifted to stare at me when I walked past its perch.

Descending the stairs, each step forced me to draw a deep breath as I squelched down. I pushed on the handle, opening the door, and I stumbled in and waved my hand triumphantly into the empty space. "The conquering hero returns!"

The bed, a bare five feet from the door greeted me as I flopped onto it, darkness finally claiming me.

Chapter 6

I woke up groggy, mouth dry, and shivering. My shirt was stained with sweat, and as I rolled over, I saw Lily seated beside me on the computer. When I shifted, the jinn looked at me and broke into a smile, helping me sit up to drink a cup of water and wash down some painkillers. Unlike last time I slept and healed, my calf ached, throbbing in pain with each heartbeat.

"What…?" I growled, shaking my head, and poked at my foot. "Why didn't it heal?"

"Whoever did that carried a magical disease. The enhanced healing I gave you can't remove it," Lily explained.

"Can you heal it?" I asked, and she shook her head, crossing her hands together as if they were tied. Right. Right. Not allowed to interfere. I guessed taking my boots off and cleaning me up wasn't considered undue interference though. Or taking off my pants. I flushed red, the increase in blood flow making me dizzy for a second. Or it could have been the fever.

"Henry?" Lily asked, placing a hand on my arm. "You need help. Magical help."

I nodded dumbly and stared at the phone the jinn was pointedly looking at. Right. Phone. Help. Except I didn't know anyone magical except Lily. I slumped back against my pillows, my eyes half closing. A sudden scream jerked me awake, making me stare at the computer where Lily's avatar had died gruesomely down a pit.

"Don't fall asleep just yet. You need to call for help."

Help. Right. I took hold of the phone, getting as far as 9-1-1 before I canceled the call. Magical help. For a moment, I stared at the ceiling, wondering why everyone always painted their ceilings a boring white. They should have colored them something more interesting, something fun. Vibrant. Red. Red like El's hair…

Holding on to that thread of thought, I scrolled to the shop's number and hit dial, then listened to the insistent ring.

"Nora's, your everyday used clothing store. El speaking."

"Henry speaking," I said and grinned at my reply.

"Henry, what can I do for you?"

"Nothing. No. Not nothing. I had something…" I frowned, trying to remember why I called her. It was funny, the way the raven-haired jinn's face was screwed up as she listened to me on the phone. "Oh, I love your hair. Your real hair. It's so much more you."

"Was that all you called me for?" El said, her voice sounding tinny over the phone.

"Yes. It's pretty. Just like you." I smiled and killed the call, happy that I'd remembered what I had done. The phone dropped from my hand, landing on the edge of the bed and bouncing off. Bounce, bounce. That looked fun, so I let myself drop too and bounced on the bed before my eyes closed.

***

"What did you do to him, Jinn!" I heard El's voice in the distance.

"Nothing, you crazed pixie. I was the one who told him to call you!"

Screams and shouts, the cackle of electricity, and then silence.

***

"Oh, Henry. You idiot," El said, as my eyes opened. My dumpy friend, clad in her featureless gray sweater swapped with an elfin apparition clad in green and brown. Hands held over my leg streamed color, arcane energy that I could now see chasing away the cold that had wrapped my leg. Warmth filled it for the first time in what seemed like ages.

Then pain.

I screamed, strong hands holding me down.

"Hold him still!"

"I'm trying, but I can't do too much. I told you we should have strapped him down!" This time, Lily's voice came from a creature of flame and smoke, clawed hands and stunning beauty that made me want to cry intermixing with my jinn, the raven-haired beauty.

Another blast of power came with pain and darkness.

***

I woke slowly this time, free from pain but dry-mouthed. I slowly sat up with a muted groan, brought a nearby cup of water to my lips, and noticed El's concerned face. I sipped at first and then gulped, greedily drinking all the water and asking for more. After the second cup, I pushed up against the bed to see Lily at the laptop, focused on her game.

"What are you doing here, El?" I finally asked. Thankfully, I seemed to be half-dressed at least. Though who had put the fresh pair of boxer briefs on me I refused to consider.

"Your call had me worried. Especially when you didn't answer. Who knows what kind of trouble you could have gotten mixed up with, especially since you have her." El nodded to Lily who stuck her tongue out without looking up. "So, I came over."

"Oh…" I frowned and touched my lower leg. No pain. Not even when I flexed my ankle. "Did you?"

"Heal you? Yes," El answered before shrugging. "Pixies have a modicum of healing magic. Now, stand up. I want to check you out."

Ignoring my initial protests and my embarrassment, the flame-haired pixie got me on my feet. For the next few minutes, El made me stand, bend, stretch, and twist as she tested my newly healed body. Finally satisfied, she had me sit at the dining table where she piled food, carefully heated in the oven, and commanded me to eat. Lily, drawn to the table, received a glare but no other admonishment from El as she dug in as well.

Any attempt at further conversation was shot down till I had stuffed myself. As I pushed away my plate, El raised a finger and said slowly and menacingly, "Now, tell me what happened. All of it."

I shivered, staring at the tiny pixie, the flint in her eyes reminding me of the one time a shoplifter had tried to get away from the store. The look she'd given him then was similar to the one she offered me now and just as effective. I spilled the details of my quest, both the failed first attempt and the second. Lily kept uncharacteristically silent through the tale, the clinking of her fork the only other noise in the apartment. Which, I had quietly noted, had a few new holes in it.

"Men." El huffed when I finished, rolling her eyes to the sky with her arms crossed. "You almost got yourself killed because of a… quest?"

I paused, giving the question actual thought. In the end, I answered her slowly. "It wasn't the quest itself. Not really. It was the decision. To stay at home training slowly or go out and do something. Anything. If I didn't make it, then, well, it was as good as having made it. You understand?"

"No."

Lily smiled slightly as El glared at me with her arms crossed over her petite breasts. Leaning forward, Lily brought the attention to her as she spoke finally. "Well, that was nice. Don't let the door hit you on the way out."

"Why, you..." El snarled.

"Lily! Stop it. She's my friend, and you need to show her some respect," I snapped at Lily.

"That little tree fairy? Do you know what she did while you were sick?" Lily spluttered, and I shook my head.

"I don't care. She's my friend, and you're going to be respectful to her, or else you can just stay in the ring when she's around," I said, glaring at Lily who returned my glare. We locked gazes for a long while before the jinn broke away, laughing softly.

"Fine, fine. I'll be nice to the... to El," Lily said. "But I do need to speak with you. Alone."

"Not happening," El said.

"This isn't for you, pixie," Lily snapped, and I sighed.

"What's this about?" I asked Lily who mouthed the word "quest" at me. Oh. I'd finished a quest which meant...

Class: Mage

Level 1 (208% Experience)

Known Spells: Light Ball, Force Bolt, Warmth, Chill, Chime, Breeze

"Nice. I can level up!" I exclaimed, and Lily winced, shaking her head.

"Level up?" El's eyes narrowed at the two of us suspiciously.

"My wish—"

"Henry!" Lily snapped at me, leaning forward. "Ixnay on the ishway."

"Oh, come on, Lily. El just saved my life. I think we can trust her," I said, which caused El to flush slightly and Lily to glare at me more. "It's my secret."

"Aaargh!" Lily threw her hands up in the air and then fell silent, which I took for tacit agreement.

"I wanted to be a mage, but I didn't want my brain dribbling out. So, I made a wish that gave me magic but would only pass the spells on in dribs and drabs as I learned to handle it. We based it off, well…" I hesitated, waving my hands to my books.

"Your role-playing games. I get it," El said, rubbing her temples. "It is the most idiotic and—"

"Genius plan ever," Lily finished, nodding firmly. "I know, right? It bypasses most of the problems wishes for magic power have and doesn't stunt his growth. Much."

"Much?" I frowned at Lily.

"She speaks of the Wizard Council. They are unlikely to be impressed by your abilities," El clarified. "The jinn is right. You should not have told me this. You should not be telling anyone this."

I blinked and then flashed El my patented Smile No. 3, the one that made me look like a kid. Okay, it was my usual smile, but it still normally worked. "But you won't tell anyone, right?"

"Oh, Henry," El said exasperatedly. "I won't. Just… stop being so damn trusting. The hidden world isn't the same as your mundane one. You cannot just do things like this."

"Okay, okay. I promise. No more telling secrets," I said, crossing my heart and flashing another grin. El just rolled her eyes while I turned to Lily. "So, level up time?"

"Yes. Hold still please. This should hurt less than the last time," Lily said consolingly, and that was when I remembered how much it had hurt.

Oh, hell.

***

"That wasn't bad," I said as I rubbed blood from my nose and gratefully accepted the painkillers from El, who had a strange look on her face.

"Next time, do it on the bed," El said, and I nodded firmly. Passing out at the dinner table and cracking my nose on the table had been a less-than-pleasant experience.

"I hear kitchen tables are quite popular," Lily said, and El flushed, looking away.

"Wait. Did you make a sex joke?" I said before I shook my head. "Never mind. I don't want to know. Now, I'm just going to see what you downloaded."

"Downloaded?" Lily said, puzzled.

I tuned them out as El explained more current lingo to the jinn and focused inward. First things first, my character sheet.

Class: Mage

Level 3 (8% Experience)

Known Spells: Light Ball, Force Missile, Heat, Freeze, Chime, Breeze, Lesser Shield, Heal, Link, Mend

The first thing I noticed was that many of my existing spells had changed name. A brief consideration showed that I still knew the lesser versions of the spells but had instead learned stronger formulas. Those spells in turn allowed me to alter the spells themselves, giving me more options. As an example, I was pretty sure I could actually cast two Force Bolts now rather than a single Force Missile. Though, controlling both Force Bolts and where they would impact would be a lot trickier.

Light Ball had not upgraded, though the intensity and duration of the spell had grown. It was no real surprise—the light spell was a pretty basic spell, and while variants on it were available, most variations were a matter of power rather than formula. The spells that I had not used or practiced, Chime and Breeze, had not changed at all.

Most interestingly, I now knew four new spells. The first was a defensive spell that layered a thin layer of compressed air and arcane energy in front of me. Intuitively, I knew that practice with both Breeze and Lesser Shield would provide me greater understanding of either. It was not a powerful defensive spell, but considering I had started with none, I was grateful for its presence. Perhaps if I'd had the spell to begin with, I would not have been as injured.

The Heal spell was, sadly, pathetic. From the spell formula that sat in my head, the spell did little more than increase the speed of my healing by a minor amount, and almost all of it focused on a small area. It was a useful spell for removing bruises and slowing, even stopping, bleeding by having the body's natural clotting properties act faster, but it was nothing like a cleric's minor healing spell. On the other hand, it was a channeled spell, with the amount of healing dependent on the amount of time it was active. If it wasn't for the fact that I would never progress with healing abilities if I didn't use it, I probably wouldn't even bother casting it at all since resting had a much more powerful effect.

The third spell was the foundation spell for scrying. At this stage, all it really did was highlight links between two objects. The closer their initial sympathetic link, the longer the range of the spell. Unfortunately, at my level, even a direct connection like blood would only highlight the connection for a few hundred meters. With practice though, the arcane knowledge involved would allow me to scry locations hundreds of miles away. Once I got the appropriate spell, of course.

The last spell was a utility spell, one you didn't see much in role-playing books because throwing around the power of gods was more interesting than fixing a hole in your pants. On the other hand, for a poor gamer like me, the spell could actually save me a few dollars. I even had a few pieces of old electronics sitting around that I kept meaning to throw away properly. Perhaps the spell would fix them?

"Did you learn anything worth your life?" El asked, and I refocused on the pixie, my lip twisting in a half smile.

"Sort of? Some of these spells might keep me alive longer," I said, which caused El to roll her eyes again.

"I have to go. I need to reopen the store," El said finally, standing up and fixing me with a look. "You aren't going to be going out and doing anything stupid, are you?"

"No. Got a whole new bunch of spells in my head. I'll want to test them out first," I replied, and El stared at me in an attempt to ascertain the truth of my words. Good thing I was telling the truth.

"Fine," El said and walked to the door, snatching her coat on the way out. "Just be careful, Henry. You don't understand the world you've entered."

"Roger!" I said, waving goodbye to the pixie.

Lily snorted at our antics, already deep into her game. I stared at the jinn for a second, trying to decide if I had any questions for her that she could answer and found none that were more pressing than testing my new spells.

As I went back to my bed, I rubbed my chin and tried to work out how to test my spells in my six-hundred-square-foot bachelor's apartment without wrecking anything. As I eyed the new holes in the apartment walls, I added "anything more."

***

It turned out that the answer to that question was the bathroom. A pot of water in the bath could steam and boil over without causing damage, and ice, well, a pot of ice really didn't make a difference where you made it. The tricky part, at least for me, was learning how to control the amount of mana I put into the spell. Unlike its lesser variants, which felt like I was pushing beanbags through rabbit holes, the new spells had a hunger for mana like a jinn's stomach.

Between waiting for my mana to recover and poking at the new knowledge in my mind, I found myself walking out of the bathroom to talk to Lily. Questions that hadn't been important till now started creeping into my mind.

***

"That orc called me a wizard, but you call me a mage. What's the difference?"

"Depends on who you ask, but the somewhat official definitions are that mages are trained to use their gifts, normally starting as apprentices. Wizards, on the other hand, are untrained arcane users who have learned to wield their powers via trial and error."

"Any other terms I should know?"

"Sorcerers are generally those who have gained their powers via demonic means. Enchanters are specialized mages—and they're almost always mages—who enchant items and spaces. Alchemists do the same with potions, but they can be wizards too. There are probably more alchemical wizards than mage actually."

"Probably?"

"Things change. And unless I use my powers, it's not as if I have a way of ascertaining what is happening around the world."

"Right."

***

Later, after freezing the pot of ice, I realized instead of a single ice cube, I'd somehow mangled the spell to create ice chunks. Definitely needed to work on the synchronicity for this spell.

"What about this Wizard Council?" I asked.

"It's mostly made up of mages, but there are some wizards too. And one sorcerer. Or at least, there was."

"The way I read it, they're not happy with me because I'm cheating the system, learning their secrets from you, and refusing to pay my dues."

"In part." Lily looked up from the laptop. For a moment, her eyes danced with flame while she spoke. "But it's more than that. Past history with jinn and mages has been fraught with tragedy. To be a mage, a powerful mage, you have to be willing to sacrifice everything. The apprenticeship itself takes decades, and apprentices are isolated from all family and friends during their tenure. The weak fall away; only the driven survive."

"And if you're that driven, you're probably not the nicest of people." I rubbed my chin and realized I still hadn't shaved.

"Yes. Most mages know our limitations to some extent. Their wishes are often more circumspect. Still, many die. Those who don't are often driven mad."

"Power-crazy assholes with wishes," I said for her. "And I'm considered one of them. Yay me."

***

My spell book was set out in front of me, a window propped open, and the bathroom fan on as we tried to ignore the smell of melted metal and plastic. I was so not going to get my damage deposit back.

"This sort of makes a bit of sense," I muttered as I read the line again. Four out of eleven words. Now, if only those words weren't the arcane equivalents of "and," "but," and "then." Sometimes, I even knew all the words in a sentence. Just not what it meant.

"That's the equivalent of a level-nine spell," Lily said without glancing up, a strand of her hair in her mouth.

"What is it for?"

"You tell me."

"The arcane runes are the same as my Force spell, so it's a Force something. But there's bits of it for distance that don't make sense—there are both distances and limits, height and width definitions." I flipped the page backward and forward, cudgeling my cerebral engine for a few more minutes, and exhaled. "It's a Force Wall."

"Good boy," Lily said and pointed to the book. "Now, back to reading."

I blew my nose again, the melted plastic making my nose run and making me truly uncomfortable as it blended with my mana headache. Ah, the glamour of spellcasting.

***

"You ignorant dung beetle!" Lily snarled at the computer as she banged the mouse against the side table she was using. The noise was sufficient to interrupt the silent contemplation of the spells in my head. The silent, closed-eyed, and very still contemplation of spells.

"Hmmmm...?" I rolled my neck to stare at Lily who pointed at the computer.

"They killed me!"

"So? You've died before. Restart or go back to your last saved game."

"No. Not the game. The players. They killed me! Just outside of town," Lily said, already seated and controlling the mouse.

"What are you playing?" I asked and ambled over to stare at the screen. I groaned quietly as I saw the familiar cartoony images and the half-sized dwarf running along idyllic green hills. "Oh no. You are not pulling anything from that into my wish."

"It's fun!" Lily said and stared at me, eyes narrowed.

"Har! Dozens of expansions in, they've had to nerf everyone constantly and keep adding expansion packs to just keep people interested."

"I bet you wish I'd made you heal like these characters do though!"

I groaned, settling in next to her to argue. Some things you just could not let stand!

"And what's nerf?"

Chapter 7

After my disastrous first quest, El took an active interest in my activities. The next evening, she showed up at my door with an agenda and a refusal to take no for an answer. Lily was not invited on this trip, a fact that the jinn did not seem to mind, other than a request for more shawarma. Over the next hour, I was introduced to the hidden-world denizens of my neighborhood. It seemed that I had, unknowingly, moved into one of the hubs of the supernatural community. While it was not necessarily better, most supernaturals liked to live and work together for convenience. The services and skills they might require—from full-body hair grooming for minotaurs to the specialized diet of dryads—made sense to keep localized.

Before each encounter, El would squeeze my triceps and growl a warning to behave myself, and in just about half the cases, I'd remember not to put my foot in my mouth. The other half generally had me alternating between squeals of geeky fanboyishness and minor eeps of terror, even wide-eyed fear in a few cases.

"Do you think you can hold it together for this next meeting?" El hissed at me as we walked up a staircase.

"It'd help if you told me what I was meeting beforehand," I said.

"Har! You almost ran away when I told you we were about to meet Leda."

"She was a medusa!" I said, my voice rising in protest.

"And the best hairdresser in the city. You nearly cost me my next appointment," El snapped and shook her head. "What? You think if she turned people to stone all the time no one would notice? Leda's kept her secret for years, but she won't if a certain someone keeps shouting about it."

"Sorry. Sorry." I lowered my voice. "You've got to give me a break here. Meeting creatures from myth is kind of out my comfort zone."

"Well, get better. This is your life now," El said as we finally reached the floor. I had to pause for a second to catch my breath before El led us to the correct doorway. Thinking better of it, El added, "Shane's a dwarf."

"Oh…" I relaxed at that. I could deal with dwarves. I mean, vertically-challenged individuals weren't exactly unusual. When the door swung open, I had a smile on my face, all ready to be polite. "GIMLI!"

Oops. But seriously, beyond the fact that Shane was lacking both his armor, axe, and helmet, he could have passed for the famous dwarf. At least as portrayed in the movies—dark-red hair and braided beard of the same color with deep-set eyes and a thoroughly unamused look on his face.

"Shane, this is Henry. He's a newcomer to our world. I've been showing him around a bit," El said after she finished extracting her elbow from my ribs.

"Hi. Sorry about that," I said. "It's just, you know, you look like—"

The glare that was shot at me shut me up. Shane nodded gravely to El before glowering at me as he spoke. "I don't have time for this. Charlie's gone missing again. I was just about to go looking for him."

"You need to keep your windows closed," El said. At my confused look, she added, "Charlie's Shane's cat."

"Oh." I paused and then realized a way I could make it up to them. "Hey. I can help. If you've got some fur, I could probably locate him for you."

El hastily added, "He's a new wizard."

"M… wizard." I nodded and surreptitiously rubbed my ribs. Damn, the pixie had sharp elbows.

"A new wizard," Shane said guardedly before he shut the door in our faces.

The pair of us traded looks while, within, we could hear loud movement. Just as I was about to knock again, the door flew open and Shane held his hand out. The hairball he dropped into my hand made me wrinkle my nose in disgust.

80

"This work?"

"Should..." I called upon the knowledge of the Link spell. A few hand gestures later, the hairball glowed, a line of red appearing before my eyes.

Link Cast

Synchronicity 63%

"Well?" Shane said, and I blinked.

"This way." I turned to take the staircase down. The line led diagonally downward, showing the shortest route from me to the cat, I presumed. Which of course didn't take into account minor things like floors, walls, and gravity. As I walked, tendrils of red would flash for a second from the hairball before dying. Each new tendril, each second that I held the original connection, drained my mana as I focused on keeping the spell tuned to Charlie.

We walked down the stairs and around the corner, though an alleyway, and out a side street to another alleyway. I barely paid attention to my surroundings other than ensuring there were no metallic death machines barreling down the road when I crossed. By the time we made it across the street, a slow-growing headache had begun to form as my mana depleted at an astonishing rate. Just as I was about to release the spell, I heard a cry of happiness behind me.

"Charlie! There you are, you horrid beast!" Shane shoved me aside as he ran forward. Charlie, rather than a feisty tomcat with a patch for an eye, was instead an elegant Persian who proceeded to snuggle into Shane's beard, almost disappearing in the dwarf's arms. "Thank you. Charlie always does this, but ever since those damn weres moved in down the street, I don't dare let him run around outside. Never know when they'd get hungry!"

"Do werewolves eat cats?" I asked, and Shane looked me straight in the eye and nodded.

"Aye. And don't let them tell you otherwise! Why, Mrs. Brindle down my hall lost her Angie just a week after those weres moved in."

El made a face as Shane continued to speak, one that was lost to him as he snuggled his cat. "Well, we should get a move on. I need to show Henry around a bit more."

"Of course, of course. I should get Charlie back in." As Shane neared me, he looked up and said, "There a way to contact you, Wizard? If I need Charlie found again, I mean."

"You can call me for now," El interjected before I could say anything. Shane just nodded, accepting this piece of knowledge with equanimity. Only when he was gone did I turn to El and raise an eyebrow. "You're not ready to let them know where you live," she explained. "For one thing, you need some wards on your home."

"Haven't learned that yet," I said, and El snorted.

"I would hope not. It takes years for an enchanter to gain sufficient knowledge to ward a building properly. Now, come on. Let's get this over with."

I followed along after the diminutive pixie, a half smile on my face as I contemplated the dwarf and his cat. It might not have been much, but using my magic for something other than killing rats or practice had actually made me feel good. Useful.

***

"El, why are we doing this?" I asked the pixie hours later. We were splitting a bowl of nachos for supper.

"Because I'm hungry," said El as she waved a nacho laden with jalapenos and cheese.

"No, not supper. The meet and greet." I nodded my head toward where our server, a long, thin praying mantis-like humanoid, took orders from a pair of frat boys. I had to smile internally as they goaded one another to hit on their server when she left. Unfocusing my eyes a little, I could understand why—the tall, leggy blonde glamour was quite the looker.

"Safety," El said and waved her hand around. "We need to get you introduced and your story straight. Until you learn to control your aura, you're glowing like a Christmas tree with all the arcane energy you're giving off. Anyone with the sight—or who has an enchantment to let them *see*, which is most everyone—can tell you're a new... wizard."

"Oh." I sat back and thought about it. If she was right and I did look like a floodlight, then there wasn't a way for me to hide my magic. Since I wasn't apprenticed, I couldn't be introduced as a mage, so I had to be a wizard, a new one at that—which set up my story and let others dismiss me. "Thanks."

"*De nada.*" El waved my thanks away.

"Why are you helping me, El?" I asked. "After the first time—"

"Oh, Henry," El said quietly. "I didn't want you to be part of this world. But since you seem bent on joining us, I might as well make sure you survive it. At least for a little while."

The last few words were said softly, so softly I didn't think El meant for me to hear them. I still didn't understand her wariness, and Lily's. So far, everyone we'd met had been nice and civil. Well, other than the orcs, but muggers were muggers. You didn't expect them to be nice. Still... "Thank you."

El flashed me a smile before she turned back to her beer and nachos.

Chapter 8

The next couple of weeks were filled with small, minor quests that were generated by the supernatural denizens of my neighborhood. Once El had finished introducing me around that evening, I'd become just another fixture, their very own wizard. What no one had told me was that wizards were relatively rare and occasionally useful to know. However, few magic users were approachable, often being the supernatural equivalent of shut-ins. After all, unlike me, most magic users had to spend hours memorizing and then practicing spells over and over again. Spending time running minor errands was the last thing on their minds.

The quests offered to me never ranged into "Fetch ten silver-capped mushrooms from the Forest of Never-Ending Anguish," but were more along the lines of "My walk-in freezer broke down. Could you chill my meat until the repairman gets here?" or "Can you please babysit my brood of a half dozen hyperactive ratkin?" By the way, if anyone ever asks you about that last one, the answer is "hell no." There's a reason Mrs. Umber had to ask an unemployed, newly developed wizard.

Unlike my rat quest, these minor quests—or errands, if you will—did not provide much in terms of experience gain. Spending an evening learning how to adjust my Light spell to cast different colored lights for a vampire-only soiree might not have been particularly exciting, once you got over the fact the vampires had no desire to drink your blood, but it was educational. And, if I did so say so myself, quite beautiful. Interesting fact—vampires were allergic to sunlight due to a specific curse by a sun god. It meant that light, even one filled with ultraviolet light, did nothing to vampires. It was why most vampires actually had a decent tan, even in winter. What better way to throw off hunters than not looking like a pale, gangly monster?

Unfortunately, Mend turned out to be significantly less useful than first envisioned. The spell actually encouraged previously separated pieces together, mending fractures and rips. It was, in some ways, very similar to the Heal spell. However, it also required a degree of finesse to work properly. A Mend spell on a broken button would fix the edges of the strings but might do so with the button on the outside. In that, like so many other things, magic was less useful than a little hard work with needle and thread. After weeks of working with magic, much of my initial excitement had worn away with the realization that magic was cool, but more often than not, mundane solutions won out. It was disappointing but at least partly explained why mages didn't rule the world; magic was useful, but so was plain old science.

All in all, the next few weeks saw a slow but gradual increase in strength and ability as I pushed my own knowledge of magic. Whether it was learning to hit and maintain a specific temperature with my spells, altering the color of light, or avoiding concussions while babysitting—those kids were vicious—I had managed to actually gain another level.

Class: Mage

Level 4 (12% Experience)

Known Spells: Light Sphere, Force Missile, Heat, Freeze, Chime, Breeze, Lesser Shield, Heal, Link, Mend, Ward

Unlike my previous level gain, there were fewer changes in my spells. I might have gotten better at controlling the spells themselves, but according to Lily, the major changes required me to improve significantly more.

Ward, on the other hand, was my first warding spell. It actually wasn't a complete spell by itself; each Ward spell had to be combined with another spell before it could be activated, and it required me to physically carve the ward into an object. A Light Ward, for example, basically created a fixed light spell that could, with a small exertion of will, be turned on or off. At least until the spell charge died.

At my current level, all I could do was put up wards that could be triggered by simple events—an exertion of magical will, the opening or closing of a door, physical pressure. I could not even chain more than one spell together at a time, a prerequisite for actual, workable wards. Still, it didn't stop me from spending half a day carving wards onto various pieces of furniture throughout the house. I only stopped when Lily promised to turn me into a lump of salt if I didn't stop.

Over the course of the few weeks, perhaps the greatest gain I saw was in the understanding of the information Lily had downloaded into my mind. I began to understand mana and magic, and how mana was just a short-form placeholder for the power of creation itself. Mages were people who were able to manipulate mana, using incantations and spell formulas to do what they desired. In truth, after speaking with Lily and El a bit, mages weren't even the most powerful or competent group. Clerics, shamans, and other faith workers could all manipulate mana just as well, though they were often restricted by the tenets of their faiths and their gods.

Furthermore, the incantations and spell formulas didn't matter. It was why there were so many branches of magic to study in the world. It was not the words themselves, but the intentions and mental energy expended that dictated the formation of the spells. By focusing the mind and that "mana muscle" that mages had, they could cast spells, channeling them through their body as appropriate to their gift. Rumors were that the most powerful mages could cast spells with just a thought. Of course, I was miles away from anything like that.

All things said and done, the last few weeks had been peaceful and surprisingly fulfilling. Running deliveries for El when I had no other quests to do, helping out in the neighborhood and receiving pay for it all, it was fun. For once in my life, I actually thought I was getting somewhere.

I should have known it would never last.

***

The first sign of trouble was the shattered basement door. The second was the raised voices as Lily argued with a stranger in our home. I formed a Force Missile in my hand, holding it low so it couldn't be seen easily, and stepped across my threshold to meet the danger. After all, that was what heroes did.

Lily was standing in front of her computer, hands on her hips and one foot tapping the ground, as she argued with my intruder. My intruder, who towered over the diminutive genie, was clad in grey slacks, a cream button-down shirt, and a long, black woolen coat. He could easily have walked around downtown and not drawn a glance, which made his presence in my rundown basement apartment even stranger.

"...you will come with me!" the stranger finished demanding when I stepped in. Like a trigger, he swiveled around to glare at me before his gaze fixed on my ring. Without even speaking, he raised his hand, fingers splaying around and twisting a few times before he jerked it toward himself. For the briefest of moments, I felt a tugging on the ring before I clenched my fist tight, and the tugging faded.

Out-of-level opponent encountered.
Please increase level before continuing encounter.

Unknown Assailant (Mage Level 187)

"No. You can't take his ring away," Lily said, snapping at the man. "I told you. It's useless."

"What in the blazes?" the man growled and raised his hand, repeating what had to be a spell. This time, there wasn't even a faint tug.

"Stop that!" I snapped at him and added, "And who the hell are you?"

"How—?" Eyes narrowed, the man stared at me and my hand while he ignored my question. With a shrug, he strode over to me and grabbed at my hand, coming to a stop inches away from my body. Reflexively, I swung the hand that held the Force Missile and watched the formed spell shatter a foot away from the man's body, a rainbow of colors rippling from the point of impact.

"A wizard," the man snarled, and he flicked a finger and pointed it at me. A Force Spear formed and shot toward my face faster than I could react. Before it reached me, the Force Spear disappeared as if it had never existed.

"What?" we both cried out in unison.

Out-of-level opponent encountered.
Please increase level before continuing encounter.

Again, the words flashed in front of my face, and this time, I actually read them. Out of level? Oh! Like the orcs.

"Genie! You did this." The man turned and snarled at Lily who smirked at him.

"Yes, I did. Told you, you aren't taking his ring," Lily said once more.

"Who are you?" I demanded again, glaring at the man as I moved away from him, courage bolstered by the fact that he really couldn't do anything. It seemed whatever Lily had done, it worked both ways and stopped me from hurting him too.

"I am Caleb Hahn, Magus of the Third Circle, and I demand you return that ring," Caleb said, drawing himself to his full height.

If he thought to intimidate me by looming, he'd chosen the wrong person. I'd grown up my whole life as the short Asian, and after a while, you either learned to ignore the height disparity or just became totally screwed over by it. I glared right back at him, my hand clenched tight as I snapped. "No. Now fuck off before I call the cops."

"The cops! You would call mundane humans on this, you unworthy peasant?" Caleb said.

"Well, yeah. You broke my door, and you are refusing to leave. I can't hurt you, and you can't hurt me." I pulled out my cell phone. "Now, you leaving or not?"

Caleb's eyes grew wide, and he spluttered a few more times, something about the sanctity of supernatural affairs, but his clarity was not helped by Lily giggling and holding her sides next to me. When I started dialing, Caleb finally threw his hands up and stalked out of the room, retreating with as much dignity as he could.

Asshole never even offered to fix my door either. Thankfully, with a little elbow grease and the Mend spell, the door was an easy patch since he had only busted the knob itself. It was after all that was done with that I had time to speak with Lily.

"So, what was that about?" I asked Lily, who was looking uncharacteristically serious when I turned to look at her.

"That was meant to be the end of this," Lily replied, waving her hand around. "But now that we've thwarted them—I love that word, thwar-ted—they'll have to regroup and think about it."

"I know what it was. I want to know what it *was about*," I said.

"Ah." Lily paused, staring at me before answering. "The ring. It was previously owned by a mage in the order. You probably realized that. They wanted the ring and me back."

"Finders keepers not a thing in the supernatural world?" I asked lightly.

"No," Lily said bitingly, glaring at me till she realized I was taking this seriously. "They will be back."

"Can they break the wish? Or am I going to be expecting a lot of, ummm... how many circles are there?"

"Seven. But they'd have to send an apprentice to deal with you," Lily said. "You wouldn't even qualify for one of their circles yet."

"But, I'm level four!" I spluttered.

"Uh huh, and the minimum level to get out of being an apprentice would be around level twenty or so, I'd say. And to actually become a member of the council, you'd have to be level forty at least. Maybe fifty," Lily said.

"Oh..." I frowned. "But my spells—"

"Are a cheat. You can cast certain spells because of what I've given you, but your understanding of magic itself is pitiful."

"Hey!"

"Could you recreate any of your spells yourself?" Lily shot back.

"Umm..." I frowned, thinking about it. I focused for a second, trying to recreate the Light spell from basics. After all, it was the spell I used the most and thus should have been most familiar with. The beginning was simple. I could remember that part easily enough. About a third of the way in, I realized I was having to cudgel my brain to extract the necessary mental gymnastics required to continue casting the spell. About halfway through, I felt the spell fizzle, the feedback sending a spike of pain through my head like an icepick through my eye. "Aaarggh."

"Told you," Lily said.

I grunted, rubbing at my eyes as the pain faded. Fine. Perhaps I relied on the ready-made, intuitive spells she had provided too much.

"It'll be a while before they actually send someone though. The council isn't very quick at making decisions or changing their minds." Lily fixed me with a glare. "However, that doesn't mean you can slack off. Once they decide to move, they will move."

"Yeah, but if I get better, my level goes up and they can throw more at me."

"You do realize that 'levels' aren't exactly accurate? I mean, it's one thing to stop a Third-Circle Mage coming at you, but if they aren't putting out magic like a sun, things start getting a bit more complicated. A mugger or a hitman, from my perspective, is only a few levels difference but from yours is significant," Lily said, and I grunted.

She had a point. And rather more importantly, I hadn't chosen to learn magic so I could hide in a corner at the first sign of trouble. If I was going to learn magic, I was going to learn it properly. Which meant… "I'm going to need better quests then."

As Lily smiled, I felt a chill go through my body.

Chapter 9

Five feet tall, red, muscular, and naked with a pair of horns, a whiplike tail, and tiny wings that couldn't support a bat, the imp raised his fist, ready pound me into the floor again in the back kitchen of the Italian mom-and-pop shop we were battling in. Thankfully, the imp was a lot like my high school bullies, all strength, no finesse, and the haymaker he threw was telegraphed from a mile away.

I ducked underneath the punch, losing a precious second as I wobbled on my feet, my balance still a bit shot from earlier blows. I twisted my fingers in a circle and pointed as I chanted the words "Force Missile." A ball of blue and green formed in the circle, shooting forward as I finished chanting and pointing, striking the imp in its chest.

Force Missile Cast
89% Synchronicity

Force Bolt does 15 damage to Lesser Imp.

The attack just pissed the imp off further, and it swung a tight uppercut that caught me in the chest, throwing my frail form backward. I smashed into the closed refrigerator door and groaned, the back of my head sending pain signals from where it had been knocked around even further.

Henry Alfred Chan Hock Tsien dealt 23 damage by Lesser Imp.

Even as I twisted my fingers around to cast another spell, the imp battered my hand away disdainfully. Through tear-filled eyes, I stared at my would-be murderer.

Lesser Imp (Level 4)
HP: 13/43

Before the monster could finish me off, a thrown cast-iron pan caught it on the back of its head. I swore I saw a little red -1 float off the top of its head, though I wasn't sure if that was just the incipient concussion or an actual artifact of Lily tinkering with the wish. The imp, distracted, turned around and stalked to its new prey.

"Do something!" Chantelle Rossi, the imp's attacker and my current quest-giver, screamed at me as she scrambled around the kitchen for more things to throw at the monster.

Reminded I wasn't part of the audience in this life-or-death struggle, I cast my Force Missile spell. Once again, I received a notification with an 84 percent synchronicity rate, more than enough to deal the damage needed to end the imp. This time, when the Force Missile hit, it cracked the monster's skull, leaving its corpse slumped against the sink. I groaned, sitting down as I stared at the blinking blue bar that indicated I had nearly no mana left.

Lesser Imp (Level 4) Defeated!

My benefactor was not taking the sudden change in fortunes in stride, instead having scooped up a pan to smash the dead monster around a few more times. Only when it did not attempt to defend itself did she stop. Chantelle stood over the dead monster, long, black hair disheveled and white blouse popped open, green blood staining it. When she turned to me, eyes sparkling with fury, her lips pulled into a snarl.

"You! You were hired to fix the problem, not make it worse," she snapped as she stalked toward me, waving the bloody pot in her hand. A piece of pasta, resiliently holding on against the tyranny of gravity, finally succumbed and dropped to the ground, landing by her feet. This, thankfully, made her pause in her tirade long enough for me to get a word in.

"Sorry! I… it was just supposed to be a level-four imp!" I spluttered as I pushed myself up, my chest aching as I breathed. Damn demon had fists like boulders.

"What do you mean 'level four'?" the raven-haired proprietress said, shaking her head. "Look at this mess. You're going to cost us more to have the place fixed up than the damage the imp was doing!"

At Chantelle's accusation, I slowly—very slowly as my neck and head were still throbbing—surveyed the room. Shattered glassware, spilled food, a few broken cupboards, and a hole in the microwave from an errant Force Missile greeted my eyes in quick succession.

"Sorry… I'll, ummm…"

"We're taking the imp's body. And don't expect to get paid!"

"But… I—"

A quick shake of the pot was enough to make me back down. A few more apologies and I finally managed to extricate myself from the kitchen and Rossi's, her family restaurant, without being beaten to death. Outside, I paused for a second to take in the beautiful, clear day and breathed in the clear, clean air. On the opposite side of the street, a few others stared at me strangely, basking in the sunlight, including a bespectacled teenager who was actually glaring. I had to smile as I relaxed and shook off the berating I had received. I was alive and learning magic. What else could I ask for?

***

As I got out of my Ryde and tapped my phone to acknowledge having been dropped off, I found myself grateful I'd decided to skip biking. My head throbbed, my back spasmed, and I found myself fumbling my keys to my basement suite. I kicked the door closed behind me, whimpered at the loud noise, and crashed on my futon.

When I woke up later that evening, almost all my injuries were healed once again. A quick perusal of the notifications explained things to me.

Henry Alfred Chan Hock Tsien is well rested. +5% Experience Gain for 4 hours.
Henry Alfred Chan Hock Tsien has gained 37 health points due to resting.

Huh. I really needed to get Lily to stop messing with the notifications, but ever since she'd seen a bill with my full name, she'd been on this kick of putting it everywhere. As my stomach growled, I got up to throw a ready-made pizza in the oven. I turned my head to stare at the jinn who was hovering over my computer. I had thought picking up a second laptop for myself would have freed up a computer for my use. Instead, Lily had just decided to take them both over and was running two different games at the same time.

"That was not a level-four imp," I grumped at Lily. Silence lingered for so long I thought she might not have heard me, punctuated only by the tapping on the keyboard and click of her mouse.

"Yes, it was," Lily said. "You just suck at fighting."

"I'm supposed to be good at it?" I muttered, shaking my head. The imp had been my second combat quest, and I had to admit, she was right. At least I hadn't gotten bitten, but it wasn't as if I'd ever had any real experience fighting for my life. Scraps with schoolyard bullies and the occasional mugging did not count after all. I wasn't a soldier or police officer or a martial artist. I was just a guy who liked computer and role-playing games and had found a magic ring.

"You ready for the next one?" Lily asked. "Goddamn noob, do your job…"

"Ummm…" I glared at Lily, but since she wasn't bothering to look up, the glare did just about nothing. In the end, I gave up. "You know, I'm new at this, but calling me a noob is a little rude."

"Not you. It's this damn cleric. Can't heal for shit. I'm dying here," Lily said, a hand briefly waving at her game. She turned her head to the side, eyeing the other game before returning to the one she was focused on. It seemed in the second game, she was flying some spaceship that was moving on autopilot, stars shifting as she kept turning and jumping. "Though, if the shoe fits…"

"Whatever," I growled. "You said you have a new quest?"

"Take your pick," Lily said, pointing to a pile of papers. I frowned, walking to them, picking them up, and scanning the headlines.

Persistent Slime Mold is Eating Away My Floors. Clean It Out! $200

Leprechaun Escapee. Capture and Return. No Corpses! 185 Gold Coins and a Brindell Tulip

Become a Hellhound Trainer! No Special Skills Required. We Will Train on the Job! Fair Compensation.

The Grey Angels Hospice is Looking for Healers! Volunteer Your Time with Our Great Staff and Residents.

Required – an Experienced Exorcist! $350

Gremlin Squatter Removal. $500

I stared at the printouts, a sneaking suspicion confirmed when I looked at the web address printed on the top. "Is this a classifieds website?"

"Mmmhmmm… hey! Give that back," Lily shouted a moment later as I pulled my new laptop onto my lap.

"Hush." I tabbed away from her game. Within seconds, I was at the site. Or what would have been the site if not for a big "Password Protected" sign. A couple seconds of fumbling indicated Lily had not saved her password either. "How do I get in?"

"You don't," Lily said, tapping furiously at her keyboard for a few seconds before turning to me. "That's way too much responsibility for you right now."

"Oh, come on. I'm just going to browse it."

"Too dangerous."

"Browsing?" I said. "I promise not to download any viruses."

"And how about spells, demonic entities, and mana taps?"

"Uhhh…" I paused, pushing the laptop away from me slightly. "Demons can come through the web?" That just sounded like a bad B-movie setup.

"Not normally, but that website isn't on the normal Internet. It's a separate dimensional nexus that the supernatural use, and the defenses that have been applied against such incursions are relaxed there. Otherwise, only entities on this dimension could post on it," Lily said.

At her words, I edged even farther away from my laptop, my eyes wide. "There are other-dimensional beings posting on that!? Like gods and demons and Lovecraft monsters?"

"And angels. Jinn. Fae. Dragons. Ice giants," Lily continued on. "Of course there are. Merl's Web is the most popular communication form right now. Not that there aren't competing sites, but Merl seems to have kept up with the times."

"Merl… Merlin?" I asked suspiciously.

"Yes. The old codger might be trapped, but he's still got his hand in the pie." Lily shook her head. "Once I got back in touch with him, he pointed me to the site."

"Merlin's alive." I sat with a thump, staring at Lily. You'd think that after months of all this, I would have gotten used to being surprised. But still… "And Arthur?"

"Dead. Or sleeping. Don't know. You'd have to ask Merl. Not that he's talking." Lily shrugged her shoulders. "He's, you know, a bit annoyed about all that."

"How about Lancelot? Gawain? The Green Knight? The Holy Grail?"

"Ques-ting," Lily drawled and pointed to the papers again.

I growled softly, but even repeated prodding had her repeating the same word again and again. Eventually, I gave up and went over the quests available. A good half of them seemed to involve killing, finding, or eradicating something. There were no "fetch" quests, probably because I received more than enough of those from El, who at least knew enough to give me exact directions. It wasn't as if I knew where to find fairy dust or three-eyed spotted mushrooms. In the end, I highlighted a couple I was willing to do and handed them to Lily.

"Right. Out then. Once I get details, you'll know."

"That's it?" I frowned, having expected, well, more details now.

"Yes. Now shoo. We're running the Virtuous Grotto, and I don't need you bothering me," Lily said, waving me away.

Kicked out of my apartment, I grabbed my jacket on the way out. Ah well, maybe El had something interesting.

***

After making my way to Nora's, I found El seated at the counter, smiling cheerfully at an unexpected mundane customer. I watched El for a second, my gaze unfocused to see her as her glamour rather than her true form before refocusing my eyes. I had to admire the svelte figure she cut, at least underneath her glamour. Though I had to wonder, what did it look like if someone saw me checking her out and was unable to see through her glamor? On the other hand, one could never tell with others' tastes.

"Henry?" Her voice brought me out of my ruminations, and I realized her customer had left. "Did you need something?"

"No." I shook my head. Then, girding up my courage, I stepped up to the counter, flashing her a smile. "Actually—"

"No."

"You didn't even—"

"Henry, I'm four hundred and thirty-six years old. I know what you were going to ask. And the answer is no," El said and smiled at me gently.

"Well, ummmm…" I paused, staring at El. I felt slightly deflated at having my advances shot down even before I'd gotten started. I looked around, awkward now, as I kicked myself for even trying. I should have known better. After all, El had never indicated any interest in me before beyond a general kindly interest in my well-being. Pretty much what you'd expect a big sister to show a little brother in fact.

"It's not personal, Henry. I might only be a lesser fae, but I am fae. I'll live for thousands of years, and well, as a human mage…" El said, shrugging her shoulders. "It's better this way."

"Oh…" I nodded slightly. I guess that made sense. I mean, the elves in the *Lord of the Rings* series were like that too. And I was no Aragorn.

"So, is there anything else you came in for?"

"Not really. I actually thought you might have something for me to do," I answered, looking back up to see El smiling at me patiently.

"Mmmm… not sure I need to remodel the shop yet."

I winced. "You heard about that."

"Just a little. Showing you around kind of tied you to me," El said.

"Yeah, sorry about that. The imp was tougher than I thought," I said, shrugging my shoulders.

"It's fine. Used to be you couldn't swing a cat without hitting a magical troubleshooter. Now, everyone wants to be an office mage or animator or enchanter," El said, shaking her head. "I guess it works out for you though—otherwise no one would hire you."

"Thanks?" I shook my head again. "Anyway, did you have anything you need me to help with?"

"Actually," El said, smiling slightly and reaching under the counter. In her hand when she lifted it was a simple, brown-paper-wrapped package.

I took it automatically, jiggling it slightly and noting a clink of glass containers before I slid it into my black messenger bag.

"Don't do that! What if it was salamander spit?"

"Ummm…"

"It's highly explosive." El sighed.

"So, is it?"

"No. And you shouldn't be asking what's in the packages. You know that," El said exasperatedly, shaking her head. "It's arthritis rub for Grandma Gail." A quick scribble and she handed me the address on a Post-it note.

"I thought I wasn't supposed to know what was in there," I said.

"You're not normally, but you're going to need to know for this. Now, be polite and nice. You're going into orc territory." El held a finger up. "Just tell them what and who you're delivering for, and they'll leave you alone. Got it?"

"You sell to orcs?" I asked incredulously.

"I sell *arthritis medicine* to everyone," El said. "What, you think I should let Grandma Gail suffer because she's green and tusky?"

"No…" I said, stepping back at the heat in El's voice.

"Get it through your head, Henry. This isn't your fantasy books. These are people with their own hopes and dreams and lives. We're just people trying to get by in a world that isn't necessarily set up for us."

"Sorry. I'm sorry. I'll do better," I said. At El's nod, I backed out and headed off to do her little courier job. Head hunched, I pulled out my phone and punched in the address to work out the fastest way to do this. One day, I'd get a car, but that would have to wait till I had a more regular and consistent source of income, one that did not rely on charity and magical windfalls.

***

Faircreek in the southwestern part of the city once hosted the city's docks. In the 1960s, the city had rebuilt the docks farther downriver, outside of the city proper, to handle the additional business. Now, Faircreek was a mixture of rundown warehouses, squat concrete buildings, and crumbling docks along with a few over-burdened homeless shelters. Dotted throughout the neighborhood were failed attempts at revitalization, the scenic concrete-and-grass walkways along the river unkept and not cleaned, a pair of soaring condos looming over their older cousins. It was no place to go if you weren't a resident, the natural resting place for those who had nowhere else to go.

Not surprisingly, even though I'd lived in the city my whole life, I'd only been down this way twice—once entirely by accident, the second on an ill-advised attempt at a hip-hop concert to impress a date. As I sat on the worn-down upholstery of the bus, waiting for my stop, I stared at the residents with new eyes, El's words still ringing in my mind.

Hunched over, hooded figures slunk from corner to corner, hands in baggy clothing. Under hoods, I caught glimpses of inhuman features—snouts, whiskers, fur, and more. Many had the barest of glamours on, just enough to pass a cursory inspection. Interestingly enough, most glamours showed the individuals as minorities. Perhaps most surprisingly was their number, one in seven, one in eight of those on the streets were inhuman—a higher percentage by far than anywhere else.

We're just people trying to get by in a world that isn't necessarily set up for us.

How hard was life for a supernatural if your funds had to go to not only food but glamour as well? If you had to cover up, hide your identity to survive? If the assholes who were casting glamour spells decided it cost "extra" to make you not look like a minority? I'd stumbled across magic and lucked out finding the golden ring, taking power by choice. Many of those I saw on the streets, they'd never had a choice.

They were somber thoughts to think as I got off the bus and glanced at my phone one last time. I walked the streets to my destination, idly noting I was a good six blocks away.

As I walked, I tried to remember all the hints about safely traversing a bad neighborhood I had ever read. Walk with purpose and keep looking around, but don't make eye contact for too long. Avoid touching, but don't act scared.

You'd think that wielding magic would have made this walk easier, but now that I could see the scales, furs, and tusks of the denizens of this city, it really didn't. It didn't help that I probably shone like a beacon to everyone else too.

I was two-thirds of the way to my destination before I encountered my first problem. A group of orcs, hanging out on the corner in hoodies, torn jeans, and leather gloves, stared at me as I neared them. The stares intensified even as I stepped to the side in an attempt to go around the group, an attempt that was foiled by a large, blocky body.

"What you doing here, Wizard?" The blocker stood in front of me, glaring down at my form.

"Uh…" I blinked and gulped, stepping back. That was a mistake as the orc stepped forward immediately, continuing to crowd me.

"Well? This ain't your neighborhood."

I opened my mouth to say something, but my throat closed with fear. While a part of me knew I was probably—probably—fine due to Lily's wish, all my lizard brain knew was that there were a half dozen large, green, and very muscular figures looking at me aggressively. A pair of hands came up and shoved me backward, sending me stumbling back into a figure I hadn't even realized was behind me.

"You going to say something, boy?"

"Delivery," I croaked out and then cleared my throat, trying again as I pulled myself straight. "Delivery for El. From El. For Grandma… ummmm…" Shit. My mind blanked on her name, the rush of adrenaline making my hands clammy. The looming figures and the casual bump against my shoulder as they crowded me made my breath tighten.

"Grandma…?" One of the orcs snorted before another smacked him on the arm with the back of his hand.

"You delivering the medicine for Grandma Gail?" the smackee asked, and I nodded in dumb relief. "Should have said so." A quick set of hand waves had the orcs stepping back, giving me breathing room. Without even waiting for me to recover, the speaker had already started walking. "Sorry about that. El never told us she was using a wizard for delivery."

"It's fine. I'm new," I muttered, relief washing through my body as we walked toward our destination.

"Oh, shit," the orc muttered just before the loud blare of a siren went off behind us.

Cruising to a stop, a police car stopped us half a block from the apartment building I was to make the delivery at. Inwardly, I cursed, getting nervous once more. It was strange how I could get nervous even if I was doing nothing wrong in the presence of police.

From out of the police car came an elf, a damn elf with pointed ears, long hair, gleaming teeth, and a smirk. A human, who glowed just like me, came to stand beside me. I frowned, staring at the pair, and after a moment, their information finally populated.

Police Elf (Level 28)

Police Mage (Level 32)

"What do we have here?" the elf said, smirking at us as he walked toward us. The orc was standing beside me, hands held to the side and away from his body, his face fixed. "A wizard and an orc walking down the street."

"Uhhh…" I said and then decided to clamp my mouth shut. Surprising fact about having conversations about the supernatural in public—no one cared. Between fantasy movies, LARPers and just normal human self-conceit, the occasional overheard conversation was easily dismissed. Still, most supernaturals weren't this blatant. Then again, this wasn't exactly your normal suburban neighborhood either.

"Witch got your tongue, Wizard?" the elf said, staring at me, baton suddenly in his hand. He moved so smoothly and quickly I didn't see it again until it was under my chin and pushing my head up. A hot flash of anger went through me, but I forced it down.

"Just doing a delivery," I said hoarsely, fighting the roiling emotions of anger, shame, and fear running through me. Damn it.

A hand went to my bag, and I automatically moved to push it aside. A second later, I found myself on the ground, a knee ground into the small of my back, one hand outstretched and the other curled around my body, pain radiating from my knee and chin where I had been slammed into the ground when the human had tossed me down.

"Trying to stop us from doing our job, are you?" A crank on my arm made me grunt in pain. The strap of my bag was pulled aside, and I felt the tension suddenly release, the bag pulled out from underneath me not too gently.

"I wasn't—"

"Lying to a police officer. Tsk…" the mage said, shaking his head. "I hate your kind. Thinking you're all something because you learned a little magic."

"I—"

"Shut up," the orc growled at me and then released a sudden exhalation of breath shortly after a meaty *thunk*.

I couldn't turn my head, and any attempt at moving resulted in another shooting pain from my arm.

"Andy, Andy, Andy, I thought you knew better," the elf said mockingly. I heard the clasp of my bag open and then the noise of the contents of my bag hitting the ground. The muffled *thunk* of the package, my notebook, and the rest of the random crap that I kept in my bag reached my ears. A short while later, I heard the tearing of paper before a dull *thunk* of glass on concrete. I found myself exhaling in thanks that all of El's packages were in ultra-tough, enchanted containers. "What is this? Hmmm…?"

A sharp jab in my back made me arch slightly.

"We're talking to you, Wizard," the mage said.

"Arthritis remedy," I said through stolen breaths.

"Really?" Indistinct noises and a loud sniff later, an open bottle landed on the ground next to me along with its lid and the remaining bottles. "Smells like shit. You peddling shit, Wizard?"

"I'm just bringing it for El," I said.

"El, El, El… that little troublesome pixie," the elf muttered. "I thought she knew better than to deal with scum like this. Well, I guess we'll just have to do something about that."

"What?" I asked as I twisted my head around. The mage let me do so briefly before he reapplied pressure, forcing me to look on futilely as the elf raised his booted foot and came down on the bottle. It shattered under his boot, his foot rising again. Anger flashed through me, at the mage and the elf and the damn orc who just stood there…

The elf raised his foot again to smash another bottle. "Now, be sure to tell El—"

"That's enough, Quinn," a low, husky, and dangerous voice said from the opposite side of my head. "You've had your fun."

"Marc," the elf said, sudden wariness in his voice. I could feel the mage above me shift his weight, turning toward the newcomer.

"Let him go," the same voice growled, and my arm was released. Footsteps shifted, and as I sat up slowly, rubbing my shoulder, I noted the policemen had backed off, staring at the newcomer. I turned my head to look as well and had to agree—the newcomer was definitely worth staring at. Where Andy, my erstwhile guide, had been big, the newcomer could have fronted for an NFL team at nearly seven feet tall and nearly half again as broad. Behind the newcomer was another trio of orcs, none as large as he was but only by a hairbreadth.

"Just making sure the wizard knows what's what," the elf said, smirking still. However, I noticed the pair had their hands near their guns now and were, in fact, moving back to their car easily. "No harm done."

Under the watchful eyes of the orcs, the pair of policeman left. I pulled together my bag, stuffed everything together, and held the broken straps in hand while my emotions raged. I could Mend them, but unlike some, I preferred to keep my magic to quieter and less public locations.

"Well, boy? You going to make your delivery?" the orc snapped at me, and I blinked, nodding quickly. I moved forward, hesitating for a second when he held a hand up to Andy to stop him from coming with me. A quick look told me his signal wasn't for me, and so I headed up the stairs.

You'd think after all that, that Grandma Gail was some mythical, powerful shaman or the power behind the throne. Instead, Grandma Gail was exactly what you'd have expected of a grandmother—old, bent, wrinkled, and in this case, green. She was more than grateful for the delivery and completely forgiving about the single broken bottle. Two hours later, filled with tea and cookies, I tottered out of the grateful orc's neat apartment, surprised to see Andy waiting for me.

"Andy?"

"I'll walk you back," Andy said and then held his hand out.

Taking the dollar bills from him automatically, I frowned as I stared at them.

"For El. For the broken bottle."

"Uhh…" I paused, unsure.

"Just take it. I should have seen them coming," Andy said, and I nodded dumbly as I fell into step with him.

"They do that often?" I asked.

"Every chance they get. Fucking pigs like to hassle us," Andy said, shaking his head. "They pick on us in particular because, well, you know."

Because they were orcs. "Sorry."

"Why are you sorry?" Andy growled at me, and I winced, ducking my head. After a moment, Andy shook his head. "Never mind. It's not your fault."

"Yeah. Assholes," I grumbled, running my finger over the mended strap. Even now, I could feel the slight raises and bumpiness from the Mend spell. At least I was getting better with the spell. Still, a part of me twisted at how easily I'd rolled over. But what was I supposed to do? They were cops. And higher levels than me. In sullen silence, the pair of us made our way back to the bus stop where we stood, brooding over our respective failures. The bus, when it arrived, found us still standing in silence.

"Take care, Wizard. Try not to get beaten up by cops again, eh?" Andy said, waving goodbye as I got on.

I had to chuckle slightly, nodding back to Andy. Well, that had been enlightening and humbling, if somewhat less than useful for my leveling. Then again, perhaps not all experience needed to come with levels.

***

Hours later, I was back home. Lily, surprisingly, was not on the computer but standing over the oven. I eyed the dark-haired genie as she stirred a pot of instant noodles and then walked to my computers without a word. On them, blue screens showed the software had updated. That was one mystery easily solved.

"Lily," I said, walking over to lean against a cupboard. "Wanted to ask you about something."

"Sure," Lily said, eyes raking over me.

I quickly explained my encounter with the orcs and the cops, finishing with: "How come the cops were able to touch me? I mean, they were obviously out of level."

"Thought it might be that," Lily said, tapping her spoon against the pot before she carefully poured the contents into a waiting bowl. "The answer is that the encounter was a social challenge, not a physical one."

"Felt pretty physical to me," I grumbled, rubbing my still-sore shoulder.

"Only because you failed your social check," Lily said, looking up at me.

"I don't really get that you know," I said. "I mean, what makes it a social encounter rather than a physical one? Aren't most encounters social till, well, they're not?"

"Mmmm… yes." Lily paused and then waved a hand to the computers before she returned to stirring the bowl. "But we're talking about your wish and the way I set it up. And I did it by watching the games. If you run into a city and start ganking the guards, you don't expect to get away with it, do you? Same thing here. The police, most legal authorities, are going to be exempt."

"But those guys were assholes," I said, grumbling. "It'd have been nice if they couldn't have grabbed me."

"And then what?" Lily said, raising an eyebrow. "Do you think the fact that they couldn't touch you would deescalate the situation? Make them decide to pack it up and go away?"

"It did for the mage," I said.

"Uh huh. And we both know he'll be back—or someone like him." Lily shook her head. "You don't want the authorities getting wind of you. Especially the mundane ones."

"I guess," I said. I looked at Lily, eyes narrowed as I voiced my other suspicion. "Still, rather convenient that the wish failed then. It must have been pretty elaborate programming for you to have set that up."

"Wasn't set up. I made the call once I saw it happening," Lily said, confirming my suspicion.

"You can do that?"

"Of course." Lily pointed to my hand and her ring that sat on it. "I'm still linked to the ring. So long as you wear it, I'll always have some awareness of you and your surroundings, ensuring encounters happen logically and according to your wish is part of my job after all."

"Huh," I said, nodding slowly. Well, that made sense, and it was what I'd signed up for. Still, knowing Lily was spying on me was just a little creepy. Then again, after a while I'd gotten used to the great god Google tracking my searches and where I traveled every day. How was this any different really? "Hey, why didn't they do something about my ring? I mean, those guys seemed like the kind who'd steal them."

"The ring has an obscuration enchantment on it. You'd have to be significantly more powerful before you could pierce it," Lily answered promptly.

"Like the mage," I said and got a confirming nod. "Then, El?"

"We walked through her wards into her place of power," Lily said, and I nodded. It still didn't explain why Lily never showed El's level to me, but I left that for now. I'd asked before and never gotten a satisfactory answer.

"We done? Because my food's getting cold."

"Yeah, yeah." I waved her back to her life as I wandered to the pile of quest notes. Might as well check out what else she had found.

Chapter 10

Life continued in this rather sedate and mundane fashion for weeks. I picked up a couple levels as I expanded my understanding of magic, learning more complex ward spells and a pair of new spells, Glamour and Illusion. It might have seemed they were the same, but glamours affected living creatures while illusions, inanimate objects. Due to a living being's natural aura, illusions were not a viable form of concealment, often breaking down before long upon interaction. Glamours, which interacted directly with the aura of a living being, were much more effective and actually altered the perception of viewers. Of course, both of those statements only held true for someone at my level; Lily had been quick to stress that powerful and skilled mages were able to cast illusions on living beings and glamours on inanimate objects as needed.

Still, I had fun playing with both spells. I often added an illusion to my messenger bag and a glamour to myself before I left for the day. Something small but noticeable—a new logo, a tiny tattoo, or highlights in my hair. Just small changes that allowed me to practice the spells without costing me too much in terms of concentration or energy, which was another major thing. These spells had to be continually channeled, like my Heal spell.

Nearly a month after I'd acquired them, nearly four months after I had acquired the ring, a new incident occurred. I should have expected it really. After all, the secret of the ring could not be kept forever. It was as I was walking out of the hospice building, after a grueling day of healing, that she confronted me. Six feet, two inches tall—towering over my diminutive five-eight—blond hair, and green eyes, the Amazon-escapee leveled a spear at my chest which I nearly walked into.

"Mr. Henry Tsien, hand over the ring or face the judgement of God!" the blonde said, spear held unwavering in front of my chest. Clad in a weird mix of armor and a nun's habit, blond peeking out from the edges, she couldn't have been older than her late teens at best. She might have held the spear competently, but her high voice and slightly breathy tones did little assure me she was serious.

"Oh, hell…" I muttered, staring at the woman. I raised my hand slightly, pushed against the blade, and frowned when it refused to budge. Well, this looked like another social encounter. Surely I wasn't expected to fight a crazy, spear-wielding nun in the middle of the streets, right? While the hospice building was somewhat out of town and in a quiet neighborhood, it still wasn't exactly inconspicuous.

"Do not blaspheme!"

"Seriously? You're holding a spear and telling me not to swear?" I goggled at the woman, shaking my head at the insanity of it all. "And don't you people have something about not attracting attention?"

"Innocent bystanders have been dealt with," the woman said.

I frowned and looked around, noticing for the first time the way the area around us was filled with a golden yellow light. I stared at the light, some of the ways it interacted with the surroundings tickling at my memory.

"Now, hand over the ring."

"No," I said as I stared at the light. On closer inspection, it wasn't diffuse in a solid format but had shades to it, and within those shades, there were gradations of that golden power. I frowned, for the harder I focused on the light, the harder it was to see it. On a hunch, I unfocused my gaze and watched as the image snapped into place. "It's a—owww. Why'd you hit me for?"

"You are ignoring me!" the blonde said, almost stamping her feet, pulling back the haft of the spear that she'd smacked my shoulder with.

"Imagine that. I'm ignoring the crazed person holding a spear at me who seems to think hitting me is going to make me do what she wants." I shook my head. Looked like my hunch was right; she wasn't actually going to hurt me. "Did your parents never teach you manners? You could at least introduce yourself before demanding things from me. Or hitting me."

"You... I am Alexa Dumough, Initiate of the Knights Templar, tasked with the retrieval of the ring you wear on your finger," Alexa said, her spear returning to point at me.

I glared at the spear as I rubbed at my injury and parsed her words together. "Huh. I thought the Knights Templar were disbanded—something to do with the King of France? And initiate? Is that lower than a squire?" Now that she had finally introduced herself, I noticed the information above her head populate further.

Alexa Dumough (Knight Initiate Level 8)
HP: 80/80

Now that she'd hit me, she'd gained an HP bar. That wasn't good. The only time Lily ever made that information appear was when she thought I would need it. Still, it did seem Lily was expecting me to have to fight Alexa, a factor I was not in favor of. It had nothing to do with the fact that she was a girl and had everything to do with the very sharp spear she held.

"I am... you, the ring! Give me the ring," Alexa finally snapped, prodding the spear forward.

I jumped backward, my eyes wide as the tip nearly pierced my chest. "Are you insane, woman!" I snapped at her, my eyes wide as I reflexively patted at my chest. "You could have—" I frowned, feeling something wet and sticky on my fingers. I looked down, seeing blood slowly trickle down my chest. "Oh, you did."

"I... I'm sorry! I didn't mean to." Alexa gasped, dropping her spear as she rushed forward. "Here, let me—"

"Stay back!" My hand raised reflexively as I called upon and cast a Force Spear, ensuring that I blunted the the newly upgraded version of my offensive spell. It hit her head on, and she stumbled as she tried to stop herself, the blow catching her on the forehead instead of chest as I had planned. The sickening crack and the sudden weightless slump had me wide eyed. I lurched forward to catch her but had to abort, the nerves in my chest finally sending me delayed pain signals.

Legs giving way under the pain, I sank to the ground and pushed back against the flowing blood. I drew a shallow breath, focusing on the Heal spell as I tried to slow my bleeding via magic and pressure. Damn it. She had barely even pushed the spear forward. How had it cut through me that easily?

The Heal spell formed and then faltered, fading away before I pushed back against the failing spell structure, reforming it in my mind. Mana flowed, more than I could use, spilling from my control as I channeled the spell into my body. I could feel my blood twist and shift, slowing and congealing while new cells grew, forming at the edges of my wound. Pain, subdued at first while I'd concentrated, exploded as my body worked to heal itself. My spell faltered and failed, and it took long, agonizing minutes before I could piece the stab wound together again. This time, when the pain came, I was ready for it. I rode the waves of pain, coasting along the edges of blanking out before the world resolved itself into a persistent headache and my mana depleted.

I pulled myself out, running fingers along the gummy and sore wound, glad to see it had stopped bleeding. It had not healed, but at least the wound had closed. Good enough, at least to get back. However, as I stared at my chest and the bloody mess that was my shirt and jeans, I had to wonder how the hell I was going to get back home. Thankfully, I had an extra pair of clothing on me, but still…

A slight groan near me had me looking up, frowning as the blonde stirred and reminded me I had another problem too. I slowly inched over to the girl, pushing the spear away from her hands before I patted her down, quickly locating a wallet with her ID and some cash and nothing else. I frowned, staring at the money and the blonde, brain turning.

***

Thank God taxi drivers had a tendency to not ask questions when you paid in cash. Of course, it helped that the illusion I cast on the spear helped reduce the strangeness of it all. Still, I was grateful when I finally got the blonde into my apartment. Her dead weight dropped unceremoniously on the floor, and I sagged against the wall.

When I finally came to, I found Lily sitting next to me and Alexa trussed up with some rope. I blushed slightly, realizing where Lily had found the smooth, silk rope, not that Lily seemed to have noticed. I might have been having a dry spell right now, but I did have interests outside of my books.

"Henry, why did you bring her back?" Lily asked grumpily.

"I couldn't just leave her there unconscious!" Moving gingerly, I crept over to Alexa and cast the Heal spell on her, only to be surprised that she had almost fully healed with nary even a bruise. Weird. Still, I hoped that meant she would be fine and no permanent damage had been done by knocking her unconscious. Unlike in the movies, knocking someone out often meant you had given them a concussion, which in the real world had severe consequences. On the other hand, the way she had healed, perhaps we weren't exactly in the "real world" as much. I was still working out how much the supernatural world changed the reality that I'd known before.

"She's an initiate with the damn Templars. And there was an illusion spell all around you that she certainly didn't cast," Lily said.

"Fine. I wasn't exactly thinking that clearly. Something about getting stabbed…" I frowned and then turned to the spear. A few minutes later, some furious scrubbing and a liberal application of bleach had ensured the spear was clear of any blood. That didn't help with the blood that had spilled in front of the hospice building, but at least this kept it out of her hands right now. Eventually, the blood would lose its efficacy as a link, thank God.

By the time I was done, Alexa had finally woken up and was sitting up. Surprisingly, after an initial struggle with the rope, she seemed perfectly calm, first checking her surroundings before fixing me and Lily with a serious look.

"I will warn you that I am trained to resist torture of all forms," Alexa said calmly.

"Torture?" I said, dumbfounded before I shook my head. "Hey, I'm not the one who did the stabbing!"

"You just knocked me out and kidnapped me," Alexa said.

"What? You'd prefer if I left you unconscious on the ground?" I asked.

"Yes."

"Told you so," Lily said, smirking at me.

"Traitor," I said to Lily before I fixed my gaze on Alexa. "Now, how the hell did you learn about the ring? And why you?"

I frowned as Alexa sat there in silence, glaring at me. While I waited, Lily walked back toward her computers, yawning slightly behind her hand. Alexa followed Lily's movements at first before she turned back toward me and caught me looking her over.

"Stop that," Alexa snapped at me.

"Sor—you know what? No. I'm not. You stabbed me," I snapped back and crossed my arms as I glared at the girl. "And looking at you to make sure you aren't going to stab me again isn't something I'm going to apologize for."

"You weren't checking the ropes, and I can't even move anyway," Alexa said, jerking her arms and making her breasts sway slightly as she did so. "You were being a pervert. I can see it in your eyes. Sister Mary was right—all of you men are perverts!"

"Hey!" I protested, though she was right. I had checked her out, but hey, I was a man. And I wasn't doing anything to her and wouldn't either.

"Well, come on then, violate me already."

"What kind of sick world did you grow up in? I'm not going to do that," I said, shaking my head.

"Oh, yeah, that's what you say now. Why else would you kidnap me?"

"I. Am. Not. Going. To. Rape. You," I snapped at her.

"Prove it."

"How?"

"Look into my eyes. I'll activate a skill of mine called Lord's Judgement, and it'll tell me all the sins on your soul, including your dirty, perverted thoughts," Alexa snapped back at me, and I growled.

"Fine!" I leaned forward, still making sure I was out of her reach and met her gaze.

"**The Lord's Judgement**." Alexa's voice had changed, gaining a timber and depth that resounded through the room. For a second, she seemed to glow with that same golden light I had seen at the hospice building. Time seemed to stretch as our gazes met, my consciousness seeping into hers, before she blinked and said, "Ewwwww."

"Wha…" I leaned back, dizziness slowly disappearing.

"Sister Mary really was right," Alexa muttered.

"Really, we're back to that again?" I asked, rubbing at my temples. "I thought your damn skill was supposed to tell you the truth?"

"Yes. It did. And I'm never doing any of that with you," Alexa said, shaking her head and looking confused. "But… you're not a bad person."

"No shit," I said and then frowned, my brain finally catching up with my emotions. "Wait, you just tricked me into letting you cast that skill on me, didn't you?"

"Finally!" Lily said, smacking the top of her forehead with the palm of her hand. "You really aren't very good at this, are you, Henry?"

"He really isn't," Alexa confirmed, smirking at me. Well, I guess I'd have smirked too if I was tied up, recently concussed, and still managed to trick my captor into… well, something. "I don't believe he actually fell for the 'innocent girl' trick."

"He's a bit of a white knight," Lily confirmed, shaking her head slightly as she continued to play on the computer.

"I'm surprised you didn't stop it though, Jinn."

"Just a spectator here mostly," Lily said. "Anyway, you seemed to have things well under control."

I growled at the pair, dragging their attention back to me. "Again, why the hell are you after the ring, and how did you know about it?"

Alexa frowned and coughed slightly. "Maybe I'd talk more if I had a drink?"

With a sigh, I walked toward her with a glass of water, keeping a close eye on Alexa. She took her time sipping on it, finally sitting back to indicate she was done. I put the glass away and sat back down to stare at her while she smiled at me.

"You wouldn't be willing to let me go too, would you?"

"No."

"Girl has to try," Alexa said, smiling slightly. It was interesting that she seemed a lot more confident here, tied up, rather than when she'd held the spear to me. I'm sure it said something about her, but what I couldn't say for sure.

"You going to answer? Or are you still playing for time?"

"Not completely oblivious, are you?" Alexa asked, and at my raised eyebrow, she shrugged. "Fine. An oracle we use learned about the ring being found. They saw you, the ring, and the city and said I had to be the one to come. And no, I don't know why me."

I grunted, keeping silent. I understood why; anyone else and they'd have been out of level and wouldn't have been able to interact with me. If I had to worry about oracles and other seers learning about the ring in this way, I had a feeling I could expect a lot more visitors soon.

"So now what?"

"I thought that was my question," Alexa said back, wiggling slightly in the ropes again to emphasize her point.

"Well, are you going to stab me again if I let you loose?" I said, frowning.

Alexa lips pursed as she turned away, her voice growing faint. "I'm sorry."

"Sorry?" I asked.

"Yes. Sorry. I didn't actually mean to stab you yet." Alexa raised her voice. "I'm sorry, all right? I, well, the martial track wasn't my thing."

"Martial track?" I frowned, and Alexa pursed her lips, shaking her head. Right, of course. Secret society so they obviously had their secrets. Still, I could guess easily enough—there were probably different ways to serve the society, and she was probably more administrative or social. Maybe magical? "So, stabbing is a no?"

"I…" Alexa paused, her voice firming. "My task is to ensure that the ring does not fall into the wrong hands. I will ensure that the scourge that is…"

Alexa's voice trailed off as she stared at Lily, the scourge of the earth who had a lock of hair in her mouth as she clicked away happily at her computer.

"Right, right. Stabbing still on the table. We'll talk about untying once it's not. Now, I'm hungry." I stood and walked to the kitchen to finish my own meal. It was only when I had brought and set the plates on the table, rice and quick stir-fried beef bowls that were ready on the kitchen counter, that I realized one rather important issue: we didn't have enough space in my bachelor pad to all eat—not at a table anyway. "Well, I'll eat first then."

"What if I gave you my parole?" Alexa asked, raising her voice.

"Hmmm?" I asked around a mouthful of rice, staring at the blonde.

"What if I gave you my parole that I wouldn't run, attack you or the jinn. Will you untie me then?"

"How do I know you're telling the truth?" I asked after I swallowed. The look Alexa shot me could have sent me under if stares could kill.

"I swear in the name of the Lord and my hope of everlasting salvation that if I am released, I shall not attempt to escape, attack you or the jinn, or otherwise act against your interest for the duration of this night, so long as I am treated with the respect and care as befits a prisoner," Alexa intoned. Again, she was sheathed in that golden light, and then it was gone, and it was just her green-eyed stare, fixed on me, waiting.

"Ummm…" I paused and looked over at Lily, hoping for some help. However, the jinn was studiously avoiding my gaze. Right—GM couldn't give advice. However, in this case, a non-answer was as good as an answer since I knew Lily would have tried something if she really thought this was dangerous. At least, I believed so. "I'll retie you just before we sleep. Deal?"

At her confirming nod, I released Alexa, who immediately stood and headed for the washroom. I felt a twinge of panic, knowing there was a window she could escape from that I'd forcibly pushed down. If she left, it might actually be for the best. I wasn't entirely sure what I was going to do with her as a prisoner anyway.

"Lily, magic question. I keep seeing this golden light whenever Alexa invokes something. I'm assuming that's another form of mana or magic? Faith magic maybe?" I asked.

"Bingo." Lily smiled at me. "Faith magic uses a different power source than your spells—the power coming direct from the gods they believe in."

"So, God is real?"

"Real enough to power her spells. Though that could be said the same for many others," Lily said.

I opened my mouth to ask for more clarification, but the door opened, and Alexa walked to the table to grab her bowl. Not ideal, but at least I had an idea about what she had done.

Dinner, not surprisingly, had been awkward. Attempts at conversation—or interrogation, as Alexa had called it—failed spectacularly, crashing like a burning blimp. In the end, I ended up spending the last few hours of the evening reading through my spell book while Alexa ran through a series of stretches before submitting to being tied once more. A simple ward spell on the rope helped satisfy me that she would not be removing it without alerting myself. Then, I dealt with the next problem—bedding for the night. A few quick reconfigurations, and I was on the floor next to the door, my sleeping bag rolled out while Alexa slept on my bed and Lily played on the laptops.

As I tossed and turned on the floor, I kept returning to my new problem - what the hell was I supposed to do about Alexa? I couldn't exactly release her since she'd be coming back to try to take the ring from me. But I certainly couldn't just hold her prisoner. If nothing else, my bachelor apartment was going to get extremely crowded rather quickly. Even as I drifted to sleep, no answers came to me.

Who would have ever thought that among my problems after becoming a mage would be the care and handling of a prisoner?

Chapter 11

"For the love of all that is holy and unprofane, get her a toothbrush and let her bathe," Lily whined the next morning, a hand held over her nose.

"I—"

"I give you my parole as I swore last night but for the day. Please, hurry. I would like not to soil myself," Alexa said, eyes wide as she crossed and uncrossed her legs again and again.

"Okay, okay," I said, stumbling over to let her loose. Once released, the woman shifted her body so fast I could have sworn she had a spell on her. The got-to-go-to-the-potty spell. While Alexa was busy cleaning herself up, I set to getting breakfast ready. Which in this case was a pot of coffee and three-day-old bread toasted and covered with butter and jam.

"Decided what you're going to do yet?" Lily asked as she looked up from the laptops. I shook my head as I brought a cup of coffee for Lily, who gratefully took it and handed me back an empty cup in return. I grimaced as I deposited the used cup in the sink and leaned against the cupboard, thinking over my options once again.

There really were only four: kill her, imprison her, let her go, or get her to give up her mission. The first option was a no go for obvious moral reasons, and well, imprisoning her was just a delaying tactic. I had to let her go really, if I couldn't convince her to give up retrieving the ring. The question was, how? That thought consumed me as I finished breakfast, a never-ending series of inane ideas—bribery, blackmail, logic, and blackmail.

"Will you stop staring at me?" Alexa asked finally, exasperated.

"Sorry. Just thinking," I said.

"About me?" Alexa perched on the only other chair in the room while I sat on the bed and Lily clicked away. "Decided that your best option is to kill me yet?"

"Seriously, what kind of training did you get?" I asked, exasperated. "I was trying to work out how to convince you to give up on taking the ring."

"Not going to happen," Alexa replied, shaking her head. "That ring—the jinn—is too powerful to be allowed to go unchecked."

"Yeah, because Lily over there is really dangerous. I think she just about cracked level eighty with her sub," I said dryly.

"That—" Alexa grimaced and shook her head. "She might be contained now but only because the ring constrains her power. If she were to be set free to do what she wants—"

"I'd continue to play these games. Maybe get a library card. Visit a few cities and some old friends. Bud and Merl are always good fun. It's been ages since I've been to Peng Lai," mused Lily as she continued to play.

"And I'm supposed to believe that?" Alexa said, her voice filled with scorn.

"Of course not. I was more telling Henry here. Give him a few ideas for trips when he levels up a bit. It'd do him good to meet some of my friends," Lily replied and looked at Alexa, smiling slightly. "Some of your people could do with meeting them too. Perhaps it'd convince you that the world isn't ending anytime soon, no matter what you think."

"That's because we keep you supernaturals in check!" Alexa snapped, to which Lily snorted and looked up, fixing Alexa with that thousand-year-old stare she occasionally got. I watched as Alexa paled, the weight of the look enough to quiet the initiate.

"Please. You do good work, but the real heavy lifting is done well above your paygrade," Lily said, shaking her head. "Not that anyone actually does much anymore. Mostly, it's just another cold war."

"I thought there were, you know, gods that just wanted destruction. Ragnarök, the apocalypse, 'eating the sun' kind of things," I said.

"Oh, yeah, there are those idiots, but they're locked down pretty tight. Any time they poke their heads out, the others give them a good smacking," Lily replied. "It's amazing what globalization has done for the general stability of the world. Once everyone got over the fact they weren't the only ones, dealing with the idiots became so much easier."

"That's rubbish. Look at World War I!" Alexa refuted Lily.

"Yes. Let's look at World War I," Lily said, tapping at her computer for a few seconds before focusing on us. "A giant world war with guns, tanks, and other newly revealed forms of destruction. And yet, no islands sank, no dark gods rose or civilizations sent back to the dark ages."

"A few million people died!" Alexa said.

"People die. Civilizations die. You get as old as most of the people you're worried about are, you accept that fact. We're not here to stop you from doing stupid things, just destroying the world," Lily said, shaking her head. "Most of us actually like this world and the way it is. Do you have any idea how boring an ice age is?"

Alexa opened and closed her mouth before she glared at Lily, falling silent. I watched the pair for a moment more before I cleared my throat, drawing attention back to me. "Anyway. Lily isn't a threat right now. She's stuck watching over me because of my wish, and I don't intend to destroy the world."

"Even if I believed that, I can't let you keep it. There's nothing to stop someone else from taking the ring," Alexa said.

"Except the Mage Council already tried." I paused, making a quick decision. "Your oracle, they sent you to fight me and not someone more senior, right? Did you ever wonder why?"

"Well… yes." Alexa frowned.

"Right, well, look…" I leaned forward and gave her the gist of the matter. I noticed Lily twitch, but I ignored it, deciding to gamble. I told her all about it, how combat with me was restricted by my wish, how I would eventually get better, but till then, the truly dangerous could not touch me.

"You're saying I was chosen because I'm as good as a four-month-old wizard?" Alexa asked when I finally wound down.

"Well, ummm…" I paused and looked over at Lily who had returned to her games. "Not exactly me—"

"No. It was your game system. Which is controlled by the jinn," Alexa said and pursed her lips. "And according to you, the Mage Council has already tried and failed to take the ring."

"Yes."

"You know, you're not exactly making your case here," Alexa replied. "Sooner or later, someone is going to manage to take it from you. Over your dead body if they have to."

"Says the woman who stabbed me," I muttered, and Alexa flushed.

"I said sorry already."

I shook my head again, the initiate a contradiction of emotions and reasoning I had yet to understand. She wanted the ring but felt bad about almost killing me. Yet, if I had to guess, without her parole, she might try again. Then again, if I thought about the entire religion, I could see how the contradictions inherent in her position could be difficult.

"What do you expect me to do?" I growled, throwing my hands up in the air. "I can't stop people from coming after me. We tried to keep this quiet, but it seems like not talking about it doesn't help. I'm doing the best I can."

"It's not enough," Alexa said, her voice growing soft. "You have your wish, and you'll be a full mage. But so long as you have the ring, you'll be a target for forces you cannot control. Give me the ring and let us handle the problem."

"And what would you do with it?" I frowned, staring at Alexa and tapping the ring with my thumb. "Are you going to lock it away? Or use it?"

"I—" Alexa paused, then spoke frankly to me. "I don't know. That is a decision that will be made by others more senior than me."

"Right. And all of them are going to be wise and smart and not try to make a wish," I said. "You said it. The ring, Lily, she's too powerful for others to use."

"You did."

"And I actually talked to her before I made my wish," I said. "And even then, look at the shit I'm in. Wishes have unintended consequences. Always."

"I'd also point out that so long as Henry lives, my strength is seriously curtailed," Lily said, pointing to me. "His first wish is quite strong and requires a significant amount of my strength to function. Even if he gave you the ring, it would be significantly less powerful. And it wouldn't help him; the Mage Council would not believe he gave up the ring voluntarily. Nor would any others that might come for it. And even once they were convinced, many of those that would come would kill him anyway to reduce future competition."

"Exactly." I nodded firmly and then paused, running the last sentence through my mind and paling slightly. "Anyway, the ring with me means we won't get stomped immediately. No guarantee with you guys."

"We are Knights Templar. We are not, not, not a nerd living in a basement bachelor suite with his gaming books and tame jinn!" Alexa snapped, standing up and glaring at me. "We have God and the Church on our side and can protect that ring."

"Except you didn't, did you?" I asked, shaking my head. "I found the ring in the belongings of an ex-Mage Council member, so you guys must have failed before."

"It was hidden from us. That the ring resurfaced, after so many years... we cannot, I cannot, let you have it, Henry. Once my parole is up..." Alexa shook her head. "I must keep it safe. Even if I have to kill you. I will not hesitate next time."

"And there we have it," I said, flopping down on the bed. "There it always ends up. All the preaching about love thy neighbor, turn the other cheek, be peaceful and pacifist. That always gets thrown away for the damn god of practicality."

"And you don't subscribe to it," Alexa said, pointing at Lily.

"Well..." I laughed, shaking my head. "I don't go about telling everyone else how to live. Also, I made a wish to gain magic powers. Whimsical and foolish seems to be more my wheelhouse. And yes, I'm a little bit of a dreamer because I'm not giving this ring up."

Alexa opened her mouth, but I refused to look at her as I continued to stare at the ceiling. For all my whining and complaining, she was right. The Mage Council, the Knights Templar, and god knows who else were coming. And so far, they'd played nice. I might have been protected, but everyone else around me wasn't. Even I could see the damn hole in our defenses. There was nothing I could do to stop them, so...

If I couldn't beat them, I'd change the rules.

***

"Lily." I squatted next to her and waited for her to look at me. I gestured to her games, and she raised an eyebrow, tapping to put them on pause or at least let her guildmates know she was gone. Seated on our only other chair, Alexa looked up with interest from the book she was reading. I ignored her, and she made no move to come closer, though she was obviously listening as I continued. "I have an idea."

"And I'm not going to like it," Lily said.

"No. But I think, well, this might work. I'm assuming I can't wish you free, right?" I nodded to the ring, and Lily's confirming nod let me dismiss that option. Not that it was very high on the list. For all that I liked the jinn, she was also someone I'd known only four months, and I would admit I was a bit of an optimist when it came to people. Fooling me would not have been hard. "Figured. Right, then we do the next best thing. We make it so the ring isn't available to anyone even if I die."

"How?" Lily asked as she raised an eyebrow.

"Well, I was thinking the sun?"

"No," Lily said, shaking her head. "Anything above the earth would spark a war among the gods. The agreements that bind them from interfering would be void."

"And under the ocean is probably a bad idea since, well, I'm sure there's Atlantis and merfolk and the like, right?" I said.

"No Atlantis," Lily said, shaking her head. "Seriously, it was just a story, but you humans…"

"Huh." I paused, assimilating that fact before moving on. It wasn't as if I could do anything about it. "So, we'll need to find a place which can't be accessed by mortals easily, preferably hidden, and that the gods won't fight over. Sound about right?"

"It'll also have to be after you're dead," Lily said. "So long as your initial wish is active, the link between myself and the ring can be easily traced."

"Right."

"You are going to make the ring disappear?" Alexa said, finally breaking in. "Think of the good it could do."

"Oh, please," I said, shaking my head. "Haven't you been listening? The ring, Lily, isn't a solution. She's just another damn problem. No offense."

"A little taken," Lily said, with a smile.

"But to make it disappear…" Alexa said, shaking her head. "Won't you trap the jinn too? Put your 'friend' in whichever location you decide on?"

"Yes." I closed my eyes and then reopened them, and Lily tilted her head to the side, her face carefully blank as she regarded me. "I think it's time for you to go."

"What?" Alexa said, startled.

"It's time for you to go. Shoo. Your parole is still active, but I don't want you here. You don't need to know the details of this wish," I said, my voice firming. "In fact, it's best if you don't."

Alexa crossed her arms in front of her body. "I—"

"Alexa, go. Either that, or I'm going to knock you out." I raised my hand as I began to call a Light spell to hand.

"You'd be breaking your side of the bargain," Alexa said, eyeing the glowing light above my hand warily. After all, while most people knew what Light spells might look like, there was no guarantee it was not hiding something else.

"So are you," I said and then paused, looking at Alexa straight in the eyes. "Please. Just go."

Alexa hesitated visibly, seeing something in my eyes that finally made her nod. She quickly gathered her things and left. At the door, she hesitated for a second, searching for something more to say. But we'd said it all, again and again.

When we were alone, I turned back to Lily, who had arranged her face into a careful, impassive mien. I smiled grimly and then tapped her on the nose, making her blink. "Well, that should work. So, here's what I was actually thinking…"

Lily stared at me, her eyes widening before they tightened, crinkling slightly. She leaned in as I lowered my voice to get her feedback on my second wish.

***

"What did you do?" El snapped at me when I finally opened the door for her. She stalked in, pushing me aside, and looked around the apartment. It didn't take her long, at which point she spun around and stabbed me with her finger. "Where is she?"

"Lily?"

"No. The other super-hot jinn who lives with you," El growled.

"Huh. You find her hot?" I raised an eyebrow and then yelped as El stabbed me in the chest again with her finger.

"Stop playing around, Henry. This is important," El said. "What did you do?"

"I solved a problem," I said, pushing her finger away and closing the apartment door. When I turned back to El, she had her hip cocked and arms crossed. "Lily's busy letting the relevant people know what I did, as per my wish."

"And what did you do?" El asked. "Because what I'm hearing is less than encouraging."

"I made a wish that will guarantee no one gets the ring if I don't die fulfilling a level-appropriate challenge after level one hundred or from natural causes," I said.

"Why?" El frowned, looking at me.

"Because if I just made the ring disappear after I died, they'd have no reason not to kill me immediately. In fact, I'd be begging them to do so. This way, they have a time limit and a goal—get me powerful enough to die without the ring disappearing," I explained.

"That just puts a target on you and lets these groups know the ring has been found," El said, staring at me.

"It was going to come out anyway. I've been attacked twice—"

Her hand rose, and El's voice grew chilly as she asked, "Twice?"

"Oh, right. You didn't know. Well, you see…" I quickly explained about Alexa to El, who gritted her teeth through the entire explanation.

When I was done, El smiled at me sweetly, leaned back, and kicked me in the balls. At which point, she ended up hopping on her other foot, cursing up a storm, as her foot had come in contact with the wish. When she was finally done, El was seated on my bed rubbing her shin.

"Next time, call me!" El growled.

"I had it under control. No one died," I said and shrugged. "Anyway, Alexa was nice, if kind of single-minded. She wasn't about to kill me."

"She stabbed you. And told you she would do whatever it took to get the ring!"

"Well, sure. But that's just her job," I said, waving my hand. "Anyway, now she won't."

"Did you just make a wish to get in her pants?" El said, her eyes wide.

"No!" I replied instantly. After a moment, I continued slower. "Look, Alexa was just the tip of the spear. The next person to come along wouldn't be as nice. I needed to make sure they wouldn't try to kill me or, you know, threaten others to get to the ring. This way, I get people like the Mage Council and the Templars watching over me so that when those idiots do arrive, they get dealt with."

"Why would they—" El paused, a chain of possibilities probably running through her mind. Outside of a few groups that would want the ring gone, any power-hungry group would actually be lining up to guard me.

"And what happens if you fail before you're level one hundred?"

"Well, then I'm dead, and it ain't my problem," I said. "But seriously, before level one hundred, I'm as safe as I can be. After that, well, they'll likely just give me a bunch of idiotic quests in an attempt to kill me."

El nodded, her long hair swaying. "It sounds well thought out mostly. But if they know about this, aren't you worried they'll try to work out the limits of your wish? Or a way to beat Lily?"

"It's a risk," I said, agreeing with her. "But it's better than doing nothing. And so long as I can level up at a decent rate, the chances are low."

"And when you die?" El finally asked. "The ring becomes the property of whoever can get it."

"Yes," I said, smiling wryly. "But I've no intention of dying anytime soon. And who knows, maybe I'll figure out a better plan by then."

"You better. We don't need another damn war," El said, shaking her finger at me.

I could only nod. After all, I had no intention of causing one either.

Chapter 12

After El had left and Lily returned, life once again returned to its prior routine for a few days. The only real change was that Lily rarely used the second laptop anymore as she was forced to pay greater attention to me and our surroundings. Since we hadn't wanted to alert everyone, we'd instead worded the wish such that she could and would check my surroundings and the buildings regularly for new interested parties. This allowed her to impart the warning before they started making trouble. At least, that was the theory.

Of course, that left me stuck up at home for the most part till everything and everyone settled. Not that I wouldn't need to head out and grab some quests again soon enough—if for nothing more than to pay rent and build up some reserves. I hated not having any real cushion, but between the numerous failed and unpaid quests and my unemployment before this entire thing, my emergency fund was looking pretty anemic.

Which made the pounding on my basement door one morning rather surprising. I frowned, peeking through the peephole to see a grumpy-looking Templar initiate with a bag slung over her shoulder standing on the other side of the door. I cautiously opened the door, noting her spear was at least capped and covered. Still, I put up my Lesser Shield first too.

"Yes?" I said.

"Let me in. This bag is heavy," Alexa said as she pushed against the door. It banged against my foot and stopped, bouncing back slightly. "Well, come on."

"The last time we spoke, you threatened to kill me," I said.

"Yes. And then you made your stupid wish, and now I'm to help you survive. So, let me in," Alexa said, pushing against the door harder.

I winced as the pressure increased against my foot, and I finally moved it away. The blonde stomped into the room, dropped her bag on the ground, and then spun to me, leveling the still-covered spear at my chest.

"Let me make this clear. I'm here to help you get to your level one hundred without dying. After that, you're someone else's problem. We're not friends. We're not even allies. We're just people with sort-of-similar goals."

"Actually, I think—" I stopped as the spear stabbed toward me, stopping a good distance away but making its wielder's point. "I get your point. But what makes you think I should trust you?" I said, crossing my arms in front of my body defensively.

"How do you intend to stop me from following you? Tie me up?" Alexa said bitingly.

"Well…" I leered at her and ducked quickly as she swung the haft at my head. Okay, I deserved that. "You know, following people who don't want you is known as stalking."

"Then you should have given the ring up when we told you to. The Brothers are watching you now, following your every move from a distance. And I'm sure there will be others soon."

"And you're what, the inside girl?"

"I'm here because I was ordered to," Alexa snapped. "Now, where do I put my stuff, and what is our first… quest? That the term?"

"Ugh. Fine. Let's find you a spot," I said while still eyeing her spear and wondering how the hell we'd handle having a third person in this apartment. At least Lily and her mystical nature seemed to skip many of the more unpleasant aspects of a mortal body. I was pretty sure I wouldn't be as lucky with Alexa.

Ten minutes later, we had her meager belongings placed next to the pile of clothing that Lily had managed to acquire on the floor. I grimaced as I made a mental note once again to look into finding a shelving unit that might work.

"No, no, no," Alexa growled as she flipped through the quest papers next to Lily. "Is this what you've been sending him on? There's no way he'll hit this… this… level one hundred with these quests. Cleaning a boat's hull? How is that even a quest?"

"It's a Viking longship that has traveled the waters of the seven realms," Lily said calmly. "You might find the barnacles a bit more challenging than you'd expect."

"Garbage!" Alexa said, growled, and tossed the paper away. "How can you justify sending him on these quests? He's a wizard! They wield the powers of creation at their fingertips, and you have him running errands like a handyman!"

Lily paused, eyes fixed on Alexa, before flicking her gaze to me and then returning to the initiate. "Well, he's been by himself thus far. No one to help pull him out of trouble if things go bad. So, yes, we've been picking safer quests that might be slightly below his level."

"I knew it!" Alexa crowed. "Give up the good stuff, Jinn."

"Whoa. I never said I was forming a party with you—" A pair of incredulous looks made me shut my mouth. Fine, yes, letting her in was pretty much my way of agreeing to this entire endeavor. But it would have been nice to be asked anyway.

"So… you're joining a party with him, right?" Lily said as she shuffled some papers around and pulled a smaller stack out. When Alexa reached for it, Lily refused to let the papers go till she received a firm nod of agreement. "Good. Then—party screen."

Alexa Dumough (Initiate of the Knights Templar Level 10) has joined your party.
HP: 120/120

"Aaargh!" Alexa staggered and dropped the sheets, holding her head as Lily invaded her body with her spells. I stepped forward for a second and then paused, stepping back. No telling what she'd do if I got too close, and a small, petty part of me couldn't help but cackle at her pain. I might have still been holding a little grudge over getting stabbed. Eventually, her breathing ironed out, and she looked up and waved her hands in front of her face. Alexa's face scrunched as she stared into the air, her eyes shifting and lips moving as she read something silently.

"Huh. Do I look like that?" I asked rhetorically. In the corner of my eye, I could still see the mini-portrait of the blonde and her health bar if I focused.

"Yes. Except dumber," Lily said.

"Thanks."

"This is your character screen thing, isn't it?" Alexa said, her face returning to normal as she turned to the two of us. "It's… infernal."

"No. Jinn," Lily said. "I should add that since you're in the same party, you cannot hurt each other intentionally. At least not for the first attack. After that, you'll be automatically booted from the party."

"No surprise attacks," I said, nodding to Lily in thanks. Smart girl.

"I'm not going to kill him. I'm here to make sure he doesn't die," Alexa growled as she collected the papers from the ground, pulling one off a plate filled with half-eaten pizza. I noted that her hands still shook slightly, but otherwise, the woman was back to business. Lily crowed in happiness when the plate was discovered and snatched the pizza slice to consume it, much to the disgust of the blonde.

"This should work," Alexa said after she perused the information a little more and thrust a piece of paper at me. "Accept it and let's go."

"Uhh…" I paused as I read over the details. "This—"

"Accept. It," Alexa snapped at me.

I ignored the glare she gave me, reading over the quest notice one last time. It was level appropriate, I guessed, if more dangerous than what I was used to.

However, Lily was right. We'd been lowballing the quests lately to make sure I didn't die. If this was level appropriate, then adding Alexa to the team should work—assuming she was telling the truth.

And I'd admit I found it hard to doubt the initiate. Not only because she was so damn straightforward, but because the entire point of the second wish was to create a situation like this. Any good role-player would tell you that you can't complete the really challenging quests without a good party. Still, I asked a few questions of Lily before I finally found myself accepting the quest. I took a little pleasure when Alexa jumped as the quest notification appeared in front of her eyes without warning.

Hey, I'd take my wins where I could.

***

"This your car?" I said, envy in my voice. It was not as if it was a Ferrari or Lamborghini, but the recent-model blue hatchback staring at me was significantly better than my feet and occasional bike.

"Not mine. It's the Templars'. You sure you don't have one yourself?" Alexa said as she got in. A few seconds of fiddling with the insides and the GPS and we were ready to leave for our first party mission.

When the silence in the car finally got too uncomfortable, I spoke up. "Maybe we should talk about, you know, the party before we get there."

"What's there to discuss?" Alexa asked. "We get to the woods, you locate the Kallikantzaroi, we kill them, and you level up."

"Is that what they teach you in knight school?" I said, surprised at the cavalier way she discussed the upcoming confrontation. I had actually hoped for more guidance. When silence just greeted my query, I frowned and looked over at the initiate. "Alexa?"

"I'm not a knight, remember? I'm not even a squire," Alexa said, her voice cracking slightly. As I stared at her closer, I realized her grip on the wheel was tighter than it needed to be, lines of tension running along her forearms and shoulder.

"Shit," I said, realizing she had told me that before. I suddenly wondered if we could change the quest. "What did you learn?"

Alexa's lips tightened before she continued, eyes focused on the road. "I'm decent with the spear and have passing knowledge of other melee weapons. I'm familiar with guns too, but we were meant to receive more intensive training later. I can be trusted not to shoot myself, but I would not be confident in wielding one in combat. I, well, I was specializing in faith healing."

"Faith. Healing." Doubt crept into my voice. "That thing where the hacks put their hands on people's heads and then shove them backward and say they're cured? And hope the placebo effect works?"

"We are not fakes," Alexa said, anger tingeing her voice. "I was learning to open myself to the power of God himself. Did you ever stop to wonder why so many still go to such events? If it was all fake?"

"I thought it was because people were idiots," I muttered.

"No. Just hopeful," Alexa said. "Many of our members move among such groups, providing what aid they can. It's not much, but it is what we can do. Other groups, other sects, have a much larger presence than Knights Templar."

The way she said the last, I got the feeling I wasn't getting the rest of that story. Or why a woman who looked like a professional wrestler would prefer to be a healer than the fighter she was built to be. Then again, who was I to complain about people playing against type?

"I guess monster combat wasn't in the curriculum?" I asked finally.

"No, the squires would have studied that," Alexa said, and I nodded slowly. Right. Right…

"Well, if that's the case, I might have a few ideas…"

***

Boarded windows with graffiti, sidewalks that smelled of piss and other unmentionables, and paint that wasn't new two decades ago greeted us as we got out of the car. Alexa locked the doors behind us, though we were more likely to have the wheels stolen if anyone was still around the neighborhood. Mostly though, the industrial complex was abandoned, too far away for most transients to live and too worn down for businesses to run after the manufacturing businesses that had been the lifeblood of the complex left. The few businesses that were here were best left unquestioned of what they actually did out here.

Even for such a place, the presence of a Kallikantzaroi clan was too much to bear. After a few pointed questions to Lily, I had confirmed that the quest had to be an extermination quest—no bargains, no deals, just death. A few more queries explained why—you didn't make deals with the Kalliks because they never upheld their ends. It had less to do with an untrusting nature and more to do with their notoriously short memory spans. You couldn't uphold a deal you couldn't remember.

Alexa took the lead once the car was parked, her spear under a light glamour to make it look like a, well, long stick. I would rather have made it disappear, but simple was better in this case. Removing the spearhead was simple and effective. A woman carrying a long stick around might raise questions but wouldn't automatically draw the police.

We walked through the industrial complex for about thirty minutes, circling worn buildings and looking for signs of the supernatural. Well, I looked for signs of the supernatural. Alexa just looked. I saw no wards, no shields or other magical markings to indicate which building the Kalliks were in, but Alexa eventually led us back near where we'd begun.

"There." Alexa pointed at a metal window grating with her spear. Upon closer inspection, I realized the grating was only held together by some well-placed bent nails. As I stared, I also realized the grass around the region was just a little thinner, sparser than the surroundings, and the window itself cleaner.

A few moments of jiggling and we had the grate off the nails, allowing us free access to the basement of the building. Alexa squirmed in first, dropping softly to the ground and moving aside to allow me to follow. The sparse light that filtered in from the dirty windows was still sufficient to show us we'd entered an old, empty office space. The mushy, moldy mattress we had landed on was the only sign of civilization. If you could call it that. A single closed door led out of the room.

Alexa moved forward carefully, placing an ear against the door and holding still. I stood back, forming a Force Spear in one hand while I layered the Lesser Shield spell in front of me. That spell, along with its equivalent ward placed on the jacket I wore, were my only forms of defense. Unlike me, Alexa had a full set of modified armor under her coat, a mixture of Kevlar and chainmail links sewn together cunningly, such that the armor barely slowed her down—or was noticeable beyond a general bulkiness.

After a short time, Alexa moved away from the door and shook her head. I assumed she meant she had heard nothing, which meant little. Once again, I wished I had a better grasp of my magical abilities. It should have, in theory, been a simple matter to cast a spell to draw noise to me. It was just a simple application of force after all. Still, in the middle of a quest was not the place to be experimenting, but I did make a mental note to test the idea for next time.

As we had no other options, we got ready to open the door. A few moments of frustrating pantomime, and another few hissed words, finally had our entry worked out. I stepped forward to open the door while Alexa ducked in immediately, spear held in front of her on guard. A moment later, I slipped in and closed the door behind us. Silence and darkness greeted us, and even as our eyes adjusted to the gloom, we still could not see far ahead.

"Light," Alexa hissed softly, and I had to agree. It might give away our position, but we needed to see. A quick pair of Light spells later and we had a couple of bobbing lights tethered to our bodies. A quick thought had me peel some loose paint from the door and slide it into a back pocket. Who needed breadcrumbs when you had a Link spell?

The light spell showed us an empty basement vault of the old manufacturing building. We had come out on a small landing, the room dropping another ten feet beneath us, filled with abandoned and rusting machines. Metal arms, hunched over snaking roller conveyor belts, dotted the floor, breaking up our sight lines.

The silence of the abandoned plant was broken by the scratching sound of nails on concrete and the slow swish of feet being dragged against the ground. In the distance, yellow eyes glinted from reflected lights as more and more of the Kalliks awakened.

Quest Update: Clear the Kallikantzaroi clan from their lair.
You've located the Kallikantzaroi clan but have alerted them of your presence. You'll need to defeat their warriors before they can be convinced to leave.

"Shit," I whispered and then realized that we weren't hiding anymore.

"Yes. Maybe we should have thought about this a bit more," Alexa said as she hefted her spear and readied it. For a moment, I considered suggesting backing into the other room, but here we had the advantage of high ground, assuming the Kalliks didn't wield any ranged weapons.

Throughout our short conversation, the Kalliks had continued to approach. At the edges of my light spell, they gathered, yellow eyes catching and reflecting the light. On instinct, I reached for my mana again, splitting my concentration a third time. I felt the mental strain and was grateful that this spell was simple. A quick gesture and the Light Sphere flew out and hung a good twenty feet away, exposing the Kalliks fully.

Hunched over in groups of five or so, the Kalliks were squat, black-furred creatures with the arms of a monkey and long donkey ears across giant heads. Sharp, curved claws caught my attention immediately as the creatures hissed at the additional light. Instinctively, I threw my other hand forward, my Force Spear arcing through the air at my command as I attacked the monsters in front of me. Something in my gut, in my hindbrain, said that these creatures weren't something that could be reasoned with or talked to.

The Force Spear was almost invisible in the meager light, the distortion in light that marked its position barely visible. The Kalliks in the direction I'd gestured twisted and shifted by reflex, but they were not paranoid enough, not until the spear landed and pinned one of their friends to the ground. The screams and roars reverberated through the plant and set my teeth on edge.

"Wha... WARN ME," Alexa snarled as she hunched and set herself as the Kalliks, spurred forward by my attack, charged us.

"Sorry!" I muttered unconsciously and focused on forming another Force Spear. Seconds, precious seconds I took to create the spear. Kalliks covered the ground before us impossibly fast, and by the time my spell was ready, the first one was halfway up the landing.

A single, beautifully executed lunge later, and the Kallik was dying on Alexa's spear. The blonde initiate's face was fixed in a snarl when she stepped back and yanked her spear out of its body, already turning to face the next attacker. A hasty block caught a swiping claw on the spear shaft before Alexa retreated to give herself room and swept the spearhead in front of her in an attempt to keep the creature back.

The clatter of claws against metal near me caught my attention, and I glanced down, seeing the broad, smashed nose and donkey ears of a Kallik near my feet as it hauled itself up above the metal railing. I gasped, brought out of my reverie, to stab with my formed spell. I kept the spell formed in my hand as the motion punched a hole in the monster, black blood flowing from the newly formed wound. A hasty swipe bounced off my Shield before I thrusted again and released the spell, the released Force Spear tearing the monster off the landing.

Beneath my first attacker, another was clambering up, ready to attack. I snarled and raised my hand, channeling Heat as I thrust my hand downward. A roar of flame and a throbbing headache appeared in conjunction, and I played the improvised flamethrower over the landing and my attackers. The Kalliks released their grips, dropping down low in fear.

Without time to form another Force Spear, I relied on my first offensive spell—Force Dart. It was not as powerful as Force Missile or Spear, but it had the advantage of having an extremely short cast time. Hands held out before me, I even abandoned my Lesser Shield so I could form spells faster. The next few minutes became a blur of gnashing teeth, glinting yellow eyes, and swiping claws as I battled to keep the creatures from climbing the landing directly while Alexa killed those that dared challenge her.

As I spun to the side again, after releasing my latest Force Dart, a hard swipe tore at my arm. Concentration broken, my spell dissipated as I stumbled backward, pain radiating from the injury. The low-level Force Shield woven into my jacket fabric saved my arm from serious damage, but as the Kallik swiped at me again, I had to throw myself backward to escape its attack. The railing hammered into my back, bringing a sharp exhalation of breath, and I stared as the Kallik raised its claw, ready to tear my throat out.

A too-human scream jarred the Kallik's concentration, making it hesitate for a fraction of a second. A thrown spearhead punched through its neck and interrupted its attack for all time. I exhaled in relief as I clutched my arm and turned to look down the landing to see Alexa as she stood weaponless and bloody amid the corpses of her attackers.

"Tha—" The ankle that was yanked out from beneath me sent me falling forward abruptly, cutting off my voiced gratitude. I landed hard and bit my tongue, blood immediately filling my mouth as a forgotten Kallik pulled itself upward, using my body as leverage. Claws pierced my skin, and I jerked spasmodically, my feet kicking out uselessly.

By the time I recovered my senses fully, the monster had squirmed two-thirds of its way through the railing, its claws dug into my feet. I slapped a hand sideways at its head pitifully, short, coarse hair and the flexible cartilage of an ear coming into contact with my skin. My hand closed around its ear as claws continued to dig into my body. I twisted and yanked upward, jerking the Kallik toward me and away from my prone body.

A moment later, Alexa was there, as she tackled the monster and sent both of them into the metal railing. Alexa snarled as she plunged a knife that I never knew she had into the monster while I pushed myself away. Seeing that Alexa had things mostly under control, I tried to form a Heal spell around the radiating pain of my wounds, but the spell formations and chants escaped my grasp with each pulse of pain.

***

I came to as a warm energy pulsed through me. As I returned to wakefulness, I noticed the pain from my wounds was gone, replaced by this comforting, warm feeling. As I attempted to sit up, I found an insistent pressure on my chest and a noise in my ears that finally resolved into words.

"Stop moving!" Alexa said and pushed on my chest again. "You'll open all your wounds again."

"Sorry," I said as I relaxed onto the cold floor again. Unable to feel my wounds as that energy flowed through me, I instead focused on my own Heal spell, letting the initial portion of the spell play through my mind. That part of the spell focused on locating injuries and assessing the damage, a magical feedback on the extent of damage that I had experienced.

The overall results were not good. I had numerous cuts and stab wounds in the back of my legs and a few in my torso, from the last Kallik that had clawed itself up me, along with the cut in my arm. Add to that numerous scrapes and bruises and significant blood loss and I was grateful Alexa's healing ability was patching me up. Unlike my own spell, it seemed to bypass minor things like blood loss and instead proceeded to fix problems directly, using the energy as its fuel source. Still, I decided not to just wait for her to be done and focused on my own spell, searching for and directing the spell to focus on the production of additional blood.

It took another few minutes before Alexa finally let me up. By that point, I had begun to shiver slightly from the cold, lack of movement, and blood loss and had to spend the next few minutes doing jumping jacks and chugging an energy drink. I resolutely kept my eyes off the Kallik corpses during this entire process.

"Did we complete the quest?" I asked Alexa while she looked on with an amused expression. I had to admit, between the blood stains, torn clothing, and low light, I probably was an amusing sight. Still, the movement was at least warming me up.

"Not yet," Alexa said. "I'm pretty sure I heard a few others moving around afterward, moving away from us."

"Okay, well, I'm ready," I said, my spells formed in my hands. It seemed a side effect of her spell was a reduction in the headache and mana weariness I experienced from casting. Before we left the landing, I spent a few minutes adding Light Spheres all around the building. Even with the added light, we saw no further signs of trouble in here.

A short and tense hour later, we had searched and prodded our way through the entire warehouse and were finally sure the Kalliks had left. A broken lock and a few fallen treasures on the way out the door told a tale of a hasty retreat. I was glad. The other signs we found indicated there had been children here. I knew I had to get harder, but killing children, even monster children, was a line that I couldn't cross. Not yet at least. Perhaps it was because they were humanoid, or that they seemed mostly sentient, but the thought of murdering them just didn't sit well with me. The quest complete notification, as usual, was just more information that we already knew. This time, Alexa only shifted a bit when it appeared.

"What are you doing?" I blinked as Alexa returned to the main nest of the Kalliks and sorted through what was left.

"Searching," Alexa said. "Ah, har!" She pulled out a wad of cash which she pocketed. A few minutes later, she had some jewelry and some other, more questionable, acquisitions. Some, I could guess, were reagents, items that people like El would like.

"Isn't this…" I frowned, searching for the word. "Wrong?"

"They left. And they probably took these off people they killed. So, no, I'm not finding it wrong," Alexa said. "How do you think the Templars finance themselves? Killing monsters isn't exactly government funded."

"Oh," I said, wondering exactly how much money you could make looting dead bodies. Then, I considered my own circumstances. "You going to share?"

Chapter 13

In the four months since I had acquired the ring, I had gained all of seven levels. In the following four weeks after Alexa moved in, I doubled my level again. There were a few reasons for this. Firstly, I was no longer struggling to figure out the new world I lived in, spending as much time questioning Lily and El about the world as I was questing. Secondly, the newer, tougher quests that we worked as a team forced me to constantly push myself, while Alexa's constant, nagging insistence on training when we weren't questing increased my productivity. Even if I hadn't been slacking off, the woman brought a focus to my training that hadn't been there before.

Not all our new quests involved violence, just a good portion of them these days. As we learned from our mistakes, we started spending a greater portion of our time studying and learning about our potential opponents before we embarked on the quests. Between Lily's extensive knowledge and the Templars' archives that Alexa was able to access, we rarely walked into a problem ill-prepared once we actually started doing our homework.

Thankfully, even Alexa understood that constant violence was a bad idea. Every couple of days, she would pick out a challenging, if nonviolent, quest to undertake. I had to admit, these quests were my favorite and ranged from spending a day layering warding spells, under the guidance of a master warder, to being magical security at a rave. I even managed to put my very first personally crafted spell into play at the rave as I muted the music all around my seat while I watched for glamours and illusions being used to sneak the underage in.

Five months after joining the supernatural world, as I lurched out of bed and got the coffee started, I had to smile as I pulled out my new character sheet.

Class: Mage

Level 14 (45% Experience)

Known Spells: Light Sphere, Force Spear, Force Shield, Force Fingers, Alter Temperature, Alter Sound, Gust, Heal, Link, Track, Scry, Mend, Ward, Glamour, Illusion, Detect Magic

---

I'd grown quite a bit in the last few weeks, and even if I'd never admit it to Alexa herself, it had mostly to do with the initiate. Of course, I wasn't the only one who had developed. Alexa had grown more confident, sure of herself and her choices during the quests. The continuous training she did in the mornings had honed her martial skills.

What puzzled me at first was that Alexa would also sneak out regularly at night or when we had called it a day. One particular evening, I decided to spend some time scrying her, using a piece of her hair, my familiarity with the woman, and a clear bowl of water. Unfortunately, once she entered the office building that was her goal, further scrying attempts were blocked. I'd admit I felt a little dirty doing it, but considering the precarious situation I was in, I felt it necessary. In the end, I spent time watching the office building and Alexa, coming to the conclusion she was reporting in to her superiors. That the office building was within walking distance of my apartment was both reassuring and suffocating. In the end, all I could do was put the entire thing to the side.

The coffee beeped, finally telling me it was ready, and I poured myself a cup before turning to the side to look at the jinn. "Lily," I called and waited for her to pause her game before I continued. "We need to talk. About my sheet."

"Oh?" Lily said inquiringly, arching one perfectly plucked eyebrow. Or shaped? Created? After all, the visage she showed was entirely artificial. I thought. I wasn't entirely sure about that, come to think about it. "What's wrong?"

"The spells. Or skills. Or, you know, this entire thing," I said. "The knowledge you are inserting into my head is beginning to diverge a bit from what I see here. Or maybe the things I understand are diverging. It's like I've got these spells in my head, but as I understand them, as I level, I realize each of the spells are just parts, components. I can alter them to do what I want if I want. Well, theoretically at least."

"Good."

"Good?"

"Of course," Lily confirmed. "It means you're beginning to understand magic properly."

"But, if these spells don't matter…" I frowned, shaking my head, trying to explain my concerns.

"Listen, Henry. Learning magic is like learning a new language. People like myself, the fae, vampires, and the kraken, we're native speakers. We grew up knowing magic, and while we might not necessarily know the finer points of grammar, we intuitively understand it and can 'speak' the language. Humans though, you're ESL. Most mages learn magic step-by-step, memorizing words and understanding the rules of grammar. It means they aren't as intuitive as we are, but they can sometimes pull off things we would never have thought of.

"You on the other hand, well, you're different. The way you're learning magic from your levels is closer to what I understand—intuitively, as a whole. But at the same time, you're human. You need to understand the rules. The spells, well, they're like memorized chapters from a book. You know the chapters and can speak them without thought, but to really understand magic, you need to analyze each sentence, each paragraph, individually."

I nodded at her words, rubbing my chin. If we took the analogy further, there were words, concepts Lily had inserted into my mind that didn't necessarily "fit" with any of the spells at first glance but actually underpinned why the spells worked. I could cast any of these spells, and even alter them, by changing specific words or adding new paragraphs. In fact, I'd been doing this without really considering the underlying structure of the spells.

"Does that mean I'm just a giant parrot? Squawking away spells whenever I need to?" I asked.

"Yes," Lily said, smiling slightly.

"Huh," I said. I'd have felt insulted, but the fact stood that I didn't understand the majority of the spells. Even my Light spell, which was perhaps the easiest spell I knew, was something I still could not cast without relying on the gifted knowledge. But the spell was more complicated than willing light to appear. First, you had to define what light was, then you had to define how much mana you'd supply to create the light. If you were creating a light ball, you had to define the space that the light itself would be in, which meant defining the sphere that the light energy was being focused into. Then, you had positioning of the spell itself in relation to yourself and the world. And that was for the simplest option, without adding in modifications for ongoing channeling and tethering of the spell to yourself.

The Force Dart was even more complicated. The spell was actually a wave of built-up kinetic energy shaped into the form of a dart, locked into space by mana, and then propelled forward by even more mana. On top of all the size, shape, and energy definitions and power requirements that the Light Ball required, Force Dart also needed to be defined according to its flight path and patterns. Still, if you looked at it that way, upgrading the spell from Force Dart to Missile was simple. I was mostly just altering the shape of the container with minor adjustments to the amount of force wielded. The Force Spear, on the other hand, was more complicated with a significantly larger container and more complex equations required as it traveled and interacted with the real world.

"We done?" Lily asked, interrupting my thoughts.

"Not really. I still think the way we have this set up isn't good," I said, waving my hand. "Maybe we should have started with a different system. Perhaps one that did better at teaching the basics."

"Just remember," Lily said. "You're asking me to try to teach you magic when I use it subconsciously. It's only because I've been owned by so many mages in my time that I even know where to start."

"Yeah, I figured," I said. "Still doesn't solve the problem."

"Well, I could put concepts into your mind and let you work it out from there," Lily said. "Hopefully you'll figure it out?"

"Uhhh… no," I stated firmly, making Lily laugh. Before we could continue the discussion, the doorknob twisted and opened, reminding me that once again, I needed to get Alexa her own key.

"I'll think about it," Lily said as she turned back to her game. "You know where the quests are."

Alexa frowned slightly and shot a suspicious glare between the pair of us. When she received no further clarification, she walked over to pick up the quest sheets. Still, from the line in her back, I had a feeling I was in for a more difficult quest.

***

Sometimes, being wrong was worse than being right. In this case, rather than a difficult quest, Alexa had located a monotonous, boring, and yet exacting quest—the unloading of a container's worth of magical merchandise. As the merchandise couldn't be physically touched, I spent the entire day moving one box after the other with Force Fingers, also known as an abbreviated form of magical telekinesis. Of course, added to the dull, throbbing pain from the constant use and concentration required from magic, I also had to contend with the icy disapproval radiating from Alexa. Not that 'anything was wrong' when I'd asked of course.

By the time we got home, I was ready to curl up on my makeshift bed and sleep the night away. Unfortunately, Lily had other ideas. Once Alexa had stomped into the bathroom, the olive-skinned jinn waved her hands at me, and a series of words appeared.

Magical Skillset
Mana Flow: 2/10
Mana to Energy Conversion: 2/10
Spell Container: 2/10
Spatial Location: 3/10
Spatial Movement: 2/10
Energy Manipulation: 2/10
Biological Manipulation: 1/10
Matter Manipulation: 0/10
Duration: 1/10

"Wha..." I said and then stopped, my sluggish brain finally catching up with me. Of course. This was Lily's solution to my problem. A series of skills that demarcated my knowledge. Still. "Why out of ten? And what's considered good?"

"Ten because I'm not doing percentages. Again, jinn, not a god. I can't read your mind, so these are rated off your shown understanding of magic,"

Lily said. "And an apprentice mage would be expected to be a three across all these areas."

"Ah." I frowned, prodding at the list before adding, "This an arithmetic or a logarithmic increase?"

"Logarithmic, I guess. It's going to get harder the more experienced you get. Not that information you need changes, but how easy it is to learn it," Lily explained.

"Thanks," I said. Well, at least this helped to solidify some of the concepts I had been playing around with. As I lay on my mattress, I could not help but prod at the list to get further information.

Mana Flow dictates your control of mana—the amount, quantity, and quality of mana you can put into a spell.

Mana to Energy Conversion is a ratio and indicates the quality of your control when converting mana to energy to affect the world. Required for most spells.

Spell Containers define the boundary of a spell. Higher levels of this skill indicate increased complexity and types of containers that may be defined.

Spatial Location defines the location that a spell may be cast. Low levels indicate the ability to cast spells within touch range. Additional levels dictate distance a spell may be cast from the caster and by visual or other methods of defining locations.

Spatial Movement dictates how a spell will or will not move. Higher levels allow spells to adjust trajectories after being cast or to define multiple variables.

Energy Manipulation indicates the caster's ability to manipulate different types of energy. Low levels indicate base understanding of energy types and forms. Higher levels will allow caster to manipulate multiple forms of energy at the same time and rarer types of energy.

Biological Manipulation indicates the caster's ability to interact and understand biological changes. At the most basic level, caster is able to sense and replicate biological matter from a healthy template. Higher levels allow the caster to alter the template, allowing replication from damaged or unhealthy biological matter or the creation of new biological matter.

Matter Manipulation indicates the caster's ability to interact and understand matter. Low levels allow the caster to replicate matter from templates. Higher levels allow the caster to alter the template, allowing replication from damaged matter or the creation of new matter.

Duration dictates the caster's knowledge of time as it relates to his spells. Basic levels allow the caster to constantly channel a spell or to cast a spell of set duration. Higher levels allow longer duration spells as well as the use of time-based triggers for spells.

All of it was self-explanatory really, though some of the hints provided by Lily gave me an idea of the kind of training I needed to conduct. Having a zero in any single area was a bit frustrating, though I had to admit I hadn't actually explored my Mend spell at all. Of course, that line of thinking, that I needed to be a "normal" apprentice with three in everything might just have been wrong. After all, I had spells I could wield without truly understanding them—the equivalent of microwave meals. Perhaps I'd be better off focusing on some other aspects of magic, like Mana Flow. Certainly, if I understood the way my levels worked, part of the reason I'd slowed down in the last week or so was because I needed to be able to physically handle more mana.

I considered the various skills, trying to line them up with the spells I wielded. Perhaps it was time to get a little more experimental…

***

It was dark when I next woke, the only light being the dual glows of laptop monitors, Alexa's unladylike snoring breaking the silence of the night. It was 3:24 a.m. I sighed as I placed my phone down and sat up, debating if I should go back to bed. A loud, insistent growl that erupted from my stomach answered that question.

"Alexa left some dinner on the counter for you," Lily said, not looking up from her monitors.

"Ah… thanks," I said and edged my way cautiously around the room to find it. Pasta. She really liked her pasta. Then again, it was precooked food. After a moment's debate, I tossed it into the microwave while I surveyed my tiny domain.

Tiny. With three people, it was only good fortune that Alexa and I never spent much time at home. Even so, there was little privacy, a fact that had begun to grate on me. Alexa seemed to handle it better, and Lily, well, Lily just played her games. The past few weeks of hard work had actually expanded my meager savings such that I, for once, had some breathing room. Perhaps it was time to find a new apartment.

As the microwave dinged, I grabbed the hot pasta and booted Lily off one of the laptops, content to do some searching. How hard could it be to find a three-bedroom location in my price range?

A few hours later, the answer was: extremely. Unless I wanted to live in a badly serviced suburb, my budget was unrealistic. While questing was an interesting way of generating funds, it was somewhat unreliable. Especially since a good third of my quests refused to complete payment, citing unsatisfactory performance. I'd have complained, but mostly they were right. I was lucky I was still being hired.

As dawn broke, I finished sending the email enquiries to a few potentials and returned the laptop to Lily while I grabbed the quest papers. Best make the selection before Alexa did. As I perused the papers, I was startled by a knocking on the door.

"Expecting company?" I said to Lily, mostly in jest as I walked to the door. Without looking, I swung it open while I said, "No, we're not interested in… what are you doing here?"

Instead of the expected door-to-door salesman, I spotted a familiar tall, sour-faced mage with slicked black hair and a cream shirt.

"You used another wish," Caleb said.

"You here to bitch or destroy more property?" I asked.

"You—" Caleb stopped, drawing a deep breath before he continued more slowly. "I am here to ensure you gain these… levels… of yours."

"At three in the morning? Seriously?" I asked.

"Is it?" Caleb paused, looking around, and shrugged. "Ah, the trans-temporal spell must have been slightly misaligned."

I stared at Caleb while filing that piece of information away. "So, you intend to babysit me?"

"No. I shall teach you the basics of magic to ensure your progress," Caleb said. "I understand you already have a protector."

"Huh. Didn't think you were the teaching type."

"Who is it?" Alexa called out as she stood at the bed, spear in hand.

"The mage who tried to kill me," I replied.

"Move!" Alexa scrambled forward, spear readied before she slowed down as she realized I was just standing there, talking. "Wait. Tried?"

"He's too high a level," I said.

"Oh…" Alexa relaxed and propped her spear against a wall before she walked to the kitchen. "Is there coffee?"

"In the pot."

"As I was saying, I am here to teach you. Now, get your gear, and we shall begin," Caleb reiterated.

"Yeah, no," I said as I turned away and walked into the kitchen. I'd have slammed the door shut, but considering my wishes didn't include property damage, I saw no reason to taunt him that way.

"Do you know what you're being offered here?!" Caleb snapped, his voice rising. "I am a Mage of the Third Circle. Apprentices the world over would sell their mothers for a chance to train under me."

"Is he always this loud?" Alexa asked as she sipped her coffee, eyeing the mage.

"You, Initiate, will be quiet. Or else you will feel my wrath," Caleb snapped. Almost in unison, all three of us rolled our eyes.

"Can't do it. She's part of Henry's party. If you started a fight with her, Henry would have to join in. So, no. She's protected too," Lily said, looking up from her laptops. "Also, you are loud. Can you tone it down? I can't hear the quest log."

Alexa grinned at Lily and stuck her tongue out at the mage. I paused, staring at the blond Amazonian before I chuckled. Sometimes, I forgot Alexa was actually quite young still. Of course, Caleb was less than impressed with us, his brows furrowing.

"Are you refusing my offer?" Caleb asked.

"No." I paused, swiftly considering the matter. Free training, even if it was with someone I disliked, was too good to pass up. And while the wishes weren't foolproof at safeguarding me, the fact stood that I was unlikely to be any safer staying here than going. "I'll take you up on it—in the mornings, when Alexa goes to her own training."

Caleb's lips thinned, obviously unhappy with the result.

"I still need to go and do quests to level up."

Provided with a fitting excuse, Caleb could only nod. "Very well. Let us begin."

***

A short walk later, I was seated in an open-plan office that consisted of a whiteboard, a pair of chairs, and a desk that faced the board, being lectured to by Caleb. Caleb had taken all of fifteen minutes to ascertain my current level of ability and knowledge before waving me to the seat behind the desk. I didn't do particularly well considering it was still in the early hours of the morning and my coffee had only just kicked in.

"Right then, it seems you are entirely ignorant about the world that you have entered," Caleb said. "We will endeavor to rectify that immediately. To begin with, do you understand why the supernatural world has chosen to hide itself from the mundane?"

I shook my head, and Caleb just huffed.

"Of course not. In truth, the question was misleading. We have not chosen to hide; humanity has chosen to ignore us."

"But the glamours and illusions—"

"Are for convenience's sake. Humanity has no desire to deal with orcs, elves, dwarves, or more. They have made this very clear numerous times in the past. Now, those who refuse to hide their visages are dealt with by the appropriate government agencies or otherwise relegated to the outskirts of society," Caleb said. "This process began in the early 1500s and was hastened by the globalization of trade. The Mage Council itself formed during that period as mages across the world met for the first time and the threats we had to deal with increased in proportion."

"Threats?"

"Yes. Threats," Caleb said. "Like your ring, the Never-Ending Gourd, the kris of Hang Tuah. The attacks by the maricoxi or the dokkaebi. Until we banded together, individual mages often found it difficult to deal with these new threats as we had no cultural knowledge to draw upon. Incomplete or incorrect as it may be, this knowledge often holds a glimmer of truth."

"But you haven't explained why the council was put together," I said, and Caleb huffed.

"I would if you would stop interrupting. Do you know how often those with magical ability are found? One in ten thousand. Of those, maybe one in ten have the ability to become true mages. If it were not for the fact that magical ability is passed on genetically, we would have died out long ago," Caleb said.

I quickly did some mental math, coming up with about sixty thousand mages in the entire world. It seemed both extremely high and yet really low. After all, at that rate, a city like mine would have slightly above twenty mages at best. When I turned my attention back, I realized Caleb had continued speaking.

"… safeguard knowledge, watch for other-dimensional threats, and deal with rogue agents," Caleb said. "We are not policemen or other guardians in general. There are numerous other agencies—both official and unofficial, like your Templar, that undertake such tasks. However, experience has shown that certain magical items and artifacts cannot be allowed to circulate in the general public."

"Like the ring," I said, and my lip twisted wryly. "Okay, lecture over. Are you actually going to teach me magic, or are you going to bore me with history till I give the ring up?"

"You—" Caleb stopped and drew a deep breath. "Fine. Let us begin with your Light Spell."

While I wasn't particularly happy to go back and practice such a basic spell, I had to admit it was better than getting a history lesson.

Hours later, as I hurried back to the apartment to grab a bite to eat before we went questing, I had to admit that Caleb was a decent teacher, even if he was constantly surprised by what I did and did not understand. Learning magic from Lily and my own experiments had been a hodgepodge affair with some basic magical knowledge missed. Of course, we didn't cover as much as I had expected since Caleb was of the view that anything that should be covered would be covered. In exacting detail.

Chapter 14

The next day, Caleb was waiting for me at his office at our scheduled time. It was actually kind of nice to leave with Alexa in the morning, having something better to do than practice my magic alone. She, of course, was off reporting and training with her people.

"We will split your lessons into two components. My lectures about the world and theory of magic and, secondly, your practical spell usage," Caleb said the moment I walked in.

"Uhh..." Caught flat-footed, that was about the only word I could utter.

"I will not have any say that even a failure of a student like you was not trained properly by me," Caleb said. "If this is unacceptable, we may call this experiment to an end."

I grimaced before finally nodding. Fine. As much as I hated boring lectures, I had to admit his practical knowledge and ability to pick out what I were missing was particularly helpful.

"Good. Now, if you are to learn magic, you should at least understand the underpinnings of it. There are numerous branches of magic, but to be a mage, one must have a least a basic understanding of it all. It is that broad understanding of magic that separates a mage from other groups like your alchemist friend," Caleb said.

I found a seat while he was speaking, content to listen and remember and take the occasional note. Thankfully, I had a very good memory for important things. However, don't ever ask me to remember your birthday. That was what electronic calendars were for.

"Now, within magic, there are numerous paths—enchanting, evocation, and alchemy being the most commonly accepted major paths."

"What about warding?" I asked.

"A subset of enchanting. The most basic form of enchanting in fact," Caleb said. "Once you grasp the basics of all three, you may begin to combine them into more complex spells or rituals."

"Rituals are hard?"

"No. A good ritual is actually easy to understand and cast. However, to understand and manipulate the workings of a ritual requires understanding of all three paths of magic. It is why the Mage Council recommends that rituals be taught later," Caleb said.

"Ah… and evocation is the casting of spells from mana, right? Things like my Force Bolt and the Light spell?"

"Yes, exactly. Now, if you'd be quiet, I'll begin the overview of each path," Caleb said, glaring at me.

I sighed and fell silent for the moment but made sure to listen. Annoying as the mage might be, he certainly knew his stuff.

***

Within days, we had fallen into our new routine. Early morning, I would make my way to his office, where Caleb would be waiting, a new lesson fully planned out. At first, my constant interruptions derailed the lessons the mage had planned, frustrating both of us. However, once I realized Caleb would, eventually, get to my questions—and if not, he had allocated time for me to ask them—matters proceeded more smoothly. It was on the afternoon of the sixth day that I finally caught up with Lily and had a moment to spare as Alexa was running late.

"Lily, I noticed I haven't actually gained much in terms of experience lately. But I'm sure I'm learning more from Caleb," I said.

"Really? How strange," Lily said, entirely focused on her laptops. However, after so many months living together, I could tell something was not right.

"Lily," I warned, and the jinn sighed, tapping quickly on the computer to put her games on hold.

"I've adjusted your experience gain lately to slow down your leveling," Lily said.

"Why?" I frowned. "Are you worried I'll hit level one hundred too soon?"

"No," Lily said. "Well, not entirely. It's more to do with your body. Have you noticed you've been getting headaches from spellcasting more frequently recently?"

"Yes," I replied. In fact, I was sporting one right now. "I figured it's because I'm using magic a lot more these days."

"You're partly correct," Lily said. "Each time I leveled you, you gained a little more access to mana. Partly from the spells and knowledge I provided and, well, partly from me adjusting the limiters. Remember, you had no real natural ability."

"I remember."

"Right. Well, you're now wielding as much mana as an apprentice mage at times, but your body hasn't had enough time to adjust to it. The headaches are just the symptoms," Lily said.

"Is it dangerous?" I asked.

"No. I noticed the issue early enough, but until your body fully adjusts to the current levels, I'm slowing down your leveling."

"So, you nerfed me," I said, my lips twisting wryly.

"Well, you are the alpha tester for this game. Rule adjustments should be expected." Lily spoke as lightly as I had, though I could see some of the tension had left her body. As if I would get upset about her taking care of me. My third lesson with Caleb had been about magical burnout, and I had no desire to end up a has been. I'd only just started wielding magic!

"How long?"

"Till you next level?" Lily shrugged. "Depends, but at least a few weeks. And you'll continue at this slower rate for a while."

I grunted, unhappy but at least glad to have an answer to the nagging doubt. With this topic exhausted, I went to the pile of quests and flipped through them. I knew Alexa had probably picked one out for me, but I liked to look them over too. It was strange how easily I had given up the responsibility of choosing the quests to the initiate, but in truth, I knew my own caution would have had me choosing lower-leveled quests.

On the other hand, with my current nerfing, perhaps that would have been a better option. Then again, many of the quests we had been doing had more specific financial benefits. It was kind of nice not having to worry as much about my budget, especially with Alexa contributing to the rent.

"Huh." I frowned, staring at the quest paper in hand. After a moment, I flipped backward and located the other quest note.

"Something interesting?" Alexa said from behind me, making me jump. I growled at her while she looked at me blankly. Though as I turned back to the papers, I saw the corners of her lips quirk up.

"Just more Devil Rats," I said. "There are two quests, both around the same area. In fact, I'm pretty sure they're near where I fought the first nest."

"Devil Rats?" Alexa took the papers from my hand. She read through the notices quickly before eyeing the bottom of the paper.

"You know what? Let's go kill them," I said suddenly, pulling the papers away from Alexa and handing them to Lily.

The jinn took them from me and, after a glance, put them back down. Within seconds, new quest notifications bloomed.

"I didn't—"

"You snooze, you lose," I said happily as I walked over to grab my jacket. After a moment's consideration, I went back and packed an additional set of clothing, cautioning the spluttering Alexa to do so as well.

***

The large, abandoned concrete office building that was our objective loomed above us as we stepped out of Alexa's car. In truth, considering a journey into the sewers wasn't required of both quests, the extra clothing and precautions were probably overkill. But since we had a car to store the bag in, I saw little harm in bringing it along. After all, being less than prepared the first time I'd dealt with these guys had been my downfall.

"I still don't get why we had to do a rat-killing quest," Alexa grumbled for the tenth time as she hefted her spear. On my suggestion, she'd brought along a shorter version of her normal weapon. This one barely reached her shoulders.

"Come on, aren't you Templars all about helping people?" I asked. As the job posting had stated, the key for the warehouse was stored in a small, locked keypad behind a bush. In moments, we had the glass doors, that led into the building open. "Ready?"

Rather than answer me, Alexa strode ahead into the sunlit entranceway. Her eyes darted sideways, taking in the disused and empty hallway before she walked farther in. She only paused for a second for me to finish tethering a Light Ball to her.

Light Ball Cast
89% Synchronicity

I was quite proud of how good I had gotten at casting the spell. Not only had I gained a better physical understanding of the motions, mentally I understood why each portion of the spell interacted the way it did. I could, with some difficulty, even cast a Light Ball without the aid of the system. Not that I was going to fool around with that right now.

"Rat droppings," Alexa said, gesturing with her spear as we checked out another empty office. This was our first visual clue that the Devil Rats were here, though the pervasive odor of rat urine assaulted our noses constantly.

"Recent?"

"What do I look like to you? A vet?" Alexa said grumpily before she strode out of the room. Before I could answer, a flash of red in the corner had me flicking my hand out. The already half-formed Force Missile flew directly at the charging rat, spearing it even as it rushed out of the hole it had hidden in. The upgraded spell speared through the monster, maiming it before disappearing.

"Trouble!" I called out hurriedly as I began forming another Force Missile. Behind the maimed rat that was still attempting to reach me, another whiskered offender was crawling out.

"I'm busy!" Alexa shouted back. It was then I realized that squeaks and the familiar swoosh of her spear could be heard from behind me. Had the damn rats tried to ambush us?

"Shit!" I snarled as my next missile missed. The Devil Rat had scrambled out of the way of my cast. It jumped, soaring toward me before it bounced off the Force Shield I swung in its way. Of course, since the Force Shield was an actual shield, I had to carefully control its size. After some experimenting, I had decided to just go with a traditional shield option most of the time and attached it to my left arm. Unfortunately, the jacket's wards just weren't powerful enough for me to rely on solely. Even as I readied another Force

Missile, my fingers flying through the complicated motions, I watched the rat before me intently.

"Eat this," I snarled as I bounced the rat off my shield again and tossed my readied spell when it landed. This attack hit, tearing through its body and leaving the monster seriously wounded. Rather than finish it or its brethren off, I stepped backward quickly to check on Alexa.

I might as well not have bothered. Rats, even Devil Rats, were no danger to my Templar friend. While she might have complained about her lack of desire to be a warrior, there was no doubt she had the training and skill to be one. The bloody pieces that littered the hallway were testament to that fact.

"Did they just try to ambush us?" Alexa asked, echoing my earlier thoughts.

"Come on, rats aren't that smart," I said, though my voice was filled with doubt. After all, they were Devil Rats, and even normal wild animals knew how to hunt in packs.

"You ready?" Alexa asked after a moment, and I had to nod. A part of me wondered if these Devil Rats had spread here from the earlier group because I had never exterminated the pack. Then again, how did you exterminate rats? Poison and pesticides, I guessed, neither of which I had access to. Of course, I was once again comparing these rats to their normal counterparts, which might have been a mistake. Sometimes, knowing only a little bit about a subject could be just as hazardous, I realized. I hadn't even taken the time to learn about the Devil Rats from Lily like I had gotten used to doing, so confident that I knew what I was up against.

By the third ambush, there was definitely no longer any doubt what the rats were doing. As we advanced up the office floors, the attacks grew in frequency. That was until we reached the third, and second-to-last, floor.

"We done?" I asked as we finished our walkthrough.

"That should be it," Alexa confirmed as she led us back toward the stairs.

"We weren't attacked," I said, and Alexa nodded again. If they weren't attacking us now, that could mean one of two things: Firstly, we'd killed all the rats there were. The second, more likely option, was that they were reserving their forces. "Perhaps we should talk about how we're going to do this."

Alexa paused, hand on the exit bar, before she turned to me, nodding for me to go ahead. While the fights so far had not been difficult, a little caution made sense.

***

"This is absolutely disgusting," I said as I stuck my finger into the lukewarm flesh of a Devil Rat. I grimaced at the slimy stickiness, the residual heat flowing and wrapping around my finger. "I'm so going to catch something from this."

"This was your idea," Alexa said, shooting one last disgusted look at me before she returned to watching for trouble.

"Don't remind me," I said and then shut up. Fingers shifted and moved, my mind stretching down familiar routes.

Link Cast
75% Synchronicity

Scry Cast
64% Synchronicity

Scry link is established.

I felt my senses expand, the link between each Devil Rat letting my mind flow down arcane routes. I frowned almost immediately and pointed to the right. Without hesitation, Alexa's spear flashed out and struck through the drywall, pinning and killing the furry spy. For precious seconds, I struggled with my spell, the split attention almost pulling it apart before I managed to reassert the necessary control. Behind my eyes, a throbbing headache exploded, a pain that at least I was used to by now.

Again, my mind rushed along the link. Above us, on the top floor. Connections. So many connections. I bounced from one to another, keeping count with each skip, the headache pulsing in time. Seconds seemed like minutes, and then I released the spell, slumping against the dirty and bloody wall unconcernedly.

"You okay?" Alexa asked, concern in her voice.

"Mmmmppphhfff," I replied—or tried to at least. I hung my head low and then blinked as I noted another drop of blood drip from my nose. Shit. I wiped it away and then leaned the other way.

"Here," Alexa said, holding a torn tissue for me. I nodded thanks as I stuffed it into my nose, thinking how silly I looked.

"I counted just over twenty before I lost the connection," I said to Alexa minutes later, when the headache had subsided.

"Are you going to be able to continue?" Alexa asked worriedly.

"Yes. We need to deal with these guys now. I'm pretty sure there's a big nest up there. If we don't do this now, they'll just spread," I said and pushed myself up.

"Too bad we can't just burn the place down," Alexa said, and I snorted. That would have definitely gotten us blacklisted. "I don't think we can take on that many, not the way we've been fighting."

"No. But these floors are all laid out the same, right?" I got a nod from Alexa. "Right then, I've got a plan."

***

The office building was laid out relatively simplistically—the main staircase was behind a fire door which led to a single corridor. Down either side of the corridor were doorways leading to smaller office spaces. From previous experience and the Scry spell, we knew the doorways on the right harbored the majority of the rats. After all, it was along that back wall that the pipes and ventilation shafts ran downward, allowing the rats to move from floor to floor with ease.

When Alexa opened the doorway, I proceeded to toss out the wooden blocks that I had pre-carved the light wards on, having activated them before we stepped in. The wards slid and bounced along the floor, lighting up the hallway even as Alexa dropped another pair of warded blocks in front of the doorway. We then waited, letting our eyes adjust to the brightened room.

As we strained our ears and breathed through our mouths, the light chittering of Devil Rats and the acrid stench of their urine and feces assaulted us. I made a mental note to look into a cleaning spell, or at least a disinfecting one, when I got back before I made myself focus. It seemed the rats refused to come out even with the provocation of the light.

Alexa stepped forward, hands tight around her spear as she edged along the hallway carefully. I followed her, my Force Shield fully cast and extended before me as we eyed the ground for gnawed-through holes in the drywall.

"There," Alexa hissed and gestured with her spear as she spotted the first hole. I nodded grimly, bending down and shifting my Shield aside as I tossed a warded block into it. I followed with a couple more rather quickly, each bearing a simple Alter Temperature spell. Each block was activated to lower the temperature around itself. After a little experimenting, I'd worked out that a single block could lower the temperature of my apartment by a good ten degrees. Putting four in there would start making the entire room entirely too chilly. In time.

Once we had dropped the blocks, both Alexa and I fell back to our prepared line of wards and waited. And waited. And waited. Did I mention that while the wards did lower the temperature, they did so only from the blocks themselves? They basically radiated the cooling effect from their present locations, which in this case meant the entire process would take quite a bit of time.

A half hour later, the rats finally rushed out of the room, obviously done with being frozen. The only concern had been if the monsters had decided to continue retreating rather than launch their attacks early. Fire of course would have been more certain, but again, we weren't about to burn down the damn building. So cold was our chosen weapon of annoyance.

The rats charged us, and the first rat hit the blocks Alexa had laid down, triggering a simple activation sequence. Like the rest of my blocks, the wards had been placed as more of an experiment than with any plan for usefulness. It was only after I had accidentally activated one—destroying the toaster in the process—that I'd decided my blocks might be useful weapons. It had taken a bit of work to get these wards right. Chaining the spell with a touch activation was simple. The tricky part was adding an on/off switch so that the wards weren't active all the time.

Now, as the Devil Rat ran right across the ward, a Force Missile formed underneath it and jutted straight out. The Devil Rat behind it was unlucky enough to cross the ward just as it finished forming, the missile spearing it in the neck. That was perhaps the biggest flaw of the wards—how long it took to form each missile. As it stood, the three warded glyphs scattered ahead of us only managed to kill one and mildly inconvenience another.

"Die!" Alexa snarled, whirling her spear around and cutting in a line as the first Devil Rats reached us. The attack knocked one aside and tore open another. Behind her, I shifted my Force Shield to lie across the floor and grow high, creating an impromptu wall. The leading rats rammed into the Force Shield with a hiss and shake of their heads, momentarily stunned. Above them, Alexa proceeded to stab at the trapped rats mercilessly.

The initial confusion and surprise lasted for a brief second, enough time for Alexa to kill a pair before the rats backed away. The first Devil Rat to jump the Shield wall was battered aside, the second took a Force Missile to the face, and then there was only one charging us, sailing through the air to land on Alexa. The initiate threw herself sideways and sent the rat flying before it could injure her through her armor. Even as the rat scrambled to its feet, Alexa's spear lashed out. I finished off the last injured monster while Alexa was dealing with hers, and then, it was over. A few minutes later, we were all set up for the next room, the cold blocks moved into it after retrieval. Even in the corridor, the chill from the first room could be felt as it slowly dissipated.

The subsequent rooms and fights followed much the same lines—a lot of waiting and a few brief moments of struggle. As my headache grew worse, I made a mental note to create some Force Shield wards for next time. I quickly added a twist to our attacks, setting up a Force Shield just in front of the Force Missile wards. That allowed the wards enough time to form and trigger, adding to the carnage. In turn, Alexa focused on batting the monsters aside as they jumped and otherwise attempted to attack us.

When we finally cleared the building, I was desperately breathing through my nose and attempting not to retch. Blood, guts, and other unmentionables littered the floor, and even Alexa only stayed long enough to ascertain no additional rats had survived before she left. As we breathed in the fresh air outside, I left a message with the building owner about the successful cleaning operation. Of course, a few of the younger rats had escaped into the wall, but those could be dealt with using mundane pesticides and traps.

"Yes, four dozen full grown. That's right. Yes. Okay," Alexa said, finishing her conversation on her phone before she turned to me. Green eyes unreadable as she stared at me, the initiate gestured toward her car.

"Can we do the other quest tomorrow?" I asked as I slid into the car, careful of where I placed my feet. Another throb and my vision narrowed again.

"Headache?" Alexa asked, and I nodded. Carefully. "Tomorrow then."

"Thanks," I whispered, my eyes shut while I dry-swallowed a pair of painkillers. Definitely tomorrow.

***

The headache from overuse of my magic subsided after a night's rest. Rather than go to class the next day, I spent the morning working on more warding blocks. The blocks themselves were simple enough to acquire. While I knew that the better material I worked with, the more powerful I could make the wards, I still went with natural hardwood rather than metal or stone. For one thing, I had no idea how I'd carve metal or stone. Art class in school had at least given me some experience with woodcarving, even if it had been ages ago. More importantly though, I just didn't have the magical oomph to need better material anyway.

Wards were simple enough in theory. A ward could be made of anything from words, characters, glyphs, or runes. So long as the mage focused and provided the underlying magical structure to the ward, you could even use stick figures. Of course, using common magical variations was simple, like walking down a well-beaten path in a forest rather than trailblazing yourself.

Bent over the block with woodcarving tools in hand, I slowly worked the first step into the block. This was the basic empowerment ward which allowed you to input mana into the entire structure. In this case, I was going with a mana storage ward, one of two types that I knew. The other was a constant channeling empowerment ward but, in this case, was much less useful. There were other more complicated empowerment wards, including ones that allowed you to passively collect mana, but I had yet to progress to that level.

Once that was finally carved into the wooden block, and the magical channels layered in, I moved onto the next step. This required me to join the empowerment ward with the spell that it was to power. Of course, to do that, you needed to carve the spell at the same time, which meant setting the parameters of the spell in the ward itself. At the most basic level, I could fix the spell with not-unalterable channels, but it was theoretically possible to create flexible wards. Many protective arrays were actually flexible spells built into the wards.

A ward was closer to a computer program in the way it worked. When creating a ward, you "wrote" the program, allowing for options while writing it. In many ways, wards were like the spells in my mind—they were set constructs that only required initiation. Of course, unlike my spells, which I could alter as I casted them, wards were unalterable except for their premade options. In this case, I was layering a Force Shield onto the wooden block.

It was this analogue that I believed Lily wanted me to experience. Being forced to consider each portion of the spells I had in my mind, and the way they interacted with my wards, developed my understanding of both warding and the spells themselves.

After layering the spell on the ward, I then had to carve in triggers. It was not enough to just have the ward. I needed to be able to control how and when they were turned on, unless I wanted them on all the time. In this case, a simple on/off switch that was manipulated by mana flow was sufficient. All that said, it took me nearly three quarters of an hour to finish creating a single ward. Thankfully, while I was channeling mana throughout the process, the amount I needed to channel was actually quite low, a tenth of what actually casting the spell would require.

It was nearly time for Alexa to get back before I was done with my experimenting, and a series of warded blocks were laid out on the floor next to me. With a flick of my hand, I activated the first and stared at it intently.

"Well, that's a failure," I muttered as I kicked at the Force Shield. While the shield itself held, physics unfortunately took a hand and sent the block skidding backward before it bounced off the wall. The small, curved shield continued to flicker as it ran the stored mana down for another thirty seconds before it died silently. "I need to figure out how to lock the shield and the block down. Though, maybe I could make a bunch of those blocks and link them together? Make a portable Shield?"

"That's a really annoying habit," Lily said from her seat.

"Huh?" I turned to Lily, frowning.

"You're talking to yourself again."

"I know," I said, refusing to apologize. Partly because it was my home. And partly because, occasionally, my mutterings actually made Lily provide a hint or two. In this case, I didn't expect any help. I was pretty certain the required spell formulas to lock the shield in place were too complicated for my current level, especially if I needed to transfer them to a ward.

"Next," I said and carefully reached for experiment number two. This one contained an altered Force Missile. Before I activated it, I cast a Force Shield around the ward, leaving just a little space for me to sneak my hand under it so I could activate the block. A moment later, the block shuddered, and a small Force Missile formed. Rather than actually flying outward, it just sat there, jutting out of the block. A few moments later, I removed the Force Shield and prodded the block, noting it had the same problem. After a moment, I decided to name this block a Force Spike block. It was a mild success; I could create the Force Spike, but like my Force Shield, it could easily be knocked sideways.

I sat back down and glared at my failed experiments. Carrying around some pre-charged blocks to run as a Force Shield might work, but Force Shield was such a mana hog that they just didn't last very long. Perhaps, with more experience and better materials, they might be useful. As for the Force Spikes, they could easily be knocked over, making them useless. Perhaps I could make them caltrops, but then I'd have to either adjust the container to activate, and form spikes around the block itself, or create four different wards.

The incessant clicking of a mouse and keyboard keys interrupted my thoughts once again, and I growled, suddenly tired. Damn it, I wanted my house back. "Can you be quiet?"

"I could if you got me a better mouse," Lily shot back. "And maybe a new keyboard."

"Go buy one yourself. I've got things to do," I said and looked at my ward blocks again, the insistent clacking reaching my ears. Click. Clack. Click.

Oh. Huh. That'd work.

***

"You sure this will work?" Alexa asked later, as we set up for the rats. This time around, we had decided on an entirely different plan of attack. Rather than walking around trying to find the rats, we were going to attract them to us.

"I trust El," I said, nudging a piece of meat a bit farther forward before I uncapped a potion. It was a simple attractant that would target the Devil Rats. It had cost more to get it specifically targeted, but since we didn't want random creatures popping in, we had happily paid for the more expensive potion. Now, I carefully poured the solution on the meat before stepping backward and surveying our preparations. We'd chosen to make our stand at the entrance hallway, with a glass door to our backs, while spread in a semicircle around us were some of my newly created Force Spikes. Ahead of them, chilling the floor and the water we had splashed on the ground, were the cooling blocks, thin layers of ice already forming around the blocks. Hopefully, the slick flooring would slow and disturb the rats enough to buy us some time.

"You sure there's only a dozen close by?" Alexa asked again.

"Yes," I replied grumpily while I stood, watching.

"Because if we get swarmed—"

"We won't be," I reassured her. They might be smart enough to plan an ambush, but they wouldn't be able to withstand the lure of the potion—or so El had promised us.

"Ah," Alexa suddenly said, her eyes fixed on red eyes that glinted at us from the shadows. Rather than approach cautiously, the rats rushed us, a dozen in total. Within moments, they hit the icy floor and slid along the ground, their feet desperately scrambling for purchase. A few bounced against the wooden blocks, knocking them about while others scrambled through the gaps to rush us. Two unlucky rats actually stepped on the spikes, the shorter and more condensed spells launching Force Darts into their bodies before disappearing.

Alexa ignored all this, instead swinging her spear as the rats approached. In turn, I backed her up with tossed Force Missiles, using the spell to harry and injure the monsters that rushed us. Minutes of fur, sharp teeth, and claws and then the battle was done, the rats lying in pieces around us.

"Well, that wasn't so bad," I said as I gulped and waited for my breathing to calm down.

"Good. Because we're going to have to do it again," Alexa said, leveling her spear at another set of eyes.

"Damn."

***

A short while later, we were staring around the mess of an entrance, privately glad we weren't going to be the ones forced to do the cleaning. Alexa squatted a short distance away, washing a few wounds with iodine and verifying she was not further injured. I was keeping watch, grateful once again I had become the backline fighter that I was. Mages were squishy—everyone knew that!

Once Alexa was done and picked her spear back up, I bent down and reached out, recasting the Link and Scry spells in quick succession. A slow, pounding headache began to form behind my eyes before I let the spell go, my lips tight. Damn Scry spell was not getting any easier to use.

"We're clear," I said.

"Good. I'm going to take a look inside," Alexa said, gesturing toward the retail complex. I frowned, my head tilted to the side.

"We're clear," I repeated.

"I know. It's not that," Alexa said. "I just want to look around."

"But—" I clamped my mouth shut as I realized Alexa was already walking in, carefully placing her feet around the puddles of blood and guts. As I caught up with her, I asked, "What's going on?"

"I'm just curious."

"Bullshit," I said. "You're looking for something."

Silence greeted my accusation. Rather than continue my line of questioning, I followed after her and waited for her to answer me. Living with two women for so long, I'd learned a trick or two. We were nearly done with our walkthrough, Alexa pausing at each office to poke around with her spear and light before leaving, before she spoke.

"What do you know about Devil Rats?"

"Big, ugly, red?" I said and shrugged. "Also, I'd rather not fight them again? Smell way too bad."

"Devil Rats are the vermin of the demonic world. They don't appear naturally… mostly. Instead, the demons that infest the rats often come from badly cast demonic rituals, escaping through badly created wards," Alexa said. "Three infestations back to back is… uncommon."

"You're worried someone's summoning demons?" I asked, and Alexa nodded.

"Huh." I rubbed my chin as I poked around further. "So, we're looking for signs of a demonic ritual?"

"Yes. Or other magical ritual," Alexa confirmed, and I sighed. Crap. As if things weren't complicated enough.

***

"Three incidents?" Caleb asked the next morning after I had explained my absence and the quests.

"In about five months," I said. "I didn't detect any other rats though. At least, not in my range." I didn't need to point out how limited my range with my Link and Scry spells were to Caleb of course.

"And you want me to look into it?" Caleb asked, peering at me imperiously.

"You did mention the Mage Council was formed to deal with extra-dimensional breaches," I said.

"Yes. For things on a larger scale. The occasional demon summoned by a wizard is…" Caleb frowned and then shrugged. "Well, it's not something we normally deal with. The local groups normally handle such matters."

"Seriously!?!" I frowned, and Caleb sighed.

"You seem to be working under a misconception. I have already informed you we're not policemen or guardians. The council is more akin to a guild. Many of us have better things to do than hunt down your random wizard."

I glared at Caleb, obviously not happy with his answer. The mage turned away, walking to the whiteboard and tapping on the table.

"Now, we were discussing the sixteen traditional formulas by Kapinsky for the positioning of a spell…"

Chapter 15

As much as I might have worried about the appearance of a demon invasion or two, the next few weeks were uneventful. No more Devil Rats were reported. Even a few late-evening excursions and Scrys had revealed nothing. In the end, it seemed the appearances of the Devil Rats had been coincidental. While uncommon, it was not unusual for the demons that inhabited the Devil Rats to sneak in via cracks in our dimension. They were small enough to do so, and if left unchecked, could eventually wear the barriers away. It was possible that an unexpected shift in the barrier had allowed a bunch of these demons to sneak in. The only thing I could do was keep an eye out for more problems and kill the Rats when they popped-up. Less of them, less damage to the barrier.

During the lull, I even had time to visit a few nice apartments and apply for two. Of course, I then ran into a rather interesting problem—proving my income. I couldn't exactly put "supernatural troubleshooter" or "mage in training" on the application forms, and "secondhand reseller" didn't look much better. In the end, we lost out on both apartments. I couldn't really say for sure if Alexa's insistence on informing the landlords that we were "in no way shape or form a couple" helped or not, but I had my suspicions.

Training continued at the plodding pace that Caleb insisted on forcing on me. I couldn't exactly say the mage was wrong in his training methods as we continued to uncover surprising gaps in what could have been construed as "basic" knowledge. Which was why we were now spending this morning walking the city and receiving a more hands-on education about ley lines and places of power after having spent all of yesterday morning receiving an academic dissertation about them.

"This is a place of power?" I asked, shaking my head as I stared at the side of a building. The mural of a floating space cat with laser beams coming out of its eyes fighting a swarm of green space aliens in superhero costumes was quite creative but not exactly what had come to mind. Wreaths and bouquets of flowers had been laid against the wall along with a single, lonely teddy bear and a scattering of candles.

"Not all places of power are places of worship. Some form due to the deeply felt emotional connection the populace has to a place. The stronger the emotion, the deeper the links." Caleb bent down and placed his own bouquet next to the group. He waved his hand over the candles, lighting them all with a careless gesture of power before he stood.

"So, not all places of worship, but a mural?" I asked.

"No." Caleb shifted some flowers to reveal a picture. "A place of mourning and reflection."

"Ah," I said. A memory tugged at me—a briefly read article about an upcoming musician, his fan base, and a tragic fight. Too young, too dumb to back down. A punch, a bad fall, and the creation of a new legend.

"Now, do you recall why places of power are important?"

"They enhance the amount of mana you can wield. The stronger the place of power, the more mana there is available to use. That lets someone with even a moderate gift wield more mana. It's why some of the most powerful places—the pyramids, the Forbidden City, Mount Rushmore—are always warded and guarded. Don't want a dumb wizard calling up a greater demon," I answered.

"Good. And that's why a competent mage studies every place of power in their city. You never know when you might require a power increase."

"Exactly how many are there? In the city," I said.

"Twelve grade-three, thirty-six grade-two, and one hundred and twenty eight"—Caleb nodded to the mural—"grade-ones."

"Nothing over grade three?" I asked, and Caleb smiled thinly.

"Nothing that you need worry about."

Asshole. Still, as Caleb walked over to the wall, I watched as he began the process of placing wards. We'd practiced it yesterday, but practice and the actual casting were different things. The first ward wasn't particularly complicated since it was an alarm ward. It involved the initial Ward glyph and a pair of Links. The first linked the ward to the place of power and the second to the board that Caleb kept. Of course, the difficult part was the triggers, ensuring the alarm itself would not trigger randomly or due to minor fluctuations in mana flow. While in theory it was simple, in practice, you had to understand not only the power level of that particular point of power but also its normal power fluctuations and the environment surrounding it. It required significant fine-tuning, which made it perfect as a training tool for me.

The second, more powerful and complicated, ward that Caleb cast once he was done with the first was one I had no ability to lay. It basically sealed the place of power, ensuring no one could use it. It was significantly more powerful and complicated. The first ward had taken Caleb a bare five minutes to lay. The second, nearly an hour. The wards glowed for a moment more, visible to everyone before they faded away from mundane sight. Unlike the wards I normally carved out, these were runic wards that were written in glowing mana script. It required somewhat more strength to invert the wards and hide them from mundane sight, but it certainly made things easier.

"Did you see?" Caleb asked finally when he turned to me, weariness etched on his face.

"The first, sure. The second..." I trailed off, shaking my head.

"Obviously," Caleb snorted. "Come, we will have you practice on the next section. And after that, you will take it as a quest of yours. Yes?"

"Yes," I agreed. It was something we had discussed already—a simple quest, one that could be approved by Lily and paid for by the Mage Council. It worked for all of us; I got paid and trained up a spell, and the Mage Council got the places of power that they couldn't be bothered to waste one of their own people on warded. All in all, it worked out quite well. I wasn't entirely certain why they cared to ward places like this since they weren't going to do more than keep watch, but that, when I asked, was none of my business. In fact, I knew Caleb normally wouldn't have sealed this place of power except for the fact that he was here.

As we walked toward the car to head to the next location, I glanced over at Caleb, curiosity warring with my usual social awkwardness. In the end, curiosity won. "Why are you doing this?"

"Hmmm? I'm sure we discussed this."

"Not the warding. The teaching," I clarified.

"Ah." Caleb paused, considering. "It is not as if your wish gave us much choice."

"But why you?" I asked.

"My initial task had not been completed. Until the ring has been returned to the council, I will not receive another," Caleb said.

"Doesn't explain the teaching," I said.

"Teaching you and raising your 'level' is the most optimal route. Once we are no longer constrained by your death, I will acquire that ring," Caleb said simply.

"Acquire. As in kill me," I said, looking at the mage's impassive face. He nodded slightly, seemingly unconcerned with that. "And you're okay with this."

"Many of us have made questionable decisions to gain the power we have," Caleb said after a long silence, his voice calm as he continued to speak. "That yours has constrained your enemies to act at a later date is almost admirable."

"Huh." I leaned back, shaking my head. I guess I somehow had a different idea of what a teacher-student relationship should be. Could be. But then again, my upbringing, my culture, set a higher importance on that relationship, almost valuing it at the same level as a familial relationship at times. To Caleb though, this was just a way of getting me up to speed so he could complete his task faster.

And of course, if he taught me, he'd know all my tricks, which would make dealing with me easier. After all, it was hard to surprise someone who'd taught you. I shivered when I realized that fact. Still, at least it explained the remoteness I always sensed when dealing with Caleb.

***

"You bring a girl to the nicest places," Alexa said as she kicked an empty beer can down the concrete path. I looked up from the ward I was currently placing, considering the desolate skate park filled with empty beer cans, discarded hypodermic needles, and other waste and had to mentally agree with her. This was a shithole and not the worst one we'd seen. After all, locations which were currently occupied were often already warded—by local supernatural organizations or the city. Admittedly, the wards that a mosque or church might use would be different than mine, but they would be no less effective. In fact, most would be significantly more complex. It was thus no surprise that my quest mostly involved dealing with these places—locations that had been abandoned.

"You didn't have to come," I said.

"I definitely did." Alexa continued to walk a circle around me. "My job is literally to babysit you."

"Didn't ask you to," I grumped. Even as I was speaking, my fingers danced as they pulled and stretched at the fabric of reality, and a portion of my mind worked the Ward spell. The days of practice I had received had given me quite a bit of confidence at casting this spell.

"No. I was ordered to." Alexa shook her head. "Child of fate and all that."

"Child of fate?" I frowned, looking at Alexa. "Keep saying that, and I'll get a big head."

"Not you, idiot," Alexa said with a roll of her eyes. "Me. Though how I got tied to you for the next little while, I have no idea."

I worked in silence for a bit since the next part was actually tricky. I didn't have a shortcut for the next part provided to me by Lily, so I actually had to manually cast the spell. While it wasn't extremely different from the Link spell—and in fact, I considered it inferior in many ways—it did have much greater range. By the time I was done, another twenty minutes had finished, and I had begun to perspire. As I stood and wiped away the sweat, I considered the initiate while I rested for a bit. The next part would be even more difficult.

"Care to explain?"

"About the child of fate? It's a term the Church uses to signify people whose presence or lack of it will alter the course of the future," Alexa said. "Telling the future is complicated. Mostly, seers can only see the major events in a person's life—the ones that have the greatest impact on others and places where numerous individuals are affected by an event. A child of fate is someone whose presence occurs numerous times in their visions and whose presence then affects those futures."

"Huh. So, you're not necessarily the agent but a catalyst? Or potentially both?"

"Yes. In fact, I'm not even supposed to know about it. It was only chance that I overheard the abbess arguing with the knights about it when I was a teenager. My choice to become a healer was not taken well."

"Chance or fate?" I said, a slight smile on my face.

Alexa snorted but did not correct me. After all, who knew? In either case, I was kind of glad Alexa had chosen to learn some healing arts. It actually made me feel safer to be with her than if she had been a typical knight.

"Time to get back to it," I said. Within moments, I had extracted the enchanted rods and placed them around the point of power. After that, I began the slow process of linking each rod and activating it. Once the rods were finally linked, the enchantment activated and proceeded to lay out the sealing ward. This was the difficult part since the rods required an external power source—namely me. I grunted as I felt the rods drawing on my gift, pulling mana from me in a steady flow.

An hour later, I finally sighed and relaxed as the rods shut down, the place of power finally sealed. Packing up after that was a simple enough matter, and when I finished, I dusted my hands off and waited for Alexa to fall into step with me. As we exited, I asked, "I have been wondering—what is it with the spear? Why not a gun?"

"A few reasons. Legality to start." Alexa smiled slightly. "You can't walk around with a gun everywhere. Here, I can just say we're part of a medieval renaissance group."

"But it's sharp!"

"Is it?" Alexa offered me the spear tip. I frowned and stared at it, then realized there was a light shimmer to the spearhead. I unfocused my eyes and saw it actually looked to be capped and blunted under the glamour. Huh. Smart.

"You said a few reasons?" I asked, more curious now.

"Effectiveness. Bullets don't hold blessings or enchantments well," Alexa said. "When you have to fight werewolves, wights, or vampires, you really want your weapons blessed. You can't even really use silver alloys. The silver content is so low it doesn't really work."

"And swords?"

"Initiates are not taught the sword till they are formally accepted as apprentices," Alexa said. "Well, not much. We're given the basics, but most of our focus is on the spear till then."

Now that Alexa was talking, I took the opportunity to question her a little more about her life before we'd met. I soon learned Alexa had grown up in one of the many orphanages supported by the Templars. These orphanages were both acts of compassion as well are recruiting grounds where gifted children were drawn into the fold. Once she started reminiscing about her time in the orphanages, the normally quiet blonde started gushing, content to relive happier memories.

In time, our conversation turned into more of a trade. Alexa was definitely curious about my life as an only child in the outside world.

"After that, pets were banned in our house," I said, finishing my story of poor Tut, the turtle. I was still sore about it so many years later. We had arrived at our next and last destination for the day. Thus far, I could only complete three a day at best, often less. "So, what's your guess?"

Alexa frowned as she surveyed the empty parking lot, a single car the only other source of company for us. A short distance away, a twenty-four-hour convenience store was the sole occupant of a strip mall. Once more, Alexa looked around, trying to discern a clue about why a place of power would be located here. However, the empty parking lot gave few clues.

"Must be a ley line thing," Alexa said eventually.

"Mmm…" was my only answer. I frowned and focused my sight. Over time, I had learned I could actually sharpen my mystical sight, allowing me to "see" more of the supernatural world. Spirits, ghosts, ley lines—all those appeared. Of course, there was a price. Within seconds, a throbbing headache made its presence known, but I was able to verify Alexa's guess. The ley line was weird, floating just about twelve feet off the ground before dipping to the earth and pooling at the place of power before sweeping upward again, its shimmering illumination a reminder of pictures of the aurora borealis. As I considered the best way to ward this rather large place of power, a shout interrupted my thoughts.

"Hey, you! What are you doing here?"

The speaker was a rather large, rotund gentleman clad in a T-shirt that depicted a bat tearing free from chains and dripping in blood. I was not able to read the stylized name on the front but had no doubt it'd be some heavy metal band. A lanky man, who desperately needed to wash his greasy long hair, flanked his left while on the right, a short, spectacled South Asian walked.

"Uhh…" I said, feeling caught by the abrupt question.

"What's it to you?" Alexa replied, squaring off with them and jutting out her chin aggressively.

"This is our place," the initial speaker said as he continued to walk toward us. As he neared, his spectacled compatriot suddenly frowned and tugged on his arm, slowing him to whisper in his ear. A moment later, the leader glared at me.

Weird. I hadn't done anything to attract his attention. Beside me, Alexa frowned at her arm where a gold bracelet rested. It had been a recent addition to her arsenal, an enchanted bracelet. When I looked at the bracelet, I noted the glow around the enchantment had increased as it activated. On instinct, I focused on the group and allowed my sight to sharpen.

Faint, so faint I had missed it in the beginning, a low glow of power shrouded each of the individuals walking toward us. I knew that glow. It was the same kind I gave off, like a beacon. Training with Caleb had reduced the glow somewhat, but still, my power overflowed my control. These guys did not suffer that same issue; their power a faint trace in the air. Unlike Caleb, I'd have had to say it was a lack of power rather than great control. I wasn't particularly surprised to see that the glow surrounded all three of them. Those with power, no matter how little, had a tendency to clump together. In a city as large as ours, those with traces of magic had a tendency to find one another, and sometimes, they even managed to form their own baby cults. As Caleb had said, none of them really had enough power to do more than light some candles, but it sure made fooling mundanes easy. Remembering the look Specs had given me, I mentally added "the sight" to their abilities.

"Really? Your parking lot? I hadn't realized that Lumin Parking had hired teenagers," Alexa said.

"You—" The leader stopped, looking at the bag I was carrying over my shoulder and then back at Alexa. "You're the ones sealing off the places, aren't you?"

"What's it to you?" I asked.

"Last warning. Get the hell out of here," Greasy Hair said as the group stopped a bare ten feet from us.

Alexa continued to look bored, though I noted how she let a hand shift to touch the concealed baton in her back pocket.

"Or what?" I asked.

Without speaking further, the pair placed their hands on the rotund boy's shoulders. Within seconds, their leader had begun chanting and moving his fingers, and in the center of his hands, floating in front of him, a small ball of fire bloomed. I had to admit I was a touch jealous. I didn't have a Fireball spell.

On the other hand, it took the combined strength of all three of them to cast it.

"Seriously?" I muttered and raised my hand. I recalled my Alter Temperature spell, quickly judged the distance to them, and then cast it.

Alter Temperature Cast
Synchronicity 83%

In a sphere that perfectly enveloped their Fireball, my Alter Temperature spell formed, and I began to forcibly lower its temperature. I watched as the trio gritted their teeth, fighting my spell, but as I had already noted, the trio possessed very little actual oomph. Hell, I doubted they individually registered on Lily's scale of mana control. Within seconds, their Fireball fizzled and died, and the three flinched back together as one as the spell snapped apart. Having failed at spellcasting before, I knew how much it stung.

"Nice party trick. Now, scram!" I said. My fingers flicked and twisted, and a Force Bolt formed in my hand, blue-and-white streaks of power running along its edge. This was a pure affectation of course since a properly cast Force Bolt was actually nearly transparent.

"This isn't over!" the leader shouted as his friends backed off, staring at me warily.

I stared at the group and then casually tossed the Force Bolt at them, guiding it to impact the ground near their retreating feet. That was incentive enough to send the trio scrambling away, and I sighed, shaking my head. "Idiots."

"Yes. So, you think they've been coming out here to do dastardly deeds?" Alexa asked, a smile dancing on her lips. "Maybe a few black magic rituals to impress the girls?"

"If they knew any, sure," I said, chuckling. "Keep an eye out? I'll ward and seal this place, and then we can go home."

"Of course," Alexa replied as she settled down to watch.

"Sushi for dinner?"

"Sounds lovely. I'll make the call."

Chapter 16

Over the next eight days, we continued to fill the requirements of our quest. Using a simple city map, we worked inward from the outer bounds of the city, tackling the more remote places of power. We'd finished just over twenty locations and spotted our teenage stalkers twice more. Since they only watched us from afar, we never took any action. Of course, after the second time we saw them, I reported their presence to Caleb. Unsurprisingly, the mage dismissed their presence as quickly as we had. It might have been arrogant, but if we concerned ourselves with pests like these, we'd never get done.

It was when we were walking back to our car from the first power point of the day that we realized pests could be extremely annoying. Alexa growled as she stared at the slashed tires of her car, garbage bags of collected litter swinging in her hands. "What the heck?"

I walked to the windshield and plucked the note that had been left under the wipers.

This is your final warning. Leave the dragon nests alone or face the consequences!

"Dragon nests?" I asked as I handed the note to Alexa.

"Another term for places of power. Ley line nodes, places of power, dragon nests, same thing," Alexa said as she balled up the paper. She moved to toss it away and then changed her mind almost immediately and stuffed it into her pocket instead. The initiate quickly popped open the trunk and deposited the collected garbage before she made the call to have her car towed away. "Next time I see them, I'm so going to teach them a lesson."

"Agreed," I said. If those kids thought slashing tires was sufficient a deterrent, they really were imagining things. After all, we were being paid five hundred dollars for every place of power we were sealing. Even if we were stuck taking taxis from location to location, we were still significantly better off.

Later that evening, I was lying in bed, idly listening to the *tap-tap* of keyboard keys as I viewed my character sheet.

Class: Mage

Level 15 (13% Experience)

Known Spells: Light Sphere, Force Spear, Force Shield, Force Fingers, Alter Temperature, Gong, Gust, Heal, Link, Track, Mend, Ward, Glamour, Illusion

Magical Skillset

Mana Flow: 3/10

Mana to Energy Conversion: 2/10

Spell Container: 3/10

Spatial Location: 3/10

Spatial Movement: 2/10

Energy Manipulation: 2/10

Biological Manipulation: 1/10

Matter Manipulation: 0/10

Duration: 2/10

As promised, Lily had nerfed my leveling for a bit. I was hoping that I could start leveling at a decent rate soon, but it was not like a video game where everything was run off a series of specific charts. Most of my 'experience' was a rule-of-thumb grant by Lily, much like most of the system. It was intensely frustrating for the munchkin in me that wanted to game the system. However, the constant channeling to the enchanted rods had given me a significant amount of practice, enough so that I had gained a couple of points in Mana Flow and Duration. Even I could tell my body had begun to adjust to the amount of mana I could wield, the headaches in the evening having reduced significantly. Unfortunately, doing the same thing over and over again wasn't helping me develop my spellcasting skills, but that was a different matter.

"Hey, Lily, when am I going to get more matter manipulation spells?" I asked, staring at my greatest weakness.

"When you're ready. You haven't even cast Mend once in the last week," Lily replied immediately. "You got to get your basics right first."

"Oh, come on. I could just get the spell and learn while I cast. Maybe a 'Create Water' or maybe a 'Mud Hole' spell."

"Mud Hole?" Lily asked, a laugh in her voice.

"Or whatever you want to call it. A Bog spell, something to slow people down," I clarified.

"Mmm… maybe." Lily blew a tendril of hair from her mouth. "I still think you need to practice what you know already rather than get more spells."

"But—"

"Did you see the quest list recently?" Lily continued, ignoring my protest.

"No. Figured we'd be doing this for the next few weeks, so I've not been looking," I replied. "Alexa will tell me if there's anything interesting."

"If she was looking," Lily answered. The aforementioned initiate having left to report the damage to her car, it left Lily and I alone in the apartment. "Might be something interesting."

I took the hint and walked over to take a quick look. I paused, sorting through the files for a moment, and looked up, eyebrows drawn downward in concern. "More Devil Rats?"

"Yes."

"Huh." I frowned and pondered the information. After a moment, I pulled out the city map we'd been using and spread it out over the dining room table. I quickly plotted the information on the new rat outbreaks, along with the older rat quests, and stared at the results. "Damn. I think I need to talk to Alexa."

"Talk to me about what?" Alexa asked as she stepped through the doorway.

"Devil Rats."

"That's... interesting," Alexa said after a moment as she stared at the map. Since we only had a single map of the city, we'd previously marked the places of power on it and crossed them out as we went along. Overlaid with the outbreaks of Devil Rats, you could tell that each outbreak was near a place of power. "Not a casual entrance then."

"No. Someone's been opening portals," I said, tapping the map. "What I don't get is why."

"To summon a demon of course," Alexa said.

"Except we never sensed any of that." I pointed to two of the places of power we had sealed, which were near the latest Devil Rat infestations. "And I'm pretty sure I would have. I sensed that imp well before I entered the restaurant, and he was pretty low-powered. I'm sure summoning something more powerful would have left traces."

"True," Alexa said. "Unless they hid it."

"Point." I grimaced. "What do we do now? I'm not exactly thrilled with the idea of trying to take on something more powerful than an imp. Even if we are protected..."

"We do nothing," Alexa said after a moment. She fished her phone out and took a quick photo of the map before furiously texting for a few moments. "Done. I've run this up the chain."

"That easy?" I asked.

"What? You want me to use a courier pigeon?"

"Wasn't what I meant," I said. Though, sending information like this over the Internet, weren't there issues about security? On the other hand, maybe she was using an encrypted app. Were there encrypted apps? "Sorry."

"It's what we do, Henry," Alexa said. "Anyway, with the ring sitting around, we have a few higher-level knights who have need for some serious work in the city."

"Oh." I recalled the people Alexa met with, her continued training in the mornings, and nodded. I guessed this made good use of the resources we had. After all, there was little point in someone following after us, what with the wish blocking most attacks. I took one last glance at the map before I turned away to check on Lily's latest progress in her game, secretly glad it wasn't my problem.

***

"Thank you, sir!" Alexa said, offering a quick peck on the scrapyard owner's cheek before she dropped onto her heels. "We won't be long!"

"No worries, miss. I'm just glad you asked. Not like those other students." The scrapyard owner sniffed and spat to the side. "Always coming in and taking their photos without permission."

"Thank you again!" Alexa waved goodbye and jerked her head toward the inside of the scrapyard. I grunted, following after the blonde. Since Caleb had cancelled our morning appointment, this was our fifth place of power today, and even under my sunglasses, the sunlight was stabbing into my eyes.

"So, what did you tell him?" I asked curiously.

"The truth. We'd been given an assignment by your teacher to check out a few locations in the city," Alexa said.

"And it made that sourpuss let us in?" I asked incredulously, recalling how grumpy the owner had been when we drove up.

"Sometimes, all you have to do is ask. All he wanted was us to acknowledge his rights," Alexa replied sunnily.

In silence, we got down to the task of locating the center of the place of power. The winding pathways in the sprawling location finally brought us to our target, which had me smiling wryly as I stared at the crusher that was smack-dab in the center. Thankfully, it wasn't running this second, but I guessed it made some sense. Countless vehicles and other mementos had bene destroyed by that crusher. All the memories, all the raw emotional baggage, destroyed and focused in that crusher again and again. Even if it was a small amount, years of use would have built up.

I narrowed my eyes, watching the slow swirl of power around the place of power as I judged how much effort would be required. After a time, I slowly nodded to myself and walked forward. From the corner of my eye, I noted Alexa had started to browse the stacks, bored.

Ten minutes later, I wiped my hand across my face, knocking my sunglasses aside slightly. I readjusted them as I looked up to call to my partner. "Hey, I'm done with the first part. Can you... Alexa?"

I frowned, staring around me. After a moment, I shrugged my shoulders and found a comfortable seat out of the sun to rest my eyes, figuring the blonde would find me when she was done. I fished out a pair of painkillers and dry-swallowed the gel pills down, cursing Alexa quietly for taking the water with her. After that, I closed my eyes to rest while I waited for the medicine to kick in.

"Probably shouldn't have pushed for five today," I muttered to myself eventually. The soft crunch of bare earth had me half open my eyes and look up as I began to berate the woman. "You know, for a... what are you—"

"Night, night!" the thin teenager said, a wide grin on his face as he swung the crowbar at my head and interrupted me. I twisted aside too late, the blow landing on top of my head and sending pain exploding through it. Even as I cried out in anguish, a second hit arrived and sent me into peaceful darkness.

Chapter 17

"You need to check on him. This isn't the movies. He could be dying over there!" Alexa's voice came to me as I woke, an unusual thread of concern running through her voice. I groaned as conscious thought returned, along with a splitting pain through my skull and a slight case of wooziness. As I opened my mouth, I felt a slight tug on my scalp, then the cracking of dried blood along with a fresh stab of pain.

"See, he's awake. He's fine," a familiar voice said. "Anyway, you supes are all protected, right? Have some healing factor working for you?"

"That's not true at all! And not if you hit him in the head. Especially not twice. What were you thinking?" Alexa snarled.

"I thought he'd just, you know, fall unconscious," muttered another voice. I recalled this voice, and a flash of anger helped clear some of the woolliness from my brain.

As I shifted, I found I could barely move, my arms, legs, and body tied to a chair. With effort, I cracked my eyes open and regretted the move immediately as ice picks were driven into my head. My eyes watered, and I whimpered as my eyes reflexively shut once more.

"Shit, I think he's got a concussion," Alexa said. "Henry. Don't fall asleep again. Do you hear me? Don't fall asleep. You might die."

"Not true actually," a third, nasally voice said. "Most recent recommendations are for an individual to sleep through minor concussions to increase healing speed."

"What part of cracking his skull is minor?!" Alexa said testily, her voice rising. "If you check my bag, the blue water bottle is a healing potion. If you feed it to him, he'll get better."

"Oooh, let's feed the wizard a potion that we don't know. How dumb do you think we are, lady?"

"Try some of it yourself first then!" Alexa said.

I tried to listen to their conversation further, but the pain in my head pushed against my consciousness, and I faded out. The next thing I knew, someone was dribbling a liquid into my mouth. After spluttering a bit, I eventually swallowed the drink rather than choke to death. You'd think a healing potion would taste good, but mostly it tasted like battery acid. Thankfully, the potion got to work right away as it cleared some of the mushiness in my brain and reduced my pain.

"Man, I should have drunk some of that. Look at the scalp go—"

"Now let us go. If you don't..." Alexa said, her voice rising.

"Oh God, you're going to threaten us now? I think you're misunderstanding the situation you're in," the leader's voice said.

"Please." I groaned. "Please..."

"Go on, Henry," Alexa said encouragingly.

"Shut up!" I said. Each word uttered was a cudgel to my poor senses. Stunned silence filled the room before laughter and giggles exploded from around me.

"You—" Alexa fell silent. However, outside of occasional snorts of laughter, our kidnappers and Alexa thankfully complied with my request.

No longer assaulted by the noise, I focused on the notifications I saw beneath my eyelids.

Henry Tsien dealt 29 damage by Wizard Wannabe.

Henry Tsien dealt 43 damage by Wizard Wannabe.

Henry Tsien has gained 24 health points due to resting.

Henry Tsien has gained 25 health points from Minor Healing Potion.

Once again, I was grateful for the increased healing rate that resting and the system had granted me. Receiving over half my health pool in damage from blows to the head was probably a guaranteed concussion. Heck, the way my thoughts kept shifting and the throbbing pain probably meant I had one, lessened as it was by the potion. However, if we had been kidnapped—and I'd have to assume we had been—lying down on the job was probably not the best option.

I focused, pulling on my mana as I called forth my Heal spell. It was a struggle, the pain and the fact that my arms were tied didn't help. I chanted the words under my breath and failed as an unexpected throb broke my concentration. Again, I tried and failed. Only on the fourth attempt did I finally get the result I desired.

Heal Cast
24% Synchronicity

Without the system help, I probably couldn't have called the spell into being at all. I groaned slightly as I felt mana quicken the healing process in my body, minor cuts and bruises fixing themselves even as the wound in my head slowly fixed itself.

"Oy! What are you doing," the leader of the teenagers asked and followed it with a kick.

I grunted, my concentration broken and the spell dissipating. The backlash was painful enough that I faded out for a second.

"Gupta. I thought you were watching him."

"Sorry. I was getting a drink," Gupta called. I mentally allocated the voice to the South Asian.

Tired of not being able to see, I started the laborious process of opening my eyes. I cracked them open by a slit, letting them adjust a bit before I stared around the room. I winced, having to pause when my head spun again as I moved too fast once more. Not surprisingly, the idiot teenagers were our kidnappers, the leader of the group glaring straight at me. The room we were in was a dull grey and made of concrete with no external windows, lit by harsh, white fluorescent lamps.

"You doing okay, Henry?" Alexa asked me, her voice low. I turned my head in the direction of her voice, craning my neck to the side to see the initiate trussed up beside me.

"What... what happened?" I slurred slightly, my throat dry.

"I heard something around the corner, and when I went to check it out, they led me on a little chase. By the time I got back, they had you. They threatened to kill you if I didn't give up too," Alexa said.

"You believed them?" I said, staring at the three teenagers who had moved away and were arguing in front of us. From what I could pick up, they were fighting over guard duties. Thinking back to their threat, I couldn't believe it. Sure, they had beaten me up, but kill me? Whatever the movies said, there was a big difference between punching someone and actually killing them. And those three...

"No. But I was scared they'd lose their grip and hurt you. Thought I'd have a chance to turn it around later," Alexa continued to whisper.

"I take it that failed too."

"They're surprisingly good at tying knots," Alexa grumbled and tugged on the arm restraints again to show me. "And they've been keeping a pretty good eye on us. But I'll get us out soon."

"Great. Then I'm going to sleep. Wake me when you're ready," I said.

Alexa opened her mouth to say something else, but the group broke up, and Gupta came back to glare at us. I shut my eyes rather than stare at him, trusting Alexa would come through. In either case, I was of no use to anyone in the condition I was in.

***

"Henry. Wake up. Wake. Up," Alexa half whispered, half hissed at me, pulling me from the comfortable darkness of unconsciousness to the painful reality of life.

Henry Tsien has gained 17 health points due to resting.

Not much of a change, but at least some. I looked over at Alexa when I opened my eyes and then followed her insistent jerking of her head to stare ahead. Gupta had been changed out with Tall-and-Thin, who was sitting on a seat with a graphic novel in his hands, watching us occasionally. The bare concrete floor had been painted on, and a very ornate, mystical-looking magic circle had been drawn on it. It looked all kinds of mystical, but with the knowledge Lily had inserted in my head, it also looked very overdone. Sure, it'd work—the same way a car in the 1900s ran. Wherever the other two were, I couldn't see them with my limited viewpoint.

"This the part they get around to killing us?" I asked Alexa.

"No one's killing anyone," Tall-and-Thin said. "We're not killers."

"Yeah, my concussion says otherwise."

"We healed you," Tall-and-Thin said.

"And we're grateful, Ozzie," Alexa butted in. "Aren't we, Henry?"

I stared at Alexa as she jerked her head toward Ozzie and tried to tell me something with her eyes. After a while, I sighed and nodded in agreement.

"If you aren't about to kill us, what's the plan? Tie us up and make us watch you guys do magic badly?" I asked.

"Oh, no. You're quite important to all this. Well, your blood," the teenage leader said from behind us. He walked around our chairs, interrupting the conversation to smirk at us. I really, really wanted to hit him now.

"Shouldn't you say that with a lisp and some fake fangs?" I asked. "Or are you guys just minions?"

"Neither," the leader growled and kicked my foot.

I winced, and he glared at me.

"It's because of you we're forced to do this. If you'd just listened to our warnings, we could have done this a lot easier."

"Zac, you're about to start monologuing," Ozzie said, dropping a hand on Zac's shoulder.

"Of course I am. That's what bad guys do!" Zac said and grinned.

"Yeah, but—"

"Relax. We've got them tied up. I told you. If they had any real power, they'd have dealt with us already," Zac said, glaring at Ozzie until Ozzie pulled his hand back. Zac turned back to us and smiled. "All we needed was the barrier to drop a little more, and we'd have been able to successfully finish the summoning. But no, you had to kill our Devil Rats. And then, you had to start sealing all the places of power too. So now, here we are."

"You're the idiots summoning the Devil Rats?" I asked. Just as suddenly, pieces started clicking into place. By their very presence, otherworldly beings frayed the edges of our reality. Creatures like the Devil Rats might do only a little, but get enough of them together, and the barriers would drop. These guys didn't have a lot of power, but boosted by a place of power and with a

212

barrier that was lowered, they might actually have been able to summon something. As I looked at Ozzie, the nagging feeling that I'd seen him somewhere before came back along with a memory. The imp.

"Are you insane?" Alexa growled. "Don't tell me you're going to summon a demon to torment the bullies who beat you up?"

"Shut up," Zac said, glaring at the blonde. "I'll let you know nobody bullied me at school." Maybe not Zac, but I noted how both Ozzie and Gupta shifted at Alexa's words.

"If you say you're summoning a devil to trade your souls for power, I'm going to save you the trouble. Those trades never work out the way you think they will." I watched Ozzie and Gupta flinch slightly, and I groaned while Zac just glared at me at first and then his friends.

"We got this. I had my dad help me draft the contract," Zac snapped.

"Your dad?" I cried incredulously. "What is he, a demon lawyer? Wait, are there demon lawyers?" I asked Alexa.

"There are, but—" Alexa paused, shaking her head after a moment. "There's no way it's his dad. We'd know of him if he was."

"My dad's the best corporate lawyer in the state!" Zac snapped even as the pair behind him goggled at the byplay between Alexa and me. "I told him I needed it for my role-playing group, and he helped draw it up."

"You got your dad, a human lawyer, to write up a contract to sign with a demon for your role-playing group." I said the words slowly, hoping Zac could hear how dumb it sounded. Then again, self-delusion was big with this kid. Maybe I needed a bullhorn and some flashing lights too.

"It'll work. And at worse, we'll just send him right back," Zac said.

"You two seem a bit saner. You do understand how messed up this is, right?" I looked past Zac, fixing my gaze on the pair of teenagers behind him. Zac growled and backhanded me, making my headache explode again and stars dance in my eyes. By the time I recovered, I was gagged. When I craned my neck to the side, I noticed Gupta finishing Alexa's gag too.

"That's better. You'll see. You've got a front row seat." Zac reached behind him, pulled out a knife and showed it to me. As I instinctively flinched backward into my chair, Zac sniggered. "Hold him."

Ozzie came forward, gripping my left arm tight before Zac dropped the knife to it and cut my arm free. A brief second later, I felt the blade bite into my flesh followed by the warmth of my blood spilling out. Rather than just leaving a single slice, I felt Zac stab it in again and twist, opening my wound and forcing a muffled scream from my throat. My arm jerked reflexively, and Ozzie had to put his weight on it to keep my arm still as it bled into the iron bucket.

"You didn't have to do that, Zac," Gupta said, his voice filled with worry. "You could really hurt him."

"Fuck him. He's just another damn wizard. The girl will give him another potion to fix him up later anyway," Zac said. "Now he knows not to laugh at me."

I glared at Zac, making a mental note to kick him in the balls a few times when I was out. Alexa next to me had struggled briefly when she'd seen the knife but now had fallen strangely silent. Praying she was working on getting us out of here, I growled at Zac to keep his attention on me, which just made him smirk.

"That's enough," Ozzie said finally, breaking the silence that had fallen over the group.

Gupta had grown a little pale, having walked away back to their magic circle to study it in detail. Zac continued to smirk at me, watching the blood flow with a little bit too much of a crazy look on his face.

"Just a little more," Zac crooned to Ozzie.

214

"No. That's enough," Ozzie said and then turned to me, meeting my eyes before he continued. "If you promise not to do anything stupid, I'll get the bandages and wrap you up."

"Mmmphhfff," I mumbled. Taking this as assent, Ozzie moved away and came back, relieved to see I hadn't tried anything. In a few seconds, he had rather expertly bandaged my wound and then tied me to the chair again using the remaining bandages. Obviously, the kid had taken some classes in first aid.

"Good. Now, come on. We can't let the blood get too cold," Zac said as he lugged the pail to the circle. I growled, watching as the group grabbed cups and dipped them into the pail. They took out paintbrushes and went to the circle with my fresh blood.

If it hadn't been my blood, I would have screamed at their laughable incompetence. You didn't need that much blood for a spell or, hell, use the circle itself. You just needed it during the sacrifice. The purpose was the link, which was as much symbolic as it was physical. Sure, more helped, but the amount they'd grabbed from me was ridiculous.

"Stop giggling!" Zac snapped at me as he looked up, and I blinked.

I was not giggling. I was not... right. That was me. I paused, forcing myself to focus again as I realized what had happened. The blood loss really was getting to me. Or was it the concussion? Maybe a little bit of both and the fact that I might actually die here.

Heal.

I needed to heal myself. I focused on that thought, pushing aside everything else, and started my spell. Thankfully, the blood loss seemed less debilitating than the earlier concussion, and the spell kicked off the first time, running through my body and completing the clotting of the wound before it began the process of fixing me.

My kidnappers were too focused on their own task now, Gupta content to stand with his back to me while Zac and Ozzie took station at the other points of the triangle in their freshly painted blood circle. I watched as they began the ritual, chanting together from the pieces of paper they held. After a few seconds, I stopped listening and focused on my spell, unable to grasp the ritual.

It had little to do with the complexities of the ritual or my lack of knowledge, though I'm sure it had something to do with it. But like their ritual circle, much of what they chanted was utter rubbish, made-up words and extra garbage that did nothing but waste time and power. In either case, I had better things to do with my time. Like heal.

I turned my head to the side slowly, careful not to shift too fast or disturb my spell I had cast. Alexa met my eyes when I looked at her, fury radiating from her body as she sat in her chair. A slight movement had me looking down, and that was when I noticed her hand shifting - back and forth ever so gently. My eyes widened, and I looked back at the idiot trio, glad to see they were caught up in their ritual.

Relieved, I focused on our kidnappers and my spell instead, stoking my concentration with the promise of coming revenge. Because what I had seen were the slowly fraying edges of the rope as Alexa cut her way free.

Chapter 18

"*Ilarx Jaa Ba!*" the trio chanted again. This was the third time that had been said, and unlike most of their ritual, those three words made my spine tighten and goosebumps appear on my skin. A part of me knew why—the words were the creature's True Name. It was the most powerful way to call a demon across the barrier and also explained why the trio felt they could do it even with their low level of power. The idiot trio must have had heaven-defying luck to have gotten the True Name of a demon.

Of course, they were also idiots. The True Name of a demon wasn't something you just let others know. It was one of those closely guarded secrets of mages the world over, and the trio had decided to chant it while the initiate and myself were in the same room.

Before I could roll my eyes yet again, the voices of our kidnappers rose in unison, indicating the end of the ritual. I glanced at the notification in the corner of my vision, my lips twisting around the gag.

Henry Tsien has gained 9 health points from Heal.

Not enough time, damn it. I had no choice now as, with the ritual over, the acrid smell of sulfur filled the room and flowed from the circle. Within moments, a demon had appeared. Surprisingly, it stood only five feet tall, its humanoid body covered in light-red scales over paler, pinkish skin beneath. In its mouth, a cigar hung, held in place by a whip-thin tail.

"You called?" the demon said.

"We have summoned you, Ilarx Jaa Ba, to make a deal!" Zac intoned immediately.

"Whoa, you can tone down the theatrics. I'm here already. And you can just call me Il," Il said, waving a hand as he turned to survey the trio. He barely spared any of them a glance before his eyes landed on the pair of us, narrowing.

"We are here… Il… to offer you a deal. A contract," Zac said, his voice losing some of its confidence.

"For your souls, right?" Il interrupted, the horned devil shaking his head. "You three for what, riches and women?"

"What we require is laid out in the document by your feet," Zac replied, gesturing to the bundle of paper.

Il reached out and tapped the document with his foot. For a second, it glowed, and then the entire document burst into flames. "Not interested."

"What? We're offering you—"

"Your souls at the end of your demise. Which will be thousands of years from now at best. Not interested," Il said with a snort. "Anyway, the market for ordinary souls like yours crashed twenty years ago and hasn't recovered. Too many damn collateralized soul obligations that weren't properly insured."

"But—" Zac looked lost, and I snorted through my gag. I glanced at Alexa who sat in her chair stiffly, staring at the demon in our midst.

"Now, for those two…" the demon said and grinned.

"Those two?" Zac asked, turning to stare at us. "I… we…"

"Come now. They are obviously your backup plan. And it's not your soul," Il said, leering at Zac.

"Zac, we can't," Gupta said, glancing down at the burned papers and then us. "This isn't what we agreed to."

Zac stood stock still, not answering his friend. Ozzie stared at Zac, an unreadable expression on his face, while the demon murmured softly, "Women. Wealth. What else do you desire? For those two…"

A tearing of cloth was heard from beside me, so soft I would never have heard it if I hadn't been waiting for that sound for minutes already. I noticed a quick motion, and then suddenly I felt the cold press of iron against my arm.

I turned my head to see Alexa sawing at my bindings. Yeah, definitely time to go.

"I can't…" Zac said, his mouth moving and then he straightened his back. "No."

"Fuck that," Ozzie snarled suddenly. "I need that money for my mom. You have a deal, Il."

"Then bring them to me," Il said, grinning as he pointed to us. "Before our prey flees."

My hand free, I raised it and conjured a weak Force Spear. I held it aloft, letting them see the swirling power, an unspoken threat. I saw Ozzie hesitate while Gupta was shouting a denial at Il and Zac was trying to talk sense to Ozzie.

"Free me then, and I'll collect them myself," Il said to Ozzie. "Free me, and our deal is complete. My word on it."

"You can't, Oz," Zac said. Struck by a thought, Zac spun to stare at Il and started speaking some gibberish again.

"Zac. Stop it, don't you dare banish him. Don't! I'm telling you—" Ozzie snarled and then looked at Il, nodding firmly. "Done."

My feet were free, and Alexa was working on the last binding on my left hand. I hadn't dared toss my spear; I didn't know if injuring Ozzie would break the spell even further. However, when I'd heard him speak, I tossed it forward. Unfortunately, my Force Spear had a dozen feet to cross and his foot only had one.

Ozzie's foot rubbed against the circle, smearing dried blood across the ground.

"Thank you," Il said to Ozzie as the demon strolled out of the broken circle, smirking openly and doing nothing to stop my Force Spear. The Force Spear picked Ozzie up and threw him backward, his body flung aside like a ragdoll as my spell collapsed. I had purposely blunted the spear when I'd cast it, not willing to kill just yet.

"Now, let's finish this," Il said as he strolled forward.

I stood quickly, tearing the last of the makeshift bandage restraint off the chair and wincing in pain. Alexa turned and stepped in front of me and to the side, crouching low with her tiny dagger held out in front of her.

"Go, Henry," Alexa snapped after she pulled the gag from her mouth.

"Mmmpff... got this," I said once I managed to extract the gag.

"Really?" Il laughed derisively as he neared us. Behind him, I could see Gupta next to Ozzie, checking him over while Zac stood, frozen in place. When Alexa suddenly stepped forward into a lunge, Il casually moved to block the attack. Both of them suddenly just stood there, staring at each other in shock.

"Told you Lily has this," I said, staring at the information that had just popped up.

Error: Your party member (Alexa) has attempted to engage in an out-of-level encounter.

"What magic is this?" Il snarled. The demon moved swiftly, trying to grab Alexa by the neck, and was once again stopped an inch away from touching her. "You are not this powerful, Wizard!"

"Not me," I said, slowly standing and smiling tightly at the demon. Behind him, I could see Zac's shocked face. "Just a friend. Now, think it's time for you to go home, no?"

Rather than reply to me, I saw Il focus. His light-red skin deepened in color as his hand tightened and the smell of sulfur intensified. Strain as he would, Il progressed no further in his attempts to injure Alexa. In turn, Alexa dropped her hand and focused on Zac and the others. Gupta had finally managed to get Ozzie up and was attempting to skedaddle.

"Fine," Il said finally as he stepped away. "You win this time, Wizard. But I will not be returning empty-handed." As soon as he said that, Il sauntered toward Ozzie and Gupta.

"Henry," Alexa said, her eyes darting between the demon, the trio, and myself. Conflict raged on her face, torn between her duty to safeguard me and her duty to protect others.

"Oh, hell," I said. Pun intended. My mind whirled while I tried to figure out what we could do. I looked again at Il's information.

Ilarx Jaa Ba (Demon Level 40)
HP: ?/?

Not a powerful demon at all. But he was still more than double my level. Even if we somehow blocked him from grabbing the three, Il would just leave and find someone else to drag back. While this was a poor summoning, Il still had more than sufficient strength to do some real damage before he finally lost his corporeal form.

"Stall him," I murmured to Alexa as I hurried to Zac. Il cast a look at me, his lips twisting slightly in amusement, but made no move to stop me. Alexa dashed forward, putting herself between Il and his prey.

"How long would it take to banish him?" I asked Zac, eyeing the pair of pages he still held in his hand.

"Uhh… a few minutes maybe," Zac replied, his voice trembling with fear. "But he has to be in the circle."

I swore silently, knowing Zac was correct. Even broken, the circle still held the power to banish the demon. Outside of it, it would require significantly more strength. Perhaps I could banish him with the ritual myself, but I couldn't be sure. The banishment might only work for those whom had initially participated in the summoning.

At the moment, the demon was glaring at Alexa, who was using her body to block him from moving closer to the pair. Her eyes narrowed as she tried to outguess the demon's intentions. It was a losing proposition though, the demon being faster than my friend.

"Get ready then." I stepped into the circle myself, conjured a Force Bolt, and then cooled the air within it. Once it was sufficiently cold, I lobbed it at Il. Immediately, the Force Bolt dissipated as it hit the unseen barrier around the demon, only the traces of chilled air remaining. Still, it was sufficient to grab the demon's attention.

Error: You are attempting to engage in an out-of-level encounter.

"You attack me?" Il said, eyebrowless brows drawing down as he stared at me, puzzled. In answer, I formed another plain Force Bolt and tossed it at the demon. When he saw the attack dissipate, the demon laughed. "It looks like your protection extends to me as well."

Error: You are attempting to engage in an out-of-level encounter.

"It does," I agreed. as I formed another Force Bolt and tossed it. Il stared at me, obviously curious about what I thought I was doing. He wasn't the only one as Alexa frowned at me.

Error: You are attempting to engage in an out-of-level encounter.
Stop this. If you keep this up, you'll lose your protection.

Finally. I formed another Force Bolt and lobbed it at Il, who had turned around to deal with the two teenagers attempting to sneak away. This Force Bolt glowed as it passed through the barrier before it smashed into the demon's back, throwing him forward from the unexpected force.

Force Bolt does 4 damage to Il.
Out-of-level encounter limitation removed.
You better know what you're doing, Henry.

"Thanks, Lily," I whispered as the information scrolled through.

Il spun around, red eyes glowing with fury, and crossed the room to grab hold of me. His hand closed around my throat and stopped, but this time, it was due to my Force Shield. I just hoped Zac did his job.

"You humans are so predictable. I could tell you were one of those idiotic heroes the moment I saw the pair of you," Il said, his hand beginning to squeeze. I grunted, feeling the Force Shield begin to strain even as Il took his time cracking it. "Did you think you could beat me, Wizard? I can see your strength."

"Fuck. You," I snarled even as my headache intensified. I felt something cut loose, a sharp pain and a light warmth ran down my lips as a nosebleed sprang.

"Pathetic," Il said as he clenched tighter.

My Force Shield shattered, the backlash making me reel. Before his hand could close on my throat, Il screamed as Alexa drove her knife into his back, the knife cutting through his body like butter. Il snarled and slapped Alexa in the face, knocking her down. As he reached down to pluck out the smoking blessed knife that had been left in his body, I raised my hand to cast another spell.

Gong Cast
84% Synchronicity

The spell was focused, channeled around the demon's head. It was so loud that even a few feet away from him, my ears hurt. As for the demon?

Gong does 7 points of damage to Il.
Stunned debuff added.
Deaf debuff added.

Right. That should have made it impossible for the demon to hear Zac at work. Il turned his attention back to me and jabbed a hand outward, reaching for my heart. I stepped back quickly, dodging the grasping hand as I chanted my next spell. A moment later, a Light Ball burst to life in front of Il's eyes, blinding him and me. The moment it did, I let my feet collapse under me, pulling my heels off the ground and letting gravity take over. Not a moment too soon as the blinded demon's hand clawed the air where my chest had been a second ago.

Scrambling on all fours, I moved around the circle that had begun to glow. I jabbed my injured arm down toward the broken spot, my fresh blood reforming the circle with added strength and boosting the banishment spell as I forced my own strength into the circle. I flexed that mystical muscle that controlled my mana flow, pushing more mana into the circle with all my might while attempting to stay in control. My head throbbed further, black spots dancing in my eyes.

As I began to consider what to do next, I felt my foot gripped from behind. Lifted off the ground from my foot, I barely escaped knocking my head on the ground as the five-foot demon proceeded to lift me up with one hand. Luckily for me, the demon was too short for what he wanted to do, so he grabbed hold of my opposite thigh.

"Let go," I snarled as I formed a Force Spear in my hand. I stabbed it into his body as I swung upward. The Force Spear dug into his light, scaled flesh, punching inward a bit. Damage notifications flickered across my eyes, but I ignored them. Il just growled and slapped my hand away. In a second, the Force Spear dispersed.

"You are annoying, Wizard," Il said, eyes narrowed as he glared at me through half-blinded eyes. "I'm going to enjoy hurting you."

The demon punctuated his words by plunging his clawed fingers into my torso, fingers closing on my intestines within. I screamed, the spell I had begun to form again dispersing. Before Il could continue his assault, Alexa, who had crawled over to us, plunged the previously discarded knife into his Achilles tendon and tugged on it, slicing it open.

Unable to support himself, the demon collapsed, his fingers still within my body. I was in so much pain even the addition of the fall and the scrabbling of fingers within my stomach added little to the misery I was in. I couldn't even form a spell the pain was so great.

Henry Tsien dealt 6 damage by falling.
Bleeding debuff received. -4 HP per minute.

Warning: Health is critically low!

"You," the demon snarled, its wound already healing, even around the smoking flesh of the blessed knife. It kicked at Alexa, who managed to get her hand up in time to shield her head. The kick caught her low and picked her up, sending her spinning out of the circle through the air, the dull thump of her landing body making me wince. "You are really getting on my nerves. This ends now."

"Yes, it does," Gupta said as he limped forward and locked hands with Ozzie. Together, the pair made a throwing motion with their hands. A tiny flame floated forward to splash against Il, who stared at them incredulously.

"You used fire? Against me, a demon?" Il said.

"We distracted you," Ozzie said and spit to the side. "Now go to hell."

"What?" Il said and spun around, finally recalling Zac.

The leader of the trio was crouched low, reading the chant. Il snarled and lunged toward Zac, coming to a stop as the circle held him in. He struck it again and again, the once-broken circle beginning to fail again. Head buried in his papers, Zac finally finished the banishment, throwing his hand forward at the end, and a small, black vortex formed in the center of the circle. It pulled Il backward, tearing apart his corporeal body. "No! You humans—"

"Got you." I coughed, clutching my stomach as I watched the demon disappear into thin air. For a second more, I stared at the space where the monster had been before I once again fainted.

Chapter 19

"I have got to stop doing this," I muttered to myself when I woke up again, my last memory of falling unconscious once more. Surprisingly, I didn't hurt, which was an extremely pleasant experience. The fact that I didn't seem to have any recurring side effects from being smacked around so much was amazing. Another surprise was that I wasn't on the concrete floor but my own bed. As I sat up, I spotted Lily tapping away at her laptops but could not find any sign of the initiate.

"She's not here," Lily said to my unasked question. "She's still getting reamed out for nearly getting you killed."

"Speaking of that..." I frowned, touching my stomach as I vividly recalled my lifeblood flowing from it.

"Alexa's people got there before you bled out completely. If Alexa didn't have her training in medicine and her faith-healing ability..." Lily said, trailing off meaningfully as her fingers stopped clicking away. I looked to meet her eyes before I was forced to look aside.

"It was pretty dumb, wasn't it?"

"It was very dumb. But..." Lily paused and then shook her head. The next moment, my status screen appeared in front of my eyes without prompting.

Class: Mage

Level 18 (48% Experience)

Known Spells: Light Sphere, Force Spear, Force Shield, Force Fingers, Alter Temperature, Gong, Gust, Heal, Link, Track, Mend, Ward, Glamour, Illusion, Summon, Iceball, Fireball

Magical Skillset

Mana Flow: 4/10

Mana to Energy Conversion: 3/10

Spell Container: 3/10

Spatial Location: 3/10

Spatial Movement: 3/10

Energy Manipulation: 3/10

Biological Manipulation: 2/10

Matter Manipulation: 0/10

Summoning: 0/10

Duration: 4/10

"Wow." I blinked, scanning through the screen for the changes—a couple of levels, a few new spells, more mana flow, control, duration, and biological understanding. "You leveled me."

"You leveled yourself. The numbers are just the reflection of reality. Well, mostly—you pushed yourself and your abilities enough that I could smooth things out a little. Fighting for your life tends to do that," Lily said.

"I guess watching someone do the summoning isn't enough to learn the basics, eh?" I said, and my lip twisted wryly.

"Nor will you yet." Caleb's voice cut into the conversation as he walked into the apartment. I frowned as I watched him put his keys into his pocket as he walked forward. "That is knowledge that you neither require nor are ready to wield."

"Caleb," I said, nodding in greeting to the Mage. "You're back."

"Yes. I leave for a few days, and I find you half-dead upon my return," Caleb said, his voice cold. "Are you attempting to break your own promise? Are you this dead set on ensuring none of us gains the ring?"

"Dead set..." Lily giggled.

"It wasn't like that," I protested, ignoring the jinn. "Though, while you're here, what happened to the idiot trio?"

"The idiot trio, as you called them, have been dealt with. The council has spoken with them, and steps have been taken to ensure they will not be able to repeat their actions. Though, I believe they will not attempt another summoning," Caleb said.

"And Ozzie's mother?" I asked, recalling the boy's impetus.

"Dying from a disease. I forget which one," Caleb answered.

"And you guys are going to help her?" I asked, my eyes narrowing, and Caleb snorted.

"Again, we are not a charitable organization. As it stands, he is lucky we let him live. Summoning a demon, even a low-level one, is a dangerous act."

I growled, shutting my mouth. Still, talking of charitable organizations, I made a note to talk to Alexa about it.

"You know, this entire incident was interesting," Caleb said as he walked toward me, his eyes slightly unfocused as he read my aura. "You risked your life and Alexa's for a group of strangers."

"That's... well..." *What heroes did.* But I couldn't say that out loud. I'd have died of embarrassment.

"Yes, moronic in the extreme. Self-sacrificial. And yet, you gave not a single thought to your friend."

"Alexa? She was about to go ahead and try anyway," I said.

"And still the jinn is not mentioned. One would almost think she was not in danger of being lost for all eternity by your death," Caleb said. I kept my face neutral as he said that, though I found myself shooting a glance at the aforementioned jinn. She continued to focus on her gaming at least.

"Well, she let me," I said finally.

"Still. Interesting, isn't it?" Caleb smiled at me tightly. "I expect you back at class tomorrow." After that last pronouncement, the mage walked out of the room, leaving the pair of us staring at each other in silence.

In the end, I flopped back down onto my bed with a light groan.

***

Alexa returned later that evening, looking worse for wear. The normally energetic blonde looked depressed, her energy shattered by the demands of her bosses. Still, she gave me a smile when she noticed me up and about, puttering around the kitchen making a lasagna.

"Any lasting damage?" Alexa asked as she came to stand beside me.

"None," I told her. "Just one second." I added the lasagna to the preheated oven and set the timer before looking at the initiate. "Thank you. For backing me up."

"Thank you for letting me act," Alexa said. "I know it wasn't an easy choice."

"Actually wasn't that hard," I admitted after a moment. I looked at the blonde, smiling slightly. "I couldn't exactly let a demon run loose. Who would?"

"You'd be surprised," Alexa said with a grimace. I almost asked if her people would have preferred it but restrained myself. Some things were best left alone. "You know, I wondered why God would let such a powerful object fall into untrained, untested hands. Now, perhaps I know why."

"Uhhh... thanks?" I said, looking away. "So... garlic bread?"

Alexa stared at me for a moment before she let the topic go and walked over to the breadbox. "Yeah, I'll get it ready."

I breathed a sigh of relief, watching my partner, my friend, help work on dinner.

Later that evening, I lay on the floor, staring at my ceiling as sleep eluded me. I'd gotten into magic because it was cool, because it had been a lifelong dream to cast spells and be a mage. The reality was every bit as cool as I'd thought it would be, but slinging spells, creating wards, and killing monsters was just the tip of the iceberg. The supernatural world was both more complex than I could ever have imagined and more mundane.

Humans would be humans. Self-interest, greed, and jealousy ruled. We might've had powers beyond the normal, but everyone was still intent on doing what was best for themselves and their groups. Well. Most everyone.

I'd done quests because it was the best way to make money and level up. But I never really thought about why I'd bothered, why I'd done it. Hell, I'd even started acting like Caleb, laughing and deriding the idiot trio because they couldn't really wield magic like I did. But, in the end, for all their own desires, they'd stepped up and helped thrust the demon back into hell.

That was the thing, power for the sake of power was vanity. The best times I'd had were when my quests actually had a purpose, when I was helping others.

Maybe, just maybe, it was time for me to start thinking less like a gamer and more like a person.

Book 2

A Squire's Wish

Chapter 1

"This would be a lot easier if I was allowed to use magic." I exhaled audibly and twisted my shoulders, my arms throbbing. Still, at least we were finally inside our new duplex. Three bedrooms, two bathrooms, hardwood floors, and a living room meant I was paying much more than I wanted. But, considering Alexa had insisted on the larger space, and she was paying half, I'd compromised. I had to admit, looking around the relatively modern, open-plan space, it looked nice. Even if all the belongings I had from my bachelor suite barely filled our new home.

"Oh please, this is barely a workout," Alexa said as she impatiently tapped her foot. The Nordic blonde was more Wonder Woman than model and had more muscles in her arms than I did, so it was no surprise she was barely out of breath.

"Mage," I said and pointed to myself as I struggled to catch my breath. Though perhaps I could do with a little more actual exercise.

"The enforcers in the Mage Council are as well known for their physical prowess as they are for their magical abilities," Alexa said. I grunted, refusing to acknowledge her point, even while being intrigued by the idea of buff magic users. I guessed real-world magicians were more like anime heroes than Raistlin. In either case, the initiate was more likely to know than I did. The Templars had been the church's sharp edge against the supernatural world for hundreds of years. They'd been occasional allies and enemies of the Mage Council throughout the years. Me? I'd barely entered the supernatural world six months ago. I still had a lot to catch up on.

"Fine. So I might be slacking off on the entire exercise bit," I muttered as I bent my knees to grab the edge of the couch once again.

"Slacking off implies you ever started," Lily said behind me, her arms full with a cardboard box helpfully labeled "books." The olive-skinned, slim and shapely jinn sauntered toward us from the front door where we'd deposited our initial run with a sway of her hips. "Where do you want these?"

"What are they?" I grunted out as we maneuvered the couch to catch the sunlight and to face where we'd decided the TV would go.

"Reference material."

"Huh?" I said as I squatted and set my end of the couch on the floor.

"Your role-playing books." The jinn held the heavy box of books with one hand as she scratched her nose, obviously not bothered with things like weight. No surprise there. Her "body" wasn't really real, just a magical construct, which begged the question why I was doing the heavy lifting, but that would open up a whole different can of worms regarding Lily's increasing agoraphobia.

"Right. We'll keep those in the living room," I said and pointed to the corner we'd designated for the bookcases. For a moment, I felt amazed as the reality of my situation hit me once again. Not the shacking up with two stunning, supermodel-level, good-looking women but the fact that I was a mage—a mage wielding magic through a wish granted by a jinn who based my entire leveling progression off a homebrew mixture of role-playing game books, single-player video games, and massive multiplayer online games. It was how my old RPG books became reference material.

"Stop delaying. We've only got the moving van till five," Alexa said, urging me out the front door.

"You sure I can't do this with magic?"

"After you left the dent in the doorway of our old apartment?" Alexa said derisively. "We can't afford to pay to fix another mistake."

"Fine." I grumbled as we reached the moving van and went for the bed stand. Alexa was not wrong. We still needed to find the money for mattresses and bed frames for both girls. Or technically, for me since I'd given my bed to Alexa. "Let's get this over with."

***

Hours later, the three of us were seated in our new living room, evening sunlight streaming in from the blinds as we preyed on four large pizzas. I shook my head, amazed once again at the sheer volume of food both women managed to put away. Admittedly, today I was putting on a good showing. Not that it was a competition.

"So, Caleb gave you today off? Alexa asked.

"Yes. After I threatened to continue using 'What Does the Fox Say?' as my training tune for Gong," I said with a grin. Since Lily basically downloaded spells into my brain at each level increase, my understanding of actual magical theory was, shall we say, erratic. It didn't help that much of the magic theory she downloaded came from millennia of magical knowledge—knowledge gained as the assistant or tool of world-class magicians. While I might have more powerful spells than my more traditionally trained counterparts, mine were also more esoteric and not as easily pliable with modern magical theory. To fix my magical shortcomings, Caleb, the master mage sent to deal with me from the Mage Council, had set up a training program. One aspect of which was teaching me to understand and manipulate the components of the spells I had in my brain.

In the case of Gong, the spell manipulated sound waves via magic. Like most spells, Gong, for all its outward simplicity, was significantly more complex internally than its final manifestation. To channel the spell, I had to control the amount of mana input, where the mana went to adjust volume and pitch, as well as dictate the location the noise would appear. All this was controlled by strings of arcane glyphs and, in some cases, actual mathematical formulas. Combined, they were known as spell formulas. Right now, my training involved learning to repeatedly cast the spell with specific target notes. I had to play a song with my spell.

Technically, I was doing this in the least mana efficient manner possible. There were actual spells that allowed its user to continually channel the spell, formulating the song in one continual cast. The problem was the spell formula for such a song was significantly more complex than the simple spell Lily had downloaded into my mind. It was kind of like the difference between playing "Chopsticks" and Mozart. When I'd asked, Caleb had displayed the simplest musical spell formula he knew for me to read just to shut me up. The formula itself was intriguing, a mixture of—

"Earth to Henry," Lily said, waving a hand in front of my eyes.

"Sorry," I said, pushing her hand away. "Was just thinking of a spell."

"Of course you were," Lily said with a snort. "Maybe you should be thinking about a quest instead. If you haven't forgotten, you're broke."

"We're broke," I said pointedly. "I still don't get why you need a room of your own. You have your ring."

"Which I've lived in for hundreds of years," Lily said, glaring at me. "You try going back to your cell. Even if the door's open—"

"Ah, right," I said and scratched my head. Sometimes I forgot Lily was basically a slave to the ring since she never actually lived in it anymore. While she had twisted my first wish to give her a way to stay out of the ring itself, past users hadn't been as careless or generous. "Sorry."

"It's fine," Lily said with a wave of her hand.

"I do not understand, however, why you cannot form your own furnishings," Alexa asked Lily.

"If you recall, I'm bound by the rules of the ring. I can't really affect the outside world in a meaningful manner with my magic without a wish," Lily said with a little bite. I guess some insults, like the Templars trying to kill me and steal my ring via Alexa, were not so easily forgiven.

"Wait. With your magic?" I said. "I thought you couldn't do it period."

"Well…" Lily paused, looking embarrassed. "It's a bit complicated."

"Complicated… like you-don't-want-to-get-a-job complicated?" I said threateningly. While I'd been scrambling to earn an income by completing requests and other small jobs in the magical community, Lily had stayed home playing computer games… and begging me to get a console.

"Well, I'm not exactly legal, am I?" Lily asked. "I don't have any proof of identification. You wouldn't want me to be deported or thrown into jail, would you?"

"That…" I paused to consider as I looked at Lily. Well, yes. She was a Middle Eastern woman in the country. Technically illegally. Then again, she was a jinn who could literally disappear with a thought, which would make for a really interesting police report. But… "Thousand hells."

"Right," Lily said with a smile when she won her point. "That's why it's better I stay back home. Also, the more games I play, the better the patches I can provide."

Once again, I noted how she also avoided mentioning her growing reluctance to even visit the outside world. I considered bringing it up and once again shied away from the topic. Tackling sensitive emotional issues headlong was not something my traditional Chinese household had readied me for.

"Please don't." Alexa interrupted my thoughts with her words. "Your last patch had him sitting at the beach picking up rocks for an hour, muttering about leveling up his 'analyze' skill."

"Hey, it's a staple cheat skill," Lily said.

"Not the way you implemented it," I said. It was only after I had spent some time talking to Lily that I realized the only way to upgrade the analyze skill while staring at rocks would have been to read books on geology first, then spend the time actually perusing the rocks. And then repeating the task over and over again.

"Everyone's a critic," Lily said and crossed her arms to glare at us.

"As the lab rat, yes I am," I said. "Let's just focus on magic, okay?"

"Speaking of that, what are your... stats?" Alexa said, almost too casually. Really, the knight initiate sucked at casual. It just wasn't something they taught at knight school. It didn't help that I knew she was asking because the Templars, like most of the other major powers in the know, were waiting for me to hit level one hundred. Once I did, the ring could finally come off my fingers without it being lost forever.

Still, she was my closest ally. And I had no reason not to show her since Caleb received almost daily updates.

Class: Mage

Level 21 (19% Experience)

Known Spells: Light Sphere, Force Spear, Force Shield, Force Fingers, Alter Temperature, Gong, Gust, Heal, Healing Ward, Link, Track, Fix, Ward, Glamour, Illusion, Summon, Iceball, Fireball

Magical Skillset

Mana Flow: 4/10

Mana to Energy Conversion: 3/10

Spell Container: 3/10

Spatial Location: 3/10

Spatial Movement: 3/10

Energy Manipulation: 4/10

Biological Manipulation: 3/10

Matter Manipulation: 1/10

Summoning: 1/10

Duration: 4/10

"You gained two levels," Alexa said in approval. "But only learned one new spell?"

"Blame Caleb," I said, disgruntled. "He convinced Lily I needed to spend more time understanding my current repertoire. He wants her to stop giving me spells entirely."

"That," Alexa said and then fell silent, compressing her lips together tightly on the sentence she had been about to utter.

"Sucks. I know." I sighed. Truth be told, I somewhat agreed with Caleb's reasoning. I'd gained so many spells, I often did not use most of them. For quite a few, I had synchronicity of less than 50 percent when I cast them, never mind linking them together. No, for a while, I needed to work on my fundamentals. If I could increase my basic magical skill set to five, I'd be considered an actual novice mage by the Council, someone who at least was worth some basic respect. Of course, the fact this was a logarithmic progression meant that once I got there, the next steps were going to be incrementally harder.

"So. Quests," Lily said leadingly, pushing forth a sheaf of papers. I groaned, staring at the quests—work orders, really—but picked them up. We needed the money.

Chapter 2

The first time I ever saw a four-hundred-pound orc charge down a football field in spiked shoulder pads and a helmet, it was an impressive and bed-wetting sight. The second time, I might've frozen in fear, wondering if I'd written my will. By the third quarter, it was routine.

"And why did we have to be here now?" I muttered, shifting on the too-hard seat. Who willingly spent their evenings unpaid, sitting on hard, metal benches—which were open to the elements—and screaming their head off at the sight of one team pummeling the other? At least when I was gaming, I did it in a temperature-controlled room with cheap, store-bought snacks on hand. "The contract's for after the game is done."

"Are you not enjoying the sight of martial excellence?" Alexa asked as the lines reset. On one side, a full team of orcs stood with control of the ball, each of them fully dressed and padded. On the other, a smaller—literally—team of dwarves stood across the field, ready to defend their turf.

"Not at all. I'm just hoping we didn't undercharge them," I said, eying the field over the cover of my book. When I had pulled it out, I received more than a few glares, but those subsided when they realized it was a spellbook. Being a mage still commanded some respect, thankfully. If not more comfortable seats.

The field itself was a torn and bloody mess, the grass and earth looking like it had been tiled by a rototiller with a grudge. Particular portions showcased the extra-violent nature of the sport, blood and guts mashed into the ground. And all over the field, I could see the light glow of mana as the illusion array ensured the mundanes were kept in the dark.

"Come on, it's not that hard. Is it?" Alexa dropped her voice to a whisper at the end, and her eyes shone with concern. Our job—my job—was to clean up the mess after the match was over. After losing their resident contracted dryad, the Supernatural Football League of Erie had contacted us. If we managed to do a good job, we'd actually have a regular contract, at least when the season was on. It'd be a nice change of pace from our regular scramble for jobs.

"Don't know," I said to Alexa just as softly. "I've never tried to manipulate this much earth and grass. Theoretically, linking multiple Healing Wards together with some direct manipulation on my part should speed up the growth of the grass. All I need to do beforehand is tamp down the earth and smooth it out, which an adjusted Force Spear should do well enough. It'd be more like a Force Plow, but it should work."

"Good." Alexa turned back to watching the orcs and dwarfs beat the shit out of each other under the guise of sport. I sighed slightly and watched the initiate for a second, seeing how she leaned forward, lips parted and eyes glinting with interest and enjoyment. Jocks. I would never understand them.

***

I frowned, adjusting the position of the warding block once again. After finally being happy with it, I moved down another twenty feet to set up the next block. Each of these warding blocks had been hand carved by me, their glyphs and spell formulas painstakingly cast beforehand. Along the field, Alexa walked back and forth, spreading fertilizer across the churned earth.

"How much longer is this going to take?" grumbled the large red-skinned, horned demon—Japanese demon that was, an oni. "Edith never took so long."

"Edith was an eighty-year-old dryad linked to the very earth itself, who had been doing this job for forty years," I replied as I pulled another block out. "And if you had confirmed the contract yesterday like we mentioned, I could have set up and buried these wards beforehand. Now, I've got to do the prep."

"This better work. For the amount we're paying you—"

"Which is two-thirds what you paid Edith," I said, staring at him. "Don't think I don't know it. But we let you do so because we aren't as good as she is."

"Whatever. Just get it done right," Ken said and walked off. I glared after the demon, my sight defocusing for a moment to see the fat, coverall-wearing figure he showed the outside world. Somehow, I felt the glamour was much more fitting for the caustic ass.

Left alone, I worked my way around the field and finally set all the blocks in place. I'd have loved to plant them deep, and perhaps I might another time, but until we confirmed the contract, I was not going to lose my warding blocks. Even if they were cheap hand-carved wooden blocks, they still took a decent amount of time to create. And if I ever wanted to increase their power, I would need to start working with some better materials. That being said, wood itself was a great material for my next spell.

Finally done, I took the next step, using a Force Plow to smooth the earth. Really, it was just a Force Spear with its container adjusted. It had taken just over three hours to work out how to create the Force Plow, adjusting the formula for the container so the spell formed the necessary shape and, more importantly, held together. Still, this was the first time I was using it for such a duration, so the worms in my stomach refused to stop shifting.

Stupid really. No one was going to die here. I'd just lose a little contract. But part of the reason I had stayed as low key—or a drudge, as my sister named me years ago—was that I hated pressure. I hated to make mistakes and lose face.

"Henry?" Alexa called after I'd been standing still for a few minutes.

"Just checking the spell over," I replied, using a lame excuse. Raising my hand, I started the casting motions required, fingers flicking, twitching, and spreading as I cast. The physical motions were technically unnecessary, as were the words I softly chanted. Magic itself was all about intention and magical formulas, with the formulas more a mental guide than necessity. But the motions and words helped. The spell slid into a universal groove, which helped reduce the cost and difficulty of casting my spell. When formed, the Force Plow was invisible for the most part. To my eyes, it consisted of three portions. The first was a slightly blunted blade that helped level the earth, with excess dirt collected in the second, covered portion. The extra dirt was then compressed into the earth by a rolling cylinder of force.

"Huh. Never seen anyone do that," Ken exclaimed, grudging admiration in his voice.

I glowed slightly at his words, though I didn't tell Ken the truth. The spell might look impressive, but it only worked because, relatively speaking, the amount of damage done to the grounds wasn't that great. I was only shifting around a foot of earth at most at each location. My spell and mana were nowhere near sufficient enough to say, compress asphalt. Yet.

Thirty minutes later, the ground was as smooth as I could make it. I paused, panting, and eyed the glowing blue line from the corner of my eyes. With a wave to Alexa, who walked the grounds again with more fertilizer, I slumped and waited for my mana to regenerate.

A part of me pointed out I should be attempting to meditate. Well, not exactly meditate. That's the wrong word, even if Caleb does use it. Cultivate? That makes it sound like I'm some Eastern immortal. "Open myself to the world" sounds too hippy-like. Whatever the case, it was a process to expand the refresh rate of my mana, of opening myself to the world's energy to draw it in. I didn't of course. Among other things, I sucked at the skill itself, and I looked like a complete fool doing it.

"Why are you stopping?" Ken asked, stomping back toward me and leaving fresh boot prints in my smooth earth.

"Two reasons. I need more mana for the next part. And we need to make sure there's enough fertilizer."

"Edith—"

"Was a dryad. She could draw nutrients from the surroundings and pour mana directly into the plants to nourish them. I can't," I said. Of course, I knew that theoretically there was a way to do so, but considering my mana pool and my lack of understanding of biological processes, I was so not going to. Healing—or in my case, accelerated growth—was already risky. Luckily, grass didn't care about cancer.

Ken rolled his big, bulbous red eyes at me again before stomping away. Once again, I took the time to check over the wards and then began the slow process of linking them together in my spell. It was not particularly difficult, just complex, casting Link and holding each Link spell in place as I cast and added another to the chain. Each one led back to me and the tuft of grass I held in my hand, forming a giant spell rectangle bordered by my wards.

When I finally cast my Heal spell, it would trigger the grass to grow, replicating and covering the churned earth with freshly grown grass. I was particularly proud of the fact that since the spell was Linked and targeted at the grass I held in hand, it wouldn't affect the various weeds, earthworms, and bugs living in the soil. It was both more mana efficient and smarter this way.

"Done," Alexa called to me and I sighed, looking into the sky as I began the last spell process. Such a simple thing, Heal Linked to the grass with wards to denote the boundaries of the spell. Even as my mana dropped, the untouched grass could visibly be seen growing while the newly tamped-down earth slowly began to sprout. I found myself swaying slightly, the spell draining more mana than I had anticipated, the loss making my face grow pale.

Linked Heal (Modified) Cast
Synchronicity 87%

"Henry," Alexa called to me as she neared, seeing my predicament.

I shook my head, knowing that if I gave up now, the spell would collapse on itself. While not dangerous—except to me—I wasn't exactly sure I could pull it off again, not with the pounding headache I'd already gained. Better to complete the job. And it was working. Already, I could see blades of grass poking out of the earth, slowly growing lusher.

"Damn it, Henry." Alexa stomped toward me and kicked my shin. The sudden pain broke my concentration, the spell unravelling. The backlash of the broken spell made me cry out and clutch at my head. "Lily warned you not to overexert yourself."

As I sat, cradling my head and eyeing the deep-red flashing mana bar, I growled at Alexa. Damn woman wore steel-toed boots. I was going to have a very big bruise there tomorrow. Yet, as my head cleared a little, I stared around the now-green fields with more than a little pride.

Magic was beautiful, complex, and amazing. Even after so many months training and learning, I still found myself marveling at the fact that I could wield such power. I could bring life to a trampled field and, perhaps most importantly, get paid.

Chapter 3

After overexerting myself spending mana, I'd been relegated to book study for the next couple days. It was frustrating, but I understood their concerns. Lily and Caleb had more than once described the dangers of mana withdrawal and overexertion. Increasing your mana pool required work, just like building muscles. The more you did and the closer you were to your limit, the more you built. However, do too much or too fast, and you created instabilities in your body. Ligaments and tendons took longer to develop in the human body than muscle mass. Mana channels and networks took longer to widen and strengthen than a body's central mana pool. My levels were, in many cases, Lily directly intervening and increasing my mana pool, but it would take a while for my body to catch up, even bolstered by her magics. Even the jinn feared directly manipulating a human body too greatly. The risks of cancer, tumors, and other unwanted mutations were not to be taken lightly.

And so here I was, lounging in my chair, working my way through another damn book. The door swung open, and Alexa walked in with a slouch from her training session. I frowned, staring at the blonde Amazon as she threw her sports bag full of workout gear, her spear, and toy weapons aside before she stomped up the stairs toward her room.

"What was that about?" I muttered.

Lily ignored my words, either because she had not heard or was refusing to hear. Our relative silence was punctuated a short while later by the slamming of a door and further large, obvious stomping. Minutes later, a door opened and then another slammed shut before the sound of water running through old pipes made its way to us.

Blessed silence ensued for all of fifteen minutes before the sound of loud stomping feet reappeared, and Alexa descended the stairs. Her short hair still slightly damp, the initiate threw herself onto the couch, forcing me to scramble quickly to pull my feet aside before they were squished. Once she was down, she sighed loudly.

"Alexa?" I asked softly. "What's wrong?"

"Nothing."

"I see," I said softly, staring at the blonde. I could push the matter, but I decided against it and instead shifted to a more comfortable position and propped my book open.

A few minutes later, a loud sigh broke the silence again.

"You know, if you have something to say, you could just say it." Yeesh. It wasn't as if I had never experienced teenage-girl syndrome, even though Alexa should have been old enough to have gotten over that period. I had to admit, it was amusing to think I was actually finding my sister's teenage youth a blessing.

"Nothing," Alexa snapped back at me before she sighed again.

I rolled my eyes and focused on my book, the silence lingering for a few minutes before it was broken by Alexa.

"I might need to leave."

"Oh?" I frowned, turning my head to the side. Considering Alexa was here because she was "fated" to be, I found her sudden decision interesting. Not that I truly believed in their oracles, but then again, I was a mage. What did I know?

"I'm getting my squire's test," Alexa said.

"Pardon?" I frowned again. "I thought you were going to be a faith healer?"

"So did I, but they feel that because of my 'involvement' with you, I should be a squire," Alexa said bitterly.

"But your healing—"

"Will become a secondary function," Alexa said, "until the jinn situation is resolved." Alexa shot a look at Lily, the jinn completely ignoring the discussion. "And maybe not then."

"Oh. I'm sorry about that," I said softly, grimacing at the fact that somehow my decisions had changed her life. Unintended consequences, they always seemed to play out no matter what I chose.

"*No es nada*," Alexa said with another sigh. "I just need to accept the will of heaven."

I paused, considering her words and then raised a hand slightly to ask the question that had been bugging me. "Is it heaven or the Templars? Because you being here is your heaven's, but making you a squire seems to be theirs."

"Our heaven," Alexa said, correcting me before she sighed. "In my case, it's the same. Or so says Templar Ignis."

I grunted, shaking my head. I would admit, the idea that anyone, especially someone I might not agree with, could have such control over my life was anathema to me. Then again, I was the guy who refused to get a proper job forever, even when my family and friends had pressured me to do so, just because I hated working for others. The number of jobs I'd been fired from before I learned my lesson was staggering. I sometimes wondered if my reason for doing so was due to my traditionally minded parents. Their views on what was "right," the pressure they exerted on me to "fit," was significant, especially while growing up. Or at least, fit in the doctor, lawyer, accountant, or engineer aspirations they had.

"When are you leaving?" I asked.

"Not sure," Alexa replied with another sigh, eyes half-closing. "Most squires receive a trial or series of trials they must pass to qualify. They're often very similar. We used to joke they'd reach into different helmets to pull out what monster and how many to kill."

"But?"

"But I'm not getting the regular," Alexa said softly. "I'm not allowed. I'm important."

"Oooh." I hissed at her words. I knew that song. The "special treatment" you got when you were unique, potentially better than anyone else. As if somehow, getting something harder and more difficult than what everyone else was doing was supposed to be a damn reward. As if the extra homework, the additional classes were "good" for you.

"Well, if there's anything I can do…"

"Thank you, but I don't want to think about it right now. Do we have any quests outstanding? Something that is easy to finish?"

"Mmm…" I paused, considering, and then waved toward the pile of papers which had accumulated in the corner. "Take your pick. Can't do much right now, but I should be okay for some light work tomorrow."

"I just want to hit something," Alexa said softly, a low growl in her voice.

"Right." I winced at her words and hoped there was a suitable quest in the pile. Because otherwise, I knew exactly what would happen. Alexa would decide I'd had enough of my book studying, drag me to the backyard, and force me to do calisthenics. And then afterward, she would make me practice on the punching bag and target pads. All to give her an excuse to use them as well.

I still had bruises on my thighs… and ribs. And that was with her hitting through the bag last time.

***

"Do you know what a large group of crows is called?" I shouted to Alexa the next day, my hand held in front of me as the Force Shield twisted and distorted before me under assault.

Mystic Crow (Level 9)
HP: 28/28

"No," Alexa said as she finished screwing her spear together. Its durable titanium-and-steel construction allowed her to break it down when not in use for easy transportation. Spear locked in place, Alexa stepped forward, the weapon held close to her body and raised toward the sky. "Can you drop your shield partially?"

"Not going to have a choice in a moment," I said with a snarl. Already, my head was ringing as my spell buckled under the repeated assaults. With an initial synchronicity rating of 38 percent, it was probably one of my worse casts in ages. But surprise and speed had factored greatly into my failure. Alexa, seeing my face distort, nodded.

A moment later, the force shield fell, and the crows descended with a vengeance. Over two dozen crows, each of them as large as a raven with glowing red eyes and claws that gleamed with an eldritch sheen, now had free and unfettered access to us. Luckily, they weren't helicopters, so many had to beat their wings and twist as they turned in a desperate attempt to reach us as quickly as possible.

Alexa thrust her spear forward, hand gliding down the end as her weapon was launched to its farthest extent and plunged into one crow's chest. A quick retraction, with a twist of her body as she did so, smashed another crow aside. The injured bird plummeted to the ground, a wing torn. Without pause, her hands shifted on the spear shaft to strike with the blunt end to beat aside another creature.

While Alexa played offense, my fingers snapped and twirled, my mind flowing through spell formulas without missing a beat. It was a simple spell at first—Gust—but I worked to combine it with another spell, Alter Temperature. Together, the pair of spells formed a gust of bitingly cold wind. I poured mana into the spell, the wind blowing perpendicular and above our forms to push the crows away from us, altering their trajectories and chilling their bones.

Gust Cast
Synchronicity 84%

Alter Temperature Cast
Synchronicity 67%

Spell Combination Success 32%

I said chilling because my spell was not powerful enough to freeze them. I swore, the combined spells I had attempted barely doing more than making the crows think it was a nice autumn day. But the gust itself at least sent most of them flying away from us, giving Alexa another shot at reducing their numbers. Most did not mean all, however. One particular bird managed to wing its way toward me, claws tearing at my hastily raised arm. Pain registered as skin parted under razor-sharp claws, skin and cloth doing little to defend me.

My concentration wavered when I was injured, but training with Caleb and Alexa over these months had some effect. I held the spell together, varying the push of mana into it to alter the strength of the breeze it generated. This shifted the crows erratically, forcing them to battle to stay on target while Alexa had her spear flickering through the air, cutting and sweeping at the birds. Soon enough, the ground was littered with injured avian creatures, forcing the pair of us to back off rather than have our feet pecked to death. Occasionally, I'd bat a too-aggressive crow aside—or attempt to—with my trusty backpack.

For a few passes, our strategy worked. Then, a badly timed gust brought a crow that had been about to miss me directly in line with my face. Panicking, I threw a punch, spearing my own hand on its claws but protecting my face. The pain and surprise made my spell fail while the bird's weight tore its body from my arm.

"Alexa!" I snarled as I kicked the grounded crow away. A flash of darkness in the corner of my eye had me throwing myself all the way to the ground to avoid another pair of crows. Alexa barely reacted to my shout, caught in the middle of a swarm of feathers. I snarled as I stood, taking things into my own hands, my trusty backpack already discarded by my feet. My fingers flicked and twisted as I used my left hand, suddenly glad Caleb had insisted I practice with both hands. Even then, the spell formed badly, the ball of flame nearly missing the bird that was a few feet from my face.

Fireball Cast
Synchronicity 43%
11 points of damage done to Mystic Crow

Literally blown off course by the spell, the crow writhed as flames licked at its body, the flash fire having caught a few of its feathers aflame. Another bird winged its way toward me, and my hasty dodge barely brought me out of range while a wing clipped my injured shoulder. As pain filled my body, I spotted a towering oak tree a short distance away.

"Tree!" I shouted to Alexa, taking off in a zigzag rush during the short break. Many crows had banked, attempting to gain altitude and speed. To give Alexa time, I turned and cast a series of Mana Darts, my left hand working smoother as I manipulated the shorter spell formula. The invisible projectiles slammed into her harassers, giving Alexa a brief moment of respite, which she used to run with me.

Under the more solid defense of the oak tree and with the ability to put our backs to it, we made our stand again, bleeding and battered. We quickly turned to relying on my Mana Darts to harass the creatures and blast them off branches when they landed while Alexa finished the birds. A few bloody and painful minutes later, we stood victorious but injured.

"That. Was. Not. Easy," I complained, stopping at each word to draw a breath. My chest heaved and sweat covered my body, running into open wounds and sending the stinging sensation through overburdened nerves. I whimpered but still focused on searching for any crows that might be late to the party.

"It was supposed to be," Alexa said, poking the last of the corpses. When she turned toward me, her eyes widened. "Your hand!"

"My head," I added and allowed Alexa to grab my arm to prod and push at my hand. I winced as she focused on the injury, a low glow filling her body and sweeping over my arm. Soon, the ache that had begun to press on me began to fade away, and the torn skin, muscles, and tendons fixed themselves under her care. I grinned slightly, grateful for her ability. The movement of my head made me wince as the mana headache returned with a vengeance. Even her healing could not fix that.

Damn, but Caleb was going to give me shit about overextending myself again.

"What a disappointing performance. A squire should have barely broken a sweat over such a simple request." The voice berating us came from a goateed, muscular man in a simple outdoor jacket and jeans ensemble. If not for the glowing, probably enchanted sword that hung on his hip, I would have thought he was a normal human. Come to think of it, he probably is a normal human—just one with training and a church backing him.

"My apologies, Templar Ignis," Alexa replied, turning slightly to offer him a half bow. She did not let go of my hand during this period though, her healing faith magic still stitching me together. Whether it was due to the lack of complete obeisance or the use of magic, I saw the Templar's eyes narrow.

"I am here to inform you about your trial regulations," Ignis said.

"That was fast," Alexa said, eyes wide.

"Is this how you speak to a Templar, Initiate? You have not been away from the camp that long, have you?" Again, the Templar's voice came with a snap.

"My apologies, Templar Ignis," Alexa replied, bowing again. Her fingers around my hand clenched slightly as she did so, the flow of magic stuttering for a second.

"Better. Due to the circumstances of your *situation*, it has been decided your trial should be modified as you were informed. You and your sorcerer will both participate in the trial. To make it fairer, you will have a broader list of requirements to fulfill." Ignis reached a hand into his jacket, and he pulled an envelope out, then tossed it toward Alexa. It landed on the ground gently, part of it staining with blood immediately.

I found myself flashing Ignis a toothy grin, as his provocation did not result in Alexa letting go of my hand.

"You have two weeks."

"Thank you, Templar," Alexa said and bowed once more.

"Hey!" I called out. When Ignis turned toward me, I continued. "What makes you think I'm going along with this?"

"You will not aid your friend?"

"You mean the person you sent to guard me without my say-so? The one who has orders to take my head if I look like I might end up going over to the dark side, ring be damned?" I asked. I stared straight at Ignis when I said the second part, but I watched Alexa from the corner of my eyes while doing so, seeing the slight flinch and feeling a sudden increase in pressure on my hand. So. I was right.

"What do you want, sorcerer?"

"Mage. And I get paid for completing quests," I said, pointing to the birds around us. "Two weeks at my usual rate sounds just about right."

Ignis stared at me, his lip curling upward in a sneer. After a moment, he jerkily nodded and turned away. I couldn't help but flash a smile. When Ignis had walked away far enough, I hissed at Alexa. "You can stop squeezing so hard."

"Oh!" Alexa blushed slightly in embarrassment, releasing her death grip on my arm.

I growled as the magic slowly tapered off. I pulled my hand back, flexing it slightly, and marveled at the crusty wound. It looked like it had undergone weeks of healing in minutes, hints of new flesh showing under the scabbed-over wound.

"Don't do that!" Alexa said, smacking my picking fingers and making me wince. Unlike my own general healing spell, hers was more directed, which meant the major damage I had taken was healed over, but the rest of my body still ached from the myriad of cuts. With a grimace, I walked to my bag and returned with the first-aid kit to start working on our minor wounds. Iodine, antibiotic cream, and gauze… lots of gauze.

"So, he was nice," I said softly once we had the majority of our wounds taken care of and wrapped. Both of us had some form of additional healing speed—mine from Lily, and Alexa's… well, Alexa's from her faith in God, I guess, but it would do us no good to bleed out beforehand. Or, you know, get pulled over by the police for bleeding everywhere.

"Templar Ignis is extremely strict," Alexa said neutrally.

"Still watching us, eh?" I shook my head. Still, there were some advantages to them watching. Among other things, the wards helped ensure that our fight in a semi-popular park in the early hours of the morning had not drawn attention.

"Most likely," Alexa said. "Come, we should rest."

"And then we'll talk about how I've been shanghaied into this?" I asked as we limped back toward her car. Our bags dangled from our hands, the letter firmly stored in one of them.

"Well, you have been *paid* to do it," Alexa said snippily.

"Angry?" I asked. After a few paces of silence, I continued. "I'd have done it without the payment, but it is nice getting paid, no?"

"Would you? It's something you'd do for a friend," Alexa said, turning to look at me, her blue eyes troubled. "I'm just your *guard*, aren't I?"

"Guard and friend," I said, shrugging blithely. "You can be both."

"Can I?" Alexa breathed her words out, her voice troubled. But this time, I did not answer her. After all, I'd said what I said. The rest, she would have to decide.

After a time, I raised my voice and said, "It's a murder. A murder of crows."

Chapter 4

"I'm not sure I should be letting Alexa choose your quests any longer," Lily said after I'd caught a quick shower and nap. Thankfully, the painkillers and nap had taken the edge off my headache. Now it just felt like a day-old caffeine headache. The three of us were now back in our sparsely furnished living room, clean and looking better off. Still, healing required food, and thus we were holding this meeting over the remnants of three large pizzas. Hawaiian for me, a meat lover's for Alexa, and a custom seafood, vegetable, and salami mix for Lily.

I laughed softly and shifted gingerly in my chair, my injured arm gently cradled in the other. "We are still getting the experience rewards, right?"

"And the money," Alexa confirmed while Lily sighed and waved her hand.

Quest complete! You successfully murdered the murder of Mystic Crows.
+187 XP
PS: Not all subjugation quests have to be finished with violence.

I laughed at Lily's note but had to admit the jinn had a point. Then again, Alexa had not been particularly interested in talking. Still, while being a murderhobo was all well and good in roleplaying games, running around killing everything you saw and stealing from every unlocked door was a good way to end up in jail in the real world.

"Well, the next few we don't have much choice on," I said, glancing at the blood-stained envelope and the pieces of paper that it once held. Lily sniffed at my words, glaring at the paper. After a moment, new notifications flashed in front of me.

New Quest Accepted – Help Alexa Complete Her Squire Trials (Chained Quest)

This is a chained quest. You must complete the sub-quests to complete the major quest. Sub-quests:

- *Investigate and deal with the sudden influx of Leprechaun's Foot*
- *Collect fifty specimens of Spotted Wynn Mushrooms*
- *Deal with the issues plaguing the Brixton Orphanage*

"Is this normal?" I asked quietly, staring at the three tasks. Considering what she had said, I expected something a little bloodier. And rote. Other than the Wynn Mushrooms, most of these looked rather specific to our city.

"No," Alexa said simply. "Normally it's more to deal with a haunting or killing a few undead. Maybe travel to Africa and kill a few shifters."

"Wait, you kill shifters?" I asked, disapproval in my voice. "I thought—"

"They were civilized? Most are, but there are roaming mercenary groups of shifters in Africa who offer their services to various warlords. And who don't bother asking the populace their thoughts when they recruit new members." Alexa's face darkened. "You'd be surprised how many charitable Christian missions include a class of initiates on their class test."

"I… see." I prodded at my own feelings, trying to decide how I felt about sending a bunch of teenagers out on a kill mission, and I found I truly had very little objections. It didn't seem that different from the government doing the same. At least in this case, they were going after known assholes. Or so I hoped.

"Guess we're special," I said, rubbing my chin. "Which one do you think we should tackle first?"

"Why don't we split it?" Alexa said, tapping the air in front of her before realizing I could not see what she saw. Being part of my party, Lily had shared a stripped-down version of my notification screen with Alexa. The party screen and Alexa's health gauge were two of the things that the wish benefitted the initiate directly on. "I'll visit the orphanage, and you talk to El about where you can find Wynn Mushrooms."

"El probably would know if anyone does," I said, agreeing with Alexa. El was my pixie friend, a used clothing shopkeeper I had known before the change. The pixie's other, less public job was buying and selling alchemical and enchantment ingredients for the supernatural population. "But it won't take me very long to finish with El. So why don't I meet you at the orphanage? That way you can meet with them first anyway."

Alexa's lips pursed and for a moment. I wondered if she didn't want me to visit the orphanage. After all, I was an evil sorcerer, at least to some strict interpretations. It'd bitten us in the ass a few times before.

"Okay," Alexa said after a moment, seeming to have come to a decision. We continued to chat for a bit, Lily providing a little more background on the mushrooms, which—I was unhappy to learn—were not known to grow in clumps. In fact, the magical mushrooms grew and thrived in areas of intense emotion. As for Leprechaun's Foot, either the jinn really knew nothing or felt it was better for us to learn about it ourselves. Myself, I was pretty sure it was the second option.

***

As usual, the window display at Nora's, El's shop, had changed again, filled with a tasteful and colorful ensemble of clothing on mannequins. The display mostly focused on women's clothing, though I did see a particular hipster ensemble with a hat, skinny pants, and a fringed jean shirt that made my lips quirk. Then again, I was wearing a shirt that had Han Solo saying: "Make it so." Perhaps critiquing other people's fashion choices might not be my best move.

Inside Nora's was the usual cluster of used clothing racks, carefully laid out to allow shoppers to browse in peace while allowing El to watch everyone. It even had a few safety mirrors set up, though only after my transformation did I notice they had been enchanted to strip away enchantments from the reflections. At least, for those who had the eyes to see.

El herself was busy at one corner of the counter, working through a pile of clothing brought in by one of her irregular "suppliers." Like myself, before my wish, they had deposited an eclectic mix of clothing purchased at garage sales, other used stores, eBay, and storage auctions. Rather than bother El, I browsed the store myself until she was free.

"Henry," El called. Out of the corner of my eyes, I saw her nod at me, and for a second, I had a sense of vertigo. At first, she looked like the matronly older woman I had known for years, a hefty brunette who always had a kind smile and an ability to pay more than other stores. Then, the flame-haired, slim beauty appeared as I stared at the pixie head-on, her glamour falling away under my Mage Sight.

"Hey, El," I greeted her, walking toward the counter.

"Here to buy or sell?" El asked.

"I could be asking for work," I replied with a smile. In my earlier days, El had kindly provided me a series of jobs collecting various enchanted material from around the city. It was low-paying work, but it was work I could manage at my lower level. Since I'd gained Alexa's help and leveled up, I'd been here much less often.

"I wish," El said with a smile. "You were one of my best suppliers, but sending a mage to collect Grimmark Gum might be overkill."

264

"Probably," I said, repressing my curiosity about what Grimmark Gum was. Getting into a discussion about it would eat up most of the afternoon. It was no surprise that with El's extensive knowledge of materials she had done as well as she had in the mystical ingredient business. The sale of her used clothing basically acted as her cover and allowed her to launder her earnings.

"Actually, I need some advice. I've got to collect some spotted Wynn mushrooms," I said, rubbing my nose. "Lily filled us in a bit on them, but I figured you might know…"

"Where to find it in the city?" El finished my sentence before she nodded slowly. "I know a few places, but the spotted Wynn are rare. How many do you need?"

"Fifty."

"Fifty?" El squeaked slightly, shaking her head rapidly. "What are you trying to do? Lay the entire New York undead population to rest?"

"Pardon?" I asked. "Isn't the mushroom for Mana recovery?"

"Wynn mushrooms are enhancers. Spotted Wynn are ten times more effective. Your Templar friends use it quite often in their censers when they do battle with the undead," El said. "They use it to disrupt their attachment to this world, and against weaker undead, it can even send them directly back."

"Oh." I frowned. Huh. "How much do they use?"

"I'm not sure, but generally about half a mushroom is enough for a single censer. You'd be collecting enough for a hundred censers, and those burn for a good hour or so," El replied.

"So, locations?" I asked after a moment. After all, it didn't matter what I wanted. What I needed was fifty specimens.

"I'm not sure," El said. "I can point you to a few locations, but Jordie's my mushroom man. He'd know better."

"Think you could put me in touch with him?" I asked after consideration. I understood El not knowing exact locations. In fact... "Do you have any in stock?"

"I could, but Jordie's not exactly the most talkative. But I've got two in stock right now," El said, eyeing me. "Link?"

"Yeah, Link spell. If Jordie doesn't work..." I shrugged. El knew enough of my abilities to know what I was going to do.

"Fine. But only once, you hear me? No collecting otherwise. And I'm going to charge you a premium," El said threateningly.

"Done." I sighed. I understood her point. Having a mage like me going around sweeping up all the alchemical ingredients was rather unfair—on her business and her collectors' livelihoods. It was one thing for me to be working as a collector for her, another to be hogging all the ingredients. The only reason mages didn't do it more often was that there was no point. Generally, most mages had better things to do with their time.

Then again, most mages weren't penniless cheats like me.

"Oh, before I forget. Leprechaun's Foot. Ever heard of it?" I asked El, recalling the other quest. We hadn't even made plans to deal with it, not knowing what exactly it was.

"Why do you want to know?" El said, her tone suddenly serious.

"Quest," I said.

El eyed me, her green-and-blue eyes hard and serious as they fixed on my face, searching for a lie that did not exist. After a moment, she relaxed and nodded. "Stay away from using it. It's bad news of the worse kind."

"But what is it?"

"Leprechaun's Foot is a luck drug. It alters your luck for the better," El said, her lips tight. "It's an old formula, renamed a few times. Karma's Whore, the Devil's Gift, Norn's Blessing. It's had a lot of names but the same formula."

"I take it there's something wrong with the way it's made?"

"Luck. Fate. Karma. However you call it, we all have some aspect of fortune provided to us, gifted if you will, from our past lives. The Foot, it requires taking from one to another, but there's no way to take, to remove such a thing without harming the original host. And the price paid by those taking it in the future is even greater," El said.

"Rule of three?" I asked curiously. It was something the Mage Council scoffed at officially but that individuals from the older traditions believed in, in one form or another. The rule of three itself was from Wicca, the belief that any magic used returned threefold. Good or bad. Which of course encouraged Wiccans to use it for good. For many supernaturals, whether it was karma or fate, the belief in old traditions certainly held true and guided their actions to some extent.

"Yes."

I paused then, somewhat awkwardly. My next question was self-evident, but it could so easily be misconstrued.

"You want to know how it's made." El read me like a book.

"Yeah," I replied softly. "Can't track it without, well…"

"No," El replied flatly. "I won't help you on that."

"Figured," I said with a sigh. Damn it. Still, if it was a drug, I knew a few people. Which amused me in a way. I knew how to get an illegal supernatural drug but had not a clue where I would purchase a bag of marijuana. Tells you the kind of life I led these days.

"Henry, be careful," El said sternly. "The type of people who make these kinds of drugs, they're not the kind you cross."

I nodded, stories of Mexican drug cartels flashing through my mind. I really didn't want my house burned down, my hands chopped off, and my balls stuffed into my mouth. Not in that order necessarily. "I'll be careful."

El sighed at my words, and I bid her goodbye. At least, to some extent, Alexa and I were protected by my wish, but there were so many loopholes in the wish that it was scant protection if someone really desired our deaths. Still, it wasn't as if we could say no. With troubled thoughts about my future and the potential for mayhem in my life, I flagged down a taxi to bring me to the orphanage.

***

The orphanage itself was a squat grey building, probably built in the sixties when the greatest architectural dream of the masses was cheap, grey, and functional. Frankly, it was depressing even looking at it, but it was functional. The murals the young children had painted on the side of the building and the well-tended flower boxes added a touch of life and color to it, that and the large—for an inner-city building—green grounds surrounding its fenced exterior. Only a small sign over the door, right below the address marker, spoke of the Brixton Orphanage's purpose.

Still, located as it was on the outskirts of downtown, flanked by tall glass buildings filled with yuppies, club kids, and the nouveau rich, I could start making assumptions about some of Brixton's troubles. The nun who let me in and had me wait in the foyer for Alexa was charming and kind but firm in keeping me from heading deeper into the building itself. Which was fine by me as it left me time to speculate if this orphanage was another feeder location for initiates. Who was I kidding? They all probably were.

I turned my thoughts over in my mind for a bit, considering how I felt about an organization that went about recruiting children to become trained killers. Generally, this was something heavily frowned upon, an act that was derided the world over for removing the "innocence" of a child. Then again, from the little I'd been told by Alexa, it wasn't as if they were making the children kill immediately. That was generally left until they were in their teens, about the same age as we'd let others go to war. It was just that the initiates had a much longer training time, and it wasn't as if they couldn't back out if they wanted to.

Then again, if all you knew was a certain lifestyle, how easy was it to leave? Cults the world over used the exclusion of the outside world to brainwash and restrict their people, ensuring loyalty. Was what the Templars doing that different? Does intent and good intentions matter when the actions themselves aren't necessarily good?

"Henry?" Alexa called to me. She walked out of the office and caught me seated on a wooden bench, thinking uncharitable thoughts of her people.

I stood as I greeted her. "Alexa. How are you doing?"

"Good. I've cleared it with the abbess for you to come in farther," Alexa said.

"So what's the problem here?"

"Two things. Firstly, they have a problem with a local developer. He keeps trying to pressure the orphanage to sell. The orphanage has barely been keeping afloat with the rising property taxes in the last few years, but the government inspectors have been coming by more regularly, fining them for the smallest infractions. Last week, the building inspectors came by for a "routine" inspection and cited a number of code requirements they had to meet—requirements they had been allowed to bypass as they were grandfathered in."

I frowned, cocking my head to the side.

"Yes, it's not normal. They're pretty sure the building inspectors and others have been paid off."

"Who?" I asked, curiously.

"The developer is named Connor Weeks," Alexa said as she led me down the quiet hallways. I was surprised that for such a large building supposedly filled with kids, it was so silent. Then again, I guessed it was class time or something. Soon enough, we arrived at a staircase which Alexa took downward, leading me toward the basement. "In either case, the orphanage began the process of having contractors come in to get back up to code and—"

"And ran into something weird," I said, finishing for her. When we exited the stairway, we entered a simple stone corridor. Immediately, I could feel the slight vibrations in mana that ran through the orphanage grow even more powerful while the small and discreet runic carvings hidden among the stonework seemed even more populous here. I grimaced, reaching out to touch one of the runes. Alexa said nothing, waiting as I let my eyes defocus slightly and traced the flow of mana through the orphanage. It took minutes before I was certain, but when I was done, I knew for sure.

"The contractors broke the runes."

"They did," Alexa said and pointed down one of the corridors. I followed the lady with the directions silently, continuing to sense the mana flow, which seemed disturbed by light touches of something darker, more bestial in it. Not human for sure. But at least it wasn't demonic.

"Do you have a feeling like they want you to fail?" I asked absently.

"Why would you say that?" Alexa said as we started spotting more and more signs of work half started and abandoned. The various construction workhorses, plywood, and tools left abandoned.

"Really? There's no way you'd be able to complete the second quest without me in two weeks, not with everything else. And as for this one…" I sighed. "It doesn't seem like something a typical squire would be expected to do."

"It isn't," Alexa said. "But then, I'm not your typical initiate, am I?"

"No, I guess not."

We finally made it to the end of the corridor, coming to what looked like a simple storage room to the untrained eye, but I noticed the numerous runic carvings over the door and along the hallway arches, some of them now marred and broken. I had to frown as some runes, even untouched, had lost their glow, seeming to have faded in their usability. "What's in there?"

"Storeroom," Alexa said and opened the door. The blonde began to step in and then visibly hesitated, her brows creasing together. "What?"

"You feel it too," I stated and pushed past her to step within. I ignored the way the hair on the back of my neck stood up, the way my stomach roiled when I walked in. I felt my muscles tensing, my shoulders tightening, and my breath shortening as an existential dread filled me. The room itself was an empty storage room, nothing to mark it from any other room except for the small runic carvings lining the ceiling and floor. Except, a number of these carvings were chipped. I stood within the room in silence, tracing the flow of mana within.

"What do you see?"

"Unlike outside, where the runes, the ritual are all passive and part of one massive spell, there are actually multiple spells here. There's a glamour hiding the majority of these runes from sight, but it has been damaged," I said, pointing to runes as I spoke. "And there's another runic set taking the ambient mana in to power these runes along with the mana that the external runes feed it. But on top of that, there's a containment rune too. These rituals…"

"Yes?" Alexa prompted me.

"They're out of my ballpark. They're significantly more complex than anything I know," I admitted. "I'd need to do some studying before I could even hope to fix this."

Alexa grimaced, but, seeing I was done with the room, happily stepped out. The moment we left, she began to relax slightly like I did. Even then, I sensed that the leakage of mana and, for want of a better word, intent from the failed containment runes were beginning to permeate the air.

"Is it dangerous?"

"Not in the short term," I said, tapping my lips. "I wouldn't necessarily want to be here in a few months, but the containment spell is chipped, not broken."

"Good," Alexa said.

"So how do we want to do this?" I asked, gesturing within. "That's a big job, but we've got two other quests to handle too."

"Let's start on the mushrooms first," Alexa finally said after some consideration. "We can work on it immediately while we brainstorm about the dual problem. I'll ask the abbess to have the contractors work on other areas for now, and we'll try to figure out what to do about Weeks. As for the drug, we'll need a sample of the Foot if what you told me is true."

"There might be someone I know," I said slowly, thinking of Andy. The orc lived in the right neighborhood, and I'd run into him a few times while doing deliveries for El. While he preferred to keep things "clean" with protection rackets, gambling, and gun running, he was in the "life" as it were. Of course, Alexa looked at me strangely, but for once, I decided not to answer her. Sometimes, it was good to be mysterious.

Chapter 5

Hunting down magic mushrooms was, frankly, a rather boring task. The challenge in acquiring the mushrooms was in the quantity required. Each location we hit only had one such stalk, which was often surrounded by other, non-spotted varieties. Of course, since we were penniless drones, we scooped up the non-spotted varieties as well while we were at it, but at the end of the day, we'd only managed to get half a dozen stalks. Most of the day itself was spent in transit as my magic led us from spot to spot. Picking the mushrooms themselves was relatively simple as their defense mechanism was passive, forcing most supernaturals to ignore them.

At this rate, collecting the mushrooms seemed to be an easily doable quest requiring only a few days. Except this was the start. Each mushroom spot was quite close together, easy to reach, but as we harvested more and more, we'd be forced to travel farther and farther, adding to the time taken. And of course, we had another pair of quests to deal with. Still, of the three quests, this seemed to be the easiest, even if it was somewhat draining for me to constantly keep Link active.

The next morning, I brought Alexa with me when I visited Andy. This time we were headed to the southwestern part of the city, where the old docks lay rotting. Without the constant flow of business, the neighborhood was a mixture of rundown warehouses, squat concrete buildings, and crumbling docks along with a few over-burdened homeless shelters. Dotted throughout the neighborhood were failed attempts at revitalization, the scenic concrete-and-grass walkways along the river unkept and littered with debris, a pair of soaring condos looming over their older cousins. It was, frankly, where I'd expect the sale of Leprechaun's Foot to do the best.

When we pulled into the neighborhood in Alexa's tiny hatchback, we received more than one interested look from the neighborhood's denizens. Hunched over, hooded figures slunk from corner to corner, hands in baggy clothing, maybe one in eight of them sporting inhuman features—snouts, whiskers, fur, and more. The others, the human denizens, were your mixture of the homeless, the working poor, the downtrodden, and the Samaritans who worked these streets. No big surprise that the pair of us—Alexa in particular with her good looks and muscular body—drew so much attention.

"You sure my car is going to be okay here?" Alexa asked softly, eyeing the individuals around us a bit worriedly. While the car itself had been mildly reinforced with a few enchantments, it was only mildly. After all, the kinds of questions you'd get for driving around with the enchanted equivalent of a tank was not worth the marginal increase in protection most of the time. It wasn't as if our lives involved car-chase scenes with machine guns spraying bullets everywhere.

"It will be," I said, looking around until I spotted a familiar face. I waved the slouching orc over, him glaring at me with the solemn defiance of a teenager. "Want to earn fifty bucks?"

"You want me to watch the *chica*'s wheels?" The teenage orc slurred, giving Alexa an obvious once-over. I watched Alexa straighten slightly, anger flickering in her eyes.

"Do that again, and it's forty." I pulled out a twenty and waved it in front of the kid. "Twenty now, the rest once we get back and the car's in one piece."

"You going to see Andy?" the kid asked, eyeing the money with interest.

"Yup."

"Okay." The kid nodded and snatched the twenty from me. Afterward, he moved over to slouch on the car itself, glowering at everyone who looked at it. As Alexa eyed me dubiously, I grabbed her arm and dragged her along.

"You sure—"

"He's just a visible marker. Now that people know we're visiting Andy, they won't touch your car," I explained softly as we walked down the street to where the orc ganger normally hung out. His stoop with his buddies, if you will.

"Are you going to tell me who we're meeting?" Alexa asked after a while.

"Patience, padawan," I said with a chuckle. When we turned the corner, I spotted a group of orcs hanging out beneath the rectangular apartment building, chatting and drinking. Out of curiosity, I eyed the street, grateful to not see any police presence here. Of course, with the way the police patrolled the streets, you never knew when things might change. As we neared the group, an orc ran in our direction but came to a stop when he noticed the pair of us.

"Henry." Andy greeted me with a toothy, tusky smile. Amusingly enough, orcs in this world came in a variety of forms. Green and grey skin, big and small tusks, with overhung foreheads and more "human" miens, there seemed to be a variety of them. Truth be told, they had distinctive species traits, but because we could, humanity had lumped them all together as orcs and called it a day. And because they were lumped together, they had decided to group together themselves. And so, the group before me was a wide variety of orcs, arising from different locations of the world. Really, only a nerd like me would recall their species' traits. After all, for someone like the Templars, all they needed to know was that the orcs bled like humans.

"Andy," I replied, gesturing back toward Alexa. "This is Alexa. She's a friend of mine."

Andy nodded slowly, eyeing the muscular blonde. His friends had parted when we arrived, the group letting us in and surrounding us in a loose semicircle now. This made Alexa tense slightly, a hand resting on her pocket where I knew she carried her extendable baton. Still, no one was drawing which was a win, at least for me so far.

"Well, if you're vouching for her…"

"I am. We aren't here for long. I just need some minor help," I said and smiled slightly at the orc.

"Har. The mage needs our help. Need someone beaten down? An office ransacked?" Andy leered at me, and for a moment, I could not tell if he was pulling my leg or actually offering—which, come to think of it, might've been the point.

"Nothing of the sort. Well, maybe a little," I said, considering what I wanted. "I'm looking for a sample of Leprechaun's Foot. Actually, possibly more than one."

The moment the drug's name hit the air, the atmosphere changed. The casual friendliness and ribbing disappeared, the group tensing around us while Andy's eyes narrowed.

"Why are you looking for that, Henry?" Andy asked, his voice a low growl. "You ain't going to use it, are you?"

"Not ingesting it," I said, raising my hands quickly as if to ward off his words. "I've got a quest, to look into the sudden increase of it on the streets. I can Link the samples, maybe get some research done then."

"So your first instinct is to buy some illegal drugs."

"Uhhh—"

"Rather than say, talk to us?" Andy asked angrily.

"Oh. Ummm—"

"Mages!" Andy harrumphed angrily and then shook his head. "The Foot's coming down from the Skulls. Green Skulls."

"Green Skulls?" I frowned.

There was a loud sigh from one of Andy's friends, who got shut down by a look from Andy, but even the orc leader seemed slightly exasperated with me. "They're another supernatural gang, werejackal based. They've been peddling that garbage for the last few weeks and expanding their base of operations aggressively. We've had a few clashes in the last few days."

"Huh," I said slowly, then glanced at Alexa for a moment. She shrugged her shoulders, a gesture I couldn't actually read. Still, I saw no reason for Andy to lie to us, so I probed for a little more, getting what information we could before we were quietly "escorted" back to our car. It was only when we were in the car itself when Alexa spoke again.

"That was… different," the initiate said.

"Oh?"

"They were a lot politer than I expected. And helpful."

"If the Green Skulls are after their streets, I'm not surprised," I said softly, rubbing my chin. "Andy's not a huge fan of people moving in on them."

"Perhaps," Alexa said doubtfully. "But are you sure they aren't lying to you?"

"For what?"

"To point you at an enemy? An enraged mage can do a lot of damage."

"Andy wouldn't—" I paused, then sighed. "Fine. He might. But I wasn't planning on going in guns blazing."

"How were you planning this?"

I paused, considering. "Maybe we should grab a cup of coffee and talk about this."

"You think?" Alexa asked with a snort.

She guided the car toward the curb when we found a coffee shop. Yeah, perhaps some planning made sense.

***

Once we had the basics of a plan down, we put it into action. We faced a few problems. Firstly, while I didn't have an outsized reputation, I had gained some notoriety in town. There just weren't that many competent mages, and even fewer willing to do work for those not swimming in cash. It meant I couldn't exactly saunter into the middle of Green Skulls territory without potentially being spotted. Alexa herself was not much better—even if no one realized she was an initiate, she was, for all intents and purposes, a mundane.

The first step then was a glamour. Unlike illusions that were static projections which altered how they looked in reality—like holographic projections—glamours worked on an individual's mind. Because illusions worked on reality, they were harder to control and thus mostly utilized on static objects, while glamours were much simpler. Unfortunately, because they affected an individual's mind, it was also easier to beat in some ways. Someone particularly perceptive, awakened, or mindful of their thoughts could beat a glamour. It was the reason why, even without trying, my mage sight cut through most glamours and showed me the true face of individuals around us.

To cast a glamour that "beat" whatever was out there, I needed to take more care and put more *oomph* than the stock enchantments peddled by apprentice mages and sorcerers on street corners. Thankfully, my glamour spell was significantly better than what most enchantments were made from, Lily having scoffed at the current state of the industry. Then again, most glamour spells were meant to deceive mundanes.

"You sure this will work?" Alexa muttered as we walked through the rundown neighborhood later that day.

Unlike the docks, the Green Skulls had a more prosperous neighborhood under their thumb, even if prosperous was a matter of degrees. Buildings here mostly had their windows in one piece, even if graffiti was everywhere and trash accumulated around us. Unlike the docks, the homeless were fewer here, their presence less desirable. On most street corners, we noted young men standing around taking cash, while children ran the goods to customers, and prostitutes smiled and strutted their stuff along the streets.

"The glamours will hold," I muttered through the corner of my mouth softly. We both had changed our clothing to something a little more worn—and less geeky in my case—courtesy of a thrift store. Both of us wore baggy hoodies, Alexa to hide her fit figure and mine to hide my skinny one. "We're just looking for now. Maybe grab a cup of coffee…" I said softly, jerking my head to the lone diner that sat on the corner.

Alexa made a face at my suggestion but shifted her trajectory slightly as we headed toward the diner. Unlike most other corners, this one was empty, bereft of drug dealers, though we passed by enough on our walk and heard their "recommendations." Sadly, we heard nothing similar to what we wanted, declining offers for marijuana, crack, and other "mundane" drugs. But at least I now had an idea of where to pick those up.

Once inside the diner, we found ourselves a seat in one of the duct-taped polystyrene booths and waited to be served. And waited. And waited. Thankfully, we weren't particularly concerned with the lack of service while we took note of the rest of the diners.

An old man sat at the bar with a plate of pie and a newspaper before him. A trio of hookers chatted quietly among themselves as they took a few minutes to relax and massage tired feet. A tired, overweight waitress in her worn uniform of pale blue and white smoked a cigarette right under the No Smoking sign. And of course, a large grouping of werejackals sat at the opposite end of the diner, their bodies in human form but shimmering with the slight hazy outline of their hybrid form behind them—at least to my eyes.

Alexa noted my gaze but didn't turn around, instead pulling the steel napkin dispenser to play around with—and, of course, adjusting it enough to glance behind her. After a few minutes, she twisted around and spotted the waitress to meet her eyes directly. With a huff, the waitress walked to our table and slapped down a pair of menus before sauntering away.

"Well, she's not getting a tip," I said with a sigh before perusing the menu. I frowned, suddenly stumped, when I realized I had no way to listen to the group speak. And speaking they were certainly doing.

"The menu's not that bad," Alexa said, mistaking my frown.

"No… just…" I sighed, then shook my head. Right. The movies always made this entire "gather intel" thing so much easier than it was. They always had the right tool for the situation, the luck to meet the right person, the skills to do it right. But here I was, sitting in a diner under a glamour that made me look like just another human, and I had no idea what to do next. I couldn't hear them speak, and I couldn't cast Link without risking them sensing my use of active magic. We could, at best, see them make a deal or two, and what would that tell us? Nothing more than what Andy already had.

"Just relax," Alexa said softly, flashing me a slight smile.

"Okay…" I sighed and closed my mouth. She was right. We had talked about this. We were only here to watch. Everything else—anything else—we learned was a bonus.

***

An hour later, after a rather unsatisfactory, sloppy burger and over-cooked fries, the pair of us finally left the diner. We'd dragged out the meal as long as we could—inadvertently helped by the lousy service—but now, we needed to leave. Either that or attract more attention to us than we wanted.

In that time, we'd learned all of nothing. That wasn't exactly true of course. We had spotted a few members of the Green Skulls. We knew what they liked to eat and that they enjoyed hanging out at the diner. In fact, it was interesting to note that the vast majority of the gang must have been men; no women had been present at the diner. Of course, there were other reasons for that. The way they'd interacted with the ladies of the night was a pretty good reason why no sensible woman would want to be around them. But in the end, it was still not particularly useful information.

When we'd left, it was alone. I clocked the pair of werejackals who came out a short couple of seconds after us but thought nothing of it. Not until I noticed they took the same corner as we did, their pace slowly increasing.

"Trouble," I said softly to Alexa.

"I noticed. Confront or run?" Alexa said.

"That…" I frowned, considering the matter. I shot her a look back in question, dithering.

"Too late." Alexa pointed subtly ahead.

I looked up and noticed another pair of werejackals, these two not even bothering to hide the fact they were coming for us. "This way."

Alexa grabbed my arm and tugged me sideways, pulling me down an alleyway. A quick look around showed us it was filled with a pair of foul-smelling garbage dumpsters, soiled clothing, and other unmentionable wastes. A single, huddled body in the corner indicated the alleyway wasn't as empty as we wished, but at least it was out of sight.

"Watch our back," Alexa said as she reached behind her and pulled her baton out. She kept it in her hand, unextended for now as she waited. It wasn't a long wait before the quartet of werejackals made their appearance with wide, almost lolling grins on their faces.

"Hello there, girlie. So nice of you to stop." One of the werejackals walked forward, a loose, cloth jacket in red and white hanging over tattered blue jeans. Obviously, he was the leader – of this group at the least if not the whole group.

"What do you want?" Alexa asked.

"Just a word," the werejackal said. "You and your boy were real curious about us. We're not real friendly with new strangers…"

"Don't know what you're talking about," Alexa said softly.

"Really. Then why'd you run?"

"Two big men chasing us down? Seemed like a good idea."

"Really? That what you think too, boy? You going to let the girlie talk for you?" the werejackal asked, taunting me.

"Yes," I said simply. With my body bladed toward the group, I could watch both sides of the alleyway, with most of my attention facing behind us. It meant I saw the van pull up at the end of the alleyway first.

"More company," I whispered softly to Alexa.

"Damn." Alexa set her feet apart and reached with her other hand into her jacket pocket. She froze when the lead jackal pulled out a gun and aimed it at her. Within seconds, the other werejackals had pulled out various weapons.

"Easy there, girlie. We don't want any mistakes," the werejackal said.

Alexa pressed her lips together but slowly eased her hand away from her hoodie. I grimaced, mentally running our options through my mind. I could throw up a Mana Shield, and it could deflect some bullets, but the sheer number and the fact that they had us flanked made it a bad option. Fighting them, well, that probably would just result in our deaths. Or severe injury at the least.

"That's better. Now, why don't you tell us the real reason you're here."

I frowned, my mind racing as I looked for a way out. Damn it, this damn quest, this confrontation was unwinnable. No competent game master would ever let you run into a situation like this. There's no way to fight…

"I told you—" Alexa paused when I laid my hand on her arm. She shot me a quizzical look that held traces of "what the hell are you doing" in it.

"Fine. I'll tell you the truth," I said, stepping forward slightly and past Alexa. When the werejackal focused on me, I continued and desperately hoped I was right. "My name is Henry Tsien. I'm the new mage."

Hisses and growls erupted from the werejackals as even more weapons pointed toward me.

I ignored them, even as I felt my back grow cold and clammy from sweat. "I have a quest."

"Better." The werejackal grinned, staring at me. "So, you meaning to mess with the Skulls? If you do, you'd be dull." Laughter erupted at that, the sing-song manner the werejackal said the last line an indicator he had probably said this a million times before.

"No. I'm here to collect mushrooms," I said. When the laughter finally died down, I gestured to my backpack. "If you'll let me, I'll show you."

"Slowly."

"Of course," I said. It did not take me long to take out my sample and show them the spotted Wynn I had collected. "These are spotted Wynn. They're good money if you can collect them, but they're rare." I noticed one of the werejackals leaning in and whispering to the lead one, but I ignored it, continuing my story. "We came here to check out this area because we heard you ran this neighborhood. Since poaching is bad…" I trailed off, shrugging my shoulders.

"You wanted to see if you could get away with it." The werejackal snarled at me.

"No. I wanted to assess your gang, see if the rumors about your drug dealing were true. If you did deal drugs, you wouldn't want to deal with a mage over a couple of mushrooms," I said simply. "I doubt the number we could scavenge here would be worth even a quarter of your night's revenue."

"Damn right," one of the other werejackals boasted before he got smacked over the back of his head by another.

"And that's the truth, is it, mage?" the leader asked, walking forward. I sensed Alexa tensing behind me, but I held my hand out backward, hoping she got the meaning. *Stand down.* We couldn't win a fight here.

"Yes," I said simply.

"See… There's only one problem with that." I found myself tensing when the werejackal neared, his face scrunching up while his gun continued to point at the middle of my chest.

"Oh?" I focused, building a Force Shield spell in my mind, holding it in abeyance for the moment.

"Yes. You smell crafty," the werejackal said, his eyes glinting as he stopped a few short feet from me.

"Well, I am a mage," I said, cursing inside. Of course. He was a shifter. Expanded senses were one of the major things they all had. Still, I had chosen my words carefully to tell the truth. Just not all of it. I just hoped it had been sufficient.

The werejackal paused for a second at my answer, then burst out laughing. It wasn't a normal laugh, more like a braying, yowling noise. A few seconds later, all his friends joined in, making the hair at the back of my neck stand even straighter. If it wasn't for the fact they'd lowered their guns when they laughed, I'd be even more worried. But still, guns were still in their hands, so I kept a close eye on them. When the laughter finally subsided, the leader stared at me again, pointing his gun back at my chest.

"Funny. Funny mage. Okay. You smell somewhat truthful. And they say don't mess with mages, so we won't. But I don't want to see your faces here again either," the werejackal said, gesturing with his gun to the side in an obvious invitation for us to leave.

I nodded and waved Alexa ahead of me. We skirted to the side of the alleyway, and the pair of us slowly shuffled past the werejackals who barely moved far enough aside to let us through. I kept myself in front of Alexa, my ability to put the primed and ready Force Shield in front of us at a moment's notice a better option than anything she could do. It seemed she agreed since I didn't get a complaint. Still, other than a sudden lunging motion by one werejackal—which managed to elicit a slight jerk from me—and a series of cackling laughter by the werejackals, they let us leave.

It was only when we finally got back to Alexa's car and were blocks away that we began to relax. I shuddered then, the adrenaline slowly leaving my body as my hands shook and too-tense muscles around my neck unclenched. I groaned softly, waiting for the after-battle effects to go away.

Damn it. That had been too damn close.

Chapter 6

We regrouped back at the duplex, safe behind magical wa—shit. I hadn't even managed to put those up. I buried my head in my hands again and forced myself to draw deep breaths. I felt my heart begin to jackhammer again. I'd risked my life before, nearly gotten killed, but somehow, staring down the end of a gunmetal barrel had driven home how little of a game this was, how pitiful my simple Force Shield was and how little it could do.

A low thump near my head had me raising it to stare at a slowly steaming cup of tea set on the coffee table, inviting me with its rich, creamy tones. I reached out, wincing slightly at the heat when I cupped the beverage in my hands and stared at Alexa, who sat across from me with her own cup.

"First. Tea? Don't you think I've been tortured enough? And secondly, how are you so calm?" I asked, at first trying for a joking tone before my voice rose at the end, escaping my control. I choked back my rising voice, drawing a deeper breath.

"Training," Alexa said simply, touching her cup to her lips before lowering it and staring at me. "Experience. Ritual. Mindfulness."

"Have I mentioned how messed up your childhood was?" I asked Alexa rhetorically. But thinking about her rather than my own reaction helped me push feelings of helplessness and rage away for a moment. I drew a breath, sitting up slightly more as I finally tasted my tea. "Ugh! What is this tea?"

"Peppermint. And you shouldn't be doing that," Alexa said.

"Doing what?" I stared at the abomination of liquid in my cup, debating why people would do this to themselves. What was wrong with simple black tea? Jasmine. Pu'er. Maybe a little dragon seed.

"Avoiding processing," Alexa said as she leaned forward, meeting my brown eyes with her blue ones. "If you have to, you have to, but we're safe. You should let yourself process your emotions. Otherwise, it'll affect your performance later."

"Performance..." I said softly, picking at her words. The initiate didn't flinch, just continued staring at me. I found myself looking away eventually, looking aside to stare at the jinn who was blatantly not listening in on us. "I just... I couldn't stop those bullets. Not even if I tried. A single Force Shield, at full strength, I could do if they were in front of us. Or behind. But if I had to split the spell, or dual cast... I don't think I could do it."

"It would have been difficult," Alexa replied.

"I felt like such a fraud. A mage. Who can't even throw lightning or fire properly. Who can't stop bullets. Who gets run off by a gang of thugs," I said softly, shaking my head. "And it was my idea to go in there, to look. Because I didn't know what else to do. I just feel so stupid."

"You're not stupid," Alexa said softly, reprimanding me. "You're just out of your depth. You're learning, but six months ago you had no idea of this world. For a civilian, you are doing amazingly well."

"Learning..." I sipped on my tea again and made a face, once again reminded about what I had in hand. "I keep doing this. Getting in over my head. Learning as I go along. Hoping I can cobble a solution together with whatever I have." I waved my hand at Lily before continuing. "We got away because I guessed it was a social confrontation, that if it wasn't, we'd have been warned. Or protected. But, maybe I—we... wouldn't.

"Because the wish I made had to be open, had to be vague, so Lily could fix things as they came up. But of course, she's limited too. I'm playing a game I can't read the rules of. There's no manual, and I was the guy who always RTFMed."

"RTFM?"

"Read the fucking manual," I replied. "But it's not a game because people die."

"No, it's not," Alexa said softly. "But it is your life."

I paused at her last words, drawing a deep shuddering breath. It was my life. And damn it, I had chosen it—chosen it and chosen that perhaps I would do something more than just live it for myself. So here I was, trying to help a friend, and not doing a good job at it. I shook my head, clutching my mug harder as my thoughts spiraled, as I searched for resolve and understanding within myself. Alexa stayed silent, sipping on her mug of tea while I worked through my emotions and the implications of her words.

"It is, isn't it?" I said softly. "Then perhaps I should stop playing…"

Alexa smiled softly, tilting her head to the side. I fell silent again, caught in my own thoughts. I was dimly aware Alexa stopped to whisper to Lily before she walked toward the stairs, pausing only long enough to place a hand on my shoulder as she left. When she did, I felt the warmth of her hand leave too, leaving me with my thoughts as the night deepened.

***

"Morning, Henry," Alexa said softly when she came downstairs the next day. I was seated on the couch, the discarded remnants of various sugary snacks scattered around me. I blinked, startling awake from the light doze I had fallen into and wincing when the stream of sunlight penetrated my eyes.

"Morning…" I grunted out, rubbing at my eyes.

"Did he not sleep?" Alexa asked.

"A bit, but he mostly sat there muttering to himself," Lily replied, looking up. I frowned, hating how she seemed to be still chipper and put together even after an all-night gaming session.

"Extra coffee then," Alexa said in reply, heading to the kitchen as she hid a light yawn behind her hand. "Should I call Caleb and let him know you'll be skipping his lesson?"

"No!" I shouted, jerking awake further. "No," I said again, more moderately. "I have questions and training I need to do."

"Oh?"

"I need to work on dual casting. Or a better shield. Or both." I spat out my reply quickly and then drew a deep breath before continuing. "Also, I think we're looking at these quests the wrong way. Or I am. I'm not playing the game right."

Alexa winced but did not stop her preparation of the coffee pot. The pot itself had been cleaned the day before, so it took her only a few seconds.

"Don't worry," I said. "I don't mean I'm thinking it's a game but that the way I've been approaching this has been wrong. I've been so caught up with the fact this is the real world, that I'm limited in what I can do, that I've forgotten the first rule of playing in a campaign—never do what the GM expects."

"The GM?" Alexa shot a look over at Lily.

"Not Lily," I said, shaking my head. "It's more of an analogy. We've been tackling these problems head on, instead of thinking creatively, like the drug."

"Go on." Alexa leaned on the counter, the hiss and burble of the coffee pot punctuating her words.

"We went and bothered the street-level gang who's distributing the drug, but what was our plan afterward? Beat them up? How long do you think it'd take before the drugs were on the street? And really, were we going to beat up a dozen gangsters and God knows how many peons?" I shook my head. "Our job is to figure out the increase in the drugs. So why not move up the chain? If we can figure out who is making it—or bringing it into town—it'd be much more effective."

"Isn't that what we had planned?" Alexa asked simply, shaking her head. "We wanted a sample and an idea of what's happening. And what makes you think they aren't making it themselves?"

"Oh." I paused, realizing she had actually thought it through a little more than I had. Oops… "But yeah, let's stop bothering the Skulls. Let's find out who's making it!"

"That's a great idea," Alexa said simply, only the barest traces of sarcasm in her voice. "How?"

"Ummm…" I paused, gathering my flitting thoughts. "Well, we should probably talk to Andy again and see if we can get some samples like we had planned at the start. Then I can look into using a Link spell. If I time it right, and they're producing or distributing it, the largest quantities should be the easiest area to locate. Might need to adjust the spell a bit…" I trailed off, my mind swirling as I played with the idea of linking it to a map or something. Or perhaps enchanting a map and then linking the sample to it so that areas with a significant magical signature would show up.

Alexa nodded slowly. "I can do that. Now that you've introduced me, it shouldn't be difficult."

"Great," I said, snapping back to reality. "The mushrooms, we should stop trying to do it ourselves. There's no rule saying we must. I bet if I spend a few hours enchanting, I can create a simple Linked spell on a compass with a low charge on it. If we hire a few people and give them that, it'll solve our problem."

"Except we don't have the money for it," Alexa pointed out.

"But the spotted Wynn mushrooms always grow with normal Wynns, right? So if we let them keep all the Wynn mushrooms, we can just keep the spotted Wynn for ourselves," I said.

"What's to stop them from shortchanging us?" Alexa asked, and I paused to consider it. There was a chance of that for sure. It wasn't as if we could watch them.

"Nothing," I said. "But I won't charge up the compasses too much, so if we think they're cheating us, we just won't charge theirs again."

"And you can build this?" Alexa asked softly, glancing sideways at the small pile of still-unpacked crafting material. Thus far, a lot of my work has been on blocks of wood because, well, I'm still learning.

"Sure," I said, nodding. "It shouldn't be too different from the wards."

"Shouldn't."

I shrugged, then brightened, looking at Lily. "Can you tell me what my chances are?"

Lily looked up from her computers for a second, pursing her lips. She stared between the pair of us before she sighed and nodded. "You can do it, given enough time. The knowledge is all there, and with Caleb's help, it shouldn't be a problem."

"How long?" Alexa asked softly, obviously concerned by that factor.

"A day or two?" I replied, semi-confidently. It wasn't as if I'd ever done this before. At her grimace, I added. "It's still faster than us tramping around ourselves, and we can always look to do that later if we can't finish this up."

"Fine." Alexa nodded. "I'm assuming you're going to need some compasses? Anything else?"

I nodded happily, reaching for the piece of paper where I had scribbled everything I thought I'd need. "I might have more after I speak with Caleb."

"Of course," Alexa said as she poured our cups of coffee, expertly mixing the drink in our preferred ratios. Alexa took hers black, but mine was filled with milk and sugar in large quantities. Lily took hers with milk but no sugar, though the cup itself was left on the counter, forcing the jinn to stand to retrieve her drink. Even if she didn't technically have a real physical body, sitting in the same spot for hours couldn't be good for her. "Any thoughts on the last quest?"

"That…" I frowned, shaking my head. "We'll need to do some research on it. If this was really a game, the developer would have some easily exploitable flaw. Maybe we could have blackmailed him or when we set a watch, we could catch him bribing the inspectors. If it was a game, the abbess would have a number of simple quests that would tell us what to kill, find, or destroy to fix the ritual."

"But this isn't a game," Alexa said. "All right then. I don't have training this morning, so I'll pick up your supplies and some samples—if Andy has any—of the drug. I'll drop it off here and then I'll do some research on Weeks. Perhaps I can find a handle on him. You get enchanting after classes."

"Sounds like a plan," I said. Once that was settled, we ate breakfast—toast and jam today—before heading out. After all, we all had things to do.

Chapter 7

"So these new quests are sufficient motivation, are they?" Caleb asked with a smirk after I had explained what I wanted from him when I arrived for class.

"Can you help me?"

"Of course I can." Caleb tapped his lips. "It is a divergence from our training plan, however. We are trying to shore up your incompetencies, not expand on them."

"It's a spell I already know!" I gritted my teeth slightly as I tried to make Caleb deviate from his planned lesson. "It's just a way to work it better."

"A spell that, at your level of knowledge, you should not be able to cast. At least until another year," Caleb said with a sniff. "Perhaps you should just consider not placing yourself in a situation where you might need to dual cast your spells."

I growled. "Oh, come on. If you help me on this, it'll go a lot faster than me trying to work it out myself. It's just the calculations to create a semi-complete sphere are killing me."

"As they should," Caleb said with another sniff. "Stretching your container in a semi-complete sphere to cover oneself is considered a significant milestone. The requirements to adjust the size, volume, and positioning of such a defense is one of the testing principles of an apprentice mage. Obviously, the thickness and dimensions of your container will alter as different amounts of mana are input. In addition, you'll need to ensure the mana flows to each portion of the container at the same rate to ensure consistent durability."

"Yeah, I got that, but the equation itself shouldn't be that different. But whenever I use the one you provided, it doesn't really work that well. It leaks mana like a sieve," I said, trying a new tactic.

"Your control must have improved if it is only leaking that badly," Caleb said with a curl of his lip. "A protective shield that covers both your front and back equally requires a different equation. While it is possible to create the initial shield container using the current formula you have, there are significantly more mana-appropriate equations. Furthermore, due to the nature of the defense, you cannot use the basic Force Shield spell formula for redirecting energy. Not even the one altered by your Lily would work. If you do, the shield itself will be too brittle."

"Really?" I frowned, tilting my head. "But isn't the formula for mana use the same? After all, the initial spell takes into consideration multiple impacts."

"It does, but you are forgetting that you are—at your level—only directing mana from a single point. Here." Caleb walked to the blackboard he kept in this office and quickly sketched the formula and then highlighted points on it. "You see? This portion…"

I kept silent, happy to keep listening. For all that Caleb disliked me, Lily, and the situation we were in, he was also a born teacher. He enjoyed talking about magic and dispensing knowledge—or perhaps lording over his greater knowledge on another. In either case, he was always intent on making sure I understood why my current thought was inefficient or just plain wrong.

"Are you listening?"

"Yes. But why is the coefficient…" I focused back on the board, making a mental note to divert him later when I needed an answer on the enchantments. Springing my need for further education on rituals was probably a bad idea, at least right now. Step by step, I would get the knowledge I needed.

***

Hours later, I walked out of the office building feeling the need for fresh air and quiet. A series of deep breaths helped calm my roiling mind, the constant high-level discussion of concepts that I barely grasped settling down as I walked back. Classes with Caleb reminded me how strange the concepts that Lily stuffed into my brain were. Initial spell casting and spell usage were at the most basic, simple form. Yet, if I dug and studied the spell itself, other concepts would slowly peel apart, making an appearance in my mind as I made use of the spell. In time, I could even modify those spell formulas to create my own version of traditional spells.

It contrasted with the way Caleb taught, in his meticulous and detailed manner, the various theories, concepts, and formulas that made up modern magic. His teaching style forced me to truly understand the relationship between each formula, each concept before I moved to the next. And, like in the last few hours, when his lessons butted against the implanted knowledge provided by Lily, it managed to drag concepts that I had yet to fully grasp to the forefront for my use. As it stood, without the implanted knowledge by Lily, it would have taken months for me to learn to cast my new, modified Force Shield. Now, I could do so in a fraction of a second.

Even if my synchronicity sucked.

By the time I got back home, unmolested, Alexa had come and gone. A series of bags had been set aside with the various pieces of equipment I had requested. A few cheap compasses purchased from the local dollar store, spools of copper and steel wire, and various pieces of tape and string were in a box. She even included the various markers I had requested, which made me happy. A few minutes later, I had that and my "enchanting tools" spread out in the middle of the living room as my first workplace area. I studied everything I had laid out, most of which were various hobby craft scalpels, knives, and chisels taken from my original tool set and what the initiate had purchased for me.

The second workplace was much smaller and temporarily set up on the island that separated the kitchen from the rest of the house. There, I had the three small Ziploc bags of goldish-yellow dust set aside on a white plate next to a laminated city map. I figured I'd get to that project later if I could figure out this one first.

Sitting at my first workstation, I ran my hands over the pieces while I worked through the spell formula in my mind. Enchanting was, technically, simple. All I had to do was Link the spotted Wynn mushroom to the compass which then needed to be linked to a power source. In this case, the power source was mana itself. Before, with my wood blocks, I chucked the mana directly into the block itself via a holding rune. I could do the same here, but the poor plastic pieces were elementally stable. I'd be spending more mana inputting the mana into the plastic than storing it, and the extraction process would be just as bad.

No. Storage would have to be done either via something like wood, which stored mana easily but could not hold much in general, or metal, which could hold significant quantities of mana but might not necessarily be easy to store or extract. Metal had an incredibly high resistance to alteration. My other option, which was where the experimenting part came in, was looking for something less traditional. I chuckled softly to myself, tapping a pack of AAA batteries.

"Baking sheet," Lily intoned before I began.

"What?"

"Put a baking sheet down. And maybe grab a pot too," Lily said. "If you remember your last experiment…"

"Oh," I said, pausing. Right. I'd melted more than one pot and wrecked the bathroom in our old place because of my experiments. Sadly, we didn't have much of a backyard, or else I'd use that. Or maybe not. Making plain blocks of wood ignite was probably going to get difficult to explain after a while.

Once I was set up again, I picked up a battery and rolled it around the palm of my hand as I considered what I wanted to try. The first attempt was to run my mana through it, gently. No attempt at storage, no carving of runes. If passage through the battery was easy, it should work. After drawing a deep breath, I focused and emitted a trickle of mana from my hand into the battery, holding it between the tips of my fingers and thumb. Just in case.

I smiled slightly when I noticed how much easier pushing mana through the battery was than I would have expected. In fact, what I was doing had nothing to do with the contents of the battery itself—except at the most basic level. What I was betting on was using the concept of batteries.

Magic was a little mysticism and a little science. Our perceptions altered how magic was used and affected just as much as the hard "rules" of magic. Like a ritual, the use of common concepts allowed magic to flow easier. Since everyone knew you could pass energy through batteries easily and store energy in them, I had theorized using an actual battery would make the entire thing easier.

"Owww!" I shouted, dropping the suddenly melting and overheated battery onto the baking sheet while waving my burned hand around. I winced slightly, sucking on my thumb as I cast a Heal spell on myself, then waited for my body to deal with the light burns. "What the hell?"

I stared at the battery that continued to bubble, my Mage Sight showing the last traces of the mana I had input interacting with the normal chemical processes that made up the battery. I frowned, reaching out to tap against the table in thought, and received a nasty shock when I accidentally touched the baking sheet.

"Owww!"

"Shhhhh!" Lily hissed at me, not even looking up from her laptops.

I growled slightly, waving my hand to shake the pins and needles away. It wasn't a horrible shock, and the Heal spell I was channeling through my body was already healing it, but it had been painful—like receiving a shock of static electricity, except ten times as bad.

"Now what happened?" I asked with a frown. Everything had been going well. I hadn't even noticed what changed, caught up in my success as I had been. If it had been a major change, I was sure I'd have noticed it. So whatever it was, it had been minor—or something that had been happening all along. As the pain in my hands faded, I grimaced and stared at the pack of batteries. There really was no way to know without testing it further.

Four batteries and a pair of slightly scorched fingers later, I sighed and leaned back in my chair. When I inhaled again, the acrid odor of melted metal and plastic from the batteries assaulted my nose. Wincing, I took the time to clean the mess, scraping the batteries off the baking sheet into the garbage bin outside before I returned.

The problem was the fact that mundane chemistry was interacting with magic—with the mana—and basically kickstarted and ran the chemical processes so long as mana was flowing through the battery. Since I hadn't kept any formed storage runes, after I took my hands away, the mana itself slowly dispersed and returned the amount within the battery to its normal, ambient amount. During the process, the battery would continue to run, overheating itself.

Now that I knew what was happening, the question was if I could do something about it. Thus far, I was leaning toward no. Even the trickle of mana I was using was overheating the battery, forcing the chemical reaction within it to work overtime. If it wasn't for the fact that my mana flow insulated me from the actual flow of electricity when I was channeling, I'd have probably noticed the issue earlier. Unfortunately, even if I managed to stop the battery from overheating now by controlling how much mana I stored in the battery, there was no guarantee I could do the same when it was linked to the compass.

So my problem was threefold. Firstly, I had to keep the battery from overheating. Secondly, I had to ensure the battery could store the mana in a decent volume. Lastly, I needed to regulate the amount of draw from the battery so that the runes I used to regulate the battery were not overridden. Easy peasy, lemon squeezy.

Pushing aside the baking sheet and batteries for the moment, I pulled the notebook close and started sketching the runes and the interactions I figured I'd need. It was a habit I had learned from Caleb, working through the necessary enchantment and links on paper before I began the laborious process of actually carving the runes and enchantments. Alongside the runes, I also scribbled down the various spell formulas I was considering, using the shorthand that had been stuck in my brain by Lily for this purpose.

The fact that I was beginning to link multiple spells—each of which were their own rune or set of runes—meant the actual process was beginning to get complicated. While there were no set designs that were correct, the process of drawing and elaborating the runes on paper firmed up the spell formula and their relations in my mind, which made the actual carving and enchanting process smoother.

"Eat," Lily said softly, setting a bowl of instant noodles next to me. I frowned slightly, noting the chunks of meat and the pitiful strings of vegetables that had been added while Lily sauntered back to her chair, a much larger bowl in her hands.

"Thanks," I said slowly, standing and stretching as my back proceeded to inform me how long I had been hunched over. I winced, swinging my arms around and doing some general calisthenics as my body adjusted before I dove into my food. Ah, instant noodles. I missed thee.

"How is it coming along?" Lily enquired, seated with a leg cocked up on a table with her bowl of noodles in her hands.

"Pretty decent," I said simply. "I have the spell formula worked out. Even tested it out…" I gestured to the burnt remnants of the paper in the pot. "The compass Link and draw aspect seems to work, at least from what I saw." Before it burst into flames from exceeding the paper's ability to withstand the mana I had flooded through it. "Now, I just have to see if I can make the battery. Worst-case scenario, I'll enchant a block of metal and use it as the battery."

"You're going to superglue a hunk of iron to the compass?" Lily asked, eyes glittering with amusement.

"If it works…"

"It's ugly."

"Not sure that's the saying," I said, which made Lily snort with amusement again, but she dropped the topic. After all, she could comment but not advise. At least, not directly.

Next was the development of the batteries themselves. Rather than enchanting each one individually with the required spells, I decided instead to save myself the trouble by creating a mana charger for the battery. By enchanting a block of wood to firstly lower the temperature of the batteries placed within and secondly control the amount of energy drawn, I could skip any complicated enchantments on the batteries themselves. I still had to enchant the batteries to store mana, but that was a significantly simpler process.

With a nod, I grabbed the soldering iron and grabbed the nearest battery. Best to get started then. As it was, soldering the design was going to be painful. It'd been ages since I actually picked up my soldering kit, and it really was not like riding a bicycle. Grimacing at the ugly beads I ended up leaving on the battery, I slowly reached out with my senses to check if the enchantment had worked.

Storage Ward Created (17% Efficiency)

"Thanks, Lily," I called out, grateful for her aid. Even if I could sense it myself, the displayed data was significantly more effective and efficient. I liked numbers, and this one at least gave me an idea of how well I'd done with my cobbled-together spell.

Now, I just had to carve out a block of wood to fit the battery, make sure the carvings for the Alter Temperature and Channel Wards were correct and then Link it to the compass. Simple.

***

"Goddamn it!" I snarled, sucking on my bleeding palm. I hated carving. I really, really hated carving. Glaring at the block, I drew a deep breath and channeled my Heal spell once again. Once again, I was grateful we had hardwood floors rather than carpet. Otherwise, we'd have lost another damage deposit from the amount of blood I'd lost. Amazing how even a relatively light cut could bleed.

"No luck?" Alexa asked when she walked down the stairs from her room, clad in a new set of clothing after her bath.

"None so far," I said with a grimace, glancing at the duo of carved and discarded blocks by the side. The first had been carved perfectly—and then I realized it could not work because I had no way of storing mana inside the block itself, making the refrigeration option impossible to work. I'd then attempted to modify it, to begin the moment I started channeling mana to store in the battery, but that had just ended up with a melted battery as the Alter Temperature rune took too long to get working.

My second attempt had not gone much better. After adding a storage rune on my mana charger, I had charged it with mana directly. That had worked well, but the reduction in temperature achieved by the initial spell had been significantly less than I had expected. After returning to the drawing board and figuring out how to adjust the spell by focusing the Alter Temperature container to just the battery location, I was working on my third block.

"Are you at least making progress?" Alexa asked as she leaned over my chair. I glanced at the blonde again, distractedly noting she'd gone for a sweater-and-sweatpants combo.

"Some. It'll get done by tomorrow at the latest," I said firmly. In fact, I did not mention I could have finished it today if I wasn't actually experimenting on these mana chargers. While it was important for my own development, we were on a timetable. "How'd you do?"

"Not much better. I spent most of the day watching his office. It's an office."

"And he didn't notice?"

"He works out of the second floor of a retail space. And there's a hairdresser who had a spot open," Alexa said simply, touching her hair hesitantly.

I turned my head and regarded her new do, a pixie-style haircut that included some very modest highlights.

"So…"

"Ummm… it's nice?" I said slowly, uncertain of what she was looking for. It was a haircut.

"It is, isn't it?" Alexa said with a smile and then straightened. "I'll make dinner."

"Great." I stared as the blonde initiate bounced off into the kitchen and then I exhaled in relief as my brain came out of enchanting fog. I barely escaped the jaws of death on that one.

Well, it did help it was nice.

Chapter 8

"You're mine," I growled softly at the wooden block the next morning. Alexa had left to see if she could dig up more information about the property developer who was interested in the orphanage while I had promised to get this enchanting job done. To put even more pressure on me, Alexa had promised to arrange the appointments with our scavengers for later tonight, which meant I needed this done.

After spending the night sleeping like the dead, I had woken up with a clearer idea of what I needed to do. Perhaps the lack of sleep the night before coupled with my experiences yesterday had clarified things, but staring at my previous day's work, I saw numerous flaws in the enchantment—over and above my poor crafting skills of course. After lacing my fingers together, I stretched them out before I bent over the wooden block, chisel in hand.

A few hours later, I finally had a working prototype. Like all prototypes, it was ugly as sin, barely functioning, and inefficient, but it proved the concept. After some tweaking and dropping nearly my entire mana pool into the charger, I was able to link it with the compass directly for the initial test. Using a simple metal clip, I made sure to link the pair together, allowing the compass to point toward the nearest spotted Wynn mushroom.

The entire contraption was, as mentioned, ugly. A plain wooden block was glued to a plastic compass which had a small spot dug out for the mushroom sample in it. The sample itself was held in place via sticky tape, which allowed me to theoretically switch out the linked material at any time. The block had numerous, badly done carvings of the enchantment runes on it while the compass had a series of gouged out runes on it as well. In the wooden block, a portion of it had been carved out such that the batteries may be inserted and linked to the entire contraption. Overall, it looked like something a twelve-year-old kid would make in a bad eighties' kids' movie. It was, in other words, perfect.

Modular Compass and Mana Battery Integrated Gadget

Efficiency: 21%

Duration: 4 hours and 5 minutes using current stored battery charge

I smiled slightly, staring at the information. Perfect. The batteries, as I figured, could hold the charge much longer than a simple block of wood or metal. If I had tried to do the same with the materials I had, I could at best store a total of two hours of work. Now, I had nearly doubled the storage capacity. If I carved a second storage channel for a second battery, I could even potentially double the lifespan. Or, and this was the genius of the concept, just hand them pre-charged mana batteries to swap out. After all, it was in the initial charging and discharging phase the batteries were dangerous. Storing them, thus far, seemed to perfectly safe.

Of course, I had to add thus far. With a grimace, I made a note to store these batteries in a cooking pot somewhere non-flammable. Just in case.

"Don't you need the initial charger?" Lily's voice woke me from my self-satisfied stupor. I still hadn't built the initial charger that regulated the batteries while I was charging them, ensuring they didn't overheat. Once it was built, I could just add mana directly to the charger, pre-charging a slew of mana batteries. On top of that, I also needed to build at least a couple more of these blocks since Alexa had booked three scavengers to arrive.

I winced slightly, flexing stiff fingers, and I stared at the next block of wood. Right. No rest for the talented.

***

Reworking the enchantments for the next couple blocks was significantly easier. Of course, I grumpily wished this was a game—or at least had easy crafting options like most games. Thankfully, everything I was doing currently required minimal actual skill. Etching, carving, and soldering were all within my wheelhouse. Blacksmithing, glassblowing, and tanning were crafting areas I was going to ignore for now. I certainly did not have the time to spend learning how to forge a sword properly, no matter how cool it would be to have a magical sword.

After I completed all three blocks, I turned to my second enchanting station. This one was significantly simpler in theory. I picked up a bottle of ink and began the process of lightly imbuing it with my mana. I wanted the ink to be mana imbued because what I wanted to do next was drawn from a magic trick I recalled seeing before.

First, Link the Leprechaun's Foot to the laminated map. Then, Link the map to the city… or the concept of the city. That, of course, was more difficult. Thankfully, as a representation of the city itself, the map did not require significant amounts of mana to achieve the link. Next, Link the drug to the ink and to the map at the same time. Then I would have to cast a Track spell while Linking that spell to the ink which was linked to the map. Lastly, if my theory was correct, all I had to do was pour the ink on the map.

Of course, creating so many Links at the same time was going to be difficult. I needed a very high level of synchronicity for this to work on each Link as their efficacy would break down along the chain. It was sort of like linking numerous pieces of wire together for electricity—you always had a loss of current the more you added. As such, while the actual theory was simple, doing it was less than simple. What the level of synchronicity I needed was… well, that was what experimentation was for.

Worse, Caleb had indicated doing something like this was considered a "simple" task for any "real" mage apprentice. Of course, at times I was uncertain how much to believe him. The mage was not above exaggerating to make me work harder.

"Ninth time's the charm," I muttered, staring at the pieces of equipment strewn around me. I took a moment to feel my mana level and sighed. Right, time for a break first. I needed at least two-thirds of my pool to do this safely, and I was just under half right now.

"Great! I'm hungry," Lily called.

"Make it yourself," I grumbled.

"But you're in the kitchen…" Lily did have a point.

"Pizza?"

"Have I ever said no?"

I dug into our freezer and quickly pulled out a frozen pizza, then turned the oven on to preheat it. Then, spotting the time, I decided to grab a second pizza, knowing Alexa would be back. Ah, the convenience of ready-made meals. I prepped the pizza sheets, pulled them aside and then took a break to hit the washroom. By the time I was done, the oven was ready and so was my mana pool.

Standing over my equipment, I drew a deep breath, forcing myself to focus again as I began the process once more. First, drug to map. Then map to the concept of the city. Mana rushed out of me in a torrent. Once the connection was made, I continued the process, carefully "sewing" the Links between each piece. In the end, I stared at the 41 percent Link efficiency I had and nodded to myself. Good enough. All that practice and previous attempts seemed to have done some good.

After drawing a deep breath, I cast a Track spell, holding the Linked aspects together through the process. My head throbbed, but I pushed it aside, the numerous portions of the spell pressing against my mind. I chanted the words of the spell softly, forced to rely only on the oral components to keep the spell together.

The ink dribbled from the bottle slowly as I poured, my mana seeming to fall with the ink itself. I gritted my teeth as a headache began to form beneath my eyebrows, but I pushed forward. I was not going to stop. As the ink fell, it began to squirm on the map, flowing to pool in larger and smaller concentrations in different places. Some of the concentrations were no more than dots, others a quarter of the size of a dime. The smallest dots even shifted slightly, most on roads of some sort when they did. When the last of the ink fell, I exhaled and put the bottle aside and grabbed my phone. A few quick photos later, I finally released the spell.

Thankfully, the ink did not run much even when it was no longer magically bound to specific locations, allowing me to take a few further photographs just in case. I smiled slightly, staring at the result. Not a bad result, for a mostly theoretical and impromptu spell. Even if it was cobbled together from the basics of other, more-established spells.

"That our map?" Alexa asked, making me jump and let out a very manly shriek.

"Oooh…" The face of a thin, angular creature in grey—who stood nearly eight feet tall—twitched, and it rubbed furiously at its ear. "Do you sing soprano?"

"That… you… When did you get here?" I asked in a low, masculine tone.

"About five minutes ago," the thin man said. "That was a great show."

"It was impressive. So those are where we need to go?" Alexa asked again, and this time, I answered her affirmatively. "Great. Corey here has agreed to your proposal."

"My... Ah! For the mushrooms," I said and grinned. I almost ran to the table, proudly showing them my latest invention. However, rather than looking impressed like with the map, the pair instead looked somewhat confused. "What?"

"It's a bit ugly," Corey finally said.

"It's effective!" I growled, shoving the compass-and-block getup at him. "Once the battery runs out, you just need to come back and swap the batteries for new ones that we'll have here. And hand us the spotted Wynn you've collected."

Corey turned the compass hand over hand, staring at the enchanted piece of equipment before he finally opened his mouth to speak slowly. "And it'll point the way to the nearest spotted Wynn?"

"Pretty much." I nodded. "Nearest and biggest. The Link spell looks for the strongest connection, so if there's a mushroom or a set of mushrooms, it'll more likely lead you there than toward a single one."

"Amazing. And it looks like you can do it for any item?" Corey asked, touching the tape.

"Sort of," I said with a shrug. "It's a bit more complicated than just choosing what I want, but yes."

"That's incredible." Corey licked his lips, a glint of avarice in his eyes. I frowned, leaning forward and tapping the table to get his attention.

"Two things. This doesn't go any further. And secondly, remember, the batteries are only chargeable by me. Unless you want to contact a real mage and ask him to play with that." I gestured at the mashed-together piece of equipment. I watched Corey's face change as he considered the fact. Most mages were arrogant asses. Asking them to work with a piece of equipment like the one he held would be demeaning for them, and no one wanted to annoy a mage.

"It's cool, man. It's cool. I was just thinking," Corey said with a grin. "I'm going to go then…"

"Go ahead," I said, waving him off. Once the thin man had gone, I raised an eyebrow at Alexa. "I thought there were others?"

"So did I," Alexa said grumpily and glanced at the clock. I guess even in the supernatural world, flakes were a thing. Changing the subject, Alexa pointed at the map. "I'm assuming the biggest ink blot is where we're going next?"

"Yes. Slowly and carefully," I said. If we were going to act against a distributor or producer, we definitely needed to play this smarter than the last time.

Alexa nodded back at me firmly, obviously thinking the same thing.

Chapter 9

"Are you sure we're in the right place?" Alexa asked softly for the second time as we drove through the tree-lined residential neighborhood. Each detached house adjoined the next in their suburban sameness, though occasional reconstruction broke the monotony of the two-story, cookie-cutter homes with their attached garages and perfectly manicured lawns.

"That's what the map says," I muttered. I had my hand on the drug as well while we slowly and carefully drove down the streets. Not too slow, just slow enough to look like a careful, civic-minded driver not wishing to run over careless children.

"This doesn't look like a drug lab…" Alexa shook her head. "Or a place to store illegal drugs."

"Well, it's not exactly illegal," I said, tapping the cyan chemical compound in its Ziploc baggie in my hand. "It's not like police are knocking down doors over Leprechaun's Foot."

Alexa pursed her lips but nodded after a moment. That was true enough. This was a supernatural drug, with supernatural enhancements. Production and effect on individuals, even at the largest level, most likely would never look like more than a blip to the federal government. As it stood, there were many more dangerous drugs to deal with affecting the mundane population. Heck, modern chemical testing probably wouldn't even see anything wrong with it.

"So…" Alexa said leadingly.

"Three doors down," I said quietly after a moment. "I'm sure it's that one."

"Are you seeing anything?"

"Noooo," I said, squinting. "Actually, yes. There's a distortion in the air around the building, like a heatwave. Reminds me of the way Caleb looks when he's channeling…" I paused to consider for a moment. "But this is a lot more stable. So less like channeling and more like it's a fixed point of distortion."

"What would do that?" Alexa asked softly, her foot barely shifting when we passed the house. Both of us stared at the simple, cream-colored building with light-brown highlights and a simple brick rooftop infested with solar panels. I wondered if the panels were to hide their usage of electricity… if they needed to use electricity. Or perhaps they were environmentalists? Supernatural, gangster environmentalists. A mind-boggling thought. Other than that, with the white curtains drawn, we could see nothing of note. Even the garage was closed, with no vehicles to give further hints.

"Looks normal," I muttered.

"Other than the magical disturbance?" Alexa said sarcastically, turning her attention back toward the road. "I think if we park up that hill, we could get a view of this house." Alexa jerked her head, indicating the hill directly in front of us.

"Sounds good," I said and started looking up directions on my phone. "And yes, normal except the magical disturbance. Pretty sure it's the Leprechaun's Foot."

"I really hate that name."

***

Thirty minutes and two wrong turns later, we found ourselves at a small, gravel shoulder on the hill. Alexa, of course, had a pair of binoculars in the car, which we took turns using to watch the house. Unfortunately, watching the building from a distance currently provided us very little information.

"How'd the investigation on the developer go?" I asked to break the silence.

"Slow." Alexa sighed. "But I'm nearly a hundred percent certain he's a blind."

"Blind?"

"Ah. You call them mundanes. Norms. Muggles," Alexa said.

"Isn't that copyrighted?"

"Who's going to tell her?" Alexa smirked, and I chuckled softly.

"So he's just being an ass?"

"Pretty much," Alexa said with a sigh. "I dug into the fines and notices the orphanage was given. They aren't exactly wrong. The rules and regulations the orphanage is in breach of are just updates on existing code. Normally, they wouldn't be applied till the orphanage needed to apply for a new license or did some work, but—"

"But it doesn't mean they aren't necessary," I said slowly. "And because it's an orphanage, it'd be harder to say: 'We don't need to bring these things up to code.'"

"Exactly," Alexa said. "I don't really know what we can do there. I've contacted a few lawyers, hopefully some of them will help us slow down the fines. That might be the best we can do about the developer. Unless we can find some dirt on him, and beyond a penchant for bribing bureaucrats to do their job, I've got nothing."

"Which leaves the fact that the contractors won't go back into the storage room because it's haunted, and you've got a series of failing rituals to contend with."

"Yes."

"Fine. That's next on the list then," I said with some resignation. Now, I really wished this was more like one of my stupid, linear computer RPGs. Most of those games involved running around and beating up the latest beholder or messing with the evil warlock. They didn't involve figuring out how to thwart the evil merchant from buying the orphanage that was annoying him. Or, well, it did, but I'd just blast him with a fireball in a game and call it a day.

Somehow, premeditated murder did not seem as fun in reality. With that sobering thought, I fell silent as the pair of us watched the house. Perhaps some brilliant idea would occur to us later.

***

"I should have brought a book," I muttered a few hours later.

"We're supposed to be watching the building," Alexa said softly.

"For what?" I asked. "I mean, they joke about how stakeouts suck, but really…"

"They do?"

"They really do." I shifted in my seat to settle my back. "I mean, what are we supposed to be doing here? Watching a house to see what? Who comes out and drives away? I swear, I could find a spell for this…"

"Mages and your spells," Alexa said.

"Come on, you can't say you're enjoying this," I said.

"Enjoy? No. But it is necessary. This is how you gather information."

"Maybe this is how you gather information, but I'm a mage," I said firmly. "I'm going to figure out a smarter way of doing this."

"Go ahead," Alexa said, getting impatient.

I nodded firmly and then fell silent, going over my character sheet and spell list to start.

Class: Mage

Level 22 (29% Experience)

Known Spells: Light Sphere, Force Spear, Force Shield, Force Fingers, Alter Temperature, Gong, Gust, Heal, Healing Ward, Link, Track, Fix, Ward, Glamour, Illusion, Summon, Iceball, Fireball, Scry

I chuckled when I noted I'd leveled up. I vaguely recalled there had been that notification while I had been working on the map yesterday, but I'd been a touch busy. And obsessed. I would admit to a little obsession. Still, as I eyed the spells, I blinked at the latest. Huh…

And huh.

I half-closed my eyes and concentrated, pulling at the spell in my mind. It came to the forefront of my thoughts with a flash, a piece of knowledge that had always been there just waiting for me to focus on it. I'd considered it a coincidence that the spell I desperately needed was right here, at my fingertips—except for the fact that, of course, I had a GM who was watching over all this. I'd bet Lily had made sure to gift this spell to me because she knew what I'd need.

Scry. A simple enough spell at the lowest levels of mastery. It actually was a compound spell like Fireball or Iceball. It built upon known spells, streamlined via specific formulas that made the spell more powerful but more restrictive. In this case, the Scry spell was built upon Link, Track, and Illusion. The Track portion basically guided the spell to the location you were looking for, Link linked the spell component you were using to an appropriate target within the location, and Illusion displayed the location. It was a triple-compound spell, one that was no more difficult to do than creating my map but more strenuous since I wasn't just linking to a conceptual city but an actual space. As such, the requirements for refinement and fidelity were higher.

Still, the Scry spell was exactly what I needed. Firstly though, I'd need a linking material—an appropriate medium. The most common items were mirrors, crystal balls, and bowls of water. Each would link to a mirror, glass, or water in the surroundings, which meant none were particularly better than the other in general. Though, from the knowledge forced into me, some were clearer than others.

Thankfully, I was in a car, so finding a mirror was a simple matter. Alexa shot me a glance when I adjusted the rearview mirror, but I decided to ignore her for the moment. Since this was the first time I was casting the spell, I figured I'd better test it out before discussing it. Wouldn't want it to fizzle out.

My fingers moved, and my mouth chanted as my mind ran through the newly provided spell formula and mana flowed through my body and out my fingertips. My perception lurched as mana flowed out of me, carrying me out of my body as the spell nearly completed. The sudden change—even if I knew subconsciously that it was about to happen—was too much for me and the spell broke, shattering around me and sending shards of free-floating mana running through me. I grunted, shuddering, and closed my eyes.

Damn it. I hadn't expected to fail at the start.

"Henry?"

"Testing a new spell," I said once I got my breath back. I leaned back for a few moments, letting my body slowly calm and the pain subside while I went over the details of the spell again. This time, I wouldn't let myself fail. Even if the out-of-body experience was weird.

Once again, I cast the spell and felt my mana leave me. I exhaled slowly and closed my eyes, feeling the lurch once more as my senses left my body. This time though, I was prepared for the feeling and continued to chant the spell, guiding my temporary self to the location. It really was just my senses, and even then, it wasn't the entirety of them. It was a vertigo-inducing moment, and by the time I had mostly adjusted, I'd covered the hundreds of yards to the house. I even overshot my location and had to retreat, adjusting the spell formulas of the Scry spell on the fly.

Sensing in this state was at the most crude, rudimentary stage. I could not see, hear, or smell anything, but I could sense where various mirrors and objects close enough to a reflective surface were. I could even sense, to an extent, the level of appropriateness for me to Link my spell. At a higher level, I would even be able to Link multiple items at the same time, but for now, I picked the highest appropriate Link item and sent my body back to the car. A fraction of a second later, I opened my eyes.

Scry Cast
Synchronicity 31%
Link 78%

Blinking away the notification, I turned to look at the rearview mirror, which now showed a new reflection. My smile held for a fraction of a second before I huffed out loud, while Alexa sniggered slightly at the image shown.

Right. Highest appropriateness meant another mirror. And where were most mirrors? In bedrooms and bathrooms. Staring at the blurry, white-tiled interior of an empty bathroom, I huffed in annoyance again. Well, at least the spell worked.

***

"Is this how it's normally done?" Alexa asked a half hour later after I'd cast and recast Scry, trying to find a good location to spy on those within. Thus far, we'd peeked into empty bedrooms, an empty closet, and an empty kitchen. Right now though, I had to wait for my mana to regenerate.

"No," I said, shaking my head as I prodded the information in my mind. "There are ways to lock onto multiple surfaces, then complete the spell. Then it's just a matter of flicking through them till you find the appropriate location."

"Why aren't you doing that?"

"Beginner here, remember? I'm having a hard enough time locking down a single location at this distance, never mind multiple. And the amount of mana required increases too, as well as the complexity of the actual spell formula." I shook my head at the thought. "Give me a bit, and I'll be able to lock down two, but for now, one and done is where we're at."

"Huh," Alexa said simply and then leaned back in her chair. A moment later, she leaned forward and grabbed her binoculars, staring ahead.

"What?" I frowned, looking at the house. It did not take me long to realize what had attracted Alexa's attention. A minivan had driven up. Unfortunately, it was one of those multi-door white minivans beloved by housewives, soccer moms, and large families everywhere. In other words, utterly useless at this distance for providing additional information. A short while later, it entered the newly opened garage.

"Can you…?"

"Already on it," I said, nodding in confirmation as I started casting Scry again. It would drop me below the 10 percent bar I'd set for myself but not too far. All it meant was I'd be eating more painkillers for the next few hours. But… "Got it. One van mirror coming up."

The mirror flickered and shifted, a new image appearing. I grimaced, making a mental note to find a bigger mirror to cart around next time since this image, drawn from the side mirror, was slightly truncated to fit everything in. With a flicker of my hand, I shifted the mirror around as distorted words came through the newly formed mirror.

"What are you doing here?" A deep, husky male voice came through first, a four-pack-a-day smoker with a cold who somehow still managed to create a feeling of dread over the communicator.

"I'm here to pick up the next shipment," a high female voice answered him. For a second, there was a flash of pale skin and an orange blouse before it was gone. I frowned, shifting the image around as I attempted to see more.

"Stop…" Alexa hissed a moment before I stopped the shifting image myself. In it, we caught our first glimpse, a female in an orange, ruffled blouse with a sneer on her lips and brown hair.

"Sold out already?" The male voice spoke again. From what I could tell, he was probably standing directly behind the mirror.

"Can't keep it on the streets. My man wants at least twice our last order," the woman said and grinned. She reached into the car, her tight pants pulling firm for a second in the image when she leaned within. I had to pause to admire the sight, a low whistle coming the other man, making me think the enviable, large, and tight posterior was being admired by more than myself.

When the lady stood straight again, this time I noted a slight grin as she exited. A bulky brown envelope was held in hand, one that she tossed over. "Same price, yes?"

The other voice chuckled. "Not going to bargain?"

"Not if you keep the exclusivity."

"Wait here." A moment later, the click of a closing door was heard. In the meantime, the young lady leaned against the now-closed van door, offering us an admirable if not particularly informative view. My fingers shifted side to side as I attempted to find a better angle and got nothing.

"Is she supernatural?" Alexa asked me as we watched.

"Can't tell. It's a good illusion if she is," I said tightly while holding the connection open. Well, glamour and illusion combined. Glamours tricked the mind; illusions tricked reality. Combined, they kept supernaturals hidden—though most of their disguises were largely glamour with the smallest amounts of illusion possible to allow supernaturals to pass common recording devices. However, the young lady in our mirror looked perfectly normal, which indicated she was either using a powerful illusion spell or wasn't using one at all.

"Bah," Alexa said softly, drumming her fingers on the wheel. A few minutes later, the door opened.

"About time," the woman said, standing. For a second, she left our field of vision, rustling and crinkling the only sound reaching us. "This looks more than double."

"Just a little extra, for our favorite customer."

"Your only customer," the woman said, a hint of aggression in her voice. The speaker just grunted in reply. A few moments later, we saw her back in our field of vision again, pulling the door open to drop a couple of brown paper bags inside.

I grunted and, as the two started exchanging goodbyes, released the spell. When Alexa turned to look at me, she noticed me breathing deeply, with sweat staining my brow, and rubbing my sore temples.

"You okay?"

"Fine. Just couldn't hold it any longer," I replied. "Give me a few hours. Once my mana's back, we can Scry it again."

"Okay," Alexa said simply. After a second's consideration, she started the car.

"I can't Track her…" I said, squinting at the house.

"I know. I was thinking we hadn't had lunch." Alexa offered me a half smile. "With your spell, we should get you fed and then come back to look again."

"Okay." I was sure there was something off about leaving the place unwatched, but considering she was doing this in consideration of my headache, I was not going to complain. And anyway, my spell was probably going to get us more information than sitting there, watching.

***

A couple hours and one plate of curried pineapple rice later, we were back at the same hill. This time around, with nearly half the likely locations already investigated, I decided I'd check out the basement level. A part of me had considered just jumping the Scry to that floor to begin with, but going below ground level actually pulled a lot more mana than staying above it. Even though the basement was technically hollowed out, the draw on my mana was still much higher than I'd care to use to start. Thus, the earlier testing.

Unfortunately, after casting the spell, I realized the biggest problem with a spell targeted to a basement that is reliant on sight: If no one turns on the lights, all you were seeing was darkness as well.

"Nothing?"

"You tell me," I said grumpily. For a brief moment, I considered if it'd be possible to cast a Light spell within the basement. It was theoretically possible. I had the spatial coordinates and even a way to see where I was casting. However, theory ran up against reality really fast. Not only would it be incredibly draining on my limited mana, it would also potentially alert our prey of our presence.

"Next?"

"Yup." I killed the spell before moving onward.

Eventually, by process of elimination, we located our targets. They were upstairs, three individuals seated watching TV in the second floor living room.

Now that we had them in view, we took our time staring at the trio. Sprawled as they were on their chairs with discarded remnants of various takeout joints and snack foods, they looked almost normal. A pair of Hispanic-looking men and a shorter, Vietnamese-looking gentleman were sprawled, idly watching the idiot box. I frowned, wanting to know which had been the speaker, but all three were silent, content to damage their minds with the drivel of afternoon TV. It was a very domestic scene if you ignored the weapons in easy reach of the three: a pair of handguns and a shotgun, with a machete also laid beside them.

"How long can you hold this?" Alexa asked softly.

"Now that it's established?" I considered, judging my mana. "Twenty minutes safely. If I meditate and focus on drawing in more mana, maybe thirty. But I'd be useless for anything—"

"Do it," Alexa said firmly. "I'll watch and take notes. At the least, I want to know who their leader is."

"All right," I said in agreement while Alexa pulled a sketchbook from her supplies within the car. She immediately started sketching while I closed my eyes and focused. My breathing deepened as I reached and opened myself at the same time, allowing the mana that surrounded us to absorb into my body even as more mana flooded out while I channeled my spell. Time lost meaning as I held the two opposing concepts in mind, focused as they were within my body.

"Time," I said softly after a while. I received a grunted agreement from Alexa, so I cut the flow of power. The spell flickered, running for a few moments more on the stored power before it wound down. As I opened my eyes, I frowned as a crunch of gravel occurred a moment later, making me turn to look at a police car rolling to a stop next to us.

326

"Crap," Alexa said. She quickly pursed her lips and then suddenly leaned over, grabbing my shirt by the side and pulling me close.

A moment later, I found myself lip-locked with the blonde as she held me tight. At first, I struggled, then my brain caught up with me. Why exactly was I struggling against the pretty blonde who was kissing me? Wait. Why was I even thinking about anything but how soft her lips were? As my brain finally caught up, I relaxed slightly only to tense again when a rapping occurred on the window. Almost immediately, Alexa released me and adjusted her blouse, her cheeks flushed.

"Wha—"

The rapping came again, my uttered exclamation not finishing.

"Window," Alexa said slightly breathlessly and then rolled hers down to smile demurely at the policeman. "Yes, Officer?"

"We received a report there was a vehicle parked here suspiciously," the officer said. I saw his eyes dart from my to Alexa's slightly flushed faces, a slight frown creasing his face.

"Oh… I didn't know that was illegal, sir!" Alexa exclaimed artlessly. She then paused, giving him big, innocent eyes as she continued. "It isn't, is it?"

"It's not illegal, miss. We're just checking that there's nothing suspicious going on," the officer replied. His attention shifted to the mirror propped up on the dashboard, the binoculars and then to the wooden warding blocks that spilled out of my backpack in the backseat. "What are you doing up here?"

"Bird-watching!" Alexa said, then flushed slightly and looked down, biting her lip.

"Bird-watching," the officer replied dryly. "Well, I'm a bit of an ornithologist myself. See anything interesting?"

I opened and shut it. Hell, I could barely tell the difference between a crow and a raven. But Alexa replied without hesitation. "Nothing rare. A couple of thrushes, a chestnut-backed chickadee, and a goldfinch."

The officer nodded his head along to Alexa's words but relaxed slightly. "Nice to see some young people taking an interest in the hobby."

"My uncle introduced me to it," Alexa said happily and smiled.

"Well, if you're just bird-watching, you have a nice day." The officer flashed a glance at the wooden blocks and then smiled at Alexa before he shot me a much frostier look. I gave him a weak grin which made the officer snort as he walked away. With the expanded senses I had, I heard him mutter as he walked off. "I know what bird he's watching…"

I coughed slightly, shaking my head, and then looked at Alexa who continued to provide a smiling demeanor until the officer had pulled off.

"What was the kiss about?" I asked quietly, touching my lips unconsciously after I finished speaking.

"Isn't that what they do in the movies?" Alexa shrugged. "I doubt he'd take the bird-watching excuse entirely, so I added to it. It worked, didn't it?"

"I thought you weren't good at lying," I said.

"I'm not. And I wasn't," Alexa said and pointed. "Thrush. Chickadee. Oooh, that's a northern fulmar."

I stared at the sudden burst of happiness on Alexa's face and then sighed. "You had the weirdest childhood."

"Uh huh." Alexa sniffed. "I'm just enjoying the beauty of His work."

Without a rejoinder, I shifted my gaze toward her sketchbook that she had dropped down the side of her seat, out of sight of the policeman. "Anything?"

"Just sketches. They didn't really talk much, but I'm pretty sure the Asian looker was our speaker."

"Ah…" I said with a nod. Well, at least we got something from this.

"We should keep watch for a little while more before we leave," Alexa said finally and flashed me a smile.

I nodded dumbly, staring at the blonde who seemed to have forgotten the kiss already. After a moment, I could do nothing more than push it aside. As they said, don't shit where you eat. And really, I doubted the initiate had any thoughts about me like that.

Chapter 10

Dinner that evening was Greek. I grabbed an order of moussaka and a double order of calamari for everyone to share, while Alexa went the roast lamb route and Lily did them all. Which, when I realized how much food that was, was a bit much. Sometimes I had the feeling Lily ate for the experience of eating more than for the physical need. I'd certainly never have to worry about kicking her out of the washroom—which was, perhaps, the only reason the three of us had survived in my old apartment.

"Right, so where are we?" I asked as I speared another deep-fried squiddy goodness. Wait, did leviathans exist? Or squiddy Cthulhu monsters?

Rather than directly answer me, Lily popped a notification in front of my eyes. I growled, swatting the box to make it smaller so I could eat and read. I had to smile that she had even added little notations of what we had managed.

Help Alexa Complete Her Squire Trial (Chained Quest)
This is a chained quest. You must complete the sub-quests to complete the major quest.
Sub-quests:

- *Investigate and deal with the sudden influx of Leprechaun's Foot (Investigated)*
- *Collect fifty specimens of Spotted Wynn Mushrooms (28/50 collected)*
- *Help solve the Brixton Orphanage issues (Have you really even started?)*

"One out of three ain't bad?" Alexa said, pointing at air and what I assumed to be the second quest line. With the scavenger working for us, we had that one covered. I might even have figured out a way to generate additional, ongoing income in the future if this worked out well.

"But two out of three would be better," I said. When there was no immediate reaction, I looked between the two ladies and then sighed. Obviously classic eighties' rock was not a selling point with this group. "Right, so we know where they're storing the Foot. Unfortunately, it doesn't look like they're manufacturing in the city. Otherwise, we'd probably spot it on the map."

"If you say so," Alexa said before she frowned. "But if they're not manufacturing them here…"

"How do we stop it from coming in?" I said, finishing for her. "It's all about supply and demand, but demand isn't something we can affect, so we got to cut off the supply. Makes me feel like the little Dutch boy and the dam."

Again, silence from the pair.

"You know, trying to stem the tide with a finger? It's not possible. Even if we burn all the product, they'll just send more."

Alexa slowly nodded, chewing on the meat-juice-soaked rice in thought. "But we don't need to stop it completely. Our job is just to reduce it, for the time being."

"And the orphanage?" Lily asked.

"We're stuck there too. We can't really make the fines go away…" I paused, considering. Well, I could wipe their files possibly. I was sure there was a spell for that somewhere. Potentially just a small electrical surge in the offices and it'd fix the issue. As for the paper records—

"Henry?"

"Ah, just thinking I might be able to erase the fines, but it's a temporary solution, isn't it?" I asked, and the pair nodded. Still, it was worth thinking about if we needed to buy ourselves some time. Time was the major problem. We had just over a week left, and we still had not found a solution. "But maybe we could con them."

"What do you mean?" Alexa asked, and I smiled slightly.

"Well, if they do all the retrofitting in every other location first, I can look it over and cast an illusion to make the storeroom look like it's been done. It won't be, but it should last the inspection, no?"

"But what about the contractors?" Alexa asked, looking troubled. "They'd know. And we'd be lying."

"Yeah, not sure about the contractors. Maybe we could lie to them and let them go after they're done because they won't finish the work? After all, they won't be able to articulate why they don't want to go in beyond it's a bad feeling, right?" I said.

Alexa protested. "But it's not their fault!"

"No, it's the orphanage's," I said. "Who hires blinds to work on a magical building? Also. Nope. That is not a word I want to use."

"They had a limited budget."

"Uh huh," I said. "And look where being cheap has gotten them. In fact, I'm not even sure having them work on the rest of the building is a good idea." I paused, considering the matter. "In fact, scrap the idea. Our next job is finding a supernatural and magically sensitive construction group to work on this."

"I don't think the Abbess will like that..."

I just stared at Alexa, letting her work out the issues herself. In the end, the blonde let out an angry huff. "You'll want me to speak with the abbess and the contractors, right?"

"Of course. It's your quest. Maybe they could do a workaround—fortify it magically and make it look like they've done the work mundanely or something," I said. "I'll hit class with Caleb tomorrow and then I'd like to do some research on the building itself."

"And the jackals?" Alexa asked, tapping her plate as she looked at me.

"You tell me."

At my words, Alexa's eyes tightened as she considered the matter. We both had the same information. In the end, Alexa said simply, "I'm going to get clarification. If all we need to do is put a temporary hold on the supply, it can be achieved by hitting the house. If they're looking for something more permanent…" Alexa trailed off, and I nodded.

Yeah. I didn't exactly have an answer to that one either. Then again, I didn't feel too bad. It wasn't as if governments hadn't been trying and failing to solve the drug problem for the last couple hundred years.

***

"Did you finish your project?" Caleb asked the next day when I arrived.

With a slight smile, I brought out a few of the failures and some pre-prepped blocks. Caleb raised an eyebrow, while I smiled at the master mage. "I thought you could take a look at my work. See if you had any comments."

Caleb tapped his lips in thought before he waved his hand, gesturing for me to start. Once I had the blocks and my equipment set aside—after a slight coughing fit by Caleb when I first pulled out my tools—I focused and started working. In a mere fifteen minutes, I had another modular compass and mana battery made. Thankfully, once I actually had the plans developed, it was easy enough to finish the work. I even threw in a new twist to some of the sigils, which seemed to increase the effectiveness of the enchanted equipment ever so slightly.

"Well, it's not the most elegant of equipment," Caleb said as he turned the block around in his hand. He tapped the batteries, a wry smile on his lips. "And it does rebuild the wheel with these batteries. But there are some interesting twists to the spells you've used, some of which I might even call genius." I began to grow pleased at Caleb's words before he added. "But then, you did pull them from your 'downloaded' spells, so it is no surprise." Caleb fished in his pockets and pulled out his wallet, drawing out four crisp bills before he handed them to me. "I will purchase this contraption from you."

"Really?" I said, my eyes wide.

"Of course. As I said, some of the mana formulas you have interlaced in the block is quite ingenious. It is much simpler to study the spells that your jinn has implanted in your mind through something like this"—Caleb tapped the mana compass—"than attempting to transcribe your explanations."

"Oh…" I exhaled disappointedly. It didn't stop me from taking the bills though and sliding them into my back pocket. "Well, if it was so bad, could you—"

"List your many failures? Of course," Caleb said. "It is what I am here for. Now, let us begin with the obvious. Your carving and handling of your tools is at best subpar. I would say it is an insult to your tools, but considering you spent all of five dollars on them, it would be too great a compliment to the tools themselves. You do realize that any self-respecting mage spends significant funds on purchasing proper equipment?"

I sighed as I pulled out a notebook, getting ready to listen to Caleb preach about the greatness and magnificence of mages once more. Proper mages. Not weird, sorcerer-mage wish hybrids like me. Because, as bad as this might be for my self-respect, the man knew his work. And—I had to admit—was probably right.

And I did kind of want a self-immolating, inscription wand.

***

"And that should be sufficient to help you improve your design by at least threefold," Caleb said, finishing his lecture.

I stared at the multiples pages of notes I had taken, of which I understood maybe a fifth of and might only be able to afford a quarter of, and could not help but nod. The sad fact was I knew Caleb had even more knowledge to impart on this matter, but considering the sheer difference in knowledge between the two of us, he'd dumbed it down.

"Once again, you have managed to distract me from the planned lesson."

"Sorry, not sorry?" I said with a smirk and a shrug of my shoulders. "I actually had another request."

"Of course you do. What is it now?"

"Rituals. I'm on a quest with Alexa, and we're dealing with a containment ritual and enchantment. It's been damaged though, so I need to restore it," I said.

"The Brixton Orphanage."

"Yes, how did you know?"

"I am the master mage in charge of this region," Caleb said with a sniff. "Part of my duties do require me to be aware of such matters."

"So do you know what is contained by the orphanage?" I asked, curiosity getting the better of me. After all, Alexa had no idea, and the Templars weren't going to tell me.

"That I do not," Caleb said stiffly. "The Templars are not forthcoming about their activities for obvious reasons. I do know that whatever is contained most likely should stay contained."

"Most likely?"

"The Templars are less forgiving than we are," Caleb said. "And considering when this occurred, well, times have changed."

"Ah…" I considered what Caleb meant. I guess society had changed since the sixties, and what was considered acceptable back then and now has altered, at least in most parts of the world. It would stand to reason that changes in social mores among mundanes would also affect tolerance levels among supernaturals. How much of a crossover, I'd have to research. But—"Is there a way to tell? There's a bit of mana leaking out."

"Hmmm… You mean the mana that is produced is tainted by the creature's or item's aura," Caleb said, correcting me. "But yes, there are ways. With your skill set… Marissa's Multibox of Telling would be best."

"The what?"

"Marissa's Multibox of Telling." Caleb walked toward his library of books. He flipped through a few before finding the one he wanted. With an absent toss of his hand, the book landed on a bookstand where Caleb then gestured at, directing a pen that had been seated on the bookstand to begin copying the spell. "Now, we were going to discuss rituals. Let us begin with an overview of your current knowledge."

I stared enviously at the scribing tool. I wanted one!

Caleb clapped his hands together. "Mr. Tsien!"

"Sorry. Overview of rituals. Right. They're just elongated spells, aren't they? Drawn onto chalk circles and boosted with various elemental items?"

"That—" Caleb drew a deep breath and glared at the wide-eyed, innocent face I returned to him. "It seems we have a lot of work to do."

***

Baiting Caleb about what he thought of my knowledge about rituals actually had a point beyond mildly amusing me. In truth, while I had some transmitted knowledge, it was mostly ancillary to the spell knowledge provided by Lily. As such, my foundational knowledge left a lot to be desired. Once again, I had to admit the way Lily had "dumped" information into my brain left me with surprisingly large and weird holes. Especially when the jinn herself was a more natural caster. Her understanding of magic had surprising gaps which at times resulted in issues on my end.

My Ward spell, for example, could not actually be directly translated to a barrier, since much of the knowledge provided to me came from a subset of Enochian magic that never bothered with rituals. So while I could—and did—figure out how to enchant with it, translating the knowledge into a ritual was outside my current skillset. And yes, the differences between a ward, a ritual, and an enchantment were small at times, but when I was altering the fundamental forces of nature, that minor gap could be lethal.

Caleb understood my issues after so many months training me. It was why he was, at times, over-thorough in his explanations. And while I saw no move in my ritual knowledge talents, I knew I had a much firmer grasp of the basics. If we kept these lessons up, in a short while, I would have a much better idea of what to do about the broken enchantments and ritual. Of course…

"Why aren't you fixing the enchantments?" I asked Caleb as we wrapped up the lesson plan.

"What do you mean?"

"Well, isn't it your job?"

"Again, you misunderstand my role. I am to watch for and deal with significant threats. While whatever is trapped by the Templars in the orphanage is of note, it is not, as you have pointed out, inherently violent. As such, it is outside of my area of responsibility. What would my life be like if I went around dealing with every minor issue third-rate sorcerers created? No. Whatever is down there is something the Templars can handle themselves."

"And if it's an item?"

"Then taking it away if it is dangerous would be simpler after its release."

"And you don't want to be bothered."

"And I don't want to be bothered." Caleb affably agreed. "You will find as you progress that many of the concerns you exhibit now are less important. They are, in fact, trivial to your progress as a mage."

"For you maybe," I said under my breath, staring at the numerous books that made up the portion of the library Caleb had brought with him. I knew he easily had hundreds more in his actual house. For "real" mages, study and experimentation were more important than going out and "leveling." Whether it was a curse or blessing, I needed to do both. Only through constant and practical use of my spells did the knowledge imparted to me become better integrated.

And truth be told, I might be a bit of a geek, but even I can get tired of reading.

***

Since Caleb had been of little use in understanding what was actually trapped beneath, I figured I would spend some time researching the building. I was curious if the enchantments had been built from the start or something that had appeared recently. It certainly seemed strange that if they were going to add an enchantment to a building, they didn't do what everyone else did: add it in the foundations, out of sight. It made things so much simpler, and stronger in most cases.

With that in mind, I made a visit to the archival room of our public library. It was only when I arrived I found out that not only did they not keep building plans, access to building plans at city hall also required me to get the permission of the owners. Oh, and there was no guarantee they'd have plans for something as old as the orphanage.

"So what can I find out here?" I asked, slightly exasperated.

Thankfully, the librarian—a thin, weedy-looking guy who looked like he needed less time in the sun—didn't take offense with my question and directed me to the microfilm section. There, he then pointed me at the various resources available, patiently explaining that no, there wasn't a web search that would give me all the information contained. And then, the bastard left me.

Four hours later, I recalled why I hated libraries. I gently dropped my head onto the giant tome that blandly described the history of social housing and welfare for children in the city. It was intensely boring, but it did at least mention the orphanage... if not in the context I required.

"May I be of assistance?" a soft voice asked me, and I twitched, tilting my head sideways. Next to me was a bespectacled, bird-headed creature with coffee-colored skin. I stared at the creature for a second, my brain trying to locate the particular type. Its feathered head bobbed slightly as the creature continued to speak. "I am Adom." Lowering his voice even further, Adom said, "I am from my lord Thoth's lineage."

"Oh..." My brain scrambled for a second, thankful for long, long D&D sessions and a rather weird obsession with all things mythological. Thoth was the Egyptian god of knowledge. Details came back from an abandoned campaign, filling in further details. Egyptian gods were generally decent, and since he was just someone from that lineage, I should treat him like any other supe. "Depends. You good at research?"

"I have some small skill," Adom said, inclining his head.

"Perfect," I said with a grin. "I need to know everything you can find about the Brixton Orphanage. In five days."

"Lord mage, I fear you misunderstand. Good research takes time," Adom said, shaking his head disapprovingly.

"I know, but I've got a time-limited quest here, so chop-chop," I said. "Not that I mean you should. Ummm... how much would I owe you?"

Adom cocked his head to the side now, regarding me for a time. "Five days of dedicated research. Rush order. Two thousand dollars."

"Two thousand!" I yelped and got glares from the few people around. I simmered down, shooting a sheepish glance back at the library attendees I had disturbed. "That's daylight robbery. One."

"Deal. Should I meet you here or at your offices?" Adom said immediately.

"Wait a second. I feel like I've been cheated here!" I grumbled. Damn it. Luckily, this was real life, or I'd probably receive negative experience for negotiating. "And here is fine. Probably for the best."

"Pleasure doing business with you," Adom said, offering his hand. I shook it while standing and walked out of the library. A thousand dollars. Gah! At least, if we completed Alexa's quest, we should still see a profit. Still. A thousand dollars.

Cursing myself, I made my way home.

Chapter 11

"Why are we doing this stakeout again?" I grumbled as we sat in the car, in a new spot overlooking the building. This was the second lookout spot we had used in the last few hours, Alexa having decided that moving more often was a better idea than having the police called on us again. Not that I disagreed, but...

"Intelligence before an attack is important. Do we have a Link?" Alexa said and prodded me. I stared at the small circular makeup mirror we had purchased for this very purpose, figuring it was easier than constantly adjusting the rearview mirror.

"Yes. The usual," I said and shifted the mirror for Alexa to look. I swear, these guys desperately needed to find something better to do than stare at the idiot box all day. Who cared what horrible food was being eaten, which long-lost cousin with amnesia was being released from jail, or how to bake a double-chocolate-fudge cake. Actually, maybe the last one.

"Let's just keep watching," Alexa said in reply after she looked.

"Fine. But what are we waiting for?" I said with a grimace. Still, I sat back and focused on feeding mana to the image while doing my utmost to draw in as much mana from the surroundings as possible.

"Either another shipment or payment. They were paid recently, so it's not likely to be the second. But if they receive a second shipment, we can hit them and destroy it. Maybe even take their money at the same time."

"You don't mean to launch the attack when the courier is there, right? Because we're a bit far away to do that..."

"No. We can take the three, but I don't know how many would be with their courier. Or when it'd arrive. Better for us to just destroy their product," Alexa said.

"Actually, I think taking their money would be better. See, the product is probably quite cheap to make, but the money they earn is, well, money."

"Why'd you think it's cheap to make?"

"Isn't that how drugs work? The product is cheap but gets marked up because it's illegal?" I asked with a shrug. "Or gets marked up because of the cost of lost product due to law enforcement, which in this case would be us."

Alexa frowned at my words but, after a moment's consideration, slowly nodded.

"Great. Then let's go home, and we'll plan the hit."

"Can we not talk about it like that?" Alexa asked. "We're not assassins."

"Fine," I said, maybe a bit pitifully. I guessed she wouldn't accept wearing black masks too?

***

"Masks are a good idea," Alexa said with a nod. "I'll put up my hair and wear a wig too."

"Wait. You're good with a mask?"

"Of course." Alexa nodded firmly. "We don't want to be caught. And you should put a glamour on us too. Just in case."

"Sure," I said, readjusting my thinking. I then stared at the sketched-out map of the house before us on my grid paper. Who said buying all this erasable grid paper for my RPG games had been a waste? Har! Though, when I had pulled it out, I'd realized how long it had been since I had a good game. Ever since my last group broke up due to interpersonal conflicts—seriously, how many times did we have to repeat "do not date in your game group" before people got it—I hadn't had a good game. Then again, I was living an urban fantasy campaign. But… well, there was still something missing.

On the grid map, we'd sketched the inner layout of the building as best as we could gather from my repeated uses of Scry. Added on to it, we had another section for the second floor. Theoretically we should have had one more for the basement, but considering we'd never seen the basement itself, it was currently empty.

On top of all this, we had a printout of the satellite image for the neighborhood and a map of the roads around the location itself including one-way streets, exits to the nearest highway, and other viable and contingency roads. I'd also taken the time to mark where the nearest police station was, though as we'd found out, the police did have a few roaming patrols.

"I'm not sure if I'm impressed or disturbed by how competent you are planning a robbery," Alexa said, watching as I jotted further information onto the map.

"Blame Shadowrun," I said.

Lily snorted at that, while Alexa looked at me blankly.

"This is so a Shadowrun job. You're even going to go in the front door, guns blazing!" Lily giggled.

"There are no guns. Wait, are there guns, Henry?" Alexa asked, staring at me.

"No guns. It's just a saying." I cocked my head sideways at Lily. "Though I'm surprised someone knows it."

"I like reading fanfic," Lily said. "And other people's recounting of their games."

"Ah…" I paused, considering the jinn. "You know, you could just sign up to play a game."

"I could?" Lily paused, her gaze turning unconsciously to the ring on my finger. After a moment, she smiled and nodded. "I could!"

"Did… did you just not realize it?"

"You try living a few millennia trapped in a ring," Lily said with her arms crossed. "I forget I can, you know, do things."

"Ahem." Alexa cleared her throat and pointed at the map. "So what are we looking at?"

"Well, if things go bad, we've got about ten minutes before the cops arrive—give or take—from the station. Probably five if there's a roaming patrol car," I said, tapping the map. "The neighborhood is mostly made up of double income earners, so I think going in during the day at around ten would be best. At night, there's a lot more people, so we're more likely to get spotted. Better to do it when everyone's out."

"Sounds fair," Alexa said.

"Right. We go in during the day. If we wait till they're all upstairs, we can walk right up to their front door. If I spend the rest of tonight, I'm pretty sure I can make the equivalent of a lockpick," I said. "Which will get us in the front door. Then we just have to—" That's when I stopped, realization hitting me.

"We'll have to deal with them."

"Right. Yeah…" My brain stuttered to a stop again, a pause that made Alexa frown at me.

"What's wrong, Henry?"

"I'm not sure about our plan. If they resist, we're going to have fight them. They've got guns and…" I paused, drawing a shuddering breath. "And I don't know if I can put them down without killing them. If I'm willing to kill them. If I can. What if I freeze? What if you get shot while I freeze? What happens if my shields can't hold up against the bullets? What if the bullets bounce and hit them? What—"

"Henry." A hand falls on my arm, squeezing it so tight, my breath hitches and my rambling stops. "You haven't killed before, have you?"

"Yes, I have," I said in protest.

"I don't mean rats. Or demons. Or obvious monsters," Alexa said. "I mean humans. Or those close to them."

"I…" I shook my head. "Why is it so different?"

"Because it is." Alexa shrugged. "We all have our own mental hiccups. It's not a bad thing. It doesn't make you weak. But I need you to think about this, very carefully. Before we make any more plans, I need you to know where your lines are."

"And if I can't kill them?" I whispered softly.

"Then we'll know. And plan around that," Alexa said.

I nodded dumbly and took my arm back from her. I realized with a shock that my hands were shaking, adrenaline setting my nerves tingling and my heartbeat rocketing without any real escape. I stumbled to the couch and sat down heavily, breathing slowly as my mind spiraled.

Could I kill? Should I kill? They were gangsters. Drug dealers. Bad people. But I wasn't the Punisher. I was no soldier who got up in the morning and chanted songs about shooting my enemies in the head. I was a gamer given a gift, and I'd mostly used it to do good. Sure, I'd been in a few fights, but killing a demon or Devil Rats wasn't morally reprehensible. They were pests. And demons. I'd have to be really messed up to have a moral problem with killing demons.

I paused, realizing I was shying away from the topic at hand once again. Killing humans. The drug dealers. Was it right? If they tried to kill me, sure. I could do that. Eye for an eye. No problem. In the heat of battle, it made sense. But here, I was planning to break into their house and fight them. It was so cold. So, wrong.

Was that why the law had differences between premeditated murder and murders of passion? Because planning and acting on a plan was so much worse? That you had to steel yourself to do it? But weren't these drug dealers doing the same? With their drugs.

Where do we—do I—draw the line? I was no saint. I wasn't going to say I would never kill. That only worked in comics. Hell, considering how much damage Batman did on a regular basis to the average mugger, in the real world, he'd eventually accidentally kill someone from a medical complication, an unknown heart condition, a seizure, a blood clot entering the brain. Humans were fragile.

But it didn't mean I was about to go around killing others. Or that I should. Somewhere, somehow, there should be a line. At least for me.

I sat on the couch, staring onto the busy city street while pondering exactly where I drew the line in my new life. Where do I, Henry Tsien, mage, decide it was okay to take a life.

***

Hours later, I looked up as dinner was set in front of me. This time around, it was Alexa's turn to cook, which resulted in tasty but simple tomato, ground-meat pasta. As the still-steaming dish sat in front of me, taunting my empty belly, Alexa took a seat before me and spoke.

"Are you okay?"

"Yes. I think. I guess, I just never really thought about what it meant," I said softly. "Getting jumped and attacked by orcs or werejackals was one thing. I could justify doing whatever I needed to do to guard myself. And if it was scary, well, what hasn't been? But breaking and entering… killing people. The morality of it is a lot greyer when it's real life."

Alexa cocked her head to the side for a time before she nodded slowly. "It's one thing I admire and pity about you, Henry. Your innocence, your optimism and belief in people. While we were taught that everyone is loved by God, we were also trained to kill, to see supernaturals as less than human. Even other humans, those who dabbled in magic and the supernatural world, were considered tainted, unworthy.

"It was simple, theoretically. I was a faith healer. It wasn't as if I was supposed to fight them directly. While we all received the training, for me, it was less real. Then I was sent to you, and we've interacted with—done quests—for the supernatural. Talked to them. Done wards for their newborns and light shows for their graduation parties. They stopped all being monsters, but…"

"But?"

"But the bad ones are still bad. The Templars are here to stop those who are bad, who are wrong. Whether it's dealing drugs or killing people, if they're human or supernatural. If they're doing evil, my job—our job is to stop them," Alexa said.

"But I'm not a Templar."

"No. You're not."

I rubbed my face again, picking up my fork to twirl the pasta around as a distraction. After a time, I shook my head and dropped it. "I don't think I can choose to do that, Alexa. I know what they're doing is wrong. I know it. But killing them when they're not trying to kill me, I can't do it."

"Then let's plan to capture them," Alexa said simply. "If we have time, I can have the Knights take them in."

"Kill them," I stated with some horror in my voice.

"Not necessarily," Alexa said. "I'm sure they'd have information we could use."

"Like?"

"Their supplier. Who they work for. Their goals," Alexa rattled off.

"Oh…" I could push her, ask what happened when all that information was given, when they had learned everything they wanted. But really, I knew that answer too. And somehow, I had to admit, I was willing to let it happen. Perhaps it was hypocritical of me, to condemn men to death but not want the blood itself on my hand. But if so, it was a level of hypocrisy I could live with. And sleep with.

"Capture." I prodded the pasta again and then firmly nodded. "If we're going to do that, I better get planning."

Alexa smiled at my words, nodding slightly and sitting backward. Off to the side, I caught Lily frowning slightly as she tapped away at her computer, but she said nothing, at least not yet.

It was only later that night when Alexa had retired for the evening and I had come back downstairs, my mind still whirling with minor alterations to the plan when the jinn spoke.

"Are you really okay with this?" Lily asked as I pushed the little robed mage and paladin miniatures around the board.

"What? The plan. Of course, I made it."

"Doing the Templars' bidding," Lily said, tapping her keyboard to pause her game and turn directly toward me. "It's not really your quest. You don't have any personal penalties for failing."

"Except I might lose Alexa."

"Except that," Lily said, conceding my point. "But while she might be friendly now, do remember that her job is to keep an eye on you and to keep you alive till you hit level one hundred, and the ring can come off."

"At which point everyone and their boss is going to come after me," I said flatly. "I remember. And that's why… That's why I need to do this."

Lily hummed slightly, prompting me to go on, and I sighed.

"I'm not a killer, Lily. I mean, sure. I've killed imps. And the demon. And Devil Rats and evil ravens. And those weird llama creatures," I said, ticking off the violence I'd conducted in my time. "But I'm not a killer. Not like her Templars. Or the orcs. Or the werejackals. I wasn't brought up to kill."

"So, you're going to make it clear to them you won't kill?" Lily asked, slightly incredulously. "How's that going to help you survive?"

"Because if I'm going to survive, I'm going to need to push myself, and killing them is easy. Simple. But my life isn't going to be simple, and this isn't going to be easy," I said slowly, reaching inside to explain a thought process I had barely grasped. "If—when I hit level one hundred, when the ring comes off, I'm going to have to fight them all. If I can learn to handle myself now with gloves on, maybe I'll be able to handle them all when the gloves come off."

Lily smiled sadly at me at my words but said nothing further. I knew—as she probably did—I had a naïve hope. But surviving when I hit level one hundred was a naïve hope. I already had two major groups gunning for me, and obviously more to come. But hope, naïve and hopeless as it may be, was all I had.

***

The drive to the drug house the next morning was quiet, tense. I found myself patting my coat repeatedly, a nervous motion as I tried to assess what the hell I was missing. It was stupid, since I had literally created a long list of everything I would need and ticked them off earlier this morning. Then I wiped down and burned anything that might be incriminating.

"Stop it. Nothing has changed since the last minute," Alexa said grumpily.

"Sorry." I put my hands down. "Right. In five minutes, I'll throw the glamour and illusion on us to hide who we are. I'll do the same with the car too, so they can't track the vehicle. Then—"

"Henry. We've gone over this a hundred times. We'll be fine," Alexa said, making me slowly fall silent. I knew she was right, but I felt the urge to snap at her, a feeling I pushed down with a surge of willpower that I was quite proud of. Truth be told, I knew I was being irrational.

"Right. Right." I fell silent, and a few moments later, I started going over the list of items I had brought with me.

"Five minutes," Alexa said, interrupting me as I mentally went over what I had brought for the umpteenth time.

I drew a deep breath and exhaled while channeling an illusion over the car. It wasn't a complex illusion, just minor changes like shifting the color of the car itself and the license plate along with removing any dents, scratches, and other, potentially identifiable material. After I sent a surge of mana into the car and completed the spell, I turned toward Alexa and nodded. Together, we tapped the small wooden enchantment I had created last night to store a simple glamour and illusion. In both cases, I went for boring and generic, making Alexa look older, brunette, and less striking while I made myself Caucasian, brunette, and older too.

As the car drew closer to the house, I took a moment to connect to the mirrors one last time to check that the three within were at their usual spots. Thankfully, they were, allowing us to carry on our nefarious task immediately.

Step one: Park the car and approach the house directly and cleanly, without acting suspicious and shifty. I made sure to grab my backpack and slung it over one shoulder, while Alexa carried her broken-down spear in a simple sports bag. When we approached the house, I moved to block Alexa from the view of any neighbors while casting a simple illusion spell over the house's video surveillance camera. A moment later, Alexa had the door open with her lockpicks.

I actually felt bad about my boast. Once I actually thought about the requirements to pick a lock magically, I realized I had neither the spells, the knowledge, nor the time to perfect an enchantable tool. Online videos showing how to move pins and tumblers were one thing, but having a force spell that could not only adjust the degree, angle, and speed of force applied to tiny little metal pieces was beyond me. Alexa had had a good laugh late last night when I started grumbling about the matter before she informed me about her skillset.

Step two was simple. Once inside, a quick scry verified our targets were still in the same location. While I did that, Alexa put together her spear, getting ready for the violence about to occur. At the same time, I ran through the spell formulas I'd created just for this moment before releasing the Scry spell. If all went well, no one was going to die.

Step three required actual action. I snuck up first, doing my best Sneaky Pete impression. Of course, I wasn't exactly trained to sneak, but I'd been a kid. Recalling the rules we'd used while playing ninja at home, I made sure not to walk in the middle of the staircase while crouching low as we ascended. When I reached the second floor, I poked my head around the corner of the staircase to see the three sprawled in the open living room, still staring at the TV.

Once again, I started a spell formula in my mind. This time I was prepping a Force Bolt, but instead of a single spherical container, I was going for a longer, cylindrical container, one that was slightly flexible. I called it my Force Rope, and in theory, the replication of the spell three times would let me wrap the three humans up without a problem.

The first two spells formed in my mind, then I began the third. Since these were all the same spell, it was difficult but not impossible, unlike triple casting three different spells. Here, at least, I just needed to concentrate on keeping the threads of mana and the spell formulas in mind.

Loud, incessant blaring of the horn from outside broke my concentration, forcing the third spell to come apart. I almost lost the other two as well, the feedback from the broken spell making me clench my teeth and let out a huff. Luckily, the noise I made was hidden by the continual honking.

"Shit. Is it delivery day?" a voice growled from above. Chairs creaked as our targets stood. I shared a wide-eyed, shocked look with Alexa as our plans came apart in moments. For a second, we both stood there in shock, footsteps coming closer before Alexa acted and rushed upward, jostling me aside gently and forcing me to struggle to hold the spells again.

"Wha—Urkk," the voice screamed, the squark and gurgled ending an auditory clue of what happened. I had no more time, no gap to consider our bad luck. It was time to act.

I strode upward, looking for and finding my targets. One was reaching for a shotgun down by his chair, the second was attempting to ward off Alexa's spear with his free hand while he vainly grasped for a handgun in his pants, and the other lay on the ground, his throat slashed. I dismissed the second, focusing on the first as I adjusted the range coordinates of my spell.

"Force Chain!" I called, releasing the spell with an auditory component. I held back the second spell, already weaving the spell formula to adjust the range to something a lot closer. Not that it was necessary. Alexa had cut the man's hand open, then swept in and kicked his bladder region, right on top of the gun which the gangster was vainly attempting to draw.

My Force Chain flew outward, wrapping the first gangster's arms and body around the lounge chair he had been sitting upon. He screamed as the chain yanked tight, plush and wooden components of the chair creaking as my hastily reconstructed spell formulas restricted his motion a little too much. He shouted in pain and surprise, a noise that set my teeth on edge. A Force Ball, located right in his mouth, worked as a useful if somewhat transparent ball gag.

As I turned toward Alexa and her opponents, I noticed she had thrust the spear into the second man's neck, this time nicking open veins and arteries. Gripping his throat, the man gurgled as his blood flowed out, unable to make much more noise than Alexa's first victim.

"Secure him!" Alexa snapped at me as I stared at the growing pool of blood. I twisted around and saw my own target had tipped his chair to the side and fallen to the ground, still bound tight as he futilely struggled toward his shotgun.

I rushed toward him and kicked the weapon away before I secured the man's feet together using a series of zip ties. I frowned, realizing I could either release him and then attempt to forcefully yank his arms together to secure them again or I could leave him as he was, tied to the chair by magic. I knew it wasn't the most secure method either. The chair was too large and plush, too pliant for there to be a truly secure binding. With a grimace, I made note to look into a sleeping spell before I recast a second Force Rope, sliding this one over both his shoulders and between his legs like a weird five-point harness.

"Come on!" Alexa snarled from downstairs. I refocused, listening to the garage doors sliding open downstairs, and hurried to the first floor, my feet making squelching sounds in the blood when I rushed past. My stomach roiled for a second, reminding me there were now two men who were dying, who I was leaving behind, but—

"I'll close the garage doors first. Have a Force Ball ready. I'll take the first person to come out. You deal with the second!" Alexa ordered me as she crouched beside the door to the garage, the garage remote still held tight in her hand. Almost immediately after it stopped grinding, she tapped the button, forcing it closed again. "Get ready."

I nodded, focusing within as I readied a Force Spear, rounding the tip to ensure it didn't kill the individual immediately. A part of me wondered if I should cast Scry to check out how many people we would be expecting, but we had only seconds left and no mirror in easy access. I discarded the idea and forced myself to draw a deep breath once again, the thrum of a readied spell riding in my mind.

"Mario!" a surprisingly high-pitched voice called from inside the garage. A moment later, the doorknob shook and the door swung open, revealing a surprised-looking human. Except, on second look, I noticed the creature had no philtrum beneath its nose, and its skin glowed slightly with a faint golden radiance. Before I could take in the creature, Alexa swung her spear at it. Only, a reflexive block with the sports bag he held in hand saved the creature from being skewered.

"Who are you!" The creature snarled, falling backward as he blocked Alexa's attacks with his bag. That golden radiance seemed to concentrate around its forehead, growing in intensity. With a snarl, I raised my hand and released the Force Spear before whatever spell, curse, or other ability was engaged.

Diwata (Level 38)
HP 138/138

The diwata jerked its head sideways in a vain attempt to dodge the Force Bolt at the last second. The Force Bolt clipped the side of its head, making the monster stumble backward, at which point Alexa's thrust tore into its shoulder. The initiate pushed forward as she attempted to keep the creature off balance, the pair entering the garage where she was shoulder-checked by a larger humanoid.

Immediately, I scrambled to the door to see Alexa pinned against wooden shelves of the garage and being punched repeatedly by a linebacker-sized orc, his polyurethane sports jacket sporting the logo of a familiar football team. But I had little time to watch, for the diwata had turned its attention toward me, the glow returning to its forehead.

"Shield!" I snarled, my hand rising and fingers splaying, and my shield took the blast of magical energy straight on. I staggered as the creature pressed its advantage and continually pummeled my spell's screen with its own magic. Over the brilliance of the attack, I squinted in a desperate attempt to see what was happening within.

Unable to see past my now-opaque shield, I raised my other hand and began to cast a Force Bolt, using the simpler version of my spell to allow me to multiply the number of Force Bolts in it. I then launched them blindly through the garage door, hoping Alexa was still in her corner. For a moment, the pressure on my Shield relented but then returned twofold. Cracks appeared all across it as my concentration wavered, my mana draining rapidly.

"Damn it!" I growled and held both hands up, flooding mana through them to reinforce the Shield. It held again, but a short, strangled scream from within let me know my friend needed my help. Fast. I swallowed, warm iron-tasting liquid sliding down my throat from a bit tongue as I forced myself to focus.

I couldn't see within to cast a spell. I couldn't even divert mana to do so. There was no guarantee my Shield and mana would last longer than the diwata within, but I had to act. I had to push in.

Push.

Oh. I kicked myself mentally and focused on the spell formula, searching quickly within my mind for the appropriate section. It was strange, how the channeled spell seemed to have a physical presence within my mind, like a glowing text twisted and wrapped together that mana flowed through. A channel I only needed to locate and adjust. In this case, the positioning portion of the spell.

I tied off other parts of the spell, fixing the sections dictating the shield's size and orientation. Using my body as the initial point for the coordinates, I pushed my now-tied-off shield forward, changing its location quickly. I basically turned the entire Force Shield into a moving projectile, one I constantly fed with mana. A loud intake of breath and a sudden pressure informed me my actions had been noticed, but too late. The impact of the Shield on the diwata's body rocked me mentally, but thankfully, the creature's attack cut off soon after impact.

I didn't relent even then. Drawing on my mana further, I shoved the Shield forward, pinning the creature onto the hood of the parked vehicle in the garage. I felt the sudden loss of pressure on the top, even as my Shield refused to move farther as its legs were crushed and trapped. The diwata let out a strangled scream even as the spell slowly dissipated. I had no time for the monster as I rushed into the garage from the house and spotted Alexa.

The initiate was doing less than well, her shoulder pinned to the wall via her own spear. The pair struggled over the shaft of it, the larger orc looming over the initiate as it dragged the spear relentlessly from Alexa's grasp.

"DIE!" I shouted as I flung my hand up and called forth an Iceball. I mentally adjusted the spell, making the container slightly sharper and more pointed, and I launched the attack into the back of the orc's head. Unfortunately, my scream alerted the creature, and he ducked even lower, letting the Iceball impact right above Alexa's wide eyes.

"Not me!" Alexa screamed but took the momentary lapse in concentration by the orc to launch a knee between its legs. The orc folded even farther, his grip loosening on the spear which allowed Alexa a chance to rip it from her shoulder properly. Even as she readied to stab the spear downward, I launched a Force Spear into the orc's lower back, the attack digging through his body and entering the bent-over creature's chest cavity from behind.

As the orc tumbled away from Alexa after a forceful push, she looked up with gratitude at me and then threw the spear. I twisted to the side, only to see the diwata stagger backward, its legs healed again with the spear in its chest.

"What?" My jaw dropped open, knowing I had seen and felt its legs being crushed by my Shield. With a shake of my head, I stumbled toward it and ripped the spear out of its body, then slammed it into the monster's chest again, piercing its heart. The creature spasmed once more and stopped, and I found myself exhaling with relief. Unlike the diwata, the orc lay on the ground, bleeding out while Alexa held a glowing white hand up to her shoulder.

"You okay?"

"No!" Alexa snapped. I nodded dumbly, staggering toward her and raising my hand to cast Heal. "Don't bother. The chainmail vest kept most of it from going in. My healing will have it fixed in a few minutes. You keep your mana."

I nodded dumbly again, grateful I didn't have to tap my already low reserves of mana.

"I'll…" I paused, considering what to do and then pointed up the stairs. Alexa's jerky nod made me smile grimly as I strode up the stairs, my heart still pounding and my hands trembling. Only when I got upstairs and ascertained the last remaining, living member of the criminal group was still tied up did I slump to the ground, my hands trembling.

Oh gods. She had nearly died. I had nearly died.

Chapter 12

It took me a few minutes to get over the sudden violence, the death we had brought upon these living, breathing, sentient humans and supernaturals. Once the initial shock wore off and the adrenaline had reduced, I stood and looked out the window. Thankfully, there seemed to be no movement from the other houses, no twitching curtains or busybody neighbors. It seemed that while our little fight had seemed intensely noisy to me, it had not drawn undue attention. Either that or someone was on the phone already making calls to the police.

In the time I took to settle, I noticed I was not the only one who had calmed—our prisoner was lying on the ground quietly, staring at me. Occasionally, I glimpsed him straining against the Force Chain before relaxing having gotten nowhere. With a grim smile, I stepped past him to collect the weapons. I unloaded the shotgun and the pistols gingerly, pocketed the bullets, and tossed the weapons into a shopping bag I had located.

"Henry?" Alexa called up to me as she ascended the stairs. "Oh, good idea. Did you find the money yet?"

"Not yet," I said. "I was, uhh, not yet." I flushed slightly, deciding not to inform her about my momentary loss of control. I'm sure she would understand. She had the previous few times I'd had a "blind moment." But still, my pride had taken sufficient battering today. "I'll take a look."

"Sure. But mind dismissing his ball gag first?"

I gestured toward the man, dismissing the simple woven ball of power that had been affixed to his mouth. The man spat and wiped his face against his shoulder once again, clearing the drool from his mouth as Alexa yanked the chair up. Only a slight hiss from the initiate gave any indication she had been injured earlier. Well, other than the bloody shirt she wore.

"Now, let's talk."

"You think I'm scared of you, girlie?"

The loud crack of the spear haft when it struck the man followed me into the bedroom as I walked in. I shut the door, blocking out the sounds from the questioning, and I began to inspect the room. Well, ransack it was perhaps a better word. Of course, I made sure to put on a new pair of gloves first, the original pair looking somewhat worse for wear after our earlier battles.

Unfortunately, the room itself held little of interest unless you had an ardent desire for smelly male socks and underwear. Which, I guess, might be a kink, but I would also guess it was an unprofitable one to cater to. For a second, I almost pulled out my phone to check, but using the greater level of self-control that studying magic had provided me, I focused on my search.

When I was done with the room, I moved to the next, and it was there I found the jackpot. A single, large safe sat closed in the closet, awaiting a master safe cracker. Of course, that was not me.

"Alexa, got a safe here," I called to the initiate when I walked out.

Alexa smiled at that, turning back toward the human with a predatory look. Bleeding from a split lip and broken nose, the man glared at Alexa and kept his mouth shut.

"Check their wallets. Or around the safe. I'm willing to bet these dumbasses have it written somewhere," Alexa said to me, her eyes focused on the man. When he glanced downward, toward the stairways, Alexa snorted. "Or maybe the fridge?"

The man's eyes widened slightly, enough that even I caught it.

"They really that dumb?" I muttered as I trooped down the stairs, taking care not to walk through the growing puddle of blood. I knew we had to do something about all that, but right now, it escaped me. I didn't exactly have any useful spells for such a situation.

In minutes, I was back upstairs holding the Post-it Note with the combination that had been handily stuck to the fridge with a Walk Away Fatty fridge magnet. I wondered which one of the three had purchased it as I spun the safe. It took me three tries, once for going the wrong way and the second for missing a number, before I had the safe open. I guess if they had been smart enough to do things like understand basic operational security, they wouldn't be crooks.

Or dead.

As I reached within to pull the stacked cash into the black sports bag I had located, my hand started trembling again. I forcibly drew a breath and exhaled, taking control of my stray thoughts and putting them aside for now. Better to avoid it.

"You think you're going to get away with this? You don't know who you're dealing with! They'll kill you. They're not human!" the man shouted, struggling in his chair. "You're crazy."

"Why don't you tell me all about it then? Who these people are," Alexa said, taunting the man.

"You don't get it. They'll kill me. And you. Or worse!"

"What's worse than death? Well, beyond torture," Alexa said, and a slightly high yelp followed her words soon after. "Hush… you don't want me to have to gag you again, do you?"

"They'll tear your soul out. They use magic!"

"You're really not very smart, are you?" I said when I walked back in the room, weighed down by the hefty bag of ill-gotten funds. "What do you think I was casting?"

The man paused, looked down at how he was held tight and then started thrashing around in his chair, screaming about the devil. Alexa grabbed a sock and shoved it into his mouth, stuffing it in before she glared at me.

"You had to remind him."

"How was I to know he was that stupid!" I said.

"You just opened their safe using a Post-it Note from their kitchen."

"Touché." With a glance at the now-still, cooling corpses, I said slowly, "We might have a problem."

"Not a problem. I've already called my supervisors. They're on their way."

"Isn't this, you know, part of your test?"

"No," Alexa said with a frown. "Why would I need to be tested on how to dispose of their corpses? Don't you know certain supernatural bodies need to be carefully handled? A mutant zombie thrown into the nearby river could cause significant problems. Better to let the experts handle it. Even Templar Ignis would not fail me over the proper use of our resources and training."

"Oh," I said, blinking. Well, duh. "So, about him?"

"They'll handle it," Alexa said. With the man secured, she walked to the couch and sat, drawing a bag toward her. From it, she extracted a pair of wallets. She opened them and perused the cards within, frowning slightly as she tossed out the driver's licenses from both.

"Problem?"

"Yes," Alexa said.

When she refused to elaborate, I walked over to take a look at the licenses. Oh. That made sense. They were from Ashland, down south. While not technically the capital of crime in our little state, it only was a technicality because no politician was going to give out those kinds of awards. It'd be like delivering a Darwin award to the mother of a child. Cruel and unnecessary.

"There a big supernatural presence down there?" I asked Alexa who let out a choked laugh, one that stopped only when she realized I was not joking.

"Is the ocean wet?" Alexa asked rhetorically. "But it's more than that. The supernaturals who hold sway there, they're the worst kind. Ancient vampires, gangs of shifters, blood sorcerers, and demonic cults all thrive in that city.

Doesn't matter how many times the mages or the Templars or anyone else cleanses the place, they just come back."

"You don't stay?" I asked.

"Limited resources," Alexa said. "We'd need to devote a significant number of people to just keep the lid on it. Never mind the fact that a small presence would just be killed in weeks. Anyway, there's always another demon cult, another ancient monster waking from its sleep, or an artifact that needs containing somewhere else."

I grimaced at the last, knowing it was a rather pointed example. Not that we had caused much trouble, Lily and me, but the potential for trouble was what made them fear us, forced them to devote their forces. Though, sometimes, I wondered if they really needed as many watchers as I felt there were.

"The drugs?"

"Are downstairs, in the van. I checked and then left them there," Alexa said.

I nodded and frowned at the bodies and the slowly growing pool of blood. With no trouble coming, I raised my hand and cast Freeze at the corpses, lowering their body temperature and freezing the blood in the bodies and on the ground. Might as well make things easier.

Alexa offered me a slight nod at that, intent on studying the content of the wallets. I watched her for a second more before deciding to head downstairs. Better to hang out in the living room, even if the curtains were drawn, than this room with its corpses. Better to put it out of mind, what I had done.

Sometimes, I wondered if I had made the right wish. If, having given up my mundane life, I also had to give up some of the same morality, some of the beliefs I had previously held. I'd become a killer, someone who took lives without thought. And even if they weren't good people, I sometimes wondered what it meant about me that I was still willing to do so.

* * *

In a few hours, Alexa's people arrived. It did not take long for them to kick us out, happy to agree we had done our part in tracking down and dealing with the latest shipment. This was but a finger in the dike, but it was sufficient, at least, to be considered completed for her quest, especially since we left them a living, breathing source. Surprisingly, they did not ask about the bag of money I carried out. Then again, it was possible Alexa had informed them of its eventual destination—the coffers of the Brixton Orphanage. Killing two birds with one stone.

Later that evening when Alexa left to donate the ill-gotten funds and check on the repairs, my thoughts once again spiraled. It was a light kick on my shin that drew my attention back from contemplating the depths of my moral depravity.

"Stop it," Lily said.

"Stop what?"

"Brooding. So you killed some bad people. It's not as if you're flaying babies to make a book cover," the jinn said as she sat on the living room table across from me, propping her head on her hands.

"That's an interesting example."

"I've had a lot of owners," Lily said unapologetically. "And you, my dear, are nowhere near the worst. Not even the most naïve. Those rarely survive the week."

I grunted, rubbing my leg. "But killing—"

"Is bad. I know," Lily said with a sniff. "That's what your modern society says, but then they still teach your soldiers how to kill, give guns to your policemen, and have the death sentence for crimes."

"So, what? Violence is part of humanity?"

"Violence is part of the world," Lily said. "Even your vegans kill plants to survive. Ask any treant and they'd call that as a bad if not worse crime than humanity's war. Humans have killed each other all their lives, for all sorts of reasons. Your body fights off viruses and bacteria every moment of your life to keep you alive. Killing, removing the threats from society's body, it's not wrong."

"But what right do I have to make that decision?" I said, grimacing.

"Did they try to kill you?"

"After we broke in!"

"After they started dealing in a dangerous, nasty drug."

"Well… yes," I said slowly. "But—"

"Did you check first? Did you see them selling the drugs? Did they go for their guns first?"

"Yes…"

"Then," Lily said, tapping me on the head, "You did your homework. You verified they were bad guys. You even went in with a plan to avoid killing them. That things went wrong is not your fault. They went for their guns. The rest was natural consequence."

"I just…" I opened my mouth to protest and was shushed by fingers on my lips. I glared at the jinn, tempted to bite the fingers which were hastily removed.

"Henry, stop thinking about how you should be feeling. Actually consider. Are you actually upset you killed them or upset because you believe you should be upset?"

"That—"

"Think! Or feel," Lily commanded me, and I grunted, leaning backward and crossing my arms over my chest. Still, I eventually repressed the surge of anger and actually considered her words.

Did I really feel bad? Actually feel bad? Maybe a little. Not for them but for whatever family they might have had. But they'd made their decision. They'd chosen to live their lives by the sword. And so, was it so surprising they'd die by the sword? Or spear in this case. Did I feel bad they'd died?

No.

I was just upset because somehow, somewhere, I thought I should be. I'd done the best I could to stop them from dying, from being killed. It hadn't played out the way I'd wanted, and now it was over. They were dead, but it wasn't something I truly regretted. Once I realized that, I found my chest relaxing slightly, tension I had carried in my neck disappearing. I grimaced, realizing what it meant but dismissed the thought a moment later. Fine. Maybe I was so focused on the type of person I should be that I got myself churned up for not meeting this random belief.

But...

"I'm still worried," I said, touching my heart. "I... They died, and they left people who will grieve for them. And I know it's their choice, but..."

"But?"

"But it's not about them," I said through a breath, my hands no longer trembling. I looked at Lily, my eyes wide, and bent to kiss her head suddenly. "Thank you. But I've got to go."

Lily looked shocked for a second at the kiss as I walked toward the exit, fishing in my pocket for my mobile phone while putting my jacket on.

"Ma? Everything's fine! I just wanted to see if you're free for dinner tonight. No, it's fine. No, I'm not getting married. Ma!"

***

Later that evening—much later—I returned and found Lily seated at her usual place in the living room, tapping away at the keyboard and moving her mouse around, occasionally shifting her gaze to the other laptop. I shut the door silently and tiptoed toward the stairs, not wanting to disturb her. I nearly made it too.

"Did you tell them?"

I paused, hand on the banister. I considered the evening—dinner with my family where my mom had cooked an extra helping of stewed soya pork, steamed bak choy, fried fish, and rice for my sudden appearance; how my parents had spoken of their work, the usual grind and politics of working in the office; and we had, as always, stayed away from the touchy topic of my employment—or lack of it. We had talked and reminisced, gossiped about my siblings and then spent the rest of the evening watching an old kung fu movie, indulging in a shared love for schlocky Shaw brothers' entertainment, but—

"No." My fingers squeezed the railing as I recalled how I lost the nerve time after time. How I failed to let them know what I was doing. The risks I was taking. The potential visit they might receive one day. "I couldn't. They were so happy to see me, and…"

"And?"

"And I didn't want them in this world," I said suddenly, heat growing in my voice. "It's beautiful. And amazing. Wondrous and magical. But they were worried because I was taking the bus home, afraid I'd get mugged on public transit. If I told them, they'd tell my siblings, and I can't—I won't, get them involved. This world, it's not something I want them in."

"It's hidden for a reason," Lily said, agreeing with me. "The world has moved on, with peace and civil order for everyone but the few and the strange."

I couldn't help but feel the corner of my lips twist at her words. I offered the jinn one last nod before I made my way upstairs to my bed, a part of me amused to realize I was part of the few and strange now. But perhaps before bed, I'd write a letter. One that might explain matters a little more. A just in case, for when and if things went bad.

Chapter 13

"Well, that was a decent attempt. At destroying the neighborhood," Caleb said acerbically, pointing to the revised ritual diagram I had created. I stared at the corrections I had made to the test ritual he had asked me to look over as part of my studies this morning. "You've got channels of power flowing in circles without an exit here, here, and here."

I blinked, following his fingers to where they traced the floating mana formulas I had materialized from the ritual circle as I pumped in a trickle of mana. I watched the flow of it, noting where his finger traced the air and the slowly growing density of mana at the locations and winced.

"Remember, always have an escape valve. No ritual is guaranteed to be done right," Caleb said. "Now release it."

I nodded and altered the formula, releasing the trapped mana back into the ether where the dangerous build-up dispersed. Unlike what most people would think, I didn't power rituals from my own mana. I kickstarted and guided it with my mana, but a ritual, unlike a spell, actually banked on drawing external mana sources to fuel it. After all, why go through all the trouble of carving, formulating, and enchanting a ritual circle if you could cast the spell yourself? You'd save yourself dozens of steps.

No, rituals were made to be powered from external power sources. It was why low-powered sorcerers with a ritual circle were dangerous. Why a runaway ritual was so dangerous. Of course, most rituals just collapsed in on themselves as the materials used to make the circle gave out before a world-ending event happened, but still, the resulting backlash from an exploding ritual circle could—as Caleb pointed out—level a city block. Not all those gas explosions out there are actual gas explosions.

"But aren't those escape valves, the gaps in the formula, weaknesses in the ritual itself?" I asked.

"They are, but if your concern is strength, perhaps you should not be attempting such a ritual anyway," Caleb said. "Just like a door is an entrance to a house, you wouldn't build a house without one, now would you? Fit your ritual strength to what you expect to contain, but always build the door."

I grunted, deciding not to argue further with Caleb. Yet, in the corners of my mind where Lily had stuffed my magical knowledge, I could see formulas and spells, rituals that had been created without any such escape valves. Bindings that were meant to last through the test of time.

"If you're done?" Caleb said, and without waiting for me to answer him, he swept his hand across the ritual, dispersing it. Immediately, the ritual circle began to shift to his commands, adjusting as the circle's enchantments and formulas adjusted to what he had in mind. It was a casual showcase of power and mastery that made me envy the mage.

"Begin."

***

Hours later, I stumbled out of the lesson with spell formulas floating in my mind, arranging and rearranging themselves while I tried to piece it all together. My brain hurt but in a good way, as borrowed knowledge slowly assimilated and I grasped what had been given to me. I was still miles away from being an actual apprentice, but…

Class: Mage

Level 23 (37% Experience)

Known Spells: Light Sphere, Force Spear, Force Shield, Force Fingers, Alter Temperature, Gong, Gust, Heal, Healing Ward, Link, Track, Fix, Ward,

Glamour, Illusion, Summon, Iceball, Fireball, Prism, Empower, Scry & Observe, Confuse

Magical Skillset

Mana Flow: 4/10

Mana to Energy Conversion: 4/10

Spell Container: 4/10

Spatial Location: 4/10

Spatial Movement: 4/10

Energy Manipulation: 4/10

Biological Manipulation: 3/10

Matter Manipulation: 2/10

Summoning: 1/10

Duration: 5/10

Rituals: 2/10

Multi-Casting: 2/10

Enchanting: 2/10

Interestingly enough, my spells had not widened significantly. Oh, I had a few more. Prism was actually just a variation of the initial Light Sphere ward but one that basically allowed me to play flashlight in multiple colors. The light itself did nothing beyond split in color, so it was more a utility spell like Fix or Track than a combat spell. But, as I've come to realize, utility spells were probably the most damn useful spells ever. It made me realize how few of them actually existed in my old RPG books. Murder hobos, we all were.

Then again, basic enchanting, which was a new added skillset, probably took care of most needs. After all, the need to layer spells on enchanted objects—like my wooden blocks—was what would make magic truly useful for the populace. When magic—or technology—reached the masses, that's when change really happened. It amused me, somewhat, that I only got Empower now, after I'd gained some basic knowledge of enchanting. Then again, perhaps it was because I had worked out how to enchant myself that Empower was available. The spell basically allowed me to temporarily place an enchantment on an object, bypassing the need to carve or otherwise layer spells on it by using the spell structure of Empower itself as the container for the enchanted spell.

Scry & Observe was just an upgrade on the Scry spell itself, a more complex version that would help with some of the problems I had encountered while using the basic spell. Among other things, I could link the spell across multiple physical objects at the same time, giving me much greater diversity. I knew the next step would actually give me a floating, observing eye, one not linked to any physical surface but that would take a bit to get there.

Lastly, and what I was somewhat stoked about was Confuse. It was my latest spell which had opened a whole new area of magic to me: mind magic. Of course, confuse was the simplest spell and basically bombarded the target's mind with numerous, random thoughts. When I'd woken up this morning with the spell in mind, I could not help but chuckle at it. First devised thousands of years ago, the spell had not altered much in the intervening years until the onset of radio and television. The latest iteration was a minor update, one that would allow me to pull from multiple, random electronic signals, turning my target into basically a giant television receiver.

I had actually considered playing around with the spell when I had time, using some of the knowledge I had garnered from Heal to create targeted neurochemical imbalances and neuron overfiring. Only problem was, I wasn't actually clear what the various portions of the spell did or, for that matter, how to alter the spell without say, blowing up someone's head.

On top of that of course was the issue of bypassing an individual's natural aura resistance. A spell like Confusion worked because it came at things in a slightly sideways fashion, but the sheer mana required to make the spell work was staggering. Unlike, say, Force Bolt, I had to directly bypass my target's aura to have the spell affect them. And while Heal did that too, in most cases, the individual either trusted me to do so and thus "opened" their aura or were unconscious. It basically made the cost lower, though, as I knew from experience, not insignificant. Either way, Confuse now gave me a way to deal with individuals without potentially having to hit, punch, or otherwise hurt them.

Whistling, I made my way back toward the house, only to be brought to a halt by an impatiently waiting Alexa.

"Where have you been?" she demanded.

"Class."

"Why weren't you answering your phone?" Alexa asked, pointing at her parked car. I scrambled to get in as she ducked within.

"Uhh…" I reached for my phone and stared at the blank screen. "Crap. Forgot to charge it. What's the problem?"

"There's an issue at the orphanage. The contractors have damaged the ritual bindings even more," Alexa said, and her lips thinned before she continued. "The abbess mentioned the children are really feeling uneasy now."

I nodded at her words, not surprised. Children were, generally, more sensitive than adults. It mostly had to do with their aura strength being significantly lower but also a wider acceptance of the world. That, unfortunately, came with a cost. It was also the reason old, cantankerous bastards tended to be fine living in haunted locations.

"Is it open?"

"Do you think I'd wait if it was?" Alexa asked with a curl of her lip. I blinked and then nodded, accepting the sense in her words.

"Any further clues about what is in there?" I asked while running through our options. Thankfully, I carried my backpack full of materials around everywhere these days, so at least I had some enchanting material to start with.

"I'm told the information is not necessary for the successful completion of the mission."

I coughed slightly, noting the frostiness in her tone. Still, I knew better than to voice my dissatisfaction. Not at this moment anyway. We had bigger fish to fry. Anyway, I would hopefully have an answer in a few days.

As we turned the corner of the street leading to the orphanage, I let out a low hiss. No surprise there was almost no foot traffic. As a mage, I was significantly more sensitive, but the pervasive chill and the hairs that stood on my forearm were something even a mundane would pick up. Unconsciously, those who could would avoid this road, leaving the area devoid of life. Even those flying rats—pigeons that is—had left the surroundings, content to peck away at discarded refuse somewhere else.

"Can the children live somewhere else?" I asked, holding my hand outward and flushing the air in front of me with my own mana. With my Mana Sight, I could see the way my mana—a pure, clean blue—interacted with the ambient mana in the air. It slowly darkened as the chill that emanated from the orphanage actively infused the newly released energy. I stopped my little experiment and looked back at the building, noting the now-visible glow of the shorted ritual circles. No surprise that a well-made ritual circle didn't glow like a Christmas tree—or a broken one—did.

"Not long-term. If we moved them out, it'd be a flag for the state," Alexa said, crossing her arms. "The abbess is planning an impromptu 'road trip,' but it's not a long-term solution. There's too many of them."

I grunted, accepting her words. Good thing it was still good enough weather that no one was going to jump up and down if they took the kids out camping or something.

"I'll see what I can do." I got out of the car with Alexa after she parked. Together, we hurried within to locate the abbess. The woman, unlike my prejudicial and preconceived notions, was neither old and dumpy nor wrinkly and grumpy. She was, in fact, just another boomer woman in a nun's habit. Take away the habit, and I probably wouldn't have given her a second look.

"Magus Tsien," the Abbess said, inclining her head slightly. "I understand you might have a solution for us?"

"I do?" I said, then coughed. "I do. Right. So we've got two problems. The overflow into the streets and the kids."

"And the breaking seal."

"That's for later," I said, waving my hand to dismiss the abbess's words. "I'll need to do a lot more study on that, but I should be able to offer the kids something to bolster their aura. And you all too."

"The staff do not require such devices," the abbess said flatly, and I nodded. Fine. I was sure they had their own methods of dealing with it. "What do you require?"

I paused, considering my options. "Let's start by creating a warding circle in a few rooms. Maybe your cafeteria and gym? Places you can bunk the children down in and where they can congregate. It'll help in the short-term while I work out portable shields."

The abbess led me to the gym immediately. It amused me that the gym also consisted of a stage, a place where the children could put on little performances for each other, but my amusement fled quickly when I reached out with my senses to test the surroundings. Damn, there was a lot of bad mana. Even if I locked everything out, I'd need to figure out a mana scrubber of some sort. Though I guess I could let the kids' own natural resistances slowly cleanse it.

Or maybe not.

"Do you have a woodshop? Or welding equipment? I'll need solder, wood, paint, and any brushes you can gather," I said directly to the Abbess who nodded her head and strode off to get going. I turned toward Alexa next while fishing out a notepad from my backpack. "I'm going to give you a shopping list. Do me a favor and pick it up from El? And swing by the house to pick up my mortar and pestle."

Orders given, I sat in the middle of the gym and started figuring out the ritual of protection. Luckily, I knew quite a few thanks to the knowledge stuffed into my head. I just had to modify the rituals slightly to take in our surroundings and ensure it worked harmoniously. I really, really needed to work on some formation flags. Sometimes, stealing—sorry, borrowing—from other magical conventions could make my life easier, but, right now, I had to work with what I had.

Unconsciously, I continued to sample the corrupted as I worked, running the mana through my system and cleansing bits and pieces as I sat there. Corrupted mana was weird. It didn't directly injure in the short-term. It was generally a milder poison, one that affected mental and emotional states first before it harmed the body. Exact effects depended on the mana corruption itself, making individuals grumpy or tired or irate. Mild headaches were part symptom, part defense mechanism on a body and soul's part. Long-term exposure to corrupt mana on the other hand could lead to fomori, to twisted and corrupted humans, but that kind of effect took years.

The abbess arrived first and deposited my requirements. I ignored her, my hands held out before me as I slowly manipulated the spell formula only I could see. No point in making it visible, so I kept the entire thing visible only to those with the sight. However, to my surprise, I noted she was staring at the space where the formula hung, the model ritual circle slowly rotating as I flooded the construct with mana.

"Interesting. So the rumors are true. You really are not classically trained."

"Nope." I slowly clapped my hands together, dispersing the formula. It worked. Now, I just needed the materials from Alexa, and I could begin. "Did you need anything?"

"Do you have a timeline?"

"When it's done?" I shrugged my shoulders. "Placing the ritual itself should be an hour or two of work. Figure an hour of prep once Alexa is back. Then I've got to repeat it for at least one more room. In between, I'll need to work out how to contain or, better, scrub the mana the building is emanating."

The Abbess frowned. "The building?"

"Yup. The ritual circle is broken but not completely. It's like a live wire that's been stripped, shooting sparks from the stripped areas but still functioning," I said, shaking my head. "If you haven't already fired your contractors, you should do it immediately. And then hire someone actually qualified."

"We have done so," the abbess said stiffly. "Standard regulations are not to use uncertified supernatural assets, but matters have progressed."

"Great. Next, this is going to be a lot easier if you tell me what I'm trying to contain."

"That information is restricted."

"I just—"

"It is restricted even from me, Magus Tsien," the abbess said, her brows lowering. "I have no direct knowledge of what is below us."

"And indirectly?"

"Rumors. Hearsay."

"Better than nothing," I said.

"Really? If you were to take insufficient precautions because of what I said, would it be better?"

"No, but I won't make that mistake," I said softly. "So…"

"A spirit. A powerful one, not malevolent by nature," the Abbess said, waving her hand around to indicate the mana overflow. I had to agree. Cold and disturbing as it might be, it was not actively dangerous. If it had been, we'd be in a lot more trouble. "But not a friend of humanity."

"Thank you. If there's nothing else, I should work on the formula for the individual works though," I said.

The Abbess nodded, indicating she would inform me when Alexa made her way back.

Once I was left alone, I sat silent in thought, turning over the information provided to me. In the end, I dismissed it. It didn't matter, not for what I needed to do now.

***

Pendants. Those were the simplest to make. A small wooden or metal strip with enchanted spell forms within. The enchantment itself was a variation of the Force Shield spell I had, just with the entire "force" section stripped out and replaced with a modified Healing Ward. I wasn't actively trying to heal them, of course, but trigger the body's intrinsic aura, increasing its effectiveness and reinforcing it with the Shield aspect.

Unfortunately, while an individual's aura was technically part of their body and thus could be healed, my own healing spell wasn't very targeted. It did help that certain spells—like Confusion and Track—had active components within their spell formula that dealt with an aura. The former to bypass, and the latter to target. It meant I could pull relevant portions of the spell together with my Shield, Heal, and Ward options to cobble together a badly made spell.

With a gesture, I finalized the spell formula and cast it, letting the spell rotate in the air in front of me, fully visible.

Aura Shield
Synchronicity 89%
Efficiency 41%

"41%?" I muttered, staring at the glowing numbers. Given a little more time and effort, I was sure I could raise the efficiency by another 20 percent at least. I knew there was a lot of wasted power, areas I'd taken from other spells that had no place in this one.

"Exactly why do you need hob dung?" Alexa asked, dropping packages by my side.

"Part of the ritual," I replied. I took a look at the packages, sorting them quickly before I pushed the bag back toward Alexa. "Can you grind the first five ingredients together and then mix them into the paint?"

"The first five..." Alexa's eyebrows furrowed as she stared at the list in her hand. "That includes the dung."

"Unless you want me to stop carving pendants," I said, gesturing at the strip of wood that sat waiting for my first attempt.

"For the children?"

"For the children."

"I hate you."

I flashed Alexa a grin as I picked up the hot soldering iron and leaned forward toward the wood. Ah, the privileges of being the specialized help.

***

By the time I was done with my first working wooden pendant, Alexa had the paint ready.

"Put this on." I tossed the block to her underhand.

Alexa frowned, gripping the four-inch strip in hand and turning it around. "How?"

"Drill a hole, thread some string," I said, waving my hand absently as I focused on the paint. It looked like the right color. "Just don't mess up the runes. Oh, and if you can drill more holes in the wood strips, I can work around them next time."

Grumbling to herself, Alexa quickly processed the wooden strip and dropped it around her neck. She tilted her head from side to side, as if trying to hear a difference. I ignored her though, since I knew it worked. After all, I had made it. And yes, tested it.

I picked up the bucket of paint and brush, muttering the spell to myself while I considered where to start. Over the entrance doors so it had the best chance to dry, and if someone walked in on me I wouldn't lose too much work? Or start in the middle of the wall to get a nice flow going?

Decisions, decisions, decisions.

Muttering to myself, I decided on the door itself and grabbed a chair to stand on. Time to get started.

"You could use a ladder…"

"Ladder smadder."

"What does that mean?"

Meh. I ignored her, propping the chair and standing to reach for the top of the doorframe. Now, where was I? Right, creating a multi-stage, room-wide ritual to contain mana from a decades-old spirit with store-bought paint, dung, and moss.

***

Breathing was hard. My chest locked tight as I dragged on the dregs of the mana within my body. The ritual had taken more from me to charge than I had expected, the corrupted mana within the building flowing into me at a significantly lower degree than normal. It meant I could not regenerate what I had used as efficiently, draining my internal stores further. And unfortunately, I didn't have a mana battery of any sort, at least nothing I could drain myself. Stupid.

Still, as I painted the last circle and dotted it, I could feel the ritual snap into place. For a second, it stuttered as it drew upon my body for its initial charge and found my lack of mana disturbing. Rather than let the ritual fail, I bit my tongue and spat the blood directly onto the paint, watching the ritual flare back to life as it drew forth the very life essence I had gifted it. Of course, it wasn't just any blood, it was blood that had a touch of my life essence. It was the reason why blood magic wasn't something you could practice on yourself continuously. It wasn't blood in terms of scientific blood but the life essence, the portion of your soul that burned and thrived. Do it too often, and you'd basically die.

But for a short burst of fuel? Nothing like it.

"Henry?" Alexa's voice came from behind me, hesitant but concerned. I ignored it as I focused on the ritual to make sure I hadn't made a mistake. Given the boost from my blood, the ritual finally managed to draw from the corrupted ambient mana and sprang to life, a protective bubble spreading across the surfaces of the room. It locked the mana within, stopping the flow of the corrupted mana from entering.

With a thump, I sat down and put my head between my legs, breathing deeply.

"Henry?" Alexa said, more urgently now.

"Pain killers." I groaned around my knees as I tried to focus on my breathing. Right. Smaller room next time.

Dry-swallowing the pills proffered, it took me another half hour before I felt human enough to speak. By that time, the corrupted mana in the room had decreased significantly since the children who had been brought into the room slowly cleansed the mana through their own auras. As I looked around, I noted how many kids there were. And the looks they were giving me.

"Do I have two heads or something?" I muttered to myself.

Alexa, hanging close by, smiled wryly. "No, but you're a mage. And they're Templars-to-be."

"Right. We're all evil."

"It's a little more complicated than that."

"But for the kids, it works out to that, eh?" I said, crossing my arms grumpily and glaring at the kids. It made more than a few look away, though one particular redheaded young teen met my gaze fearlessly. She even wrinkled her freckled nose at me.

"Just about. How's your mana pool?" Alexa asked softly. A glance upward—which really made no sense, since it was always there—and I answered her.

"Twenty-one percent. I'm going to need to meditate."

"Okay," Alexa said simply, and I flopped straight down on the floor again. After a moment's consideration, I stood back up and hunted down a more comfortable chair while ignoring the little snickers from the kids. I was no damn Buddhist monk.

Hours later, I finished the twelfth pendant and felt a crack in my back when I stretched. I tossed the enchanted device to Alexa while I took a look at the snaking sunlight from the high windows.

"This is going too slow," I said to Alexa when she got back.

"Agreed. There's nearly fifty children, and you've only got twelve done," Alexa tapped her lips. "Suggestions?"

"Money. I can't be the only one to have come up with the idea of aura-reinforcing enchantments. If we go shopping with the d… donated money, we should be able to find something," I said. "Or you will."

"What are you going to do?" Alexa asked with a frown.

"There's a fence that needs fixing. At the least, I should see if it's possible," I said.

"Pretty sure it isn't." Alexa pointed to me. "You nearly fainted doing just this room."

I hesitated but turned away from that rather uncomfortable truth. I was sure Caleb could fix this entire thing with a wave of his hands, but the damn mage had made his view on the matter entirely too clear. As it stood, I had a slim chance of putting up a ritual large enough to block the corrupted mana. For that matter… "Crap."

"Language, Henry!"

"Sorry." I bobbed my head at the glaring pair of nuns nearby while I spotted one precocious little kid mouthing my swear word. "But I realized there's no way I'm going to be able to fix the ritual either. Not, well, not as it stands."

"Because you don't have the mana."

"Right," I said.

Alexa frowned even more at my admission, looking first at me and then around at the children. "That's not acceptable, Henry. Start thinking. I'm going to go shopping."

"It…" I shut up as I watched the blonde initiate stalk off, tension radiating from every step. After a moment, I sighed and sat on my chair, propping my head on one arm as I turned my thoughts on how to power a building-wide ritual enough to fix it and then fix the ritual below. All the while not really understanding either.

Chapter 14

"Is this going to work?" Alexa asked as she stared at my most recent experiment. I looked at the staff members of the orphanage I could see, a steel chain held in their hands as they circled the large stone building and the small, fenced-off grounds that encompassed the orphanage.

"Maybe?" I said with little confidence. "Theoretically, it should work. The chain works. I can draw the mana I need from those who grip the chain so long as they're willing, but it's a lot of mana."

"It's not dangerous, right?"

"Not majorly so," I said. "I've set up the runes to disperse the buildup if we fail. It costs more mana, but the buildup is significant enough that it makes sense."

Alexa sighed while the abbess who had been watching quietly nodded her agreement for me to continue. The abbess herself was staying out of the ring, for reasons left unexplained to me. Probably a lack of confidence in my work. I'd be insulted if I wasn't making it all up on the go. Thankfully, magic—or at least magic as I practiced it—was flexible. There might be more efficient ways of doing something, but if you had the right tools to start, you could patch things together.

In this case, it was just a much, much, much larger version of the room ritual. Except, this time around, I was containing the mana rather than letting it out. It did raise a few concerning issues, like what would happen to the continual buildup, but in the short-term, at least the neighborhood could get back to its usual state.

"Ready?" I called out. I walked forward when I received confirmation, laying a hand on the chain myself while I began the process of completing the enchantment around the fence. I was using a mixture of enchantments and empowerment on the fence. The initial enchantments had been inscribed—discretely—around the fence at intervals. I enchanted and reinforced each of those glyphs, creating anchor points for the ritual. I would then empower the remainder of the spell, giving it temporary life while we worked on fixing the source.

The enchanted-and-empowered spell was a perfect blend of strength and flexibility. Rather than draining all of us attempting to affix a permanent ritual in place, the mostly empowered ritual would give us the effects without the drain. Also, it was definitely less eye-catching since empowered runes were not visible to the naked eye.

Rune after rune layered the wall as I walked, one hand on the chain and the other outstretched to the fence. A part of me knew how weird this looked—a twenty-year-old Asian man wandering the circle of a building, hand outstretched while a bunch of nuns stood around holding a metallic chain with pained looks on their faces. I was just glad the polluted mana kept passersby out of the streets, leaving few witnesses. Of course, it only needed one with a mobile phone…

But I did what I could. And hoped everything else fell into place.

What surprised me the most was how clear and abundant the mana I drew from the staff was. While I knew they had a lot from my Mana Sight, knowing and interacting with it were entirely different things. There was also an openness to the draw, to the gifting, that I had never experienced before. I made a mental note to talk to Lily about this later as it made the entire day so much easier to work from.

In a short span of time, I completed the ritual. The final lurch of it kicking in drew mana from me and the ladies quite harshly, but with the shared draw, I found it somewhat easier to handle than the first rit. I still found myself slumped to the ground at the end, exhaustion and a headache wracking my body, but at least I wasn't spitting out blood.

"Come on, let's get you back," Alexa said softly, one hand reaching under my armpit to lift me up.

"Can't. Got to get more pendants…"

"They'll sleep in the gym for now," Alexa said, dragging me reluctantly along. "You need to rest."

"But—"

"Do you want to blow up another artifact because you were too tired?"

"It was just a few wooden blocks," I muttered disconsolately, but I did let her put me in the car. It was only when she was shaking my shoulder to wake me after we'd arrived when I realized how tired I was. With bleary eyes and a thumping headache, I didn't even make it up the stairs, instead flopping straight onto the living room couch.

***

I woke to the smell of coffee the next morning. The hiss of cooking bacon and the aroma of freshly made coffee and toasted bread had me stumbling toward the kitchen table. As I sat, I realized with a shock how hungry I truly was and attacked the toasted bread ravenously. Strawberry jam and peanut butter were slathered on with wild abandon even as a cup of coffee was thumped next to me. Only when the black hole in my stomach had faded away did I look up.

"Feeling better?" Lily asked, head propped on her shoulder. At my assent, she wrinkled her nose before she grinned and waved a hand at me. "Congratulations."

Level Up!
You are now a Level 23 Mage.
You have acquired a new spell - Cleanse

You have acquired a new spell—Increase Resistance
You have acquired a new spell—Enchanted Runes
Rituals Skill increased

"Trying a new format?" I asked, mentally dismissing the notifications. Surprisingly, my head didn't throb at all from the new knowledge, though I noted I suddenly had a slew of new information in my brain. Presumably, Lily had deposited this information while I was asleep and only just now unlocked them.

"What do you think?"

"It could do without the unicorns, rainbows, and fireworks," I said, fishing one of the pieces of bacon from what was added to the plate and then juggling it from hand to hand. "Hot, hot, hot!"

"Then wait, you idiot." Alexa rolled her eyes as she returned to the grease-laden pan to add eggs.

"What's with the breakfast? Not that I'm complaining," I said.

"Lily mentioned you'd need more energy today. After the experience and mana drain," Alexa said. "Also… thanks."

"You're welcome." I finished chewing my bacon and swallowed it. "For what?"

"Helping. You didn't need to. Especially the fence," Alexa said.

"The job's to keep them running. Having the orphanage close down because everyone on the block is freaking out is probably not a great idea," I said, then paused. "Huh. Or not."

"I don't like that look."

"I do," Lily said with her head propped up on her hand and a mischievous grin playing on her lips.

"Well, they've got a problem with too-high prices and people wanting them out, right? Because the neighborhood is desirable?" I said. When I got nods, I shrugged. "If we let the mana leak out…"

Alexa hummed slightly in thought and turned back toward the pan to flip the eggs. I let her think about it for a moment while I continued to stuff my face.

"No. That'd be wrong," Alexa said finally. "We can't destroy other people's livelihoods just because it's more convenient for us."

"Heee…" I said, leaning back. "Fine. So what's the plan for today?"

"Mushrooms."

I ended up making a face at her words but nodded. It'd been a few days since Corey had dropped by, which was a bit of a concern. I mean, by now, he'd have run the mana batteries out, so he should have come by to deposit our share of the mushrooms. Since he hadn't—"Where to?"

"I have his home information."

"Great," I said and then speared another piece of toast. We would get right on it. After breakfast and my lessons.

***

Autumn was always a strange time. Everything was dying, sort of, getting ready for a winter. There were leaves on the ground, brown grass everywhere, and gutters overflowing. Yet, outside of the city, the signs of life could still be seen: the occasional darting squirrel, crows and hares scampering across a highway, and a weirdness to the mana flow, an ageing to it that made casting spells that require more concentration easier. I spent most of the drive exploring that sensation, pulling at the world's mana and dispersing the accumulation after running it through basic spell constructs.

"We should be there soon," Alexa said, and I nodded. I was surprised at how far out Corey lived. Or perhaps, I shouldn't have been. Staying next to a national park meant easy access to the woods, where herbs and other supernatural materials might be found. Alexa had picked me up right after I finished with Caleb, which meant we'd been able to skip rush-hour traffic for the most part. Still, the entire drive had taken a couple hours.

"Great." I shifted in my chair once more and dispersed the mana I held, absently checking my body for how much I was at. It was probably around 80 percent of my full, though that new full level I knew had once again increased. A quick check against my mana bar showed I was right, which made me smirk.

A turn and we were off the country road and entering a small side road. Within seconds, a large residential building appeared before our eyes. If it was a little more opulent and a little less rundown and practical, it could have been called a mansion. As it stood, it just looked like a very large, practical building. Perhaps even more surprising were the numerous plots of farmed land, each of which were separated by ramshackle fencing. I peered at the plants within, vaguely thinking I knew some of them, but I decided not to push it. After all, I knew my limits, and herbology was definitely one of them.

Perhaps just as surprising were the large number of individuals moving around the plot of land. There were at least a dozen kids rushing around, naked as the day they were born. Four feet tall and thin and grey, the mini-trolls acted just like human kids. Well, except for the one who was eating a centipede raw. As interesting were the four trolls, three women and a young male, who were working the fields, weeding, watering, and turning over the ground. When we pulled up, they stared until we exited the vehicle.

"Hi there," I said, raising my hand and offering them a smile.

"This is private property. Didn't you read the sign?" An older troll female walked up. I squinted slightly, letting the glamour she used come into focus and noted the middle-aged brunette who came into focus before I let my gaze sharpen again.

"We did, but we're actually looking for Corey," I said. A younger female troll's face twisted at the mention of Corey's name, concern quickly buried. Or at least, I hoped it was concern.

"He's not here. Please leave."

"Do you know where he might be?" I asked, pushing my luck.

"We don't know. We'll let him know you're looking for him when he's back," the matron said again.

"You don't even know who we are," I said, crossing my arms. "And he can't be harvesting any more mushrooms without more mana batteries."

"You're the mage?" The matron's tone went from coolly polite to completely unfriendly in a flash. She crossed her arms even as the younger female suddenly looked full of hope. "Leave then, Mage. You should know the courtesies required. You have been requested to leave numerous times already."

I found myself growling slightly at her words, leaning forward as I realized something was being hidden. Before I could say anything further, Alexa spoke up.

"Our apologies. We were but concerned. We'll leave now," she said. Without a further word, she got into the car and turned the engine on, leaving me staring at her. The initiate waved for me to step in when I looked at her, forcing me to choose between being abandoned or getting more information.

"What was all that about?" I growled when I sat inside.

"Courtesies and rules. We're in their home. If we continue to push things, we'll ruin our reputation," Alexa said.

I snarled. "They know something."

"They do, but if we stay after being requested to leave so bluntly, it'd be tantamount to declaring war with them. Then where would we be?" Alexa said with a snort.

"Fine…" I crossed my arms, understanding her point if not particularly impressed with the results. "How are we going to find him now?"

Alexa smiled slightly and pointed to the glove compartment as she slowly backed us away from the house. Inside, I found a small vial, one that contained a dark-red, viscous liquid.

"That's blood," I said with a frown. "Corey's?"

"Yes. Unlike you, I never trusted the troll to keep his word without some insurance," Alexa said simply. "Are you able to track him?"

I frowned again, extending my senses within the blood. It was old, though the preservation runes set around the vial had slowed its degradation. Corey's aura was still captured within, though within a few days, it'd be gone completely. I wonder what Alexa would have done then? Possibly just gotten another vial. I wanted to berate her for taking someone's blood as insurance, considering how dangerous something like this could be in the wrong hands. Then again, here we were, using it. And realistically, the amount taken was so low, it would be difficult to cast a really dangerous spell.

"Yes," I said. "Give me a few minutes. It's weak."

Alexa nodded, having the car in idle at the entrance to the road from the turnoff. I eyed our surroundings again before I fished in my backpack for the compass and drew a deep breath, getting ready to track our missing troll.

***

An hour later, we were rolling down a worn, potted country road. The singular sign indicating it was Private Property was hanging askew from a single, rusted nail. Obviously, between that, the road, and the peeling paint, it was clear the farm we were now traveling toward had been abandoned for some time. It still amazed me that buildings, especially ones so close to town, could be so easily be abandoned. Perhaps it said something of the sad state of humanity and our society that there'd be dozens of people on the streets and even more abandoned, discarded buildings like this within miles of each other.

"What do you think he'd be doing here?" I muttered, staring at the abandoned farm. Obviously, we weren't the only trespassers here in the last few years, though I had no intention of leaving my mark. I never did get the point of casual graffiti, not emotionally at least. Even if someone did want to leave a sign of their passing, they should at least do so in a manner that actually informed others of who they were because C.M. could be anyone.

"Probably looking for herbs," Alexa said, eyeing the broken windows and the single, fluttering curtain. "House or barn first?"

"Neither," I said as I glanced at the compass. It had shifted since we drew close, able to provide slightly better guidance, and was now pointing unerringly toward the small copse of trees behind the buildings. Once I explained the matter, Alexa pulled the car over and set up her spear. I, on the other hand, jittered, debating taking my backpack and loading it with more survival gear or not. In the end, I stuffed in more bottles of water, an emergency blanket, and some extra food. At Alexa's half smile at my antics, I explained. "Mages are prepared for anything."

"So are scouts, but we're not staying the night," Alexa said. "If it's longer than an hour, we go back."

"But—"

"I'm not wasting more than a day on a troll," Alexa said forcefully. "We still have a ritual that's breaking to deal with."

"He has a family who is waiting for him!" I protested.

"His wives will make do. His son looks about old enough to take on the responsibilities of the family anyway," Alexa countered as she headed into the forest. I fell into step with her, occasionally glancing at the compass and the ground. Not that I could track a herd of elephants through a glass store, but a man could hope.

"Wait. Wives?"

"Yes, didn't you see them?" Alexa turned to glance at me. "Don't tell me you mistook them for males. They're not that different."

"No, I knew they were women," I said. "And none of the stories ever mentioned female satyrs!"

"Uh huh," Alexa said.

"But wives?" I muttered, thinking about it. Well, I guess it made sense. Sort of. I mean, humans had multiple-wife cultures, so why shouldn't monsters? For that matter, I shouldn't be surprised if monsters didn't even get married. They were, literally, monsters. Though supes might be a better term, since they weren't actually monsters. Ugh. My head hurt sometimes figuring out terminology.

Alexa ignored my mutterings, focused as she was on our trek within the forest. Thankfully, there seemed to be an often-used deer track here, which we presumed had been used by Corey too. In either case, at one point, Alexa even stopped to point out a relatively clear footprint embedded in dried mud.

"It rained, what, last night?" I inquired out loud and got a nod from Alexa. With some indication we were on the right track, the pair of us sped up.

Forty minutes later, slightly out of breath, Alexa raised her hand and stopped me from stepping into the clearing. I frowned, the fading light of day making it hard to see within the forest. "What?"

"Light Ball, inside the clearing please," Alexa said simply, her spear casually leveled toward it. Rather than ask why, I muttered the words for the spell and made a Light Ball blossom within, pumping a small amount of mana in it but keeping a tether to it just in case.

Light Ball Cast
Synchronicity 94%
Efficiency 82%

The light blossomed, shedding a gentle yellow light that filled the clearing and cast back shadows. As the light reached upward, my gaze was attracted to minor movement that set leaves shivering and branches bouncing.

"Whaaat?"

"Shhhhh," Alexa hissed and then took a step backward. When she realized I hadn't followed her lead, she hissed. "Back."

"But—"

"Giant spiders," Alexa said softly. "If he's been caught, he's dead."

"That's not right," I said but followed her lead, backing off. I proceeded to pre-cast Fireball in my mind, building up the spell formulas while I had time. "In Lord of the Rings—"

"Not a book," Alexa said, cutting me off. "And Corey's not a full-blood troll. His regeneration is probably only twice or thrice as efficient as yours. He's dead. Or so close, he might as well be."

"You can't know that," I said, coming to a stop and growling softly. The Fireball formed in my mind, ready to be used, while I tied off the Light Ball and began dual-casting a Force Spear.

"No. I can't. But I'm not risking our lives for a dead troll," Alexa said.

"But…" I paused, then realized something. "He's alive. He has to be, or else his blood wouldn't be working as strongly."

My words made Alexa pause for a second before she shook her head, waving me backward. "Doesn't matter. He's not our responsibility."

"It's our fault he was looking for those mushrooms," I said, spreading my feet. "And I don't understand why you're refusing to help."

"Because he's a troll," Alexa hissed while scanning the treetops around us, her spear held in both hands.

"Who's got wives and kids. A family," I said. "Who worked for us, talked to us. Hell, even shared his snacks with us."

"Lower your voice!" Alexa snarled softly.

"Yes, do shut up!"

"I won't—" I paused, my brain catching up finally. Eyes wide, I turned toward where the third voice had erupted from and blinked. "Corey?"

"Yes. While it was nice to hear you defending me, your friend is right. We should go," Corey said, limping out from the undergrowth where the camo-clad troll with his grey skin was easier to see. I absently noted he had a bag hanging from his shoulder.

"Incoming!" Alexa snarled and side-stepped suddenly, allowing the dropping spider to miss her and fall to hang between the two of us. While she did so, she struck out and stabbed a second spider. On instinct, I released my first held spell, the Fireball smashing into the large spider and burning through its skin, sending it shaking and twisting in the air. With an abrupt, strangled shriek/squeak, it dropped the rest of the way to the ground even as its body burned from within.

"Die!" I snarled and football-kicked the small-dog-sized spider away. In passing, I absently noted the monster had red spots on its back and big, big fangs. Fangs? No, different word. I didn't have time to care. As it skidded among the dry leaves, creating a mini-tsunami of discarded vegetation, I followed up my attack with my Force Spear, pinning and killing the creature.

"Time to go!" Alexa said, having extracted her spear and now using it as a bat. As the loud, skittering noises and the rustling of the branches increased, I started backing off at speed, Force Balls conjuring beside me. As spiders dropped toward us, I fired my spell effects at the large arachnids, battering them away.

Of course, the only negative of that was since they were falling on their threads, physics eventually had its way and swung the damn monsters back toward us. After the second swinging spider nearly took me in the chest, I really sped moving backward. Thankfully, the spiders weren't willing to follow us too far from their nest. Either that or the accumulated losses from Alexa's and my repeated attacks finally made them give up.

"Where's Corey?" I asked after we had backed off another twenty feet from the point where we last saw the spiders stop. I received a shrug in reply from Alexa, and my eyes narrowed. A quick fumble and check and I realized the needle was now pointing back the way we came.

When we finally made it back to the car, we found Corey leaning against it, a cigarette between his lips.

"You left us!" I said, waving my hands.

"I did," Corey admitted unashamedly.

"We came looking for you!" I said heatedly.

"And it was real nice." Corey nodded. "But I didn't ask you to. And it wasn't me who was busy attracting the spiders. If you'd been quiet, I would have been able to sneak back out."

"Sneak?"

Corey nodded, patting his bag. "Blood blossom spider eggs. Worth a pretty penny, but their parents are very territorial. Took me days to get in and out."

While I fumed, Alexa pointed at the bag, her voice cool. "And the mushrooms?"

"Got them too. Four more. You want to take them here or for me to drop them off at your place?"

"We'll take them here," Alexa said, and Corey nodded, pulling the bag off his shoulder.

As he rummaged within, he continued. "Going to need another set of batteries. Pulled the ones you gave me out while I was working, but I'm down to one recharge."

I growled and jerked slightly, but Alexa tugged on the backpack over my shoulders. I reluctantly gave it up and watched as Alexa fished the mana batteries out, receiving the Wynn mushrooms as well as the now-defunct batteries from the troll. After confirming our next appointment, we left, leaving the troll to head back home by himself. A part of me—the nice, polite part—wanted to offer the troll a ride back. However, the grumpy, hurt, and bewildered portion won, and I stayed silent till we were back on the highway.

"How can you be so, so, blasé about that?" I asked with a slight snarl.

"He was right. He didn't ask us to rescue him," Alexa said with a shrug. "And he still got us another four mushrooms."

"But he left us to die!"

"Don't be so melodramatic. It was just a nest of blood blossom spiders. At worst, you could have burned the trees and really scared them off," Alexa said, lips parting. "Of course, I'm glad we didn't start a forest fire, but we were never really in danger."

"But—"

"Henry," Alexa said, using my name to catch my attention as she drove. "He's a troll. You're a mage. I'm a Templar. We have a nice, simple business arrangement. Stop trying to make it more than it is."

"Why'd you even agree to go looking for him if you didn't give a damn?" I asked.

"He has your compass and mana-battery system," Alexa said. "It's not exactly impossible for him to find someone else to recharge the batteries, is it?"

"No," I admitted and then frowned at the Templar. "So, that's it? You decided to follow up to make sure we got my gear back?"

"And take any mushrooms he had collected. And the breakage fee for the contract," Alexa added.

I crossed my arms and growled slightly, glaring at Alexa as my irritation grew. Gah. These, these… supes. They were all callous, annoying idiots. Business deal. I growled, falling silent as Lily's reminder resounded in my mind. As much as I sometimes thought I knew Alexa, I also had a tendency to forget that the same woman who snored in her sleep and had to be taught what Cowboy Bebop was was also a cold-blooded killer of supernaturals.

Perhaps… perhaps helping her complete her quest might not be the best idea there was. Lost in thought, I fell silent as we drove the rest of the way home.

Chapter 15

"You seem troubled today," Caleb said to me after my latest ritual attempt fizzled out, breaking at a baker's dozen of points. I prodded at the spell formulas, irritation coursing through me as I realized I had literally just looked at these lines.

"I'm fine," I said.

"No. You're in the twenty-third dimension, the elemental plane of metal and Kuala Lumpur," Caleb said, tapping the ritual. "Or your summon would be at least. And maybe portions in Johannesburg."

"Fine." I leaned back and crossed my arms while staring at the older mage. He returned my glare calmly until I broke. "I had an argument with Alexa."

"If this is a relationship issue, you may leave now," Caleb said.

"Of course not!" I said. "It's just, she treats the supernaturals like they're not, you know, human. And I can't help but think, well, does she think of me like that? Should I be helping her?"

"And you believe supernaturals to be human like you," Caleb said simply.

"Well, not exactly like me," I said slowly. "But the races, they're sentient. Good."

"Some. Some are very similar to us. Others have strange beliefs and rituals, biology that requires different things. The vampires and their need for blood, lycanthropes who lock themselves away every twenty-eight days, the ghouls who must eat corpses to survive," Caleb said. "The Templars have good reason to treat each race coldly. There is a long history of each race preying upon humanity."

"But they're not doing that now," I said stubbornly.

"True. Modern society and overpopulation have allowed many races to live in relative peace with humanity. Resources are significantly more abundant," Caleb said. "But even if as a percentage the number of malcontents has dropped, the increase in all populations has seen a total increase in attacks.

Add the slowly decreasing number of Templars as years of continued secrecy take their toll, and you begin to see how they have taken a harder line."

"But she wasn't like that earlier!" I said, crossing my hands.

"Really?"

I opened my mouth to retort but closed it, and my brain began the slow process of evaluating all the things Alexa had ever done. We'd worked a ton of quests together, but I recalled how she almost always pushed for the harder ones, the extermination quests. Almost always monsters, almost always creatures who were, without a doubt, something that needed killing. Even when we took on more mundane tasks, she never really interacted socially with our employers. Oh, she was cordial and polite, but she never tried to find out about their lives, never asked how they were doing.

"Huh."

"You object to Ms. Dumough's attitude, but have you considered that your own might be a product of your advantages?" Caleb said.

"My advantages?" I asked.

"Unlike most, you are protected." Caleb pointed to the ring on my finger, the object of magical import. "You cannot make a mistake that will see your instantaneous death. Creatures of true power are barred from attacking you, leaving you to contend with only the lowest, and those offer you the respect and wariness that is your due as a mage. Few would turn away a closer relationship with a powerful mage."

"You're saying they're friendly because I could be useful?" I asked, somewhat hurt by the implication. I wasn't exactly Mr. Popular at school, being Asian and a nerd, but I wasn't exactly unpopular either. I just had my own friends. I thought it was just a case of finding more people who were like me, like a giant convention.

"Somewhat," Caleb said. "Your power is useful, but Ms. Dumough on the other hand represents a power that has hunted and will hunt them down. Offering a business arrangement, an impersonal mien, while dealing with supernatural races allows all parties to grasp and operate on a comfortable footing."

"So she might want to be friends but doesn't know how?" I asked slowly.

"I will not speculate on her feelings, but she has good reason to be wary of the races," Caleb said. "And they, of her. As would you."

"Yeah, yeah," I grumbled. That I knew. It wasn't as if I hadn't been warned that at the end of the day, my "friend" was going to demand my ring at some point, which left me wondering, once again, if I should perhaps not help her. But I knew too the Templars would just replace her, probably with someone else, someone who might not be "fated" to be here but who was less friendly.

And in the end, I did consider Alexa my friend. Even if she didn't, me.

"If we are done, let us review the ritual you have been working on," Caleb said, tapping the table to bring my attention back to him. I sighed but nodded, focusing on the ritual. It wasn't going to draw itself.

***

Later that day, I stumbled back into our house, notebook filled with scribbled notes about the ritual and other aspects of rituals. Lunch was a hurried affair, Alexa almost dragging me off my seat as I finished my noodles.

"Okay already. I'm coming," I grumped at her, shrugging my coat on and grabbing my trusty backpack. "It's not as if the ritual is going to break right this second."

"But the contractors are arriving today," Alexa said, "and they want to speak with you."

"Contractors?"

"The supernatural ones you insisted we hire," Alexa said, ushering me into the car. Within seconds, she had pulled away from the curb and merged with traffic, her fingers drumming on the steering wheel.

"Oh, those. Glad you all finally decided to be smart about it," I said, smiling grimly. With the right group, the orphanage could probably finish the necessary work without disturbing the ritual further or, at the very least, mask it so it looked like the work was done while other, more magical means were used to create the same effect.

"It is not smart to let the…" Alexa trailed off and shut her mouth.

"The what?" I asked, prodding.

"The enemy." Alexa jutted her chin out, fingers squeezing the wheel tighter as she waited for me to explode. "Wait."

I watched all this quietly but decided not to comment, the information and her reaction no longer a surprise. Though, I had a feeling her reactions were not so much over her feelings but concern over me attacking her beliefs again.

"Who do we have coming?" I asked.

"There are meant to be three contractors." Alexa's shoulders relaxed slightly at my topic change. "The Grimwalls are bidding, as are the McClintocks and PMC."

The Grimwalls were a dwarven company, one we had actually done work for before. Good people, though I was somewhat hesitant about their level of magical knowledge. After all, the last time they ran into an unusual ward, they'd hired me to figure it out.

"The McClintocks are a group of Scottish fae. They don't do a lot of work for non-fae, but since our building is mostly stone and mortar, they are willing to give it a shot. As for the PMC, they're a multi-national corporation. We'd actually tried to hire them at first, but they had no crews available. Now, they want to assess the work before committing," Alexa explained, giving me details of the two I didn't know.

"And I'm there for…"

"To reassure them the ritual is not active, to answer questions about the rituals you created, and be our magical consultant," Alexa said.

"Har. Consultants get paid," I grumbled.

"You are," Alexa pointed out, and I shut my mouth, recalling the fact that I actually did negotiate payment earlier on. I'd actually forgotten, having delegated this entire quest under "helping a friend." Since it was an actual quest, a real job, perhaps I should stop contemplating stopping work. It'd be really unprofessional after all.

When we finally pulled up, it was to the sight of the Grimwalls stomping out, the titular-named leader literally scurrying out of the building. By the time Alexa had the car parked and I was out, the dwarves were too far for me to call to them, especially considering they seemed to be very clear in their desire to be gone.

"That's not foreboding at all," I muttered. I grabbed my bag and walked in. The abbess gave me a relieved smile when she noted my presence and quickly waved me in. "Problem?"

"The atmosphere was a bit much for the Grimwalls," she said softly, gesturing within. I nodded slowly, making a face, and took directions to find the other pair of contractors in the basement, staring at some damaged wallboards. As I walked, I sampled the increased mana corruption, the dense block of corrupted mana filling the entire building and its grounds. Obviously, our attempts at containing the corruption had worked.

Legends had the fae as beautiful, amazing creatures whose very presence could enchant and terrorize in equal measure, but it was a bit of a lie really. At least for those fae who still lived on Earth. With the ever-increasing volume of iron and the corruption and destruction of nature, pure-blooded fae had left our world long ago. Only the changelings, the thin bloods, and the lower fae were left, groups who could handle the pervasive use of technology. The fae still weren't happy with their new situation, many electing to stay in communes or in smaller towns, but they stayed. Truth be told, staring at the duo of thin bloods, I couldn't help but feel disappointed. I literally could have taken either one, dumped them in the middle of a country music concert, blinked, and have lost them.

The PMCs were somewhat more interesting. Their leader was tall and angular, his face covered by large aviator sunglasses which did little to hide his antenna or the bulge beneath the back of his coat where his wings hid. His female assistant was wearing a tank top, one leg cocked and giving the fae boys a wide grin, a red cap jauntily pressed over her long, furred ears.

"Hi there," I said, greeting everyone. Once introductions were complete, the questions started flying. It was nice to be the center of attention, especially over something I had some expertise in. It was a great ego boost, until the fae started asking questions I couldn't answer.

"No, I don't know what the eighty-third line does yet."

"You're right. That isn't a bleed-off. On second thought, it's probably Jamal's self-reinforcing transformation equation."

"I don't know if it could be bypassed. That'd depend on the inner circle which I haven't studied yet," I said finally, throwing my hands up in exasperation. I received glares from the fae at my actions, but hell. "Look, we just need you to finish the job. I'll fix the ritual eventually, but it's huge!"

"We are asking because we are not able to provide an adequate quote without sufficient information," the leading fae said, arms crossed. "You say the ritual circle is not dangerous, but you then admit you do not even understand it properly."

"Just because I don't understand what the circle is doing in its entirety doesn't mean I can't tell if it's dangerous or not," I snapped.

"Then are you willing to place your word on this?" the mothman asked, jumping in immediately.

"Yes!" I said, feet tapping with impatience. The moment I uttered my assurance, the tension in the room dissipated. I frowned, looking between the pair of consultant groups before my arm was gently yanked backward, and I was led out by an apologizing initiate.

"What?" I asked her.

"We've talked about giving your word!" Alexa said with a hiss.

"And I'll stand by this," I said and pointed at the ritual carvings around us. "Those are fine. Can't say much about the inner ritual, but so long as they avoid it, like I told them to..." I raised my voice at the last bit, making sure the contractors heard it. "We should be fine."

"Theoretically. As far as you know," Alexa pointed out.

"That's all I can offer."

"And if you're wrong, your reputation will suffer," Alexa said.

"If I'm wrong, and this place blows up, a lot more than my reputation is going to be a problem," I said, shaking my head. "No. I'll stand by my words. And if I'm wrong, I'll take the hit. But, on that note, I should be going over those rituals more. Unless you think they need me to hold their hand more?"

Alexa snorted at my words but waved me away. I took off, checking my mental map to verify the last spot I had been at as I extended my senses to encompass the slowly leaking ritual circles. Now that I was in the basement, I could sense the cold, dark mana that escaped was escaping at an even higher rate. I stared down the hallway toward the room that had been locked, my mind turning over the implications. An inadvertent side effect or an attack?

Unfortunately, I had nothing to go on, and so I turned to the external ritual, noting the areas that had been damaged and the increasingly worn areas. The initial damage was minimal, but as time passed, the ritual continued to wear itself down as the broken parts placed greater strain on the rest of the circle. In time, the entire ritual would fail.

Which was fine in itself. As I'd told the contractors, there was no chance of the external ritual blowing up. It was just a giant collector, one that focused and drew mana from the surroundings with some minor glamour and reinforcing glyphs. Part of the trick when we had created our own ritual around the fence had been in creating a one-way porous shield such that mana could still be gathered by this external ritual.

The problem was, once the external ritual failed, it would no longer power the internal, smaller containment ritual, which was the concern. Realistically, I had two choices: fix the external ritual or, failing that, modify the internal one so it did not need an external ritual. Neither was particularly easy.

Which is what brought me here, taking down notes, activating portions of the ritual so I could study the ritual formulas and then move on to the next portion.

***

Two days later, I stood before the last ritual center in contemplative silence. In my mind's eye, the ritual formulas danced, equations shifting as I adjusted the formula to patch in my fix. Eventually, I exhaled and pulled my notebook out of my pocket, canceling the latest scribbled section and writing in the new correction. With this, I should be done.

I blinked when I stepped into the sunlight a few minutes later, wincing at the harsh light hurting my eyes. Damn, I'd been down there for too long. Again.

"Are you taking a break?" the abbess asked, appearing by my shoulder like a ghost.

"No. I'm done," I said, offering her a smile.

"Done?" The excitement in her voice was palatable. "Will you be doing the ritual today?"

"No. There's a few things we need to collect," I said. Before she could ask, I pulled my notebook out of my pocket, tore the page off, and handed it to her. "The list of materials I require are here."

"We'll get it…" The abbess trailed off as she stared at the list, her jaw working silently at first before her shock finally wore off. "Isn't this a little excessive?"

"No."

"But silver dust? Eight pounds of salt, that's easy enough. Wood shavings from a two-hundred-year-old elm tree, that's—"

"It's all necessary," I said, cutting her off, my face grim. "There are three ways to strengthen and fix your ritual circle. The first is to have me do it using the materials I've requested. The second, you hire a full mage, one who has more experience and a much deeper mana pool. They'll be able to inlay the ritual formulas directly without using as many supporting materials. Or thirdly, you can find whoever put the ritual in place in the first place and have them do it.

"But I doubt the third option is viable because otherwise you'd have already taken it, and considering most mages won't work for you, the second option might not be possible either. Certainly not in the timeframe you need."

I watched as her lips pressed firmly together while my tirade continued, but I was tired, grumpy, and fed-up with having information withheld from me while being expected to make miracles happen. Perhaps there were cheaper, easier ways of completing the ritual, but we neither had the time nor did I have the inclination to consider them any longer.

"How long do you need?" I asked.

The abbess glanced at the list again and shook her head after a short while. "I do not know. Much of the material is not rare, but it is not as if we purchase these items regularly."

"Tomorrow. Or the day after. Any longer than that, and I can't promise you the inner circle will hold."

"That soon?" she asked with a hiss.

"Yes." I might be exaggerating, but I figured overestimating the wear was better than underestimating it.

"We'll get right on it."

I nodded to her, offering her a quick wave of my hand. Before I left, I checked in on the contractors—PMC being the eventual winner—in case they had any further questions. They had a few, but thankfully, unlike the mundanes, they had a clear idea of what they should or should not do. If nothing else, they just avoided the areas that were mana infused.

After that, I spent a few minutes and verified the enchantment around the gym still held before I made a couple more pendants for the kids and eventually left. It wasn't perfect, and I really hoped to clear the issue up sooner rather than later—if nothing else than to let the children make their way back to their beds at night.

It was when I was nearly home that I recalled my appointment with Adom. When I finally made it to the library, I found the figure seated at the same table we had first met, a large folder sitting across from him. I frowned, staring at the folder, but fished out the newly withdrawn payment and handed it to the supe. As I scooped up the folder, I paused.

"Is there anything I should know?"

"Of import?" Adom paused, considering. "Much of interest. Little of direct relevance to your concern. I was able to ascertain that the building had seen major renovations in the late seventies, focused on the basement area. It was marked as an extension and introduction of heating, but I understand the plans submitted were more extensive," Adom said. "However, there are no other significant notes. No burial grounds, no ley lines or previous owners of the demonic nature."

"Great!" I said with a smile and then hurried out, exhaustion wracking my body. A part of me wondered if paying that thousand dollars, money that was much needed to get exactly zero real information was worth it. Then again, perhaps it was like insurance. You hated paying for it until that one time when it panned out. Though, considering the worst case scenarios involved, I'm leaning towards never getting a payout.

Once I was finally done with delaying, I made my way home to collapse in my bed. Two long days of studying ritual formulas meant that when I did fall asleep, I dreamed of floating spell equations and a tag-team matchup of disgruntled authority figures of Caleb and the abbess taking turns berating me for my lack of talent.

Chapter 16

"No class this morning?" Lily asked, noting how slowly and languidly I was eating my breakfast.

I sipped at my coffee before I finally answered the jinn, trying desperately to banish the last of Hypnos's dust. Wait. Did Hypnos actually exist in this world? I frowned, tapping the mug of coffee in my hand with one finger. If vampires, werewolves, and the fae existed, why not gods? And if so, how the hell do I keep off their radar.

"Henry?"

"Sorry. Are gods real?" I asked.

"Real enough," Lily said. "Though they're less godlike and just beings of incredible power. Some have limits on what they can do. Others are somewhat less constrained but more… remote. The goings-on of earth and its mortals are of little concern."

"Ah…" I filed the information away before cocking my head to the side. "And no, no class today. I texted Caleb last night. I don't think I can stand another day of having ritual knowledge stuffed in my brain."

"So what are your plans for today? I notice Alexa left early."

"I understand she's helping with locating the required materials," I said. "And my plans are to turn into a giant vegetable. I still have to catch up on my reading." I pointed to the box of books that had yet to be unpacked in the corner, one labeled "unread."

"Nope," Lily said, shaking her head. "Can't do it."

"What do you mean?" I frowned. "I'm pretty sure I can."

"Nope. You've got a quest," Lily said and waved her hand.

Feed the Children

Newborn knockers require specialized sustenance. Help a mother feed her children!

mana, I noted how Lily's initial excitement had waned. In fact, if not for her darker complexion, she'd have been unhealthily pale. As it stood, there was a glazed look to her eyes that I did not like. When I guided her to take a seat in the food court without protest, I knew there was something wrong.

"Here," I said, dropping a giant cup of frozen, mushed fruits in front of her. "Drink up."

"Thank you," Lily said, sipping delicately at the drink while her hands wrapped around the cup. I sat beside her, staying silent while waiting for her to get around to speaking to me. "It's just… This looked fun, you know? On your TV."

"But it isn't?" I asked, glancing around the crowd. It was the middle of the week, so the shopping mall was not, by any reasonable standards, crowded. Since this entire mall catered to the more esoteric tastes, including a couple of fortune tellers and a martial arts gym promising to teach you the "real ninjutsu," it probably was never that busy even on weekends.

"It's okay, but…" Lily exhaled. "It's been so long since I have been allowed out, and the world, your world, is so confusing. The clothing, the fashions, the language. Magic lets me understand, to grasp the changes, but it doesn't make it any less surprising."

I sipped at my drink as I waited for Lily to continue to talk while she explained what it was that was bothering her. Even if I did have an urge to perhaps offer some suggestions, I squashed it. What could I offer a millennia-old jinn? What did I know of her experiences, of her world? Sure, she had thousands of years of history to draw upon, but so many of those years she'd spent in her ring.

"It's just a change," Lily said, turning her head to look around. "But a good one. Your food, your technology is a marvel. Magic, without mana. Magic for the common people."

I smiled slightly, following her gaze to review the fast food court. Greek food, burgers, pizza, western Chinese food, burritos, juice smashed up and frozen... and people, people everywhere reading, listening to music, watching shows on their phones and tablets. Magic, in their hands.

"It is kind of amazing, isn't it? Though I still like my magic better," I said. Real magic. Except, the more I studied it, the more I realized it too had its own rules, its own restrictions. And once again, I felt a wash of gratitude that I had met Lily. Not just for making me a mage but because of the information she had downloaded to me. Like science, every aspect of the spells was built upon the works of those before. Each spell formula had been refined by hundreds, sometimes thousands of others. At my beck and call were the formulas that master mages had produced, concepts they had refined.

Of course, there was a negative to that. In many cases, I was a monkey with Lego blocks of spell formulas. Given enough time, I could kludge something together, but the blocks weren't mine, weren't optimized. Hell, sometimes I didn't even understand the blocks beyond the barest aspects. If not for the fact that Lily was slowly feeding the simplest works to me as well as my study under Caleb, I really would be no more than a monkey bashing bricks together.

"Aye, magic is amazing," Lily said and then touched her phone. "But what you've done, the stories you've created, the technology you've created could rival a god's. I should know. I've met more than a few." I chuckled, and Lily grinned back at me. "Thank you. For letting me out with your wish. I'll always remember it."

I sipped on my drink again, ducking my head at her sincere thanks. Seeing my embarrassment, Lily smirked slightly before prodding my arm. "Now. Food!"

"We just ate... Okay, fine. Lunch."

Chuckling softly, I stood and walked toward the food options. I knew better than to ask what. Her answer would just be "everything." But as I walked away, I had to admit this was a better day than my own planned one. A quest to help others, time with a friend, and physical exercise too. What more could I ask for?

Chapter 17

As I stared at the array of stern-faced nuns before me, I had a brief moment of déjà vu. One so strong, I felt disassociated for a second, like a boat tossing on the tumultuous waves of memory. Then, reality snapped back, and I gestured at the chain we'd laid along the hallways.

"We have enough?" I asked, weariness inching into my voice. After all, we'd had to run to the hardware store twice already just to get the damn thing.

"We do now," one of the nuns said waspishly.

I ignored her tone of voice and reached out to touch the chain, sending a pulse of mana down it. I followed it as it flowed, my frown deepening as I felt the whirls and whorls, the unrefined edges where spell formulas had been compressed together or hastily completed, leaving a leakage. By the time the mana pulse had made its way back to me, it had lost nearly eighty percent of its charge. Unacceptable if I had more time. Utterly unacceptable.

But…

"All right, get to your positions," I said, dropping the chain and waving the nuns aside. I turned away from the group as they moved away, my mind focused on the other, bigger problem. In minutes, I was before the inner ritual circle room, my hand raised to test its integrity.

Bad. Even without extending my senses, I felt the psychic wind of mana blowing, the pressure being exerted by the being that was contained within the ritual. It was hidden, locked away in another dimension, but through the cracks, through the failing of the ritual circle, it was getting stronger. Much, much stronger. It felt—

"What is it?" Alexa asked when she caught me standing there, my hand extended and a frown on my face.

"Nothing."

"What is it," Alexa demanded.

"It feels like whoever—whatever is behind the circle, it's pushing with everything it's got. It's sacrificing itself—its life to get through. I think... I feel that if it fails, it's going to die," I said. "Or at least significantly injure itself."

"Good."

"Maybe," I said softly, dropping my hand.

Alexa stepped forward, putting her face inches from mine when I attempted to turn away. "What do you mean, maybe?"

"Just that," I said.

"You don't trust."

"I trust. Well, you," I said, pointing at her. "You're a good person. Even if you try to act like you're not, you're a good person. You went with me to find Corey. You let him off the hook for abandoning us. You're there with me for all of my quests, no matter what they are.

"But your people? The Templars? They're the same ones who taught you all supernaturals are evil. That the best you can do is have a business relationship with them, be polite and friendly. That in the end, we're all ravening monsters waiting for the worst to come."

"Not you—"

I held my hand up. "I'm a mage. I'm barely better than the monsters you label. At least, by your standards," I said.

"That's..." Alexa's lips tightened as she shut her mouth, unable to refute it. I could see the war on her face, the struggle between the deeply rooted beliefs in mercy and charity of her original faith fighting against the indoctrination of the Templars and their own experiences. I watched as conflict flickered across her face before she exhaled, pushing the discussion aside. "What do you intend to do?"

I paused, uncertain. In the end, I had to either blindly trust a group that had already shown itself to be somewhat untrustworthy and fanatical in their beliefs, or I could release something dangerous into the world. On that side of the equation, I had the assurance from Caleb saying whatever I released wasn't "that" dangerous, but I also knew Caleb was looking at it from the perspective of a master mage, one who saw threats in city-wide scales.

The monster I might release might only be good enough to kill a city block, but that would be little consolation to the victims. Could I, would I potentially condemn others to death? Where, in all this, did I stand? What right did I have to make these decisions?

"Is the mage done yet? Some of us have better things to do," a voice said, breaking into my thoughts, shrill and high and pitched to ensure I'd heard. My lips twisted, and I realized we'd been standing there for ages, my body wracked with indecision. Damn it.

"Let's do this," I said, gesturing for Alexa to follow me. Whatever thoughts I had, whatever doubts, I had come this far. Perhaps sealing the creature within, effectively killing it, was the wrong choice, but right now, I just did not have enough information to contradict the Templars. And for all the distasteful beliefs they had, they had spent centuries protecting humanity. Perhaps a touch of trust was reasonable.

**

"I'm starting," I called out, my hand on the iron chain while the other slowly worked the various materials into the damaged walls. Most of this prep work had been done already, the materials installed and reworked. Now, under the influence of the spell I was casting, the materials melted and shifted, adjusting themselves and accepting the ritual formulas I was installing in them.

Step by step, spell formulas hovering in my mind, Alexa next to me with my notebook for reminders when I needed them, we walked the perimeter of the building. Of course, it wasn't that simple. The building itself was broken up by hallways and rooms, forcing me to traverse around obstructions. It was at these times I'd scurry forward as the burden of keeping the ritual empowered fell upon the nuns directly.

Step by step, the ritual was patched, but as each section that had been damaged was fixed, the amount of power flowing through the ritual circle increased. The requirements for keeping the channel open jumped as our strength weakened.

"How many more?" Alexa asked as we hurried out of the boiler room.

"Two," I said shortly, saving my breath for more important things, like oxygenating my blood.

"Goo—" Alexa jerked to a halt when the entire building trembled. Eyes wide, we both stared around us as dust floated in the air, and the building slowly settled. "Earthquake?"

"Suuure?" I said uncertainly. The building moved, but it had felt wrong somehow. Before I had time to pin down exactly what the problem was, the entire building shuddered again. And then I realized, the building moved but not the floor. "What's going on?"

My answer came a moment later as a wave of corrupted mana rolled over us. I stretched my senses out, reaching toward the room, and sensed it then, the way the inner ritual circle was fracturing, the way the ritual's weaknesses were widening. I tensed, waiting as I stood there, my hand outstretched and my senses extended to the maximum.

Smash

I felt it when the impact happened that time, felt the changes in the ritual circle, the way the ritual then shifted the impact into the building itself to blunt some of the force. I felt how the ritual's cracks widened and the gush of mana as the impact faded.

"It's attacking the inner circle," I said, my eyes wide.

"It?"

"Whatever is trapped in there," I said, biting my lip. My mind spun as I searched for options and considered the ritual. I had no true understanding of the inner circle. I just did not have the ability to patch it together. Any attempt would be more likely to cause problems than solve them.

"Get the children out!" Alexa snapped to one of the few free staff members. They nodded and scurried upstairs while Alexa tried to reassure the trapped staff we would have things fixed. Of course, the way she kept throwing glances at me while she was speaking informed me she might be less certain of that than she said.

Fix the secondary ritual? That made the most sense theoretically. If we fixed it, the reinforced inner ritual might gain sufficient power to stop whatever it was from coming out. Certainly, it'd stabilize somewhat, but with the inner circle even more damaged than previously, could it hold up? Or would I be pouring power into a faulty line?

"Henry!" Alexa snapped at me as I dithered once again, attempting to divine the best solution. Unlike my gaming sessions, I had no time. No time to hesitate, no time to consider all the best options and come up with something smart and cool. I just had to decide.

I crouched, grabbing the chain from the ground and flooded my mana within, taking hold of the spell that had been supported by others. I kept my mana flowing, taking the burden off the staff while I spoke.

"Everybody leaves."

"What? No. This—"

"I can't stop the inner circle from crumbling. If we pour more power into it, I can't guarantee it won't explode. With the amount of mana that's been stored inside the circle and the compound, the chain reaction could be explosive," I said, explaining quickly even as I reached for the spell formulas I had left open. I quickly tied them off as I ran other calculations. "The staff can go. I'll shut down the ritual, maybe even… Yes, invert the ritual, pull the mana out, and disperse.

"Have them tear up the ritual at the fence when they're out. Get the kids out. I'll keep the inner ritual contained for four—no, five minutes."

"We can help you hold it up!" one of the nuns barked, but I noticed a few others had already left the chain, rushing onward to inform others.

I shook my head in negation and pointed upward. "Kids."

I saw the conflict on their faces, the struggle. Their duty to the children won out over their stubbornness and distrust. With a nod, they let go and headed up the stairs, the commotion from above slowly increasing in volume. The pounding of feet, the raised voices of children and teenagers who tumbled around in surprise, it all filtered from above and reinforced my conviction to keep this ramshackle, hodgepodge of magic holding.

Desires were weak shields against the spears of reality. With the nuns gone, I was bearing the cost of keeping multiple rituals open. Even as I shut the open connections down, finishing the patches one by one, I was also opening other areas, inverting certain aspects of the runes. The burden kept increasing, making me grit my teeth as energy continued to course out of me.

Then, blessed relief. As if someone had joined me in pushing a car, I felt mana flowing again in the chain. This mana was cleaner, brighter than the others. Not pure but lighter and hopeful. There was only one person who I knew who passed that kind of mana on.

"Alexa?"

"Don't bother asking. It's my job, remember?" Alexa said softly. Refocusing on the real world, I saw her stationed facing down the corridor, one hand on the chain, the other holding her spear, glowing with a pure, bright light.

"Thanks."

"Just do your thing," Alexa said.

And to that, I could only nod.

Chapter 18

Carry the two, multiple by eight hundred and fifty-three, integral of the result... Use Roland's Fourth Law of Motion on the result, add Kaylee's Subplanar Integration Formula but swap the third and eighth lines out. My mind swam with formulas and calculations that were one part math, one part mystic formulas, and the last part intuition. Apply vigorously to close the open ritual circle.

Next.

My left hand clenched around the chain, feeding mana into the ritual circle. My right twisted and jerked as I used a physical component to substitute for portions of the formula while I chanted aloud. Pressure continued to increase, mana dropped, and still, there were four more open connections and three areas I needed to invert.

Worst of all, we could only continue to feed the power in until I flicked the switch on the ritual. That meant the creature within the inner circle continued to bash at it without cease, not knowing we were going to release it anyway. It meant each attack sent a jarring force through the building, adding cracks that spread and knocked dust around. In addition, the blowback from the impacts toward the second ritual circle was painful to say the least and always took a few precious seconds to recover from.

Overall, even with all that, we were nearly done when the abbess finally made her way back to us. The elderly matron frowned at the pair of us, the way Alexa glowed and I was twitching and jerking as power flooded through my body.

"Will the ritual hold?" the abbess asked.

"It won't," Alexa replied. "Henry is inverting the ritual to disperse the mana. Is the circle at the fence broken?"

"It is," the abbess said with a frown. "How did this happen? You assured me the ritual would hold until it was fixed."

"I didn't expect it to be attacked," I said with a snarl while I forced my cramping fingers to continue drawing runes in the air. "I can't make accurate estimates without full information. As *I told you*."

"There is no reason to shout," the abbess said with a sniff. "And you cannot release the creature."

"What creature?" I snarled. "Don't you think it's about time to tell me?"

"No."

I growled but ignored the woman otherwise. Damn her and her idiotic rules. It didn't matter—not really, since the ritual was coming down, whether she liked it or not.

"Are you still going to release it?" the abbess asked again as I tied off the last open connection. I relaxed slightly when the burden on mana dropped, but only slightly. I still had those points of inversion to complete, and while theoretically it was simple enough to do, that was in theory. If I altered the formula wrong, we'd be looking at, best case, an uncontrolled release of built-up mana. Worst case? Probably an explosion.

Why the hell does the answer for so many things involving magic end with an explosion?

"I'm speaking with you!"

"Busy."

"We are, Sister," Alexa said, cutting in quickly before the abbess could speak again. "It's the safest choice of action. Unless you can give us a very good reason not to."

The abbess fell silent for a moment, giving me time to finish inverting the last section. Now, I just had to verify the actual spell worked before I inserted the inversions. I ran through the ritual circle and the formulas as fast as I could, only barely hearing the abbess speak.

"It's a spirit trapped within. A dark, savage spirit that was too powerful for our people to end when they fought. They managed to weaken it sufficiently to trap it within the initial ritual. After which, our men purchased the building and reinforced the original ritual with the building as you've seen," she said. "We cannot release it. The damage that will occur—"

"Too late," I said softly. "If you'd let us know beforehand, if I'd known… Maybe. But there's too many gaps in the ritual now, too much wear and tear. Even if I wanted to reinforce it, it'd probably tear under the stress."

The abbess's lips thinned and then she nodded as she stepped away from us. She clutched a large cross in front of her body, staring forward at the corridor while I inserted the formulas. At first, nothing happened, but the mana finally kicked in, the switch of the runes occurred, and while the ritual circle glowed and strained, it held.

Held and started siphoning the power from the inner circle, pulling built-up mana into the external circle where it dispersed into the air. With the ritual now powered in another format, I released the chain and the spell, the sudden release of weight making me stagger.

"Alexa…" I croaked out, waving at the chain. I could have saved my voice, since the initiate had released the chain a second after I had. Together we watched the corridor, feeling the building shake again when the creature attempted to free itself.

"How long?" the abbess asked.

"Ten minutes. Maybe less," I said and slumped to the floor with my back against the wall. Damn, my mana well was drained. Feeling within, I could tell I had barely a quarter left, and that was only because I had been doing my best to husband the mana drain. I had a feeling Alexa was not much better, though the initiate refused to sit, her spear pointed at the doorway.

"Can I do anything?" the abbess said.

"A drink would be nice," I said, then laughed softly. "Then just keep everyone back. I'll try to… bargain with it. Or something."

My last waffly sentence received a look of incredulity from the abbess and Alexa, but in truth, it was the best I could do. If the spirit came out willing to talk, perhaps we could. If not, well, I had my spells. And my wards…

Oh. Right. I had my portable wards.

With a groan, I pushed myself up and retrieved my backpack with its blocks of wood and metal. As I moved, I ignored the questioning looks sent my way by both women. Focus. I had to figure out the best way to set these up. Just in case.

***

The silence over the last couple of minutes finally got to Alexa who burst, asking, "What is going on?"

"Waiting," I said. My terse reply got me a glare, which I had to chuckle at. "The spirit's waiting for the ritual to fail completely."

"It can do that?"

"Be a poor spirit that can't sense Mana," I said.

"When?"

"Any time now." As I finished my sentence, a pop like an over-inflated balloon resounded through my soul. Corrupted mana gushed out from the room, the cold, almost slimy darkness of mana, making me shiver again. Eyes narrowed, I pushed myself to my feet. For long seconds, nothing happened, the door still remaining shut. Then with a shudder, the door collapsed outward, and a single, black snout followed by a black paw appeared.

Mentally braced for a creature from the dark, a monster of Lovecraftian proportions, a spirit of the night that sucked souls and flayed humans, I realized what exited the ritual room was so much worse.

"A *skunk spirit!*" I shouted in surprise, my eyes wide. "You trapped a *skunk* spirit?"

"Yes, a creature of darkness."

Skunk Spirit (Level 180) (Weakened Significantly. Current Level 31)
HP: 380/380

"It's a skunk!" I snapped. That explained the corruption in the mana, the way it stopped being "normal." Trapped for decades, the buildup from its scent glands, whether it was intentional or not, would have corrupted the mana around it. Since it was a spirit, its "spray" was of course mana based.

"And they are known to be monsters, even among the natives," the abbess repeated, hand clutching her cross tightly.

"Only in some cultures," I snapped. With our foe turning out to be an angry animal spirit, I was a lot less inclined to hit first and ask questions later. Stepping forward, I glared at Alexa who moved to block my way until she relented.

Having exited the room, the skunk spirit had shrunk its body slightly to better handle the small space it now occupied. It was now only the size of a large dog, the kind that fought off wolf packs before lolling in front of a fireplace, its shepherd owner seated beside it. The spirit's time trapped away with limited access to new mana had damaged the creature. Its fur was ratty, tattered and spotty in places, while its head was slightly misshapen and bleeding from a bone-deep opening. I assumed the last was from its repeated attacks against the ward.

"Brother Skunk," I said slowly, stopping a good distance away and well behind the line of my Shield Wards. I wanted—I needed to give the spirit a chance, but that didn't mean I was going to put my neck on the chopping block. "We mean you no harm."

The spirit did not speak at first, though hearing my voice made it stare directly at me. I gulped slightly, the spirit's hostility bathing my battered senses before it began to amble forward.

"Brother Skunk, I need to know your intentions before I let you go farther. Can you speak?" I said, trying again.

"It's useless. It's a dumb spirit," the abbess growled. "Kill it while it's weak, before it hurts anyone!"

"*You will die first, cross wielder.*" The spirit's voice appeared in our minds with a hiss and raging fury. But as surprising as it was that it could speak to us directly, I noted there seemed a thread of weakness in its voice, one deeply hidden but there still.

"You speak, Brother Skunk. That's great," I said, forcing a smile on my face.

"*You are no brother of mine, false shaman,*" the skunk said, "*but your actions have been mildly favorable. Leave now, and we will part without enmity.*"

"About that. You wouldn't mind telling me what you intend, do you? Just that, I'm pretty sure my friend isn't about to leave," I said, glancing at where Alexa stood silently, spear leveled at the spirit.

"*I seek revenge. For being trapped. I shall tear their bones from their flesh and feast on their bodies to regain my strength.*"

"See. What did I tell you!" the abbess shrieked. From behind her back, she pulled a vial of holy water.

"That's, umm, a bit extreme."

"*They trapped me for decades!*"

"Yeah, I get that. Their bad," I said, grimacing. The spirit was right. It had been trapped. Of course, the Templars might have had a good reason for doing so, like the creature having killed and eaten others, but I had no context for its initial imprisonment. And while I was leaning toward a knockdown, drag-out fight, I was still leery of it. Weakened as it might be, it was a nature spirit, a powerful one at that. For all intents and purposes, I was an apprentice mage with low mana and dodgy defense. If I could talk it out, I would. "I'm sure there's a middle ground. I mean, you don't go around killing everyone who annoys you, right?"

Truth be told, I was betting a lot on some half-remembered Native American stories. Not all tribes considered skunks evil, though a few did. They could also be considered protectors, guardians, and pacifist creatures. If the stories were to hold true to some extent, then the spirit before me was no more dangerous than any other wild animal.

"You ask me to negotiate, to barter. When the perpetrators of my imprisonment stand beside you." The skunk spirit twisted its head side to side, its tail swaying dangerously as it sat up high. Even from here, I could feel how the mana around me grew more and more corrupted as the mana from the room mixed with it. Casting spells in this environment was going to be incredibly difficult.

"Yeah…" I said, hesitating visibly and looking at the abbess. "You should leave."

"I will not! This is my building."

"Just go. If it gets down to a fight, you can always beat on it when it comes up the stairs." I locked gazes with the abbess. I could feel the pressure of her gaze, the resolute will behind it, but I had my stubbornness and right behind me. And a lot of adrenaline. Eventually, she broke her gaze and turned away, hurrying up the stairs but not before issuing one final warning to be careful.

I turned toward Alexa who had been watching the quietly recuperating spirit. She just looked at me, and I knew better than to request her to leave.

"That do?" I asked the spirit.

"*You still stand with the other.*"

"She wasn't even born when you were put in there. Alexa has done nothing to you, nor has she even offended you. She's just here for my protection," I said.

"*And what makes you so special, false shaman?*" the spirit asked, curiosity aroused. It padded forward, sniffing the air as it neared the ward line. I gritted my teeth, getting ready to throw it up if the creature charged. But as if it knew what the ward blocks were for, it stopped and paced next to the blocks, eyeing me first from one side, then to the next. "*I smell another spirit on you. And on her. An old one. A foreign one.*"

"Lily," I said slowly. "Look. You're free. We can work out a… a compromise and restitution for your imprisonment if you promise not to kill any humans or other, well, civilized beings." When the spirit began to bristle and aim its tail, I added hurriedly, saying, "Other than in self-defense."

"*Do you think I am that cruel, human?*"

"No. Just have to be sure, you know?" I said slowly. There were certainly some things I just wasn't supposed to tell the truth on. "So, can we deal?"

"*Perhaps. But I fear you have little to offer me.*"

I exhaled loudly when I realized we were getting somewhere. A "perhaps" meant it was thinking, and if it was thinking of it, we could talk. I grinned widely, opening my hands wide as I got ready to bargain. Right. What did skunks eat anyway?

***

"I don't believe it worked," Alexa said, awe in her voice when the nuns came trotting down with another pile of nuts, berries, and eggs. All organic of course. In fact, the children had been assigned the task of washing all the produce with distilled water just in case.

"Ixnay on the worksay!" I whispered to the initiate.

"Pretty sure that's not how pig Latin works," Alexa replied softly, "but he's eating, right?"

"Yes, but he only promised not to cause harm for the next day," I said and eyed the fur of the creature slowly unclumping and gaining a healthy glow.

"Well, yes, but…" Alexa paused, then looked at me more seriously. "Do you think he'll break his word?"

"No, but Murphy is always listening." To this, Alexa could only nod.

In wary silence, we watched as the spirit gorged itself on produce, but eventually, the first delivery was complete. What used to be a bedraggled, scruffy spirit was replaced by a sleek animal, one whose fur had been combed and unmatted. The wound itself had stopped bleeding, having crusted over, and the patches in its fur had begun growing out. Still, it was clear the spirit had only recovered mildly and was not fully healed.

"So, Spirit Skunk…" I said slowly, letting my voice trail off as it finished preening itself.

"You have completed your side of the bargain. I shall not eat the cross bearers so long as they continue to fulfill their side of the bargain. Once a week, they will provide gifts of this form," the skunk said.

"They can do that. Right?" I said the last word to the abbess who stiffly nodded, unhappiness on her face. I sighed, relaxing slightly when she did nod. As the agreement was completed, the various members of the orphanage started evacuating, opening a clear passage for the spirit to leave. While they did that and the skunk checked the bowls for anything that remained, I eyed the building and the cracks that now covered the walls. "That's not good."

"No. I've probably failed the quest," Alexa said, her face perfectly serene.

"Wait… what?" I exclaimed in surprise. And then my brain finally caught up with me. Right. The goal was to keep the orphanage open. There was no way the building inspectors were going to miss the damage or allow the orphanage to last. I eyed the spirit evilly for a brief moment before discarding the idea of making it help with the repairs. Among other things, I wasn't sure I'd trust a nature spirit to fix man-made buildings. The ensuing results were likely to be less than optimal. "Can the contractors help?"

"Not in time," Alexa said with a grimace. "The inspections were to happen this Monday. Even if they worked all weekend…"

"It wouldn't be enough," I said with a huff. Right. Could I—

"*I shall leave now, false shaman*" the skunk said, punching its words into my mind. I winced, repatching my mental defenses while offering the creature a nod in agreement. Right. Lead the spirit out. I gestured down the corridor and then walked ahead while Alexa squirreled herself in a side corridor to act as rear guard. Or, you know, stab it in the back if it tried something.

With all the staff members and kids out of the building—or out of sight at least—the three of us made our way toward the exit. There was an almost farcical moment when the spirit got stuck on the narrow stairways, squirming its body around the narrow walls and damaging them further with its rather long, sharp claws. By the time it exited the stairwell, the orphanage had another portion to fix.

When it exited, the skunk splayed its claws slightly and tilted its head side to side as it sniffed the air and its tail rose behind it. I frowned and watched the damn spirit, wondering what had it riled up now.

"You humans have destroyed the world even more. Even the stink of your people has grown," it said with a snarl.

"Eh…" I stared at the skunk spirit, struck by the absurdity of it calling anything odorous. Then again… "Our deal is still true, right?" I asked, my voice low and slow.

"Yes." The skunk snorted and took a few more steps forward. It stopped suddenly, its tail flaring again, and turned its head to face an empty spot in the garden. "I smell you!"

There was no movement at first, but suddenly a light ripple occurred. Standing in the spot where the skunk was watching, three men clad in light chainmail carrying swords and shields appeared. Thankfully, they weren't using guns. Among other things, while it was easy to enchant a gun, enchanting bullets were another matter, and since they weren't fighting a physical creature using normal bullets, even those lined with something like silver would be of little use. Even rock salt, a popular weapon against ghosts, was of little use here.

Spirits were only affected by two things reliably: magic and magically enchanted weapons. Even cold iron was a hit-or-miss subject depending on the spirit in question. Thus, it was no surprise to me the weapons and armor the Templars were wearing glowed with the light of enchantment in my eyes. What was a surprise was their presence.

Knight Templar (Level 84)
HP: 180/180

"*Betrayal!*" the skunk snarled at me, its feet shifting to pull its body away. Alexa, in the meantime, moved from behind it toward my body, crouching low with her spear held up in guard position.

"Wait! No. I didn't have anything to do with this. And, you guys! Stand the hell down," I said, noting how the Templars had moved closer when the skunk had shifted.

The lead Templar spoke up, his eyes hard and dismissive. "Initiate Dubough. You have failed your assessment. Spectacularly. It remains to be seen if you will even continue to be allowed to wear the cross."

Alexa stiffened at his words, a slight tremble appearing in her hands.

"Hey!" I said. "There's no reason to speak with Alexa that way. We did the best we could, considering you morons refused to give us further information. This could have been avoided if you'd actually been more forthcoming." When I realized what I'd said, where I said it, I turned toward the spirit and waved a hand weakly. "Though, it's good that you're free. Because you're not going to hurt anyone. Right?"

"I was wrong. You are too foolish to betray me. But if they attack, I will eat them."

I straightened slightly, trying to decide if I was more insulted or relieved by the spirit's announcement. What it didn't do was stop the Templars from continuing to close in.

With a huff, I raised my hand and focused. A Force Shield was basically a projection of power to an area that stopped further motion. One thing I had realized was that Lily's spell was slightly different from the more common shield spells used by modern mages. Most of those "froze" air directly, stilling the molecules and creating a wall to block attacks or, in other cases, used other physical elements to block attacks. The Force Shield Lily had provided me actually worked by stilling motion in the area of effect. From the outside, it looked the same, though it did offer me a few applications others might not have available.

In this case, it mattered not one whit. The Force Shield I created was basically a wall, set to appear and extend a good nine feet in the air. The size of the wall was a bit problematic, requiring a significant amount of mana, but it did halt the Templars' advances. With a bump.

"Are you acting against us, mage?" The lead Templar's hand clenched around his sword as he eyed the wall, a vein along his temple visibly throbbing and highlighting his pale-blond hair. The skunk spirit on the other hand was watching the entire thing, rather than fleeing.

"Just keeping my word," I said.

"Initiate Dubough!" the blond Templar snarled.

"Henry…" Alexa said hesitantly as she looked back at me. I saw her hand tremble as the point of her spear wavered between me and the skunk.

"What are you going to do, Alexa? Stab me?" I asked, lips pursed. I didn't put up a shield, didn't step away. It wouldn't help. I didn't have enough mana to keep two shields going, not after all this. The best I could hope for was to stop the Templars from reaching the spirit briefly while it ran away. Which reminded me… "Hey, Skunky. Time to go. If you don't, ain't my fault."

"*Skunky?*" the spirit snarled, its tail flaring higher.

I winced slightly, but I had little attention to spare for the spirit. Right now, I had a much more serious threat in front of me, one whose hesitation was visible on her face.

"Initiate. Why are you hesitating? Knock out the mage and allow us to finish this vile creature."

"It's not though," Alexa whispered softly in defiance. "It's not." Her voice grew louder. "It just wants to live. We were the ones who trapped it first. Forced it—"

"It is a pagan creature," the Templar said, his voice growing strident. "One that is likely to cause harm if left unchecked."

"And so we trap it? Kill it?" Alexa asked, her eyes tight. "It might not believe in our Lord, but it is still a creature He made, and so long as it harms no one, should we not allow it the chance to come to the Lord on its own free will?"

"It is not human," the Templar said. "It was not made in His image."

"It still lives and thinks. It can still choose." Alexa looked at the creature. "And who are we to judge him? Is that not reserved for our Lord? Especially for actions it has yet to take."

"Initiate… no. No longer an initiate," the Templar said. "I hereby declare, with the power vested in me as the Knight Templar superintendent of the third division, that Alexa Dumough, formerly an initiate of the Knights Templar, is from now on no longer a part of our order. Henceforth, any and all action taken by Alexa Dumough will have no association with the Knights Templar."

The words were like a blow to Alexa, each sentence causing her to jerk. When he finished, Alexa straightened and turned toward them, her spear aimed at the trio without hesitation or trembling. Though, as she turned away, I noted how red her eyes were and the light glint of tears on her cheeks.

"Morons," I mumbled. I'd add more, but before I could, the Templar gestured, and his buddies hammered the wall with their swords. The enchanted blades sent tangible feedback through my spell, making my knees buckle for a second before I forced them straight.

"Child!" the Templar snarled, but I noted how he did not move to attempt to harm me. Obviously they had read Alexa's reports. There was no way Lily would allow them to harm me. Well, unless she considered this a social challenge, at which point I might take a bit of damage, but they didn't need to know that.

"Oh, yeah. I'm the one with the monovision of how the world should work," I snapped. Child indeed. These guys were like five-year-olds who were so definite in their view of the world, nothing—not even logic—could sway their mind.

Another blow and the Force Shield began to crumble. Finally the skunk spirit decided it had had enough and turned tail, bounding toward the fence. This made the Templars speed up their attacks on my Shield Wall. After the second consecutive set of blows, I could no longer hold the wall and it shattered. As the skunk crouched near the fence, its lips peeled apart at the charging Templars and raised its tail. This time around, I had a feeling it wasn't just threatening.

"MOVE!" I shouted at Alexa, grabbing for her arm. I missed because the initiate—sorry, ex-initiate—had moved faster than me, having spun around, and reached for my own shoulder as she took off running for the door. I stumbled and followed along as fast as I could.

We almost made it.

The explosive spray covered ground fast, swamping the Templars first. They, unlike us, were ready for the assault, however, each of them clutching a cross around their waist that glowed with mana. The radiance from the cross covered their body, pushing against the spray and its noxious vapors. A part of me wondered how that spell managed to separate air from the spray itself—if it did. The rest of me was gagging, the vanguard of the spray reaching us already.

The door was thrust open by Alexa, and I was hauled in before it slammed shut. Not before the first wave of the spray entered though, causing the pair of us to bowl over, retching from the smell as our eyes watered and our skin prickled. Together, we staggered away from the door which was slowly allowing even more of the pervasive smell in.

"Henry..." Alexa croaked helplessly as we stumbled deeper into the abandoned orphanage. I understood her point. This smell from the spirit was more than just offensive; it was directly affecting the mana uptake and disbursement that occurred naturally. It had, basically, corrupted the mana all around, the direct effect of its earlier mana corruption multiplied a hundred times.

"The gym." I hacked and coughed as I dragged Alexa to the room. Together, we burst through the double doors and felt relief almost immediately—at least from the mana effects, though the spray that stayed on our skin continued to irritate our bodies.

"First-aid kit…" Alexa said as she stood, stumbling away. I ran my mana in a simple Heal spell, pushing the edges of the irritation away, but as I sat up, I could not help but consider how bad things were, out there.

"We can't stay here," I announced even as I fumbled my bag off my shoulder. After pulling a block out, I began the frantic process of empowering it. Thankfully, the work around the fences and the gym had provided the blueprint for the enchantment I was casting.

Empower Cast
Synchronization Rate: 82%

Cleanse Cast
Synchronization Rate: 72%

Yes! I tossed the block out, directly through the open doorway and watched as it landed in the hallway. The pair of linked spells began to work immediately, slowly grinding away at the corrupted mana. I watched for a moment to ensure the spell worked, watched the fluctuations in the spell formulas and then nodded.

Right. If I adjusted the third and eleventh line with Gaspard's Second Elemental Rune, it should stabilize and increase the speed of the mana cleansing. Lips parted, I began the process of empowering the next wooden block.

As I tossed the second block away and reached for another, I was stopped by a hand on mine. I frowned, my eyes bloodshot and my nose clogged and snotty as I stared at the blonde faith healer who had a rag and pail in hand.

"What?" I said.

"Stop. You're already low on mana. Take a few minutes, let me clean you up," Alexa said, holding the rag up. Rather than protest, I sat quietly as she quickly worked me over, swabbing me with the sharp-smelling, slightly soapy rag.

"What is that?"

"Hydrogen peroxide, dishwashing liquid, and baking soda," Alexa said. "I had to run out to the kitchen to get the last two, but luckily the kitchen is well insulated."

"How…"

"Faith healer, remember? My ability let me push the miasma away. Now, hold still."

When I tried to take the rag away, Alexa glared at me and I gave up. Rather than fight her on this, instead I focused on the next step. Two empowered cleansing blocks should be enough for the building, eventually. Of course, more would be better, but at least the doorway itself was fixed. The concern was the miasma that had spread—was spreading—throughout the neighborhood. It needed stopping.

Which meant…

Pendants. Or at least something to increase our resistance again and shield us against the miasma. I drew a ragged breath, testing my mana limits once again. The time resting while watching the skunk eat had allowed me to regenerate most of my mana, but it had taken a beating when the Templars had done their drum act on my channeled Force Shield.

If we could contain more of the miasma, the blocks I had contained and the runes around the gym would eventually deal with the mana taint, but—

"You're frowning harder than Father did when we brought back the *Evil Dead II* movie," Alexa said, prodding me sharply. "What is it?"

"That's…" I shook my head and pushed it aside. No. Not right now. "I don't have the mana. We need to fix the fence, but I don't have the mana to fix the pendants and the fence."

"Then don't," Alexa said, offering me a hand up. "I can shield us both."

"Can you?"

"Yes. I might not be an initiate, but my faith has not changed. Nor our Father's favor," Alexa said confidently.

I drew a deep breath but nodded, grabbing my trusty backpack. "Then, let's do this."

We didn't have time to wait.

Chapter 19

Outside, almost immediately, we were assaulted by the miasma. It attempted to cling to our bodies, to our skin, but the low, brilliant glow of power covering us pushed the miasma back and kept it from sticking. On the way, I scooped up the pair of blocks and dropped one off as we exited the building.

Outside, the effects of the miasma were already telling. The grass had taken on a slightly greyish tinge, the leaves on the tree curling up slightly. All around, I heard the hacking and coughing of individuals caught in the cloud, their bodies weakening as the mana they unconsciously circulated was slowly corrupted further and further.

Together, we hurried toward the fence. I found myself turning my head constantly as I attempted to locate both the Templars and the spirit. I noted neither were present, which was for the better at least. Hopefully, the skunk spirit had managed to get away. Otherwise, all of this had been for nothing. Then again, considering the amount of damage it had caused by its defensive measure, perhaps the Templars were right. Of course, that would be a better sell if the Templars hadn't triggered the entire incident by being obstinate asses, so the entire incident could be considered as wash.

At the fence itself, we quickly found the first break in the runes. I frowned at the hastily scratched out rune and grunted. Fixing it with Mend—the physical portion anyway—was possible. It would just require delicately adjusting the spell formula while it worked, a slight alteration from my usual, almost careless use of the spell.

Mend Cast
Synchronicity 64%

Minutes later, I finally had the rune fixed. When I opened my eyes, the rune was indeed fixed if slightly worse off than before. With my practiced eye,

I could see where the rune had not been mended correctly, where the lines were off, but as they said, it was good enough for office work.

"Next," I said out loud.

We moved, shifting from spot to spot on the fence until we found another broken rune. Thankfully, there weren't many, and they were mostly clustered close together. Each of them required Mend, but luckily that was not a mana-intensive spell, especially since the fixing I was doing was relatively minute. Still, toward the end, my head was throbbing again.

"How much longer?" Alexa asked, pushing against my arm slightly to get my attention.

"Just have to restart the spell," I said softly, wincing as my head throbbed. When Alexa opened her mouth to ask, I just shook my head. Instead, I suited action to my words and raised my free hand and pressed it against the runes.

Restart the spell. It was easy, since most of the runes were already enchanted. I just needed to feed enough mana into the rune structure, fill the empty spots with the actual correct spell formulas, and *blammo*. Containment ritual complete.

Simple. If I wasn't already running on fumes. If my head didn't throb like a jackhammer. If the mana around me wasn't corrupted and impossible to refresh myself from. Simple. I shuddered as mana flowed from me, drawn forth and pushed ahead by my will. My head throbbed further, my vision greying out as the light that encompassed us dimmed slightly, Alexa struggling to protect us. Simple. I licked my lips, a slight warmth and iron taste appearing on my tongue as the liquid flowed away. I reached out with my other hand unconsciously, wiping at the nose bleed even as the spell formulas danced in my mind and runes slid into place.

Simple.

With a thrum, the ritual burst into being around us. The press of mana on the ritual, a spell so intimately connected to me, made me waver. I frowned, noting how the world was leaning backward slightly and realized I was losing my balance. With a sweep of her feet, Alexa dropped me into her waiting arms and the princess carried me back into the orphanage.

"Block," I managed to cough out, waving despairingly at my bag.

After a moment, Alexa pulled the second block out and tossed it onto the grounds before dragging my limp body into the gym. Inside, she sagged to the floor, sweat matting her pale hair.

"Lily's going to kill us," she said with a groan, obviously imagining how the jinn was going to complain about my mana overdraw. I wished I could answer her, but lying on the comfortable floor, my eyes decided it was time to close.

When I next woke, it was to the insistent prodding from Alexa hours later. With the major concentration captured within the fence, the remaining escaped mana had slowly dispersed or been cleansed. That left the pair of overworked empowered blocks to finish up the job on the inside. Unfortunately, I had also left the orphanage staff with pendants, which is how the abbess had managed to make her way back to glare at us.

"I know, I know. Leave," I said with a huff.

"You and Ms. Dumough are no longer welcome," the abbess pronounced, and I sighed. Well, duh.

"Of course." Alexa bobbed her head in acknowledgement. "And I apologize again about the damage... and failing the orphanage."

"Yes, you should be." The abbess paused, then continued, her voice softer and slightly kinder. "However, the Templars have informed us that they have ensured we will be given the requisite time to complete the projects. And made a sizeable donation to deal with the inconveniences we have faced."

I paused, my eyes wide. "Wait. They could have fixed this? Then why didn't they?"

"This was a test," the abbess said, her voice calm.

"But—"

"Henry." Alexa placed a hand on my arm and shook her head.

"Why aren't you angry about this!" I said, waving a hand around. "This, this was garbage. We went through all this for nothing!"

"Garbage?" Alexa asked softly, then shook her head. "We freed a spirit that was imprisoned for decades. We helped slow the spread of a dangerous drug. And… Okay, the mushrooms weren't particularly useful."

I snorted.

"But I also learned something about myself. And them."

"What? Self-knowledge is the best knowledge?" I asked sarcastically. Sure, the test itself probably never placed the kids in any real danger, now that I knew what had been kept below. The skunk spirit might have been angry, and we might have ended up fighting it, but the abbess would never have let the children be around during such a battle. Even the mana poisoning had been a slow process, one that could easily have been fixed with a trip outdoors, but still—

"Yes," Alexa said serenely.

I glared at the ex-initiate, but in the last six hours, she seemed to have gained a sense of peace over her decision. I opened my mouth to prod her further before I shut it. There had been flash in her eyes when I was about to speak. Perhaps she might have accepted her decision and the consequences, but the pain was still there. In the end, it wasn't my place to prod her.

"Fine," I grumped and then looked at the abbess who just stared at us serenely. I sighed and waved a hand goodbye at the woman, tromping outward. "Let's go, partner."

"Coming." Even without looking around, I could hear the smile in her voice.

Epilogue

Of course it wasn't that easy. Once we got back, I had to explain the new situation to my other watcher. Caleb was less than impressed with my various explanations and the fact that I overdrew my mana, again. In fact, after some testing, he relegated me to a two-month period of convalescence and book study. It seemed my constant abuse of my body had damaged my mana channels.

As for Caleb's thoughts on Alexa? The mage did not deign to inform me.

Alexa, on the other hand, had a more arduous time of it. She had a number of belongings still at the camp which had been returned to us. In turn, Alexa returned a number of smaller items I had never noticed her owning till then, including a surprising number of explosives. Interestingly enough, the Templars allowed her to keep her spear and armor. As a mostly secret organization, none of her materials had designs on them, so they did not require cleansing.

Perhaps the greatest shock of all for the ex-initiate was the closure of her bank account and the return of a small portion of funds within it. Once I was back on my feet, I helped Alexa run a number of "adult" errands including opening a bank account and applying for a credit card. As a former ward of the Templars, she had never needed to do either herself.

Without the salary and funds provided by the Templars, Alexa quickly began running the various quests on the board that she could handle while I convalesced. If I didn't know better, I would have said she was distracting herself from the abrupt change in her. But I did, and late-night sobs from her room indicated that, newfound serenity or not, Alexa still had much to work through.

As for myself? The longer I existed in this strange new world, the more I realized how simplistic my earlier perceptions on it had been. There were deep currents, not only among the organizations that existed here but within those currents. A single misstep could pull me under. As it stood, I knew the Templars were waiting. And now, I could not help but wonder, who else?

Book 3

A Jinn's Wish

Chapter 1

Magic was wonderful, amazing, and awe-inspiring. It could destroy buildings, find lost keys, and raise a sunken ship with equal ease. Magic's only limits were the boundaries of life and the imagination and skill of its user. And even the first was arguable.

"So why is it I'm still doing dishes by hand?" I grumbled as I finished washing the bubbles from the last plate then dropped it onto the drying rack with a tinkle of glass. The small kitchen I was in held the remnants of our breakfast—store-bought frozen waffles and real maple syrup—the delectable smells lingering in the air. Cream walls and ten-year-old appliances surround me while I finish cleaning up and I wish once again there was enough money—and space—to put in a dishwasher.

"Careful. Don't chip them!" The black-haired, olive-skinned beauty I'd directed my question to didn't even look up from her video game. Some awe-inspiring, open box RPG world. More research according to Lily, but I knew it was more of an addiction. More of her way of adjusting to a world that had changed in the last fifty years of captivity in her ring.

Oh, yeah. Lily's a jinn, and until I'd released her four years ago, she'd been stuck in her ring in an abandoned briefcase. How one of the world's most powerful artifacts had found itself in an abandoned briefcase—untouched, unopened, and unknown for decades—was a mystery I had yet to solve. If someone knew—and I was sure someone did—they'd refused to tell me.

"I'd just Repair them. I got that spell down pat."

"Just because you can doesn't mean you should." Lily's tongue stuck out for a second as a stray lock of hair fell over an eye. She scrunched up her face as she focused on a platform hop between a swaying bridge and a cliff, releasing a breath of relief as she managed it. A quick flick of her finger put the game on hold. A glance showed her continuing to transition between hyper gates on her other computer. "You've grown to rely on magic too much.

Magic's an infinitely adjustable tool, but sometimes, using your hands is better. Knowing when to stop relying on magic is just as important."

I sniffed, shaking my head. "What's the point of having magic if you aren't using it?"

"To brush your teeth?"

"I was working on my fine control!"

"Getting yourself a cup of water in the middle of the night?"

"It was…" My voice dropped as I winced slightly. "Cold. My bed was warm."

"And you used four different spells to get yourself that cup."

"Just three!" I protested. Scry to shift my point of view so I could see the cup from downstairs. Levitate to move the cup. And Light because I hadn't bothered to switch on the lights.

"You forgot your Force Fingers."

To turn on the tap, of course. I'd forgotten about that. A few years ago, splitting my focus to cast four spells, even four cantrip level spells like this, would have been impossible. I'd made great strides, but maybe I had gotten a little lazy. But… "It's not as if magic is addictive. Or doing harm to my body to wield."

Lily huffed and crossed her arms. "I told you before, it's a matter of mental flexibility. If all you can see is how to use magic, you stop seeing any solutions except for a magical fix. If you want to become the strongest, you can't be limited—even by your own thoughts."

My lips curled up, a sneer forming as I instinctively fought against her recommendation. That I had fought and lost this argument already was part of the reason why I felt rather petty about this entire thing. I understood her point, probably even agreed with it to some extent. But it was a conceptual idea, one that had no real bearing on me at the moment. The kind of research and spell creation she was speaking about was for the Archmages, individuals who, if I used my own little cheat System, would be in the high hundreds. As for me, I was a measly Level 63.

Seeing that she had won, Lily turned back to her game. Before I could decide on my next step, rapid knocks came on my door. As I threw open the door, I was surprised to see Shane, a deep frown creasing his short, bearded stature. It'd been ages since I'd seen him—not since I'd managed to put a tracking enchantment on Charlie's collar, allowing Shane to track his cat. It was one of my better enchantments, especially since it drew its power source from the ambient Mana of the world.

"What's wrong?"

"There's... well. Better to show you."

"Charlie okay?" I said as I grabbed my coat off its hook.

Shane bobbed his head and stepped out. I followed the taciturn dwarf as he headed down the street. As we walked, I noticed how Shane kept turning his head, deep-set eyes growing deeper as he spotted our watchers.

"Don't worry about them," I said. "They're keeping an eye out for me."

"How many?"

"Five? No. Six groups now." I let out a huff of exasperation. Among them, the Mage Council, the Knights Templar, the Uttara Mīmāṃsā, and the FBI watched us from the various houses lining the street. I was somewhat amused that the majority of this street, and a portion of the neighborhood, had become supernatural central. "Forgot about the Druids. They're the latest."

"Druids?" Shane twitched, hunching lower. I wondered what the story was there.

I shook my head. "Don't worry about it. It's a long time before they'll do anything. In fact, this is probably the safest street in the city."

Shane grunted in acknowledgement.

I was no longer surprised by the details your generic supernatural denizen knew about my situation. One thing I'd learnt about the supernatural world was they gossiped worse than a group of mahjong players. Seriously, you'd think it was a superpower among the supernatural. But if you considered that even the biggest supernatural population was only the size of a small town, the gossip made sense. When there wasn't much in terms of laws and bureaucracy to fall upon, reputation and knowledge became the currency everyone banked on.

"Safer…" Shane fell silent.

I couldn't help but notice his body language, the way he hunched in a little, the way he kept sending glances towards me. Running around playing troubleshooter has meant that I've had to learn to read people a little better. It's surprising how much body language stays the same, even across supernatural barriers. But that might be a result of everyone forced to interact with one another constantly.

Eventually, we left my neighborhood and headed not for his, but another nearby street. There, the buildings were a mix of ground-floor retail and two-story apartment complexes, keeping the street vibrant and busy. At least, during the weekends. Weekdays, like today, things were a little quieter, though not quiet. Bisecting Spruce Street were numerous alleyways, and it was down one of those alleys Shane took me.

As we walked down the dumpster-filled alley, I couldn't help but look around. Sad to say, my life had changed significantly enough that wandering down strange alleys and looking for trouble wasn't that uncommon. From goblins living in the trash to devil rats, alleyways and garbage dumpsters were a thing.

My increased alertness was the reason I sensed the shift in Shane's demeanor. I was looking his way when he turned and plunged a knife into my chest, going straight for my heart. I shifted aside enough to avoid sudden death, but not enough to stop him from putting a bleeding hole into my lungs and tearing open a portion of my chest. A reflexive Mana Bolt punched Shane back, sending him stumbling into the wall. As if the attack was a sign, the dwarf rippled, his body elongating and lengthening even as his skin lost color and his beard shed.

"Doppelganger," I snarled.

My Force Shield caught his lunge, turning the blade. Not that the not-Shane gave me enough time to catch my breath before he stabbed at me while I clutched my wound. Only the training and the numerous near-death experiences I'd had allowed me to keep my focus on my spell. Well, that and the cheat spells Lily had stuck in my mind, allowing me to call them forth at a snap. Even so, it was all I could do to hold him off with one hand and keep my wound closed with the other.

"Time to die, warlock." The doppelganger kept attacking with one hand, but I was surprised to see him pull out an all-too-mundane grenade with the other. He stopped long enough to pull the pin on the grenade.

I was grateful for his mistake, as adjusting an existing shield was easier than casting a new one. The math, the change in the ritual runes in my mind expanded the Force Shield and curved it, making it a semi-solid, concave shield that faced the monster. Then I shrank it as fast as I could around the doppelganger even as he lobbed the grenade at me.

The too-large eyes of the grey humanoid widened in surprise and fear as the grenade bounced back. He turned to run, an action that I mimicked in order to back off as fast as I could. I did my best to contain and redirect the fury of the explosion, guiding the shrapnel and fire at my opponent, but my shield could only hold so long. And then I was on my back, staring at the stars, my ears ringing from the noise, bleeding out.

As I lay there, I couldn't help but wonder who had sent an assassin after me.

***

By the time my "guardians" arrived, I had managed to stop the bleeding with a Greater Heal spell. The accelerated healing spell started by clotting my wounds then slowly stitching the wounds closed as I held myself together. Of course, it left a big scar, but at this point, scarring was pretty much a given. Over the past few years, I had only managed to ensure that my face and neck were free of major scarring, allowing me to visit my family without serious questions. Well—except the one time I turned down a visit to the beach.

Greater Heal Cast
Synchronicity: 84%

A rather pitiful synchronicity rate, especially after so long, but I was still struggling with that spell. But unlike my normal heal spell, it had the advantage of fixing minor problems like a flooding lung.

"Wizard Tsien, do you require additional healing?" The Templar standing over me was giving me the stink-eye. He was in full tactical battle-gear, ranging from a Kevlar vest with multiple pockets, a couple of knives, a spiked stake with silver and wood, and of course, guns. Lots of guns. No sword, though the knife strapped to his thigh was big enough to be considered a short sword.

Ever since Alexa left the Templars, our brief interactions have been less than friendly.

"I'll live." I staggered to my feet, pressing at my wounds and looking at my bloody clothing. Thankfully, I'd remembered to bring my damn bag containing an extra set of clothes. Over the years, I'd had every kind of body fluid splashed, vomited, and thrown onto me. An extra set of clothes, carefully wrapped and sealed in an extra-large ziplock bag, was a minimum requirement for my lifestyle. Though getting stabbed by a friend was a new one. "Is Shane…?"

"Dead." The reply came from the Druid walking over.

You'd think a Druid would be an old man with a long, white beard and a grey or green robe. Nope. The Druid set to guard me had a carefully manicured, villain-style goatee, long hair, and mascara. Add the leather jacket with the many little spikes on it and the black T-shirt underneath, and he'd fit right in a heavy metal concert.

"Not the doppelganger," I said, shaking my head and refusing to look at the mangled remains a short distance away. "The real Shane."

"Dead," the Druid insisted. "We put out a call for his spirit once your friend went boom. Got a return signal, all strong and angry."

I swore and, having felt my body settle down a little more, began another Greater Heal. My guardians ignored my casting, paying more attention to the corpse and muttering to one another. I would have been grumpy about that, but they didn't really care what state I was in when I reached Level 100 and freed myself from my wish to Lily. It would probably be even better if I was a completely broken wreck since they still needed to kill me. Which, you can guess, was why I was a little concerned that they may have let the doppelganger in on purpose.

"*Did you sense him?*" the Templar muttered to the Druid.

"*No. Our spirits were distracted. There was another attack.*" The Druid gestured around, shaking his head. "*We only had a minor spirit watching the target.*"

"*Heat signature was correct. Dwarves and doppelgangers run hot, which is probably why they chose him,*" the Templar said, running a hand through blond hair. "*No magical resonance because it was a doppelganger.*"

"Yes. We missed it too." Caleb Hahn, Magus of the Second Circle and my mostly reluctant Magic teacher strode over, followed by two hangdog mages. I assumed those were the ones set to watch over me. Caleb turned, saw that I was done with my healing, and fixed me with a flat gaze. "They tried to open a sealed gate in an abandoned shopping mall. Thus my lateness."

"I take it you've been having trouble?" My words were somewhat muffled since I was peeling off my shirt, showing off my no longer completely pale and skinny body to everyone. Due to the added training that Alexa had put me through, I was no longer the skinny gamer I'd been years ago. Call it a little bit of vanity, but I was proud of that. Of course, I'd be prouder if I didn't have a dozen alarming scars that needed hiding.

"No more than usual for this year," Caleb said, receiving glares from the other groups.

While the Druids and Templars might not like each other, they were both clear about their dislike of the Mage Council. It had a lot to do with the fact that of them all, Caleb had the best relationship with me—and the Council itself was warming to me. They'd begun to realize that a Level 100 Mage, fed spells and knowledge long considered lost, could be a boon to them.

Already, Caleb had advanced a circle just from working with me. Watching the way I worked spells, spells that had been lost to them, had improved Caleb's knowledge at a rate that left many of his peers behind. Even if he was forced to share his knowledge, because of his position, he was still leading the pack.

As I finished pulling my new shirt over my body, I caught a glimpse of the shredded corpse. As if the stench had been waiting, I caught a whiff of the body and gagged a little. If I could have backed off farther, I would have. "Are you intending to deal with the body?"

"No." The Templar was short and abrupt.

He looked at the body once more before he stomped off, soon followed by the Druid. After stuffing my sodden shirt into my bag and covering up the blood on my jeans, I glanced at the body. Better to get rid of the evidence. As I readied myself to cast an Acid Dissolution spell on the body, Caleb pushed down my hand.

"What?"

"The body will be dealt with by some of your shyer guardians," Caleb answered.

"Who? How?" I frowned. I knew I had other watchers, but only the three I'd seen already had taken steps to actually talk to me. Repeated questions had, thus far, offered little additional knowledge.

"I am not sure, though I expect that the FBI will win this argument," Caleb said.

"FBI?" I yelped, eyes widening. "Wait. X-Files?"

"I do not believe they have an actual designation," Caleb said with a shrug. "Nor am I sure if they are actual FBI agents."

"Then…?"

"It is clear they are from the government," Caleb clarified.

Seeing that I was standing, he walked out of the alleyway, forcing me to hurry after him, as did the lower Mages. From a quick feel of their auras, I assumed they were around the sixth or so Circle—not too close to graduating but not green-nose recruits. That they offered me jealous and unhappy looks wasn't unusual, but the looks were not particularly flattering on thirty-year-old men.

Repeated interactions with those in the lower ranks of the Mage Council had shown me that my name was mud. A lot of it was due to jealousy—not only did I get the personal tutelage of a Second Circle Magician, but I also had Lily inputting spells and knowledge that the Mages had taken decades to learn. I'd managed to achieve in a few years what they'd struggled with for decades, scraping and testing, experimenting. Add in the fact that I had a wider variety of instant-cast spells, and well…

Mud. Name.

"Clear? How is it clear?" I growled by the time I caught up.

Caleb didn't bother to answer my question. "Your Mana is low. You'll need to rest. We will cancel today's training. But you should be careful from now on."

"No. Really? I should be careful about doppelgangers sticking knives in my stomach?" I snorted.

Caleb just turned aside when we neared his apartment, leaving me to walk the rest of the way back alone. Alone, grumpy, and just a little worried.

Chapter 2

By the time I got back to my apartment, I'd calmed down enough to realize that I'd never asked a lot of the questions I should have. Among other things—who sent the doppelganger? While I knew that my reluctant guardians had been hard at work keeping me safe, I hadn't realized the level of enmity I had gained. However, someone sticking a knife in my chest was a rather pointed reminder that being ignorant might not be the safest option.

On top of that, there was someone else I really needed to have a word with.

By the time I opened my door, I was fuming a little. The front door slammed before I stomped up to the living room to see the placid gaze of my jinn—my real guardian, my friend.

"How come you didn't warn me?" I snapped.

"Warn you? Was I supposed to do that?" Lily said innocently.

"Lily." I point at my chest. "Stabbed!"

"I know," Lily said, her face sobering. She turned toward me, almond eyes fixing on my own mud-puddle-brown eyes, and offered me a sad smile. "I know. But I'm bound by the rules I set up as much as you are. I couldn't tell you, because he was an appropriate threat. He didn't have a gun. He didn't have a magical weapon. Just a knife."

"Which nearly went into my heart," I snapped.

Seeing Lily flinch made my anger cool, her words reminding me once again that the jinn was bound by the magic of the ring. She could twist and turn, prod and edge the rules a little, but in the end, she was still caught. I flopped onto the couch and traced the new scar through my shirt.

"I know. I'm sorry…" Lily drew a deep breath. "I wanted to. But I couldn't. Can't. You have to be careful, have to watch out for threats of your level."

Something in the way she said it, the way she wouldn't look at me, made me sit up. "Lily—"

"I can't say any more," Lily said. "But you're in the inn."

Silence filled the room, only broken by the hum of the taxed laptop fans. In the corner of my gaze, I noted her character being PKed, left unattended in a hostile zone. That Lily didn't notice was perhaps the biggest clue as to how disturbed she was.

I finally broke the tension by leaning forward and turning on the TV screen. "So. You know, *Ascend Online 3* dropped last week. I never did get around to playing it…"

Lily perked up, eyes glowing with enthusiasm. "Oooh! I wonder if they've fixed that long travel time bug yet. Everyone complained about it in the previous edition…"

***

That was how Alexa found us later in the day, when she made it down. Ever since she'd lost her income as an Initiate, Alexa had had to find interesting and novel jobs. Since the majority of her skill set involved killing supernaturals, her first year had been tumultuous. That changed when she received a job offer at Atlantis, the hottest nightclub in town. She worked the VVIP section there, keeping the various supernatural denizens in check.

Alexa barely gave us a glance before she performed her afternoon ritual of bacon and lettuce sandwiches, coffee, stretches, and more coffee. When she flopped into a nearby chair, she only shot the game a quick glance.

"Why is there a bag full of bloody clothing left to rot?" Alexa's tone was less worried guardian and more weary roommate. "We talked about how blood sets if it's not soaked."

"I think that shirt's a goner," I said. "What with the stab hole. I can't keep using shirts that you've sewed together and having people give me that look."

"What look?"

"The one that wonders why your shirt has a suspicious-looking sewed hole where your heart should be."

"Heart?" Alexa sat up, brows drawing together. "This… Spill. Now."

I sighed, hitting the pause button—to Lily's disapproval—and turned toward Alexa to explain my most recent near-death experience. The ex-Initiate was a good listener, only interrupting twice to clarify certain points.

"Both Lily and Caleb warned you to take extra care?" Alexa confirmed. She waited long enough for me to nod before she drained her cup of coffee and walked upstairs without another word.

"Alexa?" I called after her uncertainly.

"Leave it. She'll be back," Lily said. "Can we at least finish this quest?"

"I don't think so," I said as thumps and smacks drifted downstairs.

"Bah!" Lily sighed but saved the game before crossing her arms unhappily. A moment later, she let out a yelp of surprise when she spotted her still-open laptops. "When did I die!"

In short order, Alexa came back down with a series of folders. She dropped them on the coffee table before leaving to get even more. Curiosity made me browse the carefully labeled folders, only to shiver as I read them. The Illuminati, the Mage Council, the Knight Templars, the Druidic Order, and even the Council of Shadows and Dark Races were there. Every major power I could name had their own folder, some thicker than others.

"What is all this?" I said as I picked up the folder for the Mage Council.

Personnel files of familiar faces greeted me, each file offering a detailed chart and had at least one, if not more, pictures attached. Surprisingly, the files even listed their game data. Or perhaps, as I considered the information, it shouldn't be such a surprise. After all, Lily's game data was a good, if rough, estimate of threat level.

"Everyone and everything that has taken interest in you." Alexa said, tapping the files. "At least the ones I know of. Some are, well, a bit more circumspect." To underline that, she prodded a rather thick folder that just said "miscellaneous."

"You've been keeping track of all this?" I said, my eyes widening in disbelief. "But why?"

"I am your friend, you know. Also, I like to know who might want to blow up the house I'm living in," Alexa said. "Now, you said it was a doppelganger?" I nodded dumbly and Alexa frowned, staring at the pile. "Let's split them then."

"By?"

"Ability, then likelihood of using them."

I groaned but chose to not complain, taking my stack of the pile. In truth, it didn't take long for us to separate the various groups, with some—like the Mage Council—having the ability but not motivation while others—like the Templars—having no ability or motivation. In short order, we had a small pile of likely suspects.

"The Council for Pagan Religions," I said, running my finger over the folder. I noted the numerous smaller file folders contained within it. Among them, the Druids. "Tell me again about them?"

Lily looked at Alexa, who spoke while she headed over to the coffee pot. "A more recent invention. Until the sixties or so, the various pagan religions and magic groups worked individually. But the hippie movement brought a surge of interest. Rather than stand aside and potentially miss new recruits, especially considering how small the groups had grown, the Council formed.

It has representatives from everything from the Druids to wiccans to Native American shamans."

"Wasn't there something about how the Mage Council and some of the other groups tried to suppress the Council members?" I said.

"Yeah. The beatings, Canada's residential schools for the First Nations, all of that was because the other powers were pulling strings." Alexa made a face. "Not that a lot of strings needed pulling…"

I grunted in understanding. While the amount of influence supernatural groups had on the governments of the world was not insignificant, most government policy was a matter of shared interest than a single power—or powers—calling the shot. In most cases, a supernatural group would work a bunch of human special interest groups to have policies come through. The problem with influencing entire nations was that you were dealing with hundreds, millions of people. And if you'd ever tried to organize a large dinner party, you'd know just getting people to agree on pizza or nachos can be difficult.

"So the Druids are their frontrunners for watching over me, but why do you have them in the 'potential' pile?" I said.

"I really wish you'd kept a sample of the doppelganger," Alexa said, shaking her head. "Without one, it's impossible to narrow down what it was you saw. Was it a fetch? A demonic construct using a physical change? A shui gui that took Shane's body?"

"Probably not the last," I said. "The shui gui inhabit the corpse. So it wouldn't have changed."

Alexa inclined her head in acknowledgement before continuing. "It could even be a Changeling."

"He was kind of ugly for a fae."

"Not all fae are pretty," Alexa said. "In fact, many aren't and just cover it up with glamour."

"So what you're saying is, because the Druids and the Council have access to these other supernaturals—either from their business or membership—they're on the list?" I said.

"Exactly." Alexa shrugged. "Low though. I'm more inclined to suspect the groups that haven't put someone to act as your guardian."

"Like your employers, the Dark Court."

Also known as the Council of Shadows and Dark Races. Among their many members were vampires, werewolves, naga, ogbanje, and aswang. The Council basically accepted any race or group that was inclined to "feed" on humanity and other supernaturals. Because of their liberal acceptance policy, they'd gained a rather bad reputation overall; even if they strove to police their own.

"Not the Council itself," Alexa said. "They voted already on the ring and weren't able to gain the majority they needed."

"Majority for what?"

"Anything," Alexa said, shaking her head with amusement. "A majority is required for any action. They voted to try to take the ring by force, to act as guardians, to watch you, to assassinate you, to bargain with you"—the blonde counted each thing off with her finger—"I think that's it. Anyway, there's a vote every month and nothing has come of it."

"So you're saying some of them might want to kill me," I said. "And they obviously would have the contacts."

Alexa nodded. "Which is why we should probably talk to them."

"Great." I shake my head. "Can we do it before the club opens?"

Alexa flashed me a sympathetic smile, knowing how much I hated those noisy, sweaty, alcohol-filled hellholes. Not that it had stopped me from trying them once or twice in a vain hope of getting laid. Of course, my expeditions had all ended in failure and an empty wallet. I'd admit that was probably as much a failure of my technique as anything else, but the added layer of danger from a supernatural hotspot did nothing for my desire to visit Atlantis again.

"Right. So we visit the Dark Court and ask questions. Who else do we have?" I said, turning my thoughts away from those depressing memories. And my rather long dry spell. Look, try living with two gorgeous women for two years while getting burnt, stabbed, and bitten regularly and you'll realize how morose a man can get.

"Well, because Lily gets banished if you die, we can ignore the majority of the dark cults," Alexa said, pointing at the second and rather large pile of individuals with the ability but not necessarily the motivation. After all, long-term planning wasn't their mainstay, and the desire to own the ring was their greatest motivation. "We're mostly looking at people who don't want Lily free. Or in the hands of Mage Council or one of the others."

Lily, glancing up from her computers, made a face, showing her distaste at the thought of falling into one of those group's hands again. I nodded.

"Which leaves us with… the Odd Fellows, the Alfar, the Kaaba, the Nine Unknown Men, the White Lotus and Blue Shirts…" Alexa read down the list.

I winced with each new name. Some I only knew from reputation—secret societies like the Nine Unknown Men—while others were powerful immortal groups. In a few cases, the names were individuals who had gained so much power—like Annanasi—that they warranted their own folder.

"You know, when you say it like that, it seems like more people want me dead than alive," I muttered.

"Oh, they all want you dead. Just when," Alexa said, frustration evident as we rehashed an old argument.

"Yeah, but not right now. This sounds like most people want me dead," I said.

"There's only one ring. And thus only one owner," Alexa said. "One winner. A lot of losers. And while most people who owned Lily were content to just use her for personal gain, now?" A shake of her head. "Now people understand how much she can do. And fear what she will be forced to do."

"I'm not that powerful. I mean, Lou and Mer would counteract major changes," Lily muttered.

"You're not helping your case by name-dropping them." Alexa drew a deep breath, probably pushing aside her irritation. "I've told you before, Henry, that ring is a weapon, one that no one is going to be happy is being used. The fact that you have a single wish left unnerves a lot of people."

"And also safeguards him," Lily interrupted.

"And protects you. But if they can remove the ring from play, they will." Alexa stabbed a finger at me. "Just because you want to ignore the problem doesn't mean it's going away."

"And what can worrying about it change?" I snap at the blonde, crossing my arms. "You think I don't know people want me dead? That once I hit Level 100, when the wish is over, I'll be forced to fight a battle royale? But what can I do? I can't give Lily away. I'm not going to let her be traded around, used, or stored away because people are too scared. I can't train too hard, because that'll raise my level. I can't get new equipment, because they'll know what I'm getting. All I can do is wait."

"You could spend some time learning about your opponents." Alexa stabbed the documents. "You could pay attention."

I growled, shaking my head. Even if I did, how confident was she of the veracity of her information? And, even if I wasn't studying her books, I was certainly learning at my various assignments. But even as I did, did it matter?

474

Many of these organizations were hundreds of members large. The people they sent weren't going to be the ones we knew. When they came, they'd have the information and tempo advantage. "It's not enough. It'll never be enough."

Alexa opened her mouth to protest, only to be interrupted by the beeping of a watch. We both looked at the watch Lily was shutting.

"And you're done. You've been at it for three minutes."

Alexa pursed her lips, staring at the watch before letting out a huff and ending the argument. I offered Lily a smile of gratitude, only to receive a worried look in return. Even if Lily, playing mediator had given us our time out, it was not an argument that was going away. It'd gotten so bad that we had ended up with this compromise tactic to vent. But... In the end, I found myself looking away from her too.

Maybe I was avoiding the topic because I didn't want to think about my death. But no matter how many times we argued, neither Alexa nor Lily had offered a better solution. If there was one that didn't involve magically wishing away our enemies, we hadn't come across it.

***

After everyone had calmed down, we returned to our conversation about those who might want me dead. The problem was, the list was extremely long and our actual facts were extremely short. Without the corpse and the results of any analysis, we could only work from the most basic of descriptions. And unfortunately, that description fit a wide variety of creatures.

A good two hours later, we'd gone through every document and website we could find and narrowed the list down to a half dozen types. None of which were supposed to have any real presence in the city. But globalization had brought about a large number of good and ills, including the globalization of supernatural assassins. No longer did you need to rely on the untalented and limited pool of killers and thugs in your locality. Now, with an appropriate posting or contacts, you too could hire an international assassin.

Yay.

"We're getting nowhere," I said, pushing aside my laptop. "Unless we can get the body, this is a fool's errand. And even if we did figure out who it was, it doesn't bring us any closer to who hired him."

"So what do you want to do?" Alexa said, slipping a bookmark into the book she was reading before closing it.

"We go talk to your bosses." At Alexa's grimace, I pushed on. "A good portion of our potentials are part of the Council. If someone came in, they should know. Or at least, be able to find out."

"I don't know…"

"I do," I said. "They aren't our only clue, but they are our best bet. Let's go."

Rather than wait for Alexa to respond, I strode up the stairs, grabbing my bag on the way. Upstairs, I threw in a new ziplocked bag of extra clothing, a traveling first aid kit, and looked around before deciding on grabbing my latest experiment. Puzzle ward blocks. See, wards needed two different things: the actual carved wards themselves and the power to charge them. The best option was to charge and carve the wards at the same time, to imbue the wards with the powers you needed. In fact, for the vast majority of mages, that was the only way they knew how to do it.

I wasn't the vast majority of mages.

Lily had dumped a ton of information into my brain, and after some initial teasing of the spell forms in my mind, I'd realized that many of those forms, especially when linked to a ward, were independently functional. That meant that I could, as I'd done, carve individual wards—the code of a spell—

independent of purpose and power. They were just simple blocks, but if put together in the correct sequence, they created a new ward spell.

Which was why I had three twelve-by-twelve-grid mahogany wooden frames in hand with a series of carved wooden ward blocks already inserted for a force barrier and a ziplock bag of other "code blocks" ready to alter the spell. None of the blocks were as strong as a purpose-built ward of course, but it was infinitely more flexible. No longer did I have to carry around a single block for each specific spell. I could adjust the blocks as needed.

Though I also grabbed three of my one-use blocks, ones that threw up force walls, and added them to the side pockets of my bag. Sometimes disposable wards were good. On that note, I added an inscription pen, one that I could use on most materials to carve wards into barriers.

When I looked at the corner, I spotted my staff. The staff was a new project—a long, painstaking project—and my graduation examination from Caleb. Once I finished carving it, I was to pass it to Caleb and the rest of the Mage examination committee who, if they were satisfied, would graduate me into a full apprentice of the Council. Lily found the idea of a graduation amusing and insulting at the same time, noting that in many ways, I was well past any apprentice Mage. Though even the jinn would agree that I still lacked a bit in the theoretical side. My theoretical knowledge was patchy due to the way information was passed to me by Lily.

In either case, the staff wasn't complete. I'd added a bunch of Force and Elemental multipliers throughout the staff, making any spell of that form that I cast through it much more powerful. There was also space for a Mana battery, though I'd yet to find a Mana source I wanted to add to the staff. Or, well, a Mana battery that I could afford. On top of that, there was the usual array of Link and Scry spells to ensure that no one could steal the staff and get away with it. But major spells were still on hold—partly till I was confident enough to carve them in.

"Anyway, don't need the extra firepower," I muttered as I glanced at my hands. I could cast any spell I knew far faster than any appropriately Leveled Mage that I knew. Speed was my advantage, which was why the staff was geared toward offering power. And unless I was intent on blowing up a building, I didn't need the staff.

Once I'd mentally confirmed that I wasn't going to blow up a building, the only other thing to do was grab defensive equipment. I had two major methods of defense. First was my warded jacket. Of course, I'd been stabbed in the chest while wearing it, but that was as much because I hadn't zipped it up as any fault of the jacket. And second was…

"This still seems a little girly," I said, looking at the corded bracelet I'd beaded and woven before I slipped it on. Looking like a cross between a fifth-grader's friendship bracelet—with its bright colors and pretty beads—and a cheap tourist knickknack, the spelled and warded bracelet allowed me to conjure a temporary full-body ward. The hand-woven portion had allowed me to imbue my aura into the bracelet itself, while the individually engraved colored and metallic beards directed the force ward. It was the most powerful enchanted equipment I'd ever made, and it showed.

I just wished it wasn't that colorful.

Geared and dressed, I walked downstairs to find Alexa ready. The woman looked no different than she usually did in her work clothes. An exercise-shirt-cum-bra both lifted and compressed while keeping the chaffing from her thin Kevlar-and-chainmail combination to a minimum. A dark blue shirt, untucked to hide the gun she carried at the small of her back, and the enchanted bracers completed her ensemble on the top. Blousy pants hid space for knives in her boots and padded workout bottoms while also offering comfort—just like her flat, arched boots.

"Ready?" I said.

"Yeah," Alexa said as she lifted her gym bag. A gym bag that contained a variety of other pointy and bangy toys. Of course, a simple ward on the top of the bag made sure that even if we were pulled over, no law enforcement officer would ever pay attention to it.

"Let's go. See you, Lily." I waved goodbye to the jinn, who offered one too.

Chapter 3

In the end, we went to the only people who might know who'd hired someone to kill me. The Dark Court. Or the Council of Shadows and Dark Races, as it was officially known. With that kind of name, you'd think they would be dangerous. And some were. There was only so much you could say when you needed to drink blood or eat bodies to survive. Even if they played by the rules—taking donations, hanging out in goth clubs, or running mortuaries—members did slip up. And when they did, bad things happened. Mostly to other people until someone, like the Court's enforcers or the Templars, caught them.

Locally, the Court was one of our moderate-sized powers. Most of their members tended to live in big cities, finding the gaps which humanity fell through perfect for them. Large cities let them build subcultures and groups that rarely, if ever, interacted with the rest of society. Smaller cities made it harder, and villages… Well, let's just say there was a reason their numbers had declined significantly until the recent population boom. Even now, the number of vampires, ghouls, pengallan, and more were on the lower end.

Hopping out of Alexa's tiny blue car with its impressive trunk space, I craned my neck to stare at the back of the club. We'd parked in the open parking lot next to the club, behind the fenced-off area reserved for staff. An automatic glance picked out the half-dozen closed circuit cameras on the brick building, a slightly faded mural of a dark, oppressive woods at night facing me. It was an impressive work, more so when viewed through my Mana Sight. The mural itself helped hide the numerous enchantments painted on the wall, the runes of protection, detection, and reinforcement blending right into the swirling mass. It took me about ten minutes to note that there was no way I'd be able to pierce their defenses, not at my current level of understanding.

"Henry?" Alexa asked.

"Just checking out the building," I said, squinting and dismissing the vision.

The late afternoon sun beat down upon me, making me blink rapidly as my eyesight restored to normal. It was unseasonably hot for a late autumn day, which was annoying, especially since half of my protections were sewn and inscribed into my coat. Unfortunately, I'd run out of space for a cooling ward, meaning that wearing it in the heat was sweaty and uncomfortable.

It was no wonder that so many Mages dressed like professionals with suits and trench coats—the extra layers of social formality and professionalism were a perfect cover for the enchantments and protections we all wore. However, as much as I could understand that line of reasoning, I refused to give up my sense of style. If I'd wanted to look like a constipated professional, I would have become an accountant like my parents had insisted. No. I'd sweat in my stylish black leather jacket.

"Come on, you've been here before," Alexa said, grabbing my arm and dragging me forward. She stopped after a moment and frowned, tilting her head as she looked at me. "You have been here before, right?"

"To the most stylish, expensive, and loud club in the city?" I said, looking at Alexa as if she was crazy.

After a moment, Alexa let out a chuff of laughter. "Right. Sorry. Forgot I was talking to the introvert."

"Not that much. I have gone to clubs…" I paused as Alexa rapped on the employees' entrance, the heavy security door offering a muffled reply to her insistent knocking. "But this one's a bit out of my range. I don't think they'd let me in even the back door if this wasn't the day."

"It's not that bad," Alexa muttered as the door buzzed and she opened it.

Within, the club employees' entrance was filled with metal shelving holding everything from additional tablecloths, cardboard boxes of unknown contents, and cleaning supplies. The boring cream walls were a stark contrast to the glamorous main club floor, or at least, I thought so. It wasn't as if I had

482

ever entered the club floor. As Alexa turned the corner and opened the door to the staircase leading to the basement, I noted that I wouldn't see it this time either. And if I felt a flash of disappointment, I pushed it aside. It was only a minor disappointment, one borne from having been kept out of places like this due to my class and lack of funds.

Down, down we went. We passed the mundane basement that contained all the wine, beer, stage equipment, and other goods required to keep a club of this size running. We did not stop, but to keep heading down, we had to be buzzed through the heavy security door and then again through another entrance at the bottom of the staircase. Behind the second security door was a small anteroom filled by a trio of cyclops.

For once, I was amused to note that the cyclops did not disappoint my old gamer geek instincts. Each of the cyclops was bald—mostly by choice, true, but bald nonetheless—singular of ocular persuasion, and muscled like a heavyweight bodybuilder. The only major disruption from my geek fantasy was the pair of shotguns pointed at me. At least the leader carried a club—an enchanted asp—but it did nothing to stop the sudden outbreak of cold sweat across my back.

"Alexa. The Warlock Tsien. You are expected. But I fear we must check you both," the lead cyclops said, walking forward while he held his hand down by his side.

"Sure, Nicos," Alexa said, stepping forward, only for me to pull her back.

"No. We'll see the Council without a search," I said, my voice flat. "We won't let you subject us to such an indignity."

"Henry, it's fine. That's the way we do things here," Alexa said, looking affronted at my sudden bout of stubbornness. "And Nicos won't do anything. It'll just take a minute."

"When you're working for them, that's fine. But we're here on my business," I said, eyes narrowing at Nicos, who had stopped and was no longer moving forward. "And as such, I expect us to be treated like the powers we are."

"Powers?" Nicos said, his single eye dripping with as much condescension as his voice.

"Ex-Templar Initiate Alexa Dumough and Mage Henry Tsien. Individuals with the strength to break all three of you without breaking a sweat," I said, stepping aside from Alexa and offering the trio a cold smile. "And while I can't guarantee I could take your Council, they can't touch us either. As they know."

Nicos's lips pursed in anger, but I heard a voice chirp in his ear. I saw the change in his demeanor as orders were passed over the guard's earpiece and the cyclops stepped back. A jerk of Nicos's head indicated we could pass even as the door out of the anteroom opened.

Behind the door was a new sight. The creature was dressed in a butler's traditional costume, but that did little to hide the lines of stitching that held its body together. Its skin was patchy, portions of different-colored skin stitched together to keep the creature in one piece, giving it a patchwork and pallid continence. As I stepped past the creature, my nose wrinkled as I caught the scent of formaldehyde and rot. The stench brought back memories of my grandfather's funeral, of his once strong, lively body laid out for the wake. The smell was only lacking incense smoke to complete the triumvirate.

"Welcome, Mage Tsien," the creature said, affecting a clean mid-Atlantic accent, spoiled only by the slightest lisp.

"Thank you," I said, stepping aside to let the sulking Alexa stomp in. I winced, knowing I'd have to deal with her later. Showing her up and putting her in an awkward position in her place of work would cost me. Probably about three ice cream sundaes. But for now, I had more important things to watch for. Like... "You're a Frankenstein, aren't you?"

"Yes," the creature said. "Bronislav at your service."

"Good to meet you, Bronislav," I said. "I'm surprised the Council has you. No offense meant. Just that, well."

"Most of my brothers and sisters have perished, yes," Bronislav said. "And few are created now. At least, not by the traditional methods."

"Oh?" I raised an eyebrow. "There are more... experiments?"

"Always," Bronislav said. "But the new ones, they are not Frankensteins, you know?"

"I think I do," I said as I recalled one pizza-filled late night when Lily had waxed eloquent on the different types of magical reincarnations. Alexa had her head canted to the side, listening a little to our discussion.

The Frankensteins were their very own kind, distinct from zombies, ghouls, vampires, and other magical undead. They were not empty husks given locomotion or spirits who were drawn back into rotting bodies to keep them in motion. Instead, the Frankensteins were a new form of life, given life itself in the throes of magic and science mixing, spontaneously formed through the doctor's alchemical mixture and the combination of lightning.

Newer methods of extending life via reincarnating the dead sought to bring back the dead. Unfortunately, more recent successes were but improvements upon the older forms of magic—spirits housed in less rotting bodies. Or in some cases, bodies jumpstarted and patched together to allow the spirits to survive. Revenants in bodies held together only by magic. But they were not new life.

What the doctor did was, as Lily waxed eloquent, a matter of chance and genius. Since then, spirits were drawn in, combinations of alchemical potions used, but to no avail. Life, like the Frankensteins's, refused to return. Refused to be born again. But knowing that it was possible, always did others seek to replicate the doctor's methods.

"This way." Bronislav walked us down the lounge.

Now that I was not looking at the Frankenstein, I could take in the room properly. The basement was more cigar lounge than hip-hop dance floor, with plush leather chairs, small coffee tables, and dark chrome everywhere. That there were few residents within was no surprise—like their namesakes, most of the members of the Dark Council were nocturnal by nature. In short order, we passed the bar and lounge and entered another hallway—this one more opulently done with red cushioned walls and dim lighting—to be led to a smaller room.

This room, unlike the previous ones, was a bare room, lit with fluorescent tubes and consisting of a single long conference table behind which the Council sat. That there were no chairs for us was a reminder that we were appellants. That a discreet but large drain was set in the middle of the floor very near where we stood was ominous. As were the dark discolorations around the drain itself. Rumors of self-run trials and punishments rose in my memory, and from Alexa's sudden wariness, in hers too.

"Never been here," Alexa said, her hand dropping to her side. I knew she carried her knives there, having abandoned her spear since we weren't here to fight. No matter how aggressive I might be.

"Doubt they bring good employees here," I said.

"I shall see you out when you're done." Bronislav bows to me and steps aside, leaving us to stare at the silhouettes seated behind the table. As the Frankenstein begins to walk away, he stops and adds, "And Mage Tsien?"

"Yes?"

"You are always welcome to visit the actual club. The bouncers will let you in. Though we do hope you'd dress appropriately," Bronislav said as he backed off, leaving us to deal with the Council.

Three figures sat behind the table—the Chairman and two others. The Chair I actually knew from having lit one of his family's weddings early on in my career. Eleventh wedding, and of that, a half dozen of those were to the same person. Vampires had altered the entire "death do us part" section of their vows, going instead for "till half a century has passed." After all, when you theoretically could live for eternity and were undead, a lifelong commitment became... challenging. And so marriages—or re-marriages—were a big thing among them. Having a Mage create the effect of daylight—without the burning and searing and death—was a mark of status.

Status, but not a lot of payment. Truth be told, I hadn't realized exactly how important it was back then and was taken for a ride, paid a pittance for what we did. But you lived and learned. In either case, the Chair was a known quantity, the oldest vampire in the city. Due to his age and wisdom—and yes, wealth—he ran the Council, but was known to be mostly diplomatic about matters.

The other two were unknown. One was a Native American, his skin the color of dark clay, eyes with a weight of blackest marble. Hair that fell just below his shoulders was held back by a simple stone hairband, and beside him, a cane sat. Beside the almost-normal-looking Native American was a full-blown green troll, a creature you could never see in normal daylight without a glamour. Green skin, at least nine feet tall, warts and big teeth were all present. As was a simple set of dark robes and a pair of glasses perched on its bulbous nose.

"Mage Tsien. Alexa," the Chair—Roland—said neutrally, greeting us as we approached and stood under the lights.

Now that we were in position, the trio lit up properly. If it wasn't for the fact that I could see the flow of power, the way Mana and light were manipulated to first put them in shadow, and now make us squint while revealing them fully, I'd be a little more impressed. Same with the way their words seemed to echo through the chamber. Tricks. But effective tricks, if you didn't see the enchanted wards and runes in the chamber. Nothing overt, just minor things to unsettle and unnerve.

"You come before the Council. What do you seek of us?"

I narrowed my eyes at the Chair's wording. Damn power plays. I knew this was going to happen the moment we walked in, which was why I refused to let them check me. Ever since it had become clear that the Mage Council had pretty much claimed me as one of their own, my interactions with others became complicated.

"Information." I paused, considering, but decided to play it out. "We seek information. And are willing to bargain for it."

"By the old edicts?" the troll asked as he leaned forward. That simple act was rather intimidating, when the creature leaning forward was that big.

"Hell, no!" I said, shaking my head. "One, I'm a modern-day kid. And two, I'm not an idiot."

"Pity," the Native American said.

I narrowed my eyes at him, watching the way Mana played over his body, was drawn in and escaped. The creature's aura was powerful, strong, but it was also harmonious with the Mana it drew in. And so, very much not human. There was too much "earth" in his aura, even for a shaman. Which, I was sure, the creature was too.

"Not from my viewpoint," I said. "A changeling attacked me. A skinwalker of some form. We couldn't get much from it before the Mages swooped in. But if anyone would know of a creature like that working in the city—"

"It would be us?" Roland sniffed. "Just because such creatures are under our purview does not mean we control them."

"No, but you've got your ear to the ground." I swept my gaze over the trio, trying to get a read if the news of my attack elicited any reaction. Unfortunately, none of them offered any obvious tells. Not that I would have trusted any such tells. "You can find out who hired it. I don't care about the creature as much as its employer."

"We can ask around. But what does the Mage offer?" Roland said, tapping a moleskin notebook in front of him with one manicured nail. Manicured or not, the slight unevenness and worn nature of his hands was a testament to Roland's background.

"Money. Or a service," I said, raising a finger. "By the new rules."

"We'll take the money," the troll said. "Medium-sized favor, current rate is…" He frowned, big eyebrows drawing close in puzzled thought.

"Ten thousand, three hundred, eighteen dollars on the exchange," the normal-looking one said.

My instincts thrummed every single time he opened his mouth, warning me that of the three, he was the most dangerous. I frowned, cudgelling my brain before finally I realized what the long-haired gentleman was. A Nun'Yunu'Wi. That was why he was so powerful. In fact…

"Medium…" I winced again. "You guys do payment plans?"

"No."

I sighed, reaching into my jacket and finding the envelope I'd kept my money in. A quick sorting of funds and exchange and I passed it over. Funny thing about working with supernaturals. Most didn't take checks, so keeping large stashes of cash—in this case, the majority of my savings—at home was common. Since so many of us lived in a grey market economy, a lot of money exchanged hands in that grey space too. I floated the envelope over, letting it drop onto the table with a thump.

"Thank you. You'll be informed when we know something," Roland said.

None of them even looked at the envelope. I knew they'd check it once I was gone, but trust and reputation meant that they wouldn't look. Not until later. But now, at least, we would have an answer. Maybe.

Because what I was paying for wasn't guaranteed. Just for them to ask. But it was better than nothing. I thought.

***

Outside, Alexa stayed silent until we were in the car and a block away from the club. Then she slowed the car down, pulled over, and glared at me. "Why didn't you tell me what you planned?"

"I... didn't think about it? I mean, I thought you knew that we'd be going in as, well, us. And not Alexa the employee."

"So it's my fault?" Alexa said dangerously.

I winced, knowing that tone. After living in the same house with the two women for so many years, I'd picked out a few things. One of which was compromise. Sometimes, it was better to say I was wrong than to fight to the end over something that might be arguable. And I did forget to mention it, or prepare Alexa for the problem. Even if she was, technically, the more experienced of the two of us. Sort of.

"Sorry," I said.

Alexa stayed silent for a second before offering a nod then flashing me a smile. "I am too. It's just going to be awkward now. And they'd only just started seeing me as one of them, you know?"

"I do," I said. While I and Lily might be loners by nature, Alexa was more of a people's person. She'd grown up with an organization, an entire orphanage full of people to rely on, to talk to. She had a family, a support system, and a faith she'd walked away from. Well, except the faith. That, I knew, she still held. It was just… different. "It'll be fine."

Alexa shook her head as she hit the button to open the car doors, only to pause as I was interrupted by a phone call. I frowned, a small curl of dread flashing through my stomach when I saw the name on the caller display.

Chapter 4

"Wei?" I said into the phone, offering a traditional greeting and inquiry at the same time.

"Oy! You. Call Mom. You've not called in a month, you know!" My sister's shrill voice came over the phone. Elder sisters were the same the world over, I thought. Bossy and always right.

"Has it been a month already?" I winced. I wished I could say I'd been dodging calls, but the way of Chinese parents the world over was they expected me to call them, not the other way around. It was my duty—which, as usual, I failed at. I really was not a good son. "Sorry. I'll do it tomorrow."

"You... you... you know what. We're doing dinner. Now."

"What?"

"Dinner. At the usual place." As if to entice me to come after berating me, she added, "I'm buying."

"Fine, fine," I said, wincing.

It had been months since I'd seen her. Not since the last family gathering I'd managed to make. Sometimes it was strange that I could live so close to my family and yet never really see them. I liked my family. You know, in the abstract.

In the flesh, my family was grumpy, insistent, and prone to a lot of guilt-tripping. Even if I did deserve it most of the time, I didn't want to be subjected to that kind of environment. Of course, there were advantages to showing up at family dinners—including my mother's cooking.

Once I'd explained the matter to Alexa, she insisted on dropping me off at our designated meeting place—the only decent Hong Kong dessert shop in the city. There were others around, but this was the only one that did desserts right. Whether it was because the store was owned by a family or because we had grown up eating similar desserts, my sister and I agreed there just wasn't another place that compared. Proper, pressed soybean drinks, hot tofu pudding with just the right amount of cane sugar, crispy pancakes with drizzled condensed milk. My mouth watered at the thought. Once again, I wondered why it had taken me so long to come back.

As I stepped out of the car, stretching from the long ride over, I held the door open to speak with my friend. "You sure you won't come?"

"It's a family meeting," Alexa said, shaking her head. "And your sis can get you home just as well as I can. Make sure to bring some snacks back for us."

"As if Lily would let me forget." I snorted.

Alexa chuckled as we regarded the Quest that had appeared in our joint eyesight.

Quest Received: Bribe the GM
Bring back delectable snacks for the GM.
Rewards: Variable, depending on satisfactory levels of bribes

Of course, we both knew that this particular quest wouldn't provide much in terms of experience. But bribing the GM was a long-time tradition in tabletop games, so it was "allowed," according to Lily. I still thought she was stretching the wish a little, but since it was in my favor, I wouldn't complain. Closing the door on the car, I waved Alexa off before turning around.

The dessert café was bracketed by large store-front windows that showed the fluorescent-lit interior. Within, multiple square tables lined the cream-colored wall before a single counter blocked off the dessert display and the kitchen behind. A pair of waitresses in casual clothing worked the counter and the floor. Students on a late-night food run, tired professionals, and a single four-person family filled the small café, but my sister was not among those present.

Having scoped out the location, I walked in and was quickly shown to my seat. The red upholstered chair squeaked slightly as I placed my jean-clad derriere on it and flipped open the presented menu. An order of non-caffeinated bubble tea later, I was resting quietly against the hard chair-back when my sister breezed in.

Terror of my past, annoyance of the present, my future berater stalked towards me. She barely crossed the five-foot line by a pair of inches, though you wouldn't know it as her three-inch heels took her from vertically tiny to just short. Petite or not, my sister had enough attitude to take up a room and the delicate features that had men clustering around her whenever she went clubbing.

"Hey, sis," I said, waving from my seat.

Katie—Katherine, but she hated the full name—took a seat and glanced at the menu. "You ordered yet?"

I shook my head.

"Good. You always get it wrong." Waving, she got the attention of a waitress and fired off a series of orders before turning her piercing attention on me. "You're looking good. Added a bit of muscle. And that jacket's new."

I glanced at the enchanted coat and shrugged, grateful that the enchantments were on the inside. Not that they looked like anything but weird runic glyphs, badly sewn or burnt on. One thing they didn't discuss in all the books and fantasies was how hard it was to actually do the work. I swore if I was in a proper game system, I'd have sewing at level 5 already.

"Thanks?" I said hesitantly.

"So this new job of yours is going well?" Katie said, eyes narrowing.

"It's piecemeal, but there's enough money in it." I knew the question was about more than money, though money was a big part of the conversation.

After all, it was hard to be healthy and happy when you were struggling to make ends meet. Not impossible. Just hard.

"And what is it that you do again?"

I suppressed the smile that tried to creep onto my face. I'd been purposely vague with my family. Hard to say "I run quests, make minor magical items, and occasionally kill monsters" with a straight face. Among other things, my liberal, civilized, and worrywart parents would freak out about the idea of me getting injured. Even if I did have magically gifted healing, it was just a sped-up system. Not a hand-wavey fix.

"Arts and crafts," I said. "I make things and sell them to people." That answer wasn't much better, not for an Asian family, but we make do. "And run errands for some of my richer clients."

"You know what Mama and Papa would say, right?" Katie said, eyes narrowing.

"Why do you think I stay away?"

"Avoiding the argument won't change their views," Katie said. "In fact, it makes you look like a child trying to hide a smoke."

"But talking to them won't change their minds. You know them. Have you ever won an argument?" I countered, shaking my head. "Easier to just keep them in the dark."

"And at arm's length?" Katie opened her mouth to berate me further but was interrupted as the food arrived. When the waitress left, I picked up a sesame ball and dropped it on her plate. "This isn't over!"

"Food first." I popped one of the balls into my mouth.

Katie sighed but dropped the conversation, allowing us to focus on the dishes. In short order, we were done, replete and less angry.

"Henry, you need to call and visit more. Staying away hurts them. You know that. I know you know that, so why?"

I grimaced but stayed silent, not having a particularly good answer.

Katie sighed, shaking her head, and pointed at me. "Ever since you started this new job, it's been like that. And don't think we haven't noticed the new scars and the muscles. Are you part of a triad? A gang?"

"Of course not!"

Katie smiled slightly at how fast I replied, taking it for the truth it was. I was just grateful that I hadn't tried to overthink the question, since the Mage Council could be considered a weird cult. Not a triad or gang, but, you know.

"Then where are you getting all this money? I don't believe you're earning that much just 'running errands.'"

"Well, I don't care if you don't believe it. It's the truth." I paused, then added, "Okay, not just running errands. I get a bunch from selling my stuff."

"Your… stuff." Katie waggled her eyebrows, and I snorted.

"Not that kind."

"True. You have no chance at earning a living that way," Katie said.

I sniffed, but I had to admit I was grateful that we had shifted our talk in a new direction. For a time, we turned to happier things, like discussions about Katie's lack of a love life as she pursued her career in the banking industry, about old friends and past experiences. We talked like family did, about nothing important and everything. And I couldn't help but forget some of my worries, forget about the fact that someone had tried to kill me earlier that day. I reveled in the normalcy of the conversation, and my sister, the smart woman that she was, noticed it.

Eventually, the waitress gave us a look, hinting that it was time to free up her table. I paid for the bill, making sure to leave a generous tip. An act that made Katie raise an eyebrow, though she didn't pursue it.

Our congenial atmosphere lasted until she dropped me off at home. Then she put a hand on my arm, growing serious. "Henry. Call them. And… consider trusting us. Whatever is going on, you know we'll support you."

I flashed her a quick, wry smile and nodded, detaching my arm from hers as I opened the door. Family, obligation, responsibilities. I was never good at them. Not at home, not in person. But I'd try to call them more often, even if I had to lie. Because for all that I wanted it otherwise, might want it otherwise, my life was not one I'd drag them into.

Chapter 5

The next morning, we pulled up at the scene of the crime. Not mine, since that one was still blocked off by government representatives and my guardians. No, the original crime. Shane's murder. Of course, I didn't know exactly where he had been killed, but his home was our best bet.

We approached the apartment, having parked Alexa's car a distance away. The ex-Initiate had her gym bag slung over the shoulder of her inscrolled winter jacket. It was rather nice of her friends from the Templars to send that to her for Christmas last winter, even if the note guilting her for leaving had been rather passive-aggressive. Still, the coat was both armored and imbued with faith magic, such that she was better protected against malicious magic than even I was.

The flat was in one of those concrete block, low-income buildings that had been built in the 1960s and never really updated. Even the wallpaper in the corridors was faded and stained from years of use, no matter the amount of care taken for it. For all its wear, it was obvious the inhabitants of the building took good care of it. The floors were swept and mopped, the scent of a cleaning fluid assaulting my nose as I walked down the well-lit corridor.

Shane's apartment was one of the larger ones, a legacy of how long the dwarf had lived there. Staring at the green door, it took me only a moment to locate the spell ward that subtly turned away unwanted visitors. This one was still intact, traces of its user still glowing.

"Are we going in?" Alexa asked impatiently. Breaking and entering had a tendency to put the ex-Initiate on edge, especially since she'd lost the protection of her order.

"One second," I said, touching the ward. I manipulated it, pulling forth the ward's aura.

I nodded after a second, releasing the ward, having memorized the traces of the magical signature still left on it. The ward had degraded such that I wouldn't be able to track its caster, but if they used magic near me, it'd probably be possible to figure out who they were. Most likely, the ward maker was dead, killed by my hand yesterday. But... you never know.

After that, breaking in required two spells—one to bypass the ward, the second to open the locks. Magic made crime way too easy. It was one of the reasons why we policed each other so much—when the governments got involved, they had a tendency to overreact. Or, perhaps, because we never gave them a chance to properly react, they didn't have a middle ground.

When I move to step in, Alexa pushes me aside, shooting me a glare that I duck my head to avoid. She enters, the buckler she carried in her gym bag on her hand while a shorter stick was held in the other. That stick, I knew, could extend to form a point of Mana-imbued force. It was one of my better inventions, though the charge could only hold for about ten minutes.

It was a good thing too that Alexa went ahead, as three steps into the apartment, she was attacked by a crazed ball of fur. She caught the attacker on her shield, holding its claws away from her face. A few struggles and three deep scratches later, I had the cat suspended in mid-air, snarling at us.

"Forgot about Charlie," I said.

"I didn't," Alexa said, glaring at the deep scratches on her wrist.

She waved for me to deal with the feline while she scouted out the rest of the apartment. By the time she had come back, I'd set up a small force wall to keep the cat contained. Alexa caught me browsing through cupboards, looking for the remainder of Shane's cat food, when she got back.

"Do you mind opening the window?" I said, gesturing outward.

Agitated and abandoned, forced to stay at home—which he hated—Charlie had proceeded to make his distaste known. Cat urine, vomit, and feces made the interior of the apartment rather horrendous for all right-thinking, breathing creatures.

Alexa quickly complied then poked her head out the window, eyeing the fire escape before walking back, carefully. Shane's residence was, beyond its feline-induced chaos, relatively neat. The dwarf had been a collector of puzzle blocks and rocks. All across the room were mason jars filled with rocks, all of them placed in a haphazard manner with no sense—at least to my eyes—for the kind of geology they contained. As for Shane's furniture, most of it was worn and marked, the few cushions split, stuffing falling out. But beyond that, there was a mild discomfort in being in the room, one that I only twigged on later.

Everything was a little bit smaller than it should be. I wasn't that tall, but Shane was—had been—a dwarf. So… yeah. Chairs were a little lower, tables fitting perfectly for someone four and a half feet tall. Even the stepstool kind of made sense.

"So now what?" Alexa said, eyeing the content cat after I'd refilled its bowls.

"Now we look for a clue."

"And what would that look like?"

"If I knew, I'd have a clue."

Alexa groaned but proceeded to help. After we finished up going through the living room and pantry together, she relegated me to the bedroom, saying how weird it would be to go there herself. While I was browsing through sock drawers and finding contents that were all too typical, I heard a shout from Alexa.

"What is it?" I said, walking over, relieved to have left the bedroom.

"Appointment book!" Alexa said, waving at the desk she sat behind. "I think I've narrowed down his death day."

I nodded, taking the book from her. We were already certain that Shane hadn't died here. Death had a tendency to release a large amount of energy and emotions, ensuring that any practitioner of the magic arts could pick out a recent death. Unless steps were taken to disperse both the lingering death aura and the magic release. But those actions also often left their mark.

The appointment book was neatly organized, and it was clear why Alexa was certain of the day of death. Shane had a tendency to leave notes on appointments and on the day itself at the bottom of each finished day, making the appointment book part calendar and part diary. On the day in question, there were no additional notes—and it was also two days ago. Which made it well within our expectations.

"The White Scarves?" I frowned, tapping the only appointment of consequence. Unless he was taken while running groceries, that was our best bet.

"It's the Chinese group. Tong? Triad?" Alexa scratched her head. "Secret society turned supernatural group turned sort-of gangsters?"

"I know who they are. I just don't know where they are." I paused, considering. "One second." A brief phone search later, I nodded, tossing the appointment book back onto the table. "Got it."

"You ran a search on them? What did you type in? 'Supernatural secret societies, Chinese'?" Alexa said.

"Sort of, yeah. The associations are sort of like the Yakuza. They've got meeting places that are official and meant for their members to join. Clan associations, secret societies, whatever. Since the White Scarves aren't actually a triad, it was easy finding them," I said. "We should probably finish up here, but that seems like our best option."

Alexa nodded, turning back to looking around the office for further clues. As for myself, I went back to poking around the bedroom, checking under the bed, looking for other tell-tale problems. Only when I was done, finding little else but dust bunnies and a small safe that contained a gun, did I remember something important.

"Lily, don't I get a Quest or something?" I said to the empty air, knowing that the jinn was watching over me.

Of course, she couldn't talk to me directly, but I got a reply anyway.

Quest: Do What You Were Going to Do Anyway
Find the people who put a death warrant out on your head and deal with them.
Failure: Death
Reward: You live. Also, a Level Up.

The quest notification was within expectation. The reward was much less so. I felt my mouth dry before I swiped the quest away. Like any good game, rewards were offered based off difficulty level. If Lily was willing to give me a full level, especially considering how hard the levels were getting these days, she was expecting survival to be a chore.

"Why do I have a quest telling me to keep you alive?" Alexa said, catching me staring into mid-air as I pondered this new information.

"Sorry. Lily. Do we…" I licked my lips, and paused. "Are you sure you want to do this?"

"Do what?"

"Stick with me. You don't have to…" I trailed off as Alexa glared at me. "You're free, you know."

"And run off when my friend needs me? The devil take that." Alexa snorted. "Even if the Templars don't think I'm suitable anymore, the Oracle meant for me to be here. And here I'll be."

I blinked, recalling what Alexa said. And realizing that for all the time we'd been together, she hadn't brought up that. That reason why she had first come into my life. And yet, even if she wasn't an Initiate, even if she was no longer a Templar-to-be, her faith in both the Oracle and what she was meant to do was unshaken.

"Thank you," I said, offering her a half-smile. I hoped that she was choosing right.

We stayed silent until I got out of the bedroom and spotted Charlie, curled up in the corner and looking content. The cat had gorged himself on the food and water and now slept peacefully.

"What do we do about Charlie?"

Alexa frowned. "Did Shane have friends? Someone who could take care of him? Family?"

I shook my head, glancing at the mantel. There were pictures of his departed mother. Outside of that, he had no other pictures, no brothers or sisters. "His clan?"

Alexa slowly nodded. "We should check."

"Yeah…"

Resolved and somehow sadder than ever, we scooted out of the late dwarf's apartment. It was a sad thing, to die and have no one to take care of your pets. Or belongings. Or…

"Hey," I called, stopping Alexa as we walked to the elevator. "I'll be right back."

"What?"

I waved away Alexa's question while trying to recall if the kitchen had any garbage bags. Then I headed back to Shane's bedroom and sock cupboard. Some things… well, it was the right thing to do.

Chapter 6

We pulled up across the street from the White Scarves's meeting place, a non-descript double-story retail building with shuttered windows and a single wooden door on the outskirts of our two-block Chinatown. The building had a small, almost hidden sign reading the "White Scarf Chinese Cultural Association," the only thing denoting what lay within. Officially, Chinatown started a block away, though like most communities, the official Chinatown was really only comprised of overpriced restaurants, tourist shops, and a few grocery stores.

We sat and watched the building for a few minutes after Alexa parked, eyeballing the location and its various wards. Magic itself was like mathematics. Even if the symbols used to indicate the formula were unknown, they all had the same logic underlying the symbology. While it took me a bit of time to figure out the symbols, I worked them out.

"Nothing too unusual," I said. "Wards of reinforcement. Pest control. Ignorance. There's also an attack ward, but I can't tell what it does. Lots of lightning though."

Alexa grimaced but finally opened the door. Together we exited the car and headed for the building. After we knocked on the door for a bit, it was finally opened.

"Members only," the portly, mustached man inside snapped at us before he started closing the door.

"I'm here to speak with the White Scarves," I said, putting a hand on the door. Unfortunately, my actions did nothing to stop the door from continuing to swing close.

"No."

When the door was nearly closed, Alexa slapped her palm against it with a thump, putting the closing to a halt. She pushed, sending the man stumbling back.

"The Mage wants to speak with your people." So saying, she scooted past me and strode in, before freezing three steps in.

"Alexa?" I blinked as she stood frozen and I managed to squeeze past her. Only to see what had stopped her. "Oh."

A half dozen men sat around foldout circular tables, bottles of beer and bowls of sesame seeds spread before them. Each of the men was looking at us, the barrels of revolvers and pistols pointed directly at us.

The portly man sneered. "Members only."

"Yeah, no," I said, flicking my hand sideways. That was not the way I'd wanted to play it, but now that we were there, I wasn't going to let my friend be filled with lead. Power swelled as I formed but did not cast my Force Wall, ready to catch their bullets. Really, they should have just shot us if they intended to make use of those guns. "We're not here to cause trouble. We just have a few questions."

"Members—"

"Only. I got it. Look. You aren't going to shoot us. Especially not when your silencing wards are down."

"Our wards aren't—" The door warden's eyes widened as he saw the light show happening along the edge of the property. The wards weren't actually down, but as a mundane, he wouldn't know.

"So. Your bosses. Or we can just stand around all day," I said.

The door warden's lip curled up, and he walked to the staircase and ascended. He was gone for long minutes, minutes that we spent under the barrels of guns. Of course, I didn't waste that time, edging my body sideways so they couldn't see my fingers as I manipulated the spell forces, burning new linked wards around the building and beneath the concrete under our feet.

Force Ward Cast
Synchronicity: 86%

Disruptive Ward Cast
Synchronicity: 37%

Spell after spell, I layered defenses around their defenses. Layering protection around us. Just in case things went bad. It was how smart magicians worked, taking the time to set up a scenario they could win. I also, however, kept a close eye on how much Mana I had, knowing I'd need it if things went bad. You never really know how things would play out, which was why instant-cast spells like the ones I used were still preferred over wards and enchantments.

When the door warden finally made his way down, he looked entirely put out. A few gruff words of command later, guns were put away and we were escorted up the stairs. I had to admit my back itched the entire walk up, wondering if there was a hidden order to shoot us. It was only as I was nearly at the top of the staircase that one of the heretofore-silent men below spoke.

"Damn banana."

I stiffened, and Alexa, somehow sensing the change in my movement, looked back. I shook my head, dismissing her concerned look as I refocused on what was important. Like our coming meeting.

***

A simple reception area greets us when we make our way up, and then we're led past a board room to an office. Behind a brown desk featuring a monitor and one of those underpowered, overpriced mini-desktops sat a fifty-something Chinese man, his half-balding head of hair combed back where traces of grey appeared. He looked up from his keyboard, hidden behind paper and a trio of photograph stands.

Beside him stood another Chinese man. Unlike his officemate, he was larger, a man who obviously saw the inside of a gym on a semi-regular basis. Muscular, but with a layer of fat that appeared when one got older and lazier. The T-shirt denoting a boy band concert of some form stood in stark contrast to his large, intimidating demeanor. Powerful—in a mundane way. But mundane or not, he was armed with the highest variety and quality of enchanted equipment I'd seen. Everything from the bracers on his wrists and ankles to his necklace and hairband were enchanted. The knife in his boot and the gun on his hip were all powered too, and the shining pair of rectangles in his pockets told me that he'd probably enchanted the individual bullets in the gun.

"Mage Tsien. You came into our house, demanding answers. Why?" The seated man looked directly at me then flicked a dismissive glance at Alexa, who had stepped away to regard the enforcer.

"I'd be happy to answer your questions, but I'd also like to know who I'm talking to," I said.

"You can call me Manager Kim. And this is Brother Lu," Kim said.

"Okay. Firstly, thank you. I'm sorry we pushed in when we weren't meant to. We just have a question about Shane Travertine. He was supposed to visit you a few days ago."

"We heard of the attack on you. And his death. You think we had something to do with it?" Lu asked, his voice accusatory.

"No. I just need to know why he came," I said. "And what time he left."

"None of your business," Lu said.

Alexa shifted at his words, but I held up a hand, stopping her from moving.

"Look, I know it's none of our business what he did here. But you know he died, right?" When I received a nod from Kim, I continued. "Well, I want to find out why he died. Surely you don't begrudge him that."

"He's dead. Doesn't matter to him."

"I bet his ghost wouldn't say that," I said.

The pair exchanged glances, looking slightly worried. I wasn't surprised they were concerned. After all, ghosts were annoying. Few of them had the strength to do any real damage, but having one haunt you could be frustrating. And potentially dangerous, if you had a newborn. The reflection in the window that Lu sat with his back to showed the pictures of his new, happy family.

"He never seemed like one to haunt. And his clan will deal with him," Lu said, but I heard his trace of uncertainty.

"I just need a confirmation he arrived and when he left," I wheedled.

"Two p.m.," Kim said, shaking his head. When I moved to thank him and leave, he held up a hand, stopping me. "Why did you betray your people?"

"What?"

"You have chosen to be a... Mage," Kim almost spat the word, shaking his head. "Aligning yourself with the Western Imperialists. Why?"

"What are we, in a bad nineties Hong Kong film?"

My words made the pair glare. Alexa looked stern to anyone who didn't know her, but I saw her slight amusement at my words.

"You joke, but you betrayed your people. Learning rubbish magic from those who destroyed our very foundations. Why did you not join us?" Kim slapped his hand on the table. "Do you not care that they destroyed our people, weakened us so that we had to leave our motherland just to survive?"

"Not really."

How could I explain that what I learnt from Caleb was mainly magic theory, concepts and history rather than detailed casting. For the most part, I didn't even use sixty percent of what he taught. Sure, some of the fundamentals were useful, but the magic theory that Lily deposited in my brain was often more sophisticated and complex than anything I learnt from Caleb.

Even if I could explain that, I wouldn't. For the last twenty levels, I'd be dumbing down what I knew and cast so that I wasn't showing my entire range of knowledge to Caleb. As it was, I startled the Mage repeatedly with the way I combined spells. Or, more truthfully, the way Lily taught me to combine spells.

"I joined the Mages because they came to me and are teaching me," I said. "They offered protection and lessons. If you all came, well…"

"Well?"

"I might have chosen to learn from you. But I didn't even know you guys were here till now," I said flatly. "Which kind of tells me you aren't much of a power. In this city at least."

Lu shifted, a hand drifting toward the butt of his pistol. Alexa's eyes narrowed, though Lu's motion looked more an unconscious threat than a conscious one. Still, unconscious or not, it was a threat.

"We might not have much presence in this city, but we are still strong in Asia. You would do well to not underestimate us," Lu said.

"I'm not. Just stating a fact." And I meant it. It had taken Lily a bit to figure out how to classify Lu, but he was within range to be a threat for me. Being a mundane and having enchanted equipment meant he could theoretically end me without her interference.

Lu (Level 47—Human)
HP: 100/100
Mana: 0/0

Kim at least was in the tens, a normal human by Lily's standards. But as the Manager, the local boss, his danger was not in how hard he could hit but the number of people he could send to do the hitting. Because at the end of the day, no matter how much magic I wielded, I was still a squishy human underneath.

"And if you're threatening us, you might as well get in line," Alexa said, snorting at the pair.

"There is no line, Templar," Kim said scornfully. "If we want you dead, we will not hesitate. And your actions have driven many to seek such action."

"Actions?" I frowned, cocking my head. "Look, we've been rude here, but killing us seems a little much, no?"

"Not this. That… genie of yours. She is a danger. To all of us," Kim said, shaking his head. "Her presence is a danger. If we did not have our own artifacts, we would be concerned."

Faction Information: White Scarves

Formerly based in mainland China, emigrated to Taiwan, as did many other secret societies due to purges by their Socialist Republic of China. One of eleven major secret societies in Taiwan who control the majority of supernatural activity within the country. Has multiple branches worldwide, though none have the same strength as the main quarters. Known for using internal and external magic sources, based on misconceptions formed from Taoist and Legalist magical theory.

Known Artifacts: Yi's Bow and Arrows, the 24 Ocean Calming Pearls, the Golden Brick

I grunted as Lily finally updated their faction information. It was amusing, since most of that was knowledge I would never have gotten if not for the fact that she had decided that a Wikipedia entry of factions was part of the game experience. Their artifacts were all just powerful enchanted objects—able to level the playing field, but to call them a similar strength to my ring was a bit of an exaggeration. Still... a Golden Brick?

"Sure, sure," I said, deciding to give them face. "I can understand how Lily could be a concern. But she's not going anywhere, not for a while. But your warning is well taken."

"Lily." Lu snorts. "You really do like your white friends."

"First, Lily's a jinn. She's not white or brown or... whatever. Secondly, you're an ass," I said, glaring at him. "Lastly, I do like my friends." Turning on my heels, I walked to the door and nodded to Alexa. "Let's go."

I saw Kim try to say something, but I was incensed enough that I didn't stop. There was no point in talking to them anyway. I'd met enough racist asses on both ends of the spectrum. Some, having been beaten down enough, decided to play the victim card unceasingly. It was always worse when they hung out with their own, staying with others who shared their background, race, and views. Never trying to see a different viewpoint, never traveling. That process of creating silos created echo chambers of beliefs, reinforcing their belief that their hurt, their pain was more important than any others'. And it was true enough that we all justified our pain and playing the victim. But at a certain point, you just had to keep moving.

We only spoke once we were a distance away in the car. And more to focus on something else, something worth talking about.

"They know about Lily," I said. "They know people are coming after us."

"Picked that up. Sounds like it's not just one group, if they've picked that up too," Alexa said, her frown creasing. "I wonder how many."

"I don't know. But I think we know someone who might. And might be willing to tell us."

"You don't mean…"

"I do."

"You…" Alexa huffed then muttered something under her breath. Still, she took the next turn, heading away from the house.

At least we'd confirmed—at least we thought we had—that Shane had been alive when he left the Scarves. If the names of those after us were being bandied around so much, we might have another clue.

Chapter 7

Nora's hadn't changed. Even if I hadn't been back in a few months, the clothing store was the same. To mundane eyes, the used clothing store was filled with cheap, well-kept clothing brought there by thrifty individuals, dumpster divers, and locker clearers like I had been. The only incongruity were the wooden cupboards lining the walls, cupboards that were rarely opened when non-magical individuals were around. Simple "ignore me" wards along the cupboards ensured that no one paid attention to them. Of course, the wards were so low-powered that any supernatural and a few Gifted individuals would automatically ignore the spells. But that too was by design.

After all, El had to find customers for her real business somewhere. As the foremost material merchant in the city, El was both a great salesperson and collector. And while it was mostly Mages who made use of her services, she did dabble in other enchanted objects too. Or knew who would sell or trade them. Which meant she had a ton of connections throughout the city.

"El!" I waved to her after walking in, wrinkling my nose slightly as I noticed the incense. I let my eyes unfocus for a second to see what kind of glamour the pixie was using. The old matronly woman that I'd known before flashed into focus, along with her humdrum pink-and-green flowery dress, a piece of clothing that could have been taken right off her racks. Then I let my Mage Sight reassert itself and the redhead, pointed-long-eared pixie came into focus. "Got a moment?"

"Just doing inventory," El said, wrinkling her nose in such an adorable look that I wanted to say aww. "Stupid business is doing better."

"Huh?"

"The clothing business. I think there's going to be a recession again," El said, shaking her head. "Every time, we get more customers here before a recession. Means I go through inventory faster and have to buy more too. I need to hire again."

Drawn into the conversation, I went over to the counter where she was sorting clothes and leaned against it. "So do you hire supes because of your other business?"

"Of course. But you'd be surprised how hard it is to hire properly. Anyone with any ambition is always snapped up by others. Even if you find someone good, in a few years, they're gone. Either for a better job or… well."

Knowing El as I did, a lot of her hires probably came from the bad side of the tracks—orcs, goblins, and others who weren't trendy enough to be considered a "dark race" but who still suffered the consequences of not being passable as a human. Stuck living on the edges, many of them found legal work difficult, and so ended up dabbling in illegal or supernatural work. Neither of which was safe.

"Sorry to hear that."

"Forget sorry. Want a job?" she asked.

"No."

"Bah. Ever since you got your magic, you've gotten all kinds of posh." El sniffed, teasing me. She looked at Alexa, raising one elegant eyebrow at the blonde.

"No, thank you. I'm not very good at…" Alexa hunted for the right word.

"Fashion?" I added helpfully before yelping as she kicked me.

"Why are you here?" El said, turning the conversation back.

"Ah. Ummm… have you heard about Shane?" I said, lowering my voice.

When El indicated she hadn't, I winced and told her the story. In the silence that flowed through the store afterward, a pair of shoppers came in, chatting merrily as they browsed through the women's racks.

I eyed the girls, teenagers who had no clue what we had been speaking about, and dropped my voice a little. "Anyway. I was hoping you'd heard of people going after me."

"After you?" El shook her head. "There's been talk of your levels and Lily, but no one mentioned an attack. I'd have told you otherwise."

"Yeah… think you could look into it?" I offered her a smile, mocking myself as I did so. "We're out of leads right now. At least till someone tells us what's going on. But I'm not a fan of being a mushroom, you know?"

El nodded then straightened. "Oh hell. I got to deal with them."

Stomping off, the little pixie headed toward the pair of shoppers who'd gone extremely quiet. I cocked my head to the side, only to have my arm grabbed and myself pulled away.

"What?"

"Shoplifters."

"Oh." I sighed and let El deal with them.

Outside, Alex and I stared at one another, debating what next to do. It wasn't as if I had a clue.

As my stomach rumbled and the evening light slowly darkened, I sighed. "Let's go eat."

***

One of the advantages of visiting El was that we managed to swing by my favorite Greek restaurant, a place where they served both quantity and quality. The lamb shoulder was fall-off-the-bone succulent, and the rice was cooked just right, herbed and soaked in butter and the lamb juices by the time we made it home. I might have splurged, picking up both calamari and moussaka to share with Lily, along with her own dish of lamb. Alexa got a large Greek salad which she'd eat before stealing much more delicious food from the two of us. What could I say? We'd corrupted the woman.

Dinner was good, if subdued. As much as I liked to think I'd gotten people wanting me dead, having them actually act on it was another thing entirely. I'd mostly been putting the danger out of mind, figuring I'd seriously think about it when I hit Level 80 or so before. But it could be that my continued progression had triggered concerns about exactly how powerful I would be at Level 100.

I was packing up the leftovers when I asked the question that had been on all our minds. "What now?"

There was a deep and uncomfortable silence that stretched and stretched. No one had anything to offer. Should we just go back to normal? Should we keep knocking on doors, hoping something will give? Should I ask Caleb, our only source into our guardians, and hope he'd deign to tell us something?

"Well, we could…" Alexa opened her mouth, then seemed to change her mind. "I could ask my friends? In the Order."

"Are they still talking to you?" I said, eyebrow rising.

"A few, but they're not really connected to this. Most are, well, most are still training…"

Right, that made sense. Her friends would be Initiates like her, people she might have grown up with. Which meant they'd probably not know much, if anything.

"No. Not yet. I mean, they're unlikely to know anything, right?" Alexa nodded. "Let's table that for now. I'll bug Caleb tomorrow…"

I paused, a sense of pressure coming from the door. I was alerted before the door was knocked upon, the individual behind it so strong that his aura was like a physical thing.

When I looked at Lily, she smiled. "Don't worry. Well out of your Level."

I couldn't help but nod in gratitude. If she hadn't been smart enough to block off individuals of power from interacting with me directly, I'd have lost the ring—or my life—a long time ago. Even so, people had been finding ways around the entire thing, especially lately.

When I opened the door, staring back at me was a trio, each of which were as powerful, if not more so, than Caleb. The first was a small woman with greying, long brown hair, a flowery dress covering a bony body. She absently picked at the fraying edges of her dress's long sleeves when I opened the door, ignoring me entirely. She could be someone's mother, if not for my magic senses.

On the other hand, the big man standing at the forefront—presumably the one who had knocked on the door—could have just walked off a lumberyard. Red and black plaid shirt, big bushy beard, and thick, steel-toed shoes completed the ensemble as he glowered at me from nearly a foot over my head. I had to admit, I stepped back just from the suffocating physical presence he exuded.

As the last member of the trio, the Native American man looked the most normal. Clad in a simple shirt and jean ensemble, he had a green windbreaker over his torso and hands stuck in his pockets. But as an indicator of his strength, the glow of the fetish around his neck was powerful enough to make me dial down my sensitivity. It was kind of like looking at a Third Circle Mage's staff in action. Just a little too much for a casual evening.

"Mr. Tsien, may we come in?" the man in front spoke, not giving me more time to review the group.

"Uhhh... who are you?" Not that I couldn't guess, not with all the hints, but always good to ask.

"I am Druid Osian Carr. This is Witch Milli Cook and Doctor Chunta David. We're part of a group of concerned individuals," Osian said.

"Doctor?" I frowned, looking at Chunta.

"Medical. I prefer to go by that," Chunta clarified.

Well, I would too if I'd spent half a million dollars for an education. Then again, he was old enough that maybe he'd had it cheaper. If not easier.

"Yeah, I guess." I stepped back and waved them in while Lily moved her computers out of the way.

As each of them passed through my wards, they set off a small light display, their sheer presence affecting my wards and straining them. My wards weren't badly made—they weren't great, but they weren't horrendous—but each of the visitors was the magical equivalent of a nuke. The sheer amount of energy they output, just by being, was enough to make my wards react.

"This is the jinn, is it?" Milli said as she walked into the living room, staring at Lily.

While the others might be taking in the room or our notes or Alexa casually leaning against the wall and her spear, Milli was solely focused on Lily. She stared at Lily with an intensity that she had not showcased before and was unconsciously stirring the ambient Mana and spiritual realms. I saw how my wards reacted as the spirits and ghosts the Witch, and probably seer, interacted with rose to do her unconscious bidding and were blocked.

"Yes." Lily tilted her head.

Suddenly, the light show around my wards stopped. The wards themselves were protected as Lily sent the spirits and ghosts running away. There was no ripple of power, no magical warning. She just looked and they ran.

"You're the one, aren't you?" Milli said, nodding then walking over to the most comfortable seat in the house—mine—and flopping down. "Do we get tea? I like tea. But none of that flowery stuff. Real tea."

I was a bit whipsawed by the change as both of the other extremely powerful personages took seats on my lounge, giving me drink orders. Rather than fight it, I got out the cookies, Cheetos, and other snacks from our last gaming day and drinks. Chunta was a cola drinker, while Osian had a beer. He wrinkled his nose a bit at the beer we handed him, muttering something about worse than water, but I was more than content to ignore him. As if I could have afforded craft beer.

"So. What are the three founding members of the Pagan Circle doing in my living room?" I said when I was finally seated.

"Just two," Milli said, offering me a half-smile. "I was a late comer."

"Right, right. But—"

"We'd like to speak with you. And your jinn," Osian said, leaning forward and taking our attention with that small movement. "The attack on you was well coordinated. The follow-up nearly took us by surprise as well."

"Follow-up?" I squeaked.

"Yes. Another group tried to sneak close to your residence while we were paying attention to the initial attack. Luckily, Milli learnt of the matter and the suborned pair of Mages," Osian said, shaking his head. "We managed to deal with the matter, but it seems your enemies have grown more persistent."

"Must have been quiet," I said softly. "I never even noticed."

"A simple isolation spell." Except there was nothing simple about a spell that could conceal the equivalent of a magic battle right outside my door, no matter what Osian said. Even if it was possible, there was nothing simple about it. "But that—or our losses—was not what we came to talk to you about."

"Then what is?" I said, tilting my head.

"We are here to talk about your future," Osian said. "We assumed that when you ... Level up, you would be independent. A free agent. You've shown, in the past, disdain toward authority and organizations. But recently, you and the Mage Council have been flouting your relationship."

I frowned. "Caleb's teaching me."

"And your upcoming graduation," Osian added. "Do you intend to join them?"

"I… well…" I leaned back, my mind spinning. Pieces that I hadn't really put into place found their place and I exhaled, swearing. "Of course. You all think I'm going to join them and give them Lily's ring."

"On your death, yes. Or worse, lend the jinn's magical knowledge to them." Osian took a sip of the beer and made a face, putting it down. "That's not a good thing, especially for us."

"Especially for you?"

"We"—a hand waved toward the three of them, but I knew it really meant their group—"are representatives of a group, a series of teachings that don't fit with your Mage Council. They might not think we're evil, but—"

"But they're the bigger organization and eventually they'll stamp you out?" I kind of knew what he was talking about. Caleb had a tendency to be arrogant, and the rest of his people were even worse. Much worse. "You're worried they'll keep drawing others away, draining you of your people? Eventually killing your traditions?"

"If I was teaching them, that'd be the best," Lily said, shaking her head. "Your magics, all of it, are so damn inefficient."

"Lily—"

"No. Let the jinn speak," Chunta said, fixing Lily with his gaze. "Let her tell us how we are failing."

"It's not a matter of failing. It's the fact that you are not very good at what you're doing," said Lily. "Oh, you might have picked up a few new tricks and maybe even made some progress, but the way you handle power is so inefficient. Your ancestors were doing better two hundred years ago."

"Are you blaming us for losing some of our knowledge?" Chunta growled.

"Blaming? Did I ever say blame? No. I just said you guys have lost much of the magic you had and are busy recreating it." Lily pointed at each of the three. "All of you have so much power, you set off Henry's sloppy wards."

"Hey!"

"And it's not even a case of you throwing your weight around. None of you can actually control your auras." Lily sniffed disparagingly. "All of you, from Mages to Druids, you're so busy fighting over whose magic is better, whose magic is more correct or more traditional, that you ignore what's best. Mer, Yup'ik, Solomon, none of them would ever have been so sloppy. Magic is about will and training. It's about formula, vision, and practice. And all of you guys, you keep thinking that your way is the best. But the best, the smartest, the most powerful—they stole and used and adjusted from every tradition.

"So, yeah. If I was teaching them, the Mage Council would steal your 'people' and they'd be best. Because I'd teach them how to do real magic, not the party tricks you're so proud of."

"I told you. She's a demon," Chunta said, leaning back, his earlier anger gone as he looked at his friends. For a man who had angered and set off Lily's rant, he seemed entirely unconcerned about her. "She cares nothing for our people or our traditions. It is best that she is destroyed."

"I do not agree," Osian said, shaking his head. "While she might be blunt, she's correct that we all have lost much knowledge. If she—if Henry—is willing to teach us some of our old magic—"

"Bah, the boy has already been corrupted by her and the Council," Chunta said. "Too much danger. Let them die."

"Hey!" I said, rapping my fingers on the table. "We're right here, you know."

"Deciding their fate was not what we were charged with by the Circle. We are here to investigate," Osian continued to speak to Chunta, ignoring me.

In her seat, sipping on her cup of steaming tea and seeming above it all, Milli stayed silent as the boys argued.

"I said, I'm right here," I said, rapping the table harder. "So why don't you guys try talking to me rather than making guesses?"

And then I got my wish, as both of them turned to regard me. My throat went dry as they looked at me as if expecting me to speak.

I struggled for a second and cleared my throat before I spoke. "Look. I don't know about tradition or what magic is better. Well, I do, sort of. Because Lily is right. She teaches magic, pure magic. I've got… information, spells, data rattling around my head. And sometimes what I learn from the Mages isn't right, and what I have works better.

"And yeah, I'm taking their apprentice test. But that's because they offered to let me take it. Offered to teach me." I drew a deep breath and plunged on, not entirely sure where I was going with this, but knowing that I needed to finish talking before they decided to interrupt me. "And you guys never did. You just watched over me, thinking somehow I'd join you guys for some reason? Hell, I never even talked to you or your guardians. As far as I could tell, you guys wanted me dead as much as the Templars did.

"So maybe I figured the Mage Council was my only choice because they were the only ones to offer another option. Now that you're actually talking to me, well, things have changed, no? And maybe we'll be able to talk about different choices. But even if there isn't, why does everyone think I'm going to go lockstep with the Council? They're a bunch of arrogant asses."

I ran out of breath and grabbed my cup, draining it to fill my dry mouth and to find something, anything to do. When I set down my cup, the trio were sharing looks between one another before standing.

"What?" I said.

"I believe we've learnt all we needed to," Osian said.

Chunta snorted at me, striding to the door, not even waiting for his companions to catch up. Alexa watched over the group as they left—a little more politely in the other two's cases, but just as quickly. In short order, the three of us were alone once again.

After I flopped onto the couch with a newly retrieved can of pop, I placed it on my head and groaned softly. "I screwed up, didn't I?"

"I'm not sure there was anything you could ever do," Alexa said, letting the window blinds she'd been peering out of close.

"Osian and Milli looked to be open to changing their minds—"

"Milli was here to see me," Lily said. "I don't think whatever you did or said made a difference. Once she gauged my strength, she'd made up her mind."

"How…" I clamped my lips shut. I wasn't sure I agreed with her evaluation. Certainly, I didn't see anything that Milli had done that warranted that belief. "But is it because I'm getting close to the Mages? Is that the reason for all this?"

Alexa shrugged. "Maybe. Or it could be a good excuse. It could be that the deals are done, that the balance of those wanting you dead has tipped."

I sighed plaintively. "Hopefully they'll reconsider. Maybe, maybe they'll even help."

Alexa looked at me pityingly but eventually relented. "Maybe."

Chapter 8

"Fancy seeing you here this early," I greeted Caleb, my sort-of teacher. And it was early—we'd barely started breakfast before the knocking on the door.

"What did you say to the pagans?" Caleb snapped, pushing his way in.

I sighed again. One of the aspects of my wards were that I'd keyed them to allow in those with no hostile intent. While it'd be simple enough for someone at Caleb's level to spoof the spell, he—like our earlier visitors—was still limited by Lily. And anyone at my strength level would find it hard to beat my wards.

"What happened?" I said, growing serious. I saw how agitated the Mage was in the way he looked at me, the way he stomped past me, barely even glancing at Lily or Alexa in their morning clothes. Which was a bit of a sight since Lily was in a pink bunny onesie and Alexa was already dressed for her morning exercises.

"They withdrew their support this morning," Caleb said, lips pursing. "As did two-thirds of those watching over you. Even the Templars have indicated that the Orders are in discussion if they should continue to support us."

"Wait. What? I thought they wanted the ring..." I looked at Alexa. I wasn't entirely sure why they wanted the ring. They'd never really explained it.

At my look, Alexa shrugged.

"They did. But they're not as large as they used to be, and there are concerns that losing more people to protect, well, you isn't worth it." Caleb's eyes narrowed as he continued. "I've been called back to speak to the Council itself. On the same topic."

My jaw dropped. "Are you guys abandoning me too?"

"No. Not if I have anything to say about it," Caleb stated. "But some assurances would be reassuring."

"Assurances on what?"

"That you'll join us. That when you're done with the ring, you'll pass it on to our safekeeping." Caleb raised a finger. "No matter what they say of us, we are good at keeping the really bad artifacts out of circulation."

"Bad artifacts?"

"Yes. Like Blackbeard's Chest. Muhammad's Pot. The Strangling Rope of Kuching."

"Never heard of them."

"Exactly!"

Rather than reply to Caleb, I looked at Lily, who shrugged. "He's not wrong. The Mage Council's Vault of Unending Space is well-known to be very secure."

I gave Lily a curt nod before looking at Caleb, muttering to stall for time as my mind swirled, "You know that the reason we're getting so much pushback is because the Mage Council is trying to take it all. Everyone's worried that I'm tilting too much in your favor. That it isn't going to be a fair competition in the end and you guys are all going to pile on."

Caleb shrugged. "Lily's knowledge is certainly a draw for us. As is the ring and the powers it holds. But understand, we're as interested in you. Despite your unorthodox introduction to our world, you've adapted well. Your magic—your spells—give you an unprecedented flexibility, especially compared to our own apprentices. Already we're adjusting the lessons we provide from our reports. I expect great things from you. As do many on the Council."

I noted how Caleb was avoiding the point I was trying to make, trying to butter me up. Not that it didn't help. The usual taciturn Mage was actually complimenting me, which was a nice change. But… "I don't know. You're pretty nice, but I'm not sure I'd want to be made part of your Council. I barely know them."

"Then meet us."

I shook my head. "Not yet."

Caleb's eyes narrowed. "If you don't provide us any reassurance, trying to convince the Council to dedicate more resources will be difficult. At best. We might even be forced to back off."

"I know."

Caleb stared at me, letting his gaze do all the talking. But I refused to turn away from him or change my mind, and in the end, Caleb walked out, tutting to himself. I stayed serious till he was gone, then I broke into laughter as Lily mimicked Caleb's last moments, tutting and tapping her foot, arms beneath her breasts.

"Stop. Please," I said.

"But I'm so disappointed in you," Lily whined in a gruffer voice.

Alexa giggled, covering her mouth, and I laughed. For a time, we shared a laugh, then we turned to our food. Only when we were done and cleaning up did we turn our thoughts to our visit.

"Are you sure you don't want to meet the Council?" Alexa said, cocking her head.

"Mostly. They're... dangerous," I said. "Even if Lily can kick any one of their asses—"

"Or all of them!"

Ignoring Lily, I continued. "Going into their place of power would put even her at a disadvantage. They've had hundreds of years to layer defenses. I'm not sure even she could stop them from killing me if they wanted to."

"Right..." Alexa cocked her head to the side. "Sorry, I'm just used to Lily being, well, Lily."

"She's powerful, but not omnipotent," I said. "Until I can escape by myself, I won't put myself in such a situation."

"But we're going to lose all our support." Alexa looked at the door and what lay behind. "Do you think the government…?"

"They'll stay out of it." After placing the dish in the drying rack with the rest of the plates, I wiped my hands dry and stepped away from the sink. "That's their modus operandi, no? They leave us to deal with one another, while keeping an eye that things don't get out of hand. It's too much trouble to get rid of us, especially when the supernatural world is slowly dying out."

Alexa made a face but had to agree. As powerful as magic was, as powerful as we were individually, humanity had the numbers and the technology to more than even the odds. It was why the supernatural world lived peacefully alongside humanity. For the most part. There were still a few countries run by supernaturals, but it was often in the background, as puppeteers rather than the face.

"Then what do we do?" Alexa said as she poured herself another cup of coffee.

"Well, the Mages and the Order haven't left yet. So I figure we should look at what we can do to upgrade our defenses," I said, looking around our house, eyeing the now-quiet wards. To make sure we didn't have to pay the damage deposit, when I created the wards, I'd actually painted them on using a metallic paint. Where I could, on particularly worrisome areas—like our front door and the frame—I'd carved into the wood itself. But for the most part, the wards were anchored by paint and Mana, which I had to admit was not the most powerful method. "For that, we'll need more—"

"Money." Alexa nodded. "I'll go find some quests then."

I nodded, walking over to my computer. Time to check the good old job board.

Tao Wong

***

It was interesting how more and more work had transferred over to the job board in the last couple of years. At first, only edge cases and those desperate for trivial help posted on the board. But as people got used to it, more and more jobs were posted. It helped that Bast, the board owner, had upgraded functionality and now, everyone who used the board had their own profile. Jobs were graded according to their difficulty, and those looking to take the jobs were also graded on their profile as they completed each job publicly.

To keep up with the growth of the job postings, Bast had even taken to outsourcing the work, with each local region having their own moderators who reviewed profiles, made sure no one doubled-up on profiles, and that all jobs were appropriately categorized. The last was probably the biggest concern, since a badly categorized job could lead to harm or a failure due to no fault of the job-taker. It was why ratings had been created for both sides.

The last reason the job board was popular was due to the fact that all high-tier jobs were verified by Bast herself, which made taking those jobs much less risky. Of course, to get the right to do those jobs—or post them—the various groups had to work themselves up, ensuring a high clear rate on the board.

All of which meant I had a chance to view the wide variety of jobs now available for someone like me. It was part of why El didn't see me that much anymore, since I was rather busy. This time around though, I changed my filter settings.

Normally, I filtered for complex, decently paying jobs with no violence involved. Since I wasn't a traditional RPG character, I didn't need to kill things to Level up. And while combat would increase my Level, it was only because I was getting better at casting spells under duress—combining knowledge that had been inserted into my brain with the knowledge that I'd learned and teased apart in my studies. It wasn't because I was getting some weird "experience" from fighting.

As such, I generally avoided violent missions. Of course, as one of the stronger supernaturals in town—at least, stronger freelancing supernaturals—I often ended up dealing with the really nasty problems anyway. But most of those were by personal request rather than choice.

Today was different.

Today, I looked for jobs that were high paying and could be completed in a day or less. Which, obviously, meant no gathering jobs, no ward reinforcement or enchantment fixing, no alchemical potions needing to be brewed or artist's show being developed. No. It meant dealing with the kind of things that the sane didn't want to deal with.

A supernatural fungal infestation in an alchemist warehouse that had grown semi-sentient and carnivorous.

An escaped chimera.

A new gang of redcaps making their presence known in the south west, mostly preying on teenagers by selling the latest drug.

Reports of a shadow creature moving in and out of bedrooms in a local neighborhood. Leaving behind the occasional smothered corpse and a lot of nightmares.

There were other reports, but these were the best paying. Over the next few hours, I reviewed information about each job. Just because a job was generally correct in its initial description did not mean that the details didn't paint a different picture.

The fungal infestation post had been up for three months, with two others having attempted to clear the infection. Initially, the in-house alchemist had come up with a potion to destroy the fungus and it had worked. Except for a small, unnoticed portion that had escaped the cleansing. When the fungus came back, it was resistant to the alchemical potion and the two other potions the in-house alchemist came up with. By that point, the warehouse had to be abandoned and the job put up. The first applicant to try to cleanse the warehouse was a shaman who'd brought numerous spirits to play, destroying the spiritual nexus of the fungus. Of course, that didn't work that well—for one thing, the spiritual body of a fungus was both nearly non-existent by nature and also quite hardy. The fungus had, once again, managed to escape total destruction. The next job-seeker was actually a group of sentient slimes who'd scoured the entire location. Until the fungus, having mutated again, drove the slimes away by destroying half of them.

"So. Carnivorous, semi-sentient, able to fight off slimes. And the job is rated a high C." I snorted in amusement. It might have started as a simple D rank problem, but by now, the job was approaching Bast level of attention. "Not touching this one with a ten-foot pole. Especially since the damn company still wants their goods 'intact.'"

Next up was the redcaps. A quick review of the job had me steering clear. Among other things, it looked like the reason why it was paying so much was because the local neighborhood supes had spotted a lot more mundane heat. Considering my current problems, getting entangled in a sting operation wasn't a good idea. Better to let that play out.

The shadow creature, on the other hand, was a nighttime problem. It was also inconsistent, which meant I'd need to access the homes of people who might—or might not—believe I was there to help, set up wards, and try to track the creature. If I was lucky, there was enough of a signature for that to happen. More likely, I'd be forced to set up large scale tracking wards and hope to catch it. Either way, not a quick solution. Which meant it shouldn't have been categorised as a 'quick' job. The joy of job hunting – no one ever categorised things properly.

That left the most dangerous—a solid C+ bordering on B—quest. Killing the chimera. The good news was, it had everything I needed—its lair was known, the payment was in an escrow account already, and I only needed to kill it because the chimera had gone feral. The bad news was that it was a chimera, which meant my magic would be less than useful due to its natural resistances.

"Alexa. Chimera?"

The blonde blinked, absently drying her hair after her shower. "Are you asking what they are or if we should fight one?"

"Fight. There's a quest for it."

"I'll have to do most of the work…" Alexa grinned. "Like usual."

"Funny. Let's get ready. And bring your net."

***

The chimera had gone to ground close by where it had escaped—in High Park, a small oasis of greenery in our urban jungle. The park was popular among joggers and hikers since it consisted of a trio of rolling hills with a jogging track circling the lower areas of the hills and rising over them occasionally. It was a good three mile workout if you ran the entire park, and I'd been there a couple of times during the summer months with Alexa.

Inside the park, off the main path, were dirt trails, kept in condition for those looking for more of a challenge and a greener run. I had to admit I much preferred jogging on the paths. The lack of tripping hazards and cobwebs to the face made me happy.

Alexa, on the other hand, was perfectly at ease walking on the dirt trails, her spear shaft used as a walking stick as we made our way deeper into the woods. We walked forward in silence, keeping an eye out for potential trouble, even if the job posting had indicated the chimera was lying low for the moment.

By the time we left the well-trod path, signs of the chimera's presence were making themselves known. First and foremost was the lack of noise. Not that the park was that noisy, but the occasional bird call, the scamper of a squirrel, or the buzzing of insects was gone entirely. None of them wanted anything to do with the chimera.

Next was the smell. It started out subtle, a hint of wet dog, and grew until it almost choked me with its intensity. That the smell was as much in my mind from the corrupted Mana the creature exuded did little for my gag reflex. Still, at least we knew we were on the right track.

"Net?" I said, gesturing to Alexa.

The blonde nodded and pulled off her bag, getting her equipment ready. I unslung my bag from both shoulders too, pulling the zipper wide but not reaching for any of my warding blocks. We'd discussed our optimal strategy on the drive over, and now, we needed to get close to verify its presence.

As a magical construct, chimeras had a few notable characteristics that made them difficult opponents for Mages. They were highly resistant to any magic cast on and at them. Even a spell like Mana bolt or fire bolt would find its effectiveness greatly reduced as the miasmic Mana the chimera exuded corrupted and broke down the spell forms. Closer to the chimera's body, the bolt would deflect or shift away, the power within dispersing. In some cases, chimeras were known to even gain strength from magic wielded against it. The most effective means of dealing with a chimera was via overwhelming force, using elemental bolts or force pushes and releasing the spells just before hitting the creature.

Because of the corruption and miasma and because of the chimera's original magic nature, scrying and tracking spells were of little use. The delicate spell forms broke down in short order around the creature or places it lived, and would alert the monster of our presence. Add in the fact that doing so would allow it to taste the "flavor" of my magic, and checking up on it magically was contraindicated.

The other aspect of chimeras that made them difficult to deal with were the sheer variety. The common image of a lion, goat, and dragon-headed creature was not wrong, just incomplete. Chimeras were magical constructs formed from multiple creatures smooshed together. The results were as varied as the insane mages and "scientists" who put them together. There was a small but healthy industry of "branded" chimeras—formulations of creatures that were sold as pets and guard dogs. In this case, we were facing one of the latter, its control spells damaged beyond repair after an "incident."

No. I didn't know what the incident was. And I hadn't asked.

Once Alexa was ready, wearing her armored coat and a scalemail skirt that ended just above her armored knees, we crept closer. The ex-Initiate had screwed on her spearhead and carried the weighted net in hand, gently pushing aside foliage with the tip of her spear.

As I ducked under a branch and grimaced as an unseen cobweb swept over my face, I spotted the hole the chimera had made its lair. A small mound of dirt fronted the hole that went under a fallen tree, the insides of the lair dark and uninviting. I held up my hand and pointed at Alexa, who nodded, both of us crouching a little to stay hidden. Seeing no movement, I frowned, debating our options.

If the chimera had left its lair, placing wards was a waste of time and could allow it to catch us. On the other hand, if it was in there, a series of wards were the safest way to capture it. On the third, non-existent hand, as I glanced at the darkened spots on the leaves around the lair, if the creature was out hunting, people were in danger.

I looked at Alexa, who lifted her net, gesturing toward the lair. I nodded, deciding to stick to our tentative plan. We split apart slightly, doing our best to sneak toward the lair. Unfortunately, I was paying too much attention to the lair itself and not enough to my footing. I stepped on a dry branch, sending a resounding crack through the still forest.

I froze. Alexa didn't as she rushed forward, swirling the net to make it open slightly. As I tensed, waiting for the creature to jump out, Alexa skidded to a stop near the exit. She paused, peering into the darkness before turning toward me, already shaking her head. I sighed, relaxing, and saw her eyes widen in shock.

Instinct from long years of practice had me throwing myself forward even as I formed the spell for a Force Wall. But as the spell formula rose in my mind, it felt slippery, twisty, refusing to come together with the same fluidity I was used to.

The chimera hit my upper back, making my graceful roll turn into a sprawl that jarred my head and left me with the taste of dirt and leaves in my mouth. The chimera was heavier than I'd expected, the ursine-canine mixture adding muscle and bone mass to the monster. Thankfully, the spelled duster kept it from doing any real damage, even as I desperately rolled to the side.

Force Wall Cast

Synchronicity: 31%

I splayed my fingers in front of my face, the Force Wall catching the slavering chimera just before it tore into my face. For the first time, I caught sight of the monster clearly. Wide jaws. A pair of extra-long canines on both the upper and lower levels of its teeth. A short tongue dripping frothy saliva. Two angry, tiny eyes stared at me as it snapped at the Force Wall again.

Somehow, between my turn and the chimera adjusting its body for balance, I had managed to squirm it half-off me, its long and low-slung black-furred body resting only half on top of me. Even so, I felt the enchantments on my jacket activate as it pushed against the weight.

As I squirmed to get away and held it off with the Force Wall, I felt the spell formula squirm and twist, refusing to hold still as the chimera's essence ate away at my spell. A sharp pain and another hit my legs, like a hard stick slamming into them that left a stinging sensation behind. The attacks made the spell wobble as my concentration slipped. As I glanced down, I noted the trio of tails—each long and muscled, like a snake's body—and the way they whipped at my feet. If not for the enchantments I'd sewn into my jeans, I would have severely bruised thighs and calves. Or worse.

Another lunging snap caught only by me shrinking the size of the Force Wall again. The attack rebounded the chimera's face, smooshing its snout flat before it raised its head for another attack. Only to have a spear catch it in its upper body, thrown by my brawny friend. The spear took the creature just behind its foreleg, throwing it off me through sheer momentum and allowing me to roll away.

Alexa pounded over to me, already waving her net above her head as I came up to my knees. A languid toss of the net caught the back of the creature's body and part of the haft of her spear. The chimera squirmed away, getting to its feet and shaking its body to dislodge the spear and net. Too bad for it, it was my turn.

"Bog ground," I snapped and pointed down, my fingers flicking and twisting before splaying.

Multi-Linked Spell Bog Ground Cast

Synchronicity: 64%

The spell took effect, conjured elemental water filling the ground beneath the monster. At the same time, the viscosity of the ground decreased, sinking the chimera. It struggled, which made it sink faster. I didn't try to hold the spell together, sending a surge of Mana into the container before releasing it to begin my next spell. Bog Ground was actually a multi-linked spell, one that linked Summon, Alter Temperature, Force Fingers, and Decrease Resistance together. Because of that, the complicated spell began to break down the moment I released it.

Next up, I formed an Ice Spear and threw it at the monster. The Bog Ground spell had dispersed, leaving the ground dry and hard and the chimera knee deep. The shard of ice slammed into the chimera's chest as it struggled free, throwing it backward. Hopping over, machete in hand, Alexa threw a cut that lopped off an ear, making the chimera howl once again.

With it trapped, injured, and surrounded, the rest of the fight was never in doubt.

***

Cleanse was such a powerful and useful spell. As I cleaned away traces of the fight and the blood on us, Alexa looked at the remnants of the chimera. She wrinkled her nose as the body parts continued their accelerated decay, leaving behind a ghastly smell and patches of meat and innards.

"Do we need to bring anything back?" Alexa said, looking entirely unimpressed with the thought of poking her fingers into that mess.

"Nah. We should be good. If there're concerns, they'll scry the location."

Nodding, Alexa finished cleaning her blade and waved me on. Together, we headed back for the car while I mentally spent our rewards. Getting sorted would be expensive.

Chapter 9

"Easy come, easy go," I muttered, staring at the handful of change I had left.

Splayed around the living room were the purchases I'd made, the vast majority coming from El, while the remainder had been picked up at the local hardware store. After some consideration, we'd decided against reinforcing the wards in-house. The time cost involved in developing thicker and more powerful wards was too high.

Rather than do that, I had chosen to work on a portable safeguard. That was why our coffee table had been pushed aside and the beginning of our warding circle rolled out on the floor. For the base, I'd decided to go with leather—specifically troll leather. The material had been carefully cured and still kept a little of its regenerative properties, allowing it to keep its pristine condition.

Having finished contemplating my poverty once again, I turned back to the leather. I was using a beam compass to draw out the edges of the circle on a giant sheet of paper pinned to the leather itself. Once I'd drawn the various runes in pencil, making sure I had enough space for everything, I would then have to enchant the entire thing.

Unlike most of my other wards, the portable shelter would be a short-lived defense. It wasn't meant to last forever. In fact, with the amount of power I intended to pump through the thing, I figured it'd burn out within five minutes even if no one attacked it. But those five minutes would allow the secondary enchantments to kick in.

Of course, before I could make the secondary enchantments, I needed to make sure the primary ones worked. Around me were the discarded pieces of paper from previous attempts. Each time, a minor mistake—or a better idea—spoiled my work. As I finished with the compass, I leaned back and sighed in relief. Step one, done.

"You know, this is the second day you've been at this," Alexa said, shaking her head as she leaned against the wall. "And you wanted to build more weapons, right?"

"I do. But this is more important," I said, pointing at the leather. "As you know, defensive enchantments are always stronger if they're pre-laid. I can cook up a powerful spell without a thought, but a properly enchanted circle could eat any attack of mine and laugh. It's why all-out attacks against a Mage's Tower were so rare. Anyway, I'll be done soon."

"You haven't even started inscribing the runes."

"But I've worked out what I want. Did you get the rest of my stuff?"

"Yes. Crushed deathwatch beetles, the extracted poison of a naga, and the lymph glands of a Chupacabra," Alexa said, wrinkling her nose.

"Great. I wrote the instructions somewhere…" I cast around, moving papers till I found the necessary document and waved it at the blonde. "Here. Follow instructions."

"I—"

"Lily!" I waited for the jinn to acknowledge my call before going on. "Can you watch Alexa and warn her if she does something wrong?"

Lily made her way down the stairs, her face furrowed with concentration. I waited while she tested the restrictions on her ring and the wish before she grimaced. "Yeah. I think so."

"See. Easy!" I cheerfully exclaimed to Alexa, who made a face at me.

I laughed, having passed on the most time consuming and smelly job. Of course, I could do it myself—and often did—but as Alexa had pointed out, we were short on time. Better to finish this now than to wait.

***

Staring at the slowly drying piece of enchanted leather, I eyed the magic circle critically in the waning light of evening. Not that the living room was dark—in fact, it was brighter than day with all the lights I had turned on. The various enchanted materials we'd mixed had been added to gold and silver dust before I had taken the time to carefully inscribe the entire thing. Rather than waste time painting it on, I'd used magic to keep the mixture melted and stirred while Force Fingers carefully guided the slow-flowing mixture in the correct paths. All the while, I infused the mixture with my Mana and enscribed the runes with the spell formula.

The process had drained me more than any other enchantment I'd ever done and had taken the better part of four painstaking hours. The final result, to my eye, was perfect. Unfortunately, to the jinn's exacting nature, it was less so.

Enscribed Runic Portable Abode Cast

Spell Fidelity: 87.4%

Enchantment Durability: 34%

Max Duration: 6.7 minutes

Portable Abode

This portable abode is a travesty of magic and intent. Rather than building a permanent safe location, this abode focuses on thickening the defensive walls of the abode, ensuring that it can withstand a strike even by an Archmage. Or so the creator thinks. Currently, this is an incomplete enchantment with a loss of 5.8% efficiency due to unfinished connections in the center.

Creates a 5' x 5' x 8' protected location when triggered.

"Harsh," I said, eyeing Lily.

"But fair." Lily shook her head. "I would have preferred something more traditional. But I understand your thinking."

I nodded. The second enchantment, the one I'd yet to complete, was a teleportation enchantment. It was basically a Linked enchantment with a spatial component. The goal was simple—you stepped into the circle, triggered the abode, and the protective walls came up. In the meantime, the teleportation enchantment made the connection to your teleportation location before sending you over.

The reason why I'd built it to last five minutes—rather than just a simple teleportation circle—was because teleportation was an incredibly complex spell. In fact, it was so complex that I couldn't actually do it. Not real teleportation.

So instead, I was going to cheat. The plan was to use Link, Anchor, and Summon spells to sidestep the concept of teleportation. Rather, I'd Summon us to the new location, with the individuals within the circle taking a short ride through another dimension. Much, much safer than an actual teleportation spell.

Still insanely dangerous, but much safer.

"Now that you've completed that perversion, what's your next plan?" Lily said, looking at the trio of plastic tubes I had resting to one side.

"Oh. Those. One-off-use wands," I said, grinning. "Except I've got this idea that rather than generate the air itself, if I use hollow plastic, I could just put a Gust spell within."

Lily's eyes narrowed in thought, but before she could hint at what I was doing wrong, a knock on our door drew us away. It was just the two of us, since Alexa was at her night job.

"Trouble?" I said, wandering over to the door while grabbing my staff. I'd leave it out of sight, behind the door, but I'd grown a little paranoid over the last few days.

"It normally doesn't knock," Lily pointed out.

"Huh. True." I opened the door.

Outside, to my surprise, a bike messenger stood, his hand raised to knock again. "Mr. Henry Tsien?"

"Yes?"

"Document for you." The messenger handed me a clipboard to sign before he relinquished the simple envelope.

"Thanks."

I was closing the door before I realized the poor fellow expected a tip. Unfortunately, I didn't have my wallet on me. Magical staff, sure. But wallet, no. Shaking my head, I closed the door fully and walked back to Lily, eyeing the purple envelope. For a small envelope, it had a certain heft and stiffness that spoke of high quality, thick paper. An invitation—old school too, with a seal on the back.

"Weird." I waved the paper in front of Lily's face.

When the jinn saw the seal on the back, she stiffened. The seal was dark red, a slight smear of color running and, as I raised the envelope further, gave off the slightest tingle of magic. Not enough for me to worry about a magical attack, though there was definitely magic in play here.

"Do you recognize it?"

Rather than answer directly, Lily nodded stiffly. When I realized I wasn't going to receive any further information from the jinn, I walked over to the kitchen counter and carefully set aside the mail. I grabbed my bag, pulled out my modifiable warding tablets, and flicked them around until I had the enchanted runes ready. Once I'd placed the envelope within my bag, I released a surge of power into the warding tablet and sealed the envelope away.

Once that was done, I focused and cast Force Fingers, manipulating the envelope to open it. As I broke the seal, a flicker of power escaped, rotating around as the notification spell hit the edges of my barrier and then, unable to escape, self-destructed. My eyes narrowed before I pulled out the card within.

The invitation was on fine purple paper, the note within written in a cursive script reminiscent of medieval Bibles rather than the functional cursive we'd been taught. I cocked my head, deciphering the words before turning the card around to check for a post-script. Finding nothing on the back or in the envelope, I released the Force Fingers spell while leaving the envelope trapped.

"How interesting," I muttered. "I didn't realize Rihanna was a magic user."

"*Rhiannon*! You ignorant, pop-culture-loving nerd! Rhiannon. The fae goddess!" Lily gave up on being quiet, only to clamp her mouth shut when she saw my crinkled eyes and choking laughter. Once I'd managed to get a hold of myself, she continued. "It's not a laughing matter. She's the queen of the fae. You can't turn down that invitation."

I cocked my head as I sobered up and pointed at Lily. "How powerful, exactly, is she?"

"Individually?" Lily played with a strand of hair as she walked away, tapping a few buttons to continue mining with her ship before she answered, her voice soft. "We don't count things that way. Didn't. Once you hit a certain… point, it's hard to really compare. Powerful enough, Henry. That should be enough for you."

I grunted, tapping the envelope again. "And why is she inviting me? Us?"

Lily shrugged, not offering an answer. Or perhaps unable to.

In either case, I looked at the invitation and waved at it. "So I'm assuming that's safe?"

When I got no answer from Lily, I sighed and pumped a little more Mana into the shield. Better to be safe than sorry then. I had the address memorized at least. Grabbing a pad, I scribbled a note for Alexa then got dressed. Considering the invitation requested an audience ASAP and Lily's reaction, letting them wait was a bad idea.

***

There were many places I'd expect to find a portal to Faery. A standing stone circle on a mist-enshrouded hilltop. Perhaps, if you were a Tolkien fan, the elves might be watching the opera or theatre—you know, refined and snooty. I would even accept a park or a secure warehouse, one that allowed large movements of people without issue—especially if they lay in a confluence of ley lines.

What I did not expect was for it to be inside a comedy club. Getting in was easy. All I had to do was pay the very reasonable door charge. That I was getting in toward the last half of the show meant that the door person was willing to give me a discount too. Inside, I headed to the bar opposite the stage, eyeing the dimly lit, half-filled room. I wrinkled my nose slightly as the smell of stale popcorn and alcohol mixed with the raucous laughter.

I ordered a beer and leaned against the bar. So. This was the address. And I assumed if I flashed the invitation, I'd have been led where I needed to go. But without it, I needed to work out by myself where I had to go. As I chuckled appreciatively at a joke about a chicken, a boat, and a college party, I let my Mana Sight activate.

It was always in play, to some extent. A Mage's ability to cut through most glamours, to sense Mana was always on. But there was a difference between looking and seeing—a shift of perception and attention. I stopped just looking and actually saw, letting the swirl of ambient Mana register in my consciousness. In short order, I chugged down half of the bottle, fortifying myself with some alcoholic courage, and headed for the washroom.

Pity I'd miss the rest of the act. But needs must when the fae called.

I made it most of the way down the corridor, bypassing the washrooms and heading for the "employee only" entrance before I was caught. The bouncer seemed to materialize from nowhere, his seven-foot, linebacker body form drawing my attention only when he leaned forward and put a meaty paw in my way.

"Employees only," he growled, his voice resounding in my chest like a rising drumroll.

Now that he'd moved, I could see him properly for what he was—a troll. A fae troll, not the German ones which are called the same but are an entirely different species. These guys are big, big eared and nosed, with magic in their blood and the strength of the mountains in their bones. In other words, he could have squashed me if he'd grabbed me.

"I'm invited," I said and held up a hand, letting a light spell form around my hand.

The troll watched my hand. "Mage Tsien."

Statement more than question, but I nodded. The troll dropped his hand, letting me by, and I walked to the door. A push let me in, leading down a corridor that shimmered before my eyes. I squinted slightly, realizing that the split in the corridor was both illusionary and true—one a magical road for those who could make it and another, the mundane route for the norms.

I exhaled, shaking my head at the casual use of magic. At the fact that the road to Faery wasn't a standing stone but an illusion in a comedy club. And because where I was going, I had never been before. As I stepped onto the road, a hand dropped onto my shoulder, forcing me to blink.

"Lily?" I gaped at my friend. "How…?"

"We are between and betwixt," Lily said. "Some rules are relaxed. And we were both invited, were we not?"

I was surprised by her presence, knowing how little Lily liked leaving the house. Even after all these years—which for the immortal jinn was probably an eyeblink—it was still uncommon for the jinn to voluntarily leave our house. Yet as we strode along the twisting cobblestone road, mist rising to brush against our legs, I found myself comforted by her presence.

"You do remember your stories about the fae, don't you?" Lily said, brushing dark hair back across her ears as she hunched in her favorite hoodie. It said "Let me show you true magic" with a book underneath.

"Yeah…" I scrambled through my memories. "They don't speak untruth, but they can lie via leading statements. Their promises are binding—as are mine. No eating food or drink, or taking gifts. Or offering them, because that'll create obligations."

Lily made a face, then waved. "Mostly. The first one is a lie, and the others have… refinements. But I don't have time to teach you court etiquette."

"Nor could you," I said, cocking my head.

Lily's shoulders rose in a nonchalant shrug. Out of conversation topics for the moment, I eyed our misty surroundings, devoid of sound the way only a mist-filled land could be. Everything, even my own steps, was muffled, while my ability to see had dropped from tens of feet to a few feet.

As we continued onward, I noticed how the mist was slowly growing less dense, more and more of the world becoming clear. Trees in the distance firmed up, their brown barks deepening even as their leaves danced on subtle wind. They shimmered, and I squinted, slowing down as I tried to grasp their meaning.

"Ooof." A hand grabbed mine and pulled my gaze away as Lily stumbled. I helped her regain her balance before she offered me a sheepish smile. "Loose stone."

"Oh…" I looked at the smooth cobblestones beneath my feet and then at the guileless jinn, before drawing a deep breath and setting my mental defenses higher. Even the trees were a danger here.

Because Faery was not part of Earth. Once, perhaps it had been, but now, it was a different land entirely. Much like Avalon, it existed in a parallel dimension, one reachable via such faery roads and circles, but separate and untouchable. It was a magical land, and as I walked, I sensed my magical senses, my sight, shivering and waking. The light here was brighter, the Mana more intense, the smells more potent. It was like taking a half dozen shots of energy drinks at one go, the way it made my body wake. I found myself smiling, even as I reached for the calm that I'd learned to exist in to cast magic.

An awning rose up from the hill without warning, the portable court blocking the light from the—two!—suns while those within lounged, laughed, and ate. The fae that stood in the tents were tall, reminiscent of Tolkien's elves but subtly different. Inhuman with sharp teeth and cunning eyes, while looking elegant and refined at the same time, clad in courtier clothing at least three centuries out of date. And in the center of the mobile court was a single chair where a woman lounged, clad not in courtier clothing but practical riding clothes. As I entered the tent, the group hushed.

For a moment, I froze, but subtle pressure on my arm that Lily had yet to release had me moving forward. I paused in front of the riding figure and bowed low. And then, catching Lily's beckoning hand beside me, went lower.

"Rise, Mage Tsien. It's a pleasure to see you too, Auntie." Rhiannon's voice was low, rough. Her accent was hard to place, her diction clear and distinct.

"Auntie?" I mouthed to Lily, who shushed me with her eyes and flicked her gaze back to the queen. Or god. Depending on who you asked.

"Thank you, Queen Rhiannon," I said, deciding on the lesser status. After all, she wasn't acting like a goddess to those present, but a queen at most. So I'd go with that. Also, it made my heart feel a lot better to deal with a supernatural fae queen rather than a goddess. "I received your kind invitation. Though—"

"You are wondering why I brought you here?"

"Yes, Your Majesty."

"We do not, normally, interact with the mortal world. Our time there has passed," Rhiannon said, her eyes twinkling slightly. "But you attracted our attention when you made inquiries about one of our former citizens."

"I did?" I blinked, then realization caught up. "The doppelganger."

"The Changeling," Rhiannon corrected gently but firmly.

"My apologies for the slip of tongue, Your Majesty," I said. "But I had thought Changelings could only… well, is that not normal?"

"An aberration. Changelings take a single form, but this one altered," one of the courtiers said, his hair the violent purple one only saw on Teletubbies and bad '80s cartoons. "A mutation caused by the pollutants in your world."

"Iron?" I guessed.

"If only that were the only poison in your world." The courtier sniffed and opened his mouth, his hand rising, body leaning forward as he worked up to an epic rant. Only to be shut down by a single walnut tossed at his head by Rhiannon.

"Hush. My aunt has no desire to hear you rant. Nor I."

"My apologies, my queen." The courtier bowed low.

Dismissing him, Rhiannon looked at me. "So. What do you seek from us?"

"Knowledge, if you will." I mentally ran through what I needed. "Knowledge of who hired the Changeling would be gratefully accepted. If you have it. If not... I would not dare ask for more."

"Polite, aren't you?" Rhiannon's eyes crinkled in amusement. "Not like your last... three masters?"

"I believe you're thinking of others. My second-last master was quite respectful. But I don't think you met him," Lily said softly.

"Oh, of course. I forget. You've had so many."

My eyes narrowed at the barbed words, and I glared at the woman. Queen. Fae. Whatever. Bitch was better. But I kept my tongue in my mouth because Lily had warned me not to anger her, even as much as declining her invitation. Which Lily hadn't said for the Mage Council.

"I know nothing of this Changeling's activities. As I said, we have little to do with your world anymore. At least, not officially," Rhiannon said. "Only a few things interest us these days."

I stilled, wondering what she meant. But seeing that she had no information for me, I bowed again. "Thank you for your time then, Your Majesty."

Rather than dismiss me, Rhiannon fixed Lily with a playful, indulgent smile. Like a cat staring at a struggling mouse. "Tell me, Aunt, have you told him who you are really?" At Lily's silence, she turned to me. "Have you asked her?"

I shook my head before realizing I didn't need to answer the damn woman.

When I opened my mouth to say that, she cut me off. "Of course not. Her masters are always in such a rush to use her powers, for their wishes, that they never ask what the price of those wishes are. Well, almost all of them."

"I know the price, but Lily's..."

Free? Even I could not say that word with a straight face. She had freedom, more than she'd had for many years, centuries, maybe ever since she was trapped in the ring. But she was not free. *Content?* Maybe. Though perhaps distracted was a better word. Distracted by games, my TV, by virtual reality and a million other things that kept her from thinking of, well, freedom.

For the first time, I considered how Lily might feel. Knowing that my death would send her to an abyss. Forever.

But even as I considered those words, Rhiannon spoke. "My aunt is not who you think she is. She was trapped not because she was too powerful, but for what she did. What she is." Rhiannon leaned forward. "You see her as a friend. A confidant. Do not be fooled."

"Rhiannon." Lily's voice was cold, angry.

The threat was clear, but Rhiannon ignored her. Ignored her because Lily was, in the end, powerless to do anything.

"You are quiet." Rhiannon's lips curled up, her eyes gleaming with amusement. "Good. You are listening. Then hear this, Mage. The one whose magic you use, whose knowledge you borrow? She is Lilith. Eldest of our kind. Mistress of magic, mother of monsters, the first rebel."

"Oh, please!" Lily rolled her eyes. "Not those lies again."

"Lies?" Rhiannon's lips curled. "You are the one who formalized, who began the rituals of magic. Whose experiments created the first jinn from the very blood that flows through your veins. You destroyed towns and wiped out settlements because they angered you."

"They tried to kill me!" Lily snapped.

"And they all deserved it?"

"Well..." Lily fell silent, shaking her head. "It was a long time ago. I was—"

"Powerful. A rival for the dragons themselves. And since then, you have grown only more powerful," Rhiannon said, looking at my hand where the ring rested. "Trapped, perhaps, but each year, each decade, you grow in strength and knowledge. Refining your magic."

"Now I'm being condemned for studying the only thing I can?" Lily said, clenching her fists. "Henry, I'm not—"

"You are. Lilith. And you're friends with creatures from legends and have a goddess who calls you auntie," I said, offering the jinn a half-smile. "I'm not dumb. I figured that one out a while ago." As Lily's jaw dropped, I turned back to Rhiannon and offered her a bow. "Thank you for your warning, Your Majesty. If that is all?"

Rhiannon's lips tightened. The mouthy courtier stirred, looking at me predatorily but made no move. We stood there in silence as I waited for Rhiannon to dismiss me. Or attack me. Either or.

In the end, the bounds of tradition, of the fae's word and their rules of hospitality, held. Rhiannon flicked her hand, sending me off, and I hurried away, only wiping my brow when I was out of sight. Perhaps she had considered killing me. Perhaps she had just intended to warn me. But I decided there and then never to return to Faery. Not without a lot more firepower anyway.

Beside me, a silent jinn walked. Until we stepped across the threshold and the ring's bindings forced her to disappear once more. Leaving me in peace, but with doubts. For while I knew who she had been, the question of her fate rose once more.

As much as I liked Lily, there was a reason why she had been locked up. A reason why so many feared her. And a reason, in the end, for me to keep the ring to myself. Because at least I knew what I would do with it.

Chapter 10

There was blessed solitude when I walked to the light rail train twenty minutes away. The entire journey would take just over two hours, more than enough time to think. More than enough time to…

That was where my thoughts stuttered to a stop. Truth was, I was not sure what I was supposed to think. I had known who Lily was for a long time. Suspected that her imprisonment were for crimes. Even if Lily wasn't exactly the Lilith from the Bible, it was likely much of her story was taken as inspiration. The same way the great flood might not mean the flooding of the world but a specific location. Of course, knowing that there are angels and faith magic had… well, let's say that I am agnostic.

None of which was an answer to my problem—if it was a problem—or solved my concerns about Lily. Or the ring. Even if she was properly punished—and a couple thousand years of imprisonment and forced servitude seemed a tad harsh—I was not entirely sure there was any way for me to free her. A glance at the ring made me wince as I recalled the only time I'd ever looked at the ring properly. The most complex enchantment I'd ever done had been the wards on our house. It'd taken over three months, spaced between classes and jobs and was, in my view, as good as, if not better than, the enchantments on my staff. There were multiple levels to the house enchantment, from increasing the durability of the walls to blocking scrying, alerting me of scrying attempts that couldn't be blocked, attack wards, and more.

Now, if one took the complexity of that ward, multiplied it by a thousand, stuffed it into the space of a single ring, you would get a glimpse of how complex the enchantment was. The fact that the ring was drawing power from an unknown source was even more frightening, since disrupting the enchantments themselves could have explosive consequences. Literally.

I swiped my card at the rail station and headed up the stairs. I was fortunate enough to get an empty car that pulled away moments after I got onboard. I found a side seat and pulled out my warding tablet to adjust and empower it. The modified Force Bubble sprung into existence, anchored around the ward and offering me some peace of mind.

"Damn fey," I muttered, looking about the empty rail car.

I was seated parallel to the walls and the doors, the few horizontally aligned seats empty but unappetizing in their restriction. Perhaps it was the look in that fey's eyes or perhaps it was the memory of being targeted, but I felt the need for space. For... freedom.

But that's not something Lily would ever have. Not while I held the ring. Not while anyone held the ring. And yet, who was I to judge? While I was not entirely oblivious, I knew I was not the best at reading people. Someone, sometime, decided this was a just punishment. Someone—or someones—more powerful, more skilled than me.

Yet could any punishment that read "for all eternity" ever be just? What kind of action, what sin could justify a punishment that lasted forever? And if no crime could justify eternity, then had Lily suffered enough?

Was what she was going through punishment or containment? Was she trapped because she did something wrong or because we—they—feared her? Feared what she could do? We didn't let nukes walk around unwatched. Why would people—jinn—be any different? Yet trapping her, punishing her...

Was it punishment for the crime or do we hope of redemption? In the belief that people would, could, change? Perhaps that was the question. Perhaps that was the answer, if it was a punishment. If we saw her enslavement as a punishment, then the question was is it just? But if we saw it as a way for her to redeem herself—eventually—then the question was, did I think she had changed? Do I think people could change?

My mind spun around in circles and whorls, forced to contort around my inconclusive thoughts. I couldn't figure out an answer. Maybe because there was no right answer. It's not a math problem where one plus one equaled two. It was a human problem, where one plus one might equal happily ever after or a gunshot to the foot.

I was so caught up in my thoughts that I hadn't noticed the train pull to a stop or the new passengers. Didn't see them even as the doors closed and trapped me with them. Didn't notice the gun that came up and fired as the train pulled away from the station.

The bullet punched through the air, hitting the Force Bubble. The idea for the ward was stolen directly from a scifi series. Anything moving slowly—a clap on the shoulder, a gesture from my hands—only slowed and angled away slightly. But the higher the momentum of the motion, the faster something moved, the greater the force my ward applied to it. It was a useful ward to use while I was in public, since it was only mildly disconcerting for mundanes caught in its vicinity. Unfortunately, I'd yet to work out a stable formula for movement, so it was only useable when the ward center was still.

The bullet hit the edge of the Force Bubble and slowed perceptibly. A lateral force was applied to the bullet, shifting it away from the center of the ward and making it fly by my face, leaving a sting of wind behind. They were smart enough to shoot for my head—avoiding my enchanted jacket—but that made the target much smaller. Even a small force was enough to make the shot miss, though the retort from the gun was still painful to my ears, even when slowed and distorted by my now-glowing modular ward tablet.

Instinct took over as I formed a Force Wall before me. Fingers snapped and twisted as I blocked off the area just outside of my Force Bubble. As the wall formed, it struck aside the gun barrel, sending the next shot up into the roof of the train. A mental command turned off the strained ward, the tablet glowing with light as it ran out of the Mana I instilled in it. Through my semi-opaque Force Wall, I stared at my attackers.

Three individuals. Clad in black business suits and shades at night, all of which spelled trouble. Of course, the trio of silencer-equipped pistols pointed at me was another good indicator. They were a mix of races—Hispanic and Caucasian—and ages, with the youngest a teenager. The kid's gun came back down to point at me and the shield I had formed, targeted straight at my face. Then they opened fire and my Force Wall flickered, points of impact spreading and rippling even as bullets ricocheted away.

Gunman 1 (Level 37)
HP: 100/100
MP: 0/0

Gunman 2 (Level 45)
HP: 100/100
MP: 0/0

Gunman 3 (Level 59)
HP: 100/100
MP: 0/0

Non-magical gunmen. Mortal, but dangerous nonetheless as assessed by Lily. That probably meant training—special forces or worse. After all, a normal cop on the beat was only in the low 20s and that's because he had a gun in hand and some modicum of training.

As the trio realized they were not getting through my Force Wall—not with their bullets ricocheting around—they stopped firing. They took turns dropping their magazines and reloading while keeping their guns pointed at me, faces impassive. A shard of a broken bullet seemed to have caught Gunman Two across the cheek, as a thin line of blood dripped down his face, ignored.

"Who are you people?" I said, keeping my spell formed as I mentally prepare a second and third backup.

Those bullets were unenchanted. They also had quite a bit of kick—especially compared to the pop-guns most gangers use—but nothing my Force Wall couldn't handle. Their only chance was lost when they missed me the first time. So I could afford to fish for information.

Rather than answer me, the lead gunner looked sideways, ignoring the screams and shouts of horror from passengers in other cabins. I followed the gunner's glance and spotted the upcoming stop, the way they eyed the doors.

"Come on. Just tell me. Who wants me dead?" I said.

Again, I got no answer. I noticed the pair at the back angling their bodies as they dropped their off-hands, taking them out of my view. Then the train slowed down, wheels grinding and shrieking, drowning out shrieking voices as it swayed ever so slightly.

"You failed. So tell me who sent you."

No one answered. But the doors hissed open and the passengers in the other cars rushed out. So did my attackers, though not before they tossed a pair of small oblong objects at my wall. I didn't have time to register what they were as I released my spell. The gunmen got their feet in the doorway and slammed headfirst into the Force Walls I'd formed around the car, hemming them in.

Force Cube Cast

Synchronicity: 89%

Durability: 1238

Foreheads smashed, bodies piled up against the wall and bounced backward. Their eyes widened, the youngest glancing back at the discarded items. I followed his gaze, spotted the grenades, and winced. Before everything became chaos.

***

In the resulting bedlam of two grenades exploding in a contained space, I sneaked out of the train via the untouched back doors. I couldn't hear anything but the incessant ringing in my ears, bag slung over my shoulder as I cast a simple Glamour that changed what I looked like. I combined that with an Illusion for the security cameras, though I was not entirely sure how useful that'd be with the cameras in the rail car having already caught a glimpse of me.

Then again, I was sure my other guardians would cover it up. If they weren't the ones who'd sent my attackers. Because… well, I was not entirely sure who else had three trained, mundane killers with access to high explosives and silenced weapons. Then again, with the militarization of our society, that number was rather higher and more depressing than I liked considering.

Behind me, as I hurried away on foot, I left the burnt and wrecked shells of my enemies, corpses torn and twisted by the rebounding explosive force of the grenades. I'd created the cube to contain them, to potentially get some answers. I hadn't expected a grenade, and even now, I could feel how low my Mana was, how drained I'd been reinforcing the spell as the explosion rebounded. Even if I had grown more powerful, even if the Force Cube was one of my more complex spells—which I would never have tried casting if they hadn't given me the time to do so—it was still tiring to use.

As I hurried out of the chaotic station, I couldn't help but feel a little guilty at the deaths I'd caused, the collateral damage that was done. I hated killing, and even if I hadn't done it myself, their deaths were painful. Still, if there was one thing I'd learned, it was that at least two groups were after me. Because whoever had sent the doppelganger wasn't likely to use something this mundane.

Letting out an exhalation, I ducked into a nearby alleyway and recast both spells, cloaking myself in magic. It was time to get home. Quietly.

***

"You're not allowed out without me," Alexa stated. There was no anger in her voice, though she stared at me till I offered her a nod. Once I got back—later than the night-shift-working ex-Initiate—I'd been grilled in detail about my encounter.

"The police offering any more news?" I asked, tilting my head toward the TV that wasn't on a superhero TV show or console game, but the local news for once. Even if I'd contained the blast, the damage done to the train and the ensuing disruption was more than enough for the local news to jump on it.

"No," Alexa said.

Unasked and unanswered was the question of whether I should be packing an extra bag for a long, long talk with the police. And maybe jail time. I hoped not. While I did have a bucket list, jail wasn't on it.

Leaving might be an option, but that meant abandoning our house and the wards. Even if I did leave, it'd be a temporary solution. Sooner or later, my enemies would find me.

"So…" I let my voice draw out, looking at Alexa and the silent Lily.

"I'll…" Alexa frowned then shrugged. "I'll ask around. See if I can learn if you're in trouble. If we can learn who it is."

Lily offered me a half-smile, then flashed the old Quest again. The one that asked me to stay alive. I couldn't help but snort, wishing this was a game. One that railroaded you with clues, rather than a stupid puzzle one where the solution might be right in front of you—or in a portion of the map that you'd missed half the game back.

"I guess I'll just rest for now," I said, feeling the lack of Mana sending another wave of exhaustion through me. Being low on Mana and paranoid had drained me, putting me on the edge of sleep.

The pair offered me a smile, waving me away as I stumbled up the stairs. I barely even glanced at the notification that told me of a Level increase, knowing it didn't help.

Perhaps, perhaps a solution would present itself when I awakened.

Chapter 11

Two days passed in tense silence, Alexa's few contacts unable to offer us any assurance. Even our attempts to speak to our governmental guardians were thwarted—the ever-present service vans that had been parked on our street for months gone.

We'd been left in the dark, so I spent my time working on the enchantments. I finished the portable shelter, then worked the portable flamethrowers while we waited for the next shoe to drop. Alexa had taken a leave of absence from her job, though they'd hinted that she might not be welcome back. Actions had consequences, and mine had lost her her job.

When a knock came on the door, I didn't move from my work table, having nearly completed the weapons. After I was done, I planned to work on my staff. The layered defenses available on the staff would be greatly appreciated, even if—unlike the flamethrowers—I'd have to power the staff myself.

When Alexa lead Caleb into the room, I looked up, blinking in surprise at the Mage. "You're back."

"I am. I come bearing conflicted news," Caleb said. "The Council is unwilling to risk further manpower on an untested warlock."

"Mage," I said, glaring at Caleb. I might not have been trained by the Mage Council, but I was a Mage. Bette than their apprentices.

"Warlock in their eyes. Many do not believe what I have reported, are unwilling to accept your potential," Caleb said. "It is why I have bargained for you to take the apprentice examination early."

"What?" I said.

"Pack your staff. We must leave if we are to make it to the examination." Caleb gestured to the staff propped up beside me as my next project.

"I'm nearly done," I said, gesturing at the tubes.

"Those things?" Caleb took one glance and sniffed. "They're cumbersome and not worth the Mana invested. You should have spent your time on the staff."

"Funny. But I like having more tools." I looked Caleb over, shaking my head. "Not as if you don't have your own enchantments."

"They are accessories. Useful but unimportant compared to a proper staff," Caleb said. "That we are forced to leave them behind by modern-day fashion does not reduce the staff's functionality."

"Yeah, yeah, yeah. Heard it before."

"You are right. Now, come."

I dithered for a moment, not entirely sure I wanted to commit. But what choice did I have? At least the Mage Council was still willing to help. No matter how much I grew, no matter what Level I achieved, I'd still be outnumbered. As much as I might have disliked the Council, I needed them. I needed an organization at my back.

Letting out a breath, I grabbed my staff and stood.

Alexa cleared her throat, drawing my attention. "Didn't we agree to something?"

"Sorry. You're right. Is she allowed to come?" I looked at Caleb, who shook his head.

"Can you guarantee his safety?" Alexa asked, looking pointedly at Caleb.

"During the trial, yes." Caleb cocked his head. "I can take you to the grounds. Outside. If he fails—"

"We're on our own," Alexa said. "I'll get my spear."

I tossed her the pair of finished flamethrowers. "Add this too."

The blonde nodded, heading upstairs to get dressed and armed. Caleb sniffed, tapping his foot only to be brought up short when Lily stood.

"Leave us, Mage," Lily said.

"I'm—"

"Waiting outside."

Caleb narrowed his eyes, but when I cleared my throat, he relented and left, leaving Lily and me to stare at one another.

"We haven't… talked since, you know," Lily said awkwardly. "About me. About my… crimes."

"Were they crimes?" I said.

Lily nodded.

"Were they bad?"

Lily nodded again.

"Bad enough to be put in a ring for all eternity?"

"I… don't know."

I nodded. "Yeah, thought so. We don't have much to talk about then."

Lily flinched, looking at the tops of her feet.

I winced, realizing how harsh that sounded, and put a hand on her arm. "Lily." When she looked up, I offered her a small smile. "It's fine. Whatever you did, it was a long time ago. So long it's probably not relevant anymore." When Lily flinched, I raised an eyebrow. "Never mind. It's still not relevant. You're you now. Not… whatever."

"We're still friends, right?" Lily said, sounding timid.

"Don't have a choice, do I?" I said, trying for teasing.

When Lily shrank back, I winced and decided to shut up. I hugged the jinn, feeling the tension in her body that slowly relaxed and went away. Eventually Alexa cleared her throat, reminding me that I had to go.

"We're friends. Now and forever. Promise," I said. "But I got to go."

Lily nodded, pushing me away. I headed off, catching her words just before I left.

"Good luck."

***

Mundane. That's a good description of my magical existence. No magical carpets, no teleporting rings, just a black four-door sedan that takes me out of the city and down the highway. Alexa's seated in the back, dressed in her armored jacket and skirt, spear taken apart and laid out beside her. I'm up front with Caleb, watching as he guides us down the road with expert ease.

"No enchantments on the car?" I said, having finished looking it over.

"It's a rental."

As I said. Mundane.

"You should consider going over what you have learnt. There is no time to fix your staff," Caleb said. "But some last-minute cramming would not hurt."

"Actually, did you know that research has shown that last-minute cramming might actually be more detrimental than studying?" I flashed Caleb a smile, only to have him glare at me briefly before turning his gaze back to the road. "Fine. If I fail, you know who I'm going to blame." When the silence grew colder, I added, "Me."

"You're really not as funny as you think, Henry," Alexa said.

I grumbled under my breath but closed my eyes, calling forth what I knew about the examination. There were three sections in an apprentice exam. The first was theory—which mostly consisted of a written examination where I had to expound on formulas. This was my weakest area, and the area Caleb was hinting that I work on. While Lily might dump information into my mind, the way she did so was specific to spells, such that I often found myself missing important areas of learning. Or at least I used to. Lessons with Caleb and more spells had helped patch those holes. If I had to describe it, it'd be like learning high school mathematics—algebra, differential equations, logarithmic charts—and then realizing that you'd never learned how to do long division. Or, say, angles in a circle. Gods, I hated those.

The second portion of the examination I was much more blasé about. That was the practical examination where you were asked to show your command over magic. Apprentices were scored on the effects of their spells, and since I was, in terms of actual casting, much more advanced, I expected to get close to full scores. Even spells that I might not "know," I could recreate by linking multiple aspects.

The last portion would be dealt with while I was writing the examination. That was where my staff would come into play, where I would provide the staff to them for review. They'd test the staff, reviewing it for flaws before marking it. I was much less certain of my results there. While I had some Master-level work in the staff, I was also still trying to make other portions of it work.

Still, I thought, overall, I should pass. But maybe a little more review of the theory would be best. Because passing wasn't my goal anymore. I needed to be so good that they wanted me in the Council, that they were willing to put in real effort.

Resolved to do more than just pass, I went over my spells and the theories in my mind, allowing time to pass.

***

Since I'd refused to go to the Mage Council's headquarters, the examination was being held in one of their many safe houses. In this case, it was a working horse farm. Stable? In either case, the farm had about four fenced off areas for the horses, a big stable, and another, larger covered riding ring on the right of the road. Dominating the entire location was the double-story white ranch house with its large windows and blue curtains. A trio of vehicles were parked outside, the truck being the only practical farm instrument. The other two were sedans like ours, city vehicles by the lack of dents and dirt.

Of course, my attention was drawn to the presence of the three examiners standing on the house-spanning front porch. How did I know they were my examiners and not stable hands? Well, their Levels for one.

Patricia Fitzgerald (Level 173)
HP: 180/180
MP: 1783/1894

Nicholas Diaz (Level 183)
HP: 141/147
MP: 1084/1147

Muhammad Black (Level 171)
HP: 201/204
MP: 997/1473

"Are all examiners that high level?" I muttered to Caleb as we got out of the car. I could feel the power radiating out from them, and Patricia had a half-dozen more enchantments on her than Caleb did. Obviously she didn't agree with his "the staff is the best thing ever" line of thought. I thought I might even like her.

"No. Your case is unique. They are the head examiners for the three closest regions," Caleb said.

Caleb stayed silent until we were close to the group, then he introduced us and them to one another. Of course, I didn't mention that I knew their names already thanks to Lily. Be a little rude.

"The Templar must stay outside." Muhammad stated that with a glare at Alexa.

"Ex-Templar," she said.

"There is no such thing," Muhammad snapped before running a hand across curly, close-cropped hair, glancing at my hand with Lily's ring. "The jinn is not here?"

"She stayed behind." Caleb added, after glancing at the ring, "In a manner of speaking."

"Good. The staff?" Nicholas held out his hand before inclining his head toward Patricia. "Mage Fitzgerald will guide you to the examination room."

I stepped forward and handed over my staff, giving it one last glance before following Patricia into the house. She strode past the living room into the single barren office right off the corridor. On the worn, bulky office table, a paper had been set, along with a single line exercise book.

"Two hours."

I acknowledged her words and walked over, fishing some pens from inside my jacket before putting the jacket over the back of the chair and getting comfortable. Patricia looked me over once again then walked out, shutting the door. I felt the spell that sealed the room and triggered the protective enchantment. For a moment, fear clutched at me—until I noticed the trigger that would turn the room-sealing enchantment off from the inside. Right. Not a prison, just extra careful against cheaters who might be getting help from others.

I snorted, tapped the workbook, and flipped over the examination questions. Best to get to it then. I scanned through the first question and clicked my pen, composing my thoughts. Time to get to it.

Two hours went by in a blink. I wrote and wrote, answering questions as quickly as I could. At first, the questions were easy to answer. The equivalent of basic math. But by the time I got toward the last couple of pages, the complexity made me frown, my brow furrowing as I struggled to provide responses. Some of it was history, context dependent. Others required knowledge of spell formulae and theorems I only vaguely recalled, or had puzzled out the basic portions of. I was so caught up in answering, I didn't notice the door opening, the release of the wards.

"Time is up." Patricia stood beside the table, hand held out for me to hand her the notebook.

I blinked, staring at the words I'd scribbled, and saw a notification that had my eyes narrowing in thought.

Experience Gained for Theorem Exploration!
+27,489

"Oh, you tricky bastards," I said, looking at Patricia's impatient mien and the last few pages. I scooted back slightly as I reached forward with both hands, gripped the last few questions, and ripped out the pages. I saw Patricia hiss, and as I set the pages on fire, I barely felt the trace of power as she extinguished the flames. I felt another wave of power, and I stopped trying to destroy the paper. "You just copied my answers, didn't you?"

Patricia sniffed. "We will not be marking the torn portions."

"Bullshit." I tossed the notebook on the table, ignoring her still-extended hand, and stood. Sons of bitches caught me out, making me think I was taking an apprentice exam but instead testing me for what I really knew. Testing me for the things that Lily had taught me behind their backs.

I stalked out of the house, only to see Caleb waiting for me. His lips pursed at my glare, but I wasn't about to be mollified. "That was no apprentice test."

"The initial part was," Caleb said, holding up his hands. "I did not know they were going to test you like that. But it's good, it means they're taking you seriously."

"Or trying to trick Lily's knowledge out of me."

"Knowledge that you would have to share anyway, if you joined us," Patricia said, appearing from behind me. "I have marked your examination."

"Already?" I said, surprised.

"Yes. Your basics are spotty, but much better than most of our Apprentices, I will admit. You also have, as Magus Hahn has informed us, quite a degree of knowledge in some advance application of spell theory."

I narrowed my eyes, hearing the but. "But?"

"Theory is insufficient to prove your ability. And it seems your work with the staff is, at best, average," Patricia said.

Once again I narrowed my eyes in suspicion at the Mage. I was not entirely sure I agreed with her assessment, knowing what I did of the Mage Council. Alexa, seated on the hood of the car, looked at me and I carefully shook my head to keep her seated. No, nothing that she could help with here.

"So what? We finishing this?" I said, deciding to see what else they wanted. Or needed.

"This way," Patricia said, stepping past me and heading for the indoor riding circle.

I followed, the giant white canvas flaps billowing in the wind as I walked into the bare earth riding circle. The riding circle was empty but for a series of enchanted staves located at the borders of the stable. As I stepped in, I felt the enchantments kick in, sealing me within.

A hand came up, generating a shield across my body even as I put distance between Patricia and myself. I continued my scan of the location, noting the presence of the other examiners and my staff, held casually in one tester's hand. A jerk of my fist triggered the return protocols in my staff, making it lurch through the air to slap into my hand.

"Calm yourself," Caleb said, holding up a hand. "The enchantments are to ensure that no damage is done to the surroundings."

I looked at the Mage and saw that he and Patricia were not making any threatening moves. Neither were the other examiners, truth be told. And… well, that made sense. I found myself flushing in embarrassment even as I pushed down the emotion. After all, they could have warned me. Unlike most of their apprentices, I dealt with more violent and dangerous situations regularly.

"Now what?"

"Now you show us you can handle yourself," Nicholas said, waving toward the center of the room.

A second later, a giant ball of glowing light, made from criss-crossing verses of spell formula, appeared. My eyes narrowed. I was surprised he'd managed to conjure something so complex with a wave of his hand—until I noticed the small tripod and globe beneath the actual globe itself. Ah. An enchanted object.

"You want me to read the spell formulas?" I guessed, cocking my head as I tried to follow the scrolling information.

Tough, especially since I could only see portions of the spell. Though even a quick glance told me that multiple spells were involved in the creation of the globe. In fact, some of those spells looked familiar—like that Fire Bolt one…

A fraction of a second later, a Fire Bolt formed in the center of the spell globe and shot toward me. I batted it aside with my shield, frowning. The spell was quite weak, so weak that it probably wouldn't have killed me. Probably.

"What the hell?" I said. That was not how the examination was supposed to go.

"You will need to read, anticipate, and understand the spells formed by the globe and counter them. The testing globe will continue to release spells at timed intervals. Points will be awarded for spells that are blocked or counter-spelled," Nathan said. As he finished, next to the spell globe, a scoreboard appeared with the number 001 on it. "You will need to score a minimum of a hundred to pass."

When I opened my mouth to ask further questions, an Ice Bolt formed around the globe and shot toward me. Once again, I batted it away, watching as the points went up by another one.

"A word of warning. As time goes on, the spells you will have to deal with grow more complicated," Mohammad said, offering me a thin smile.

I growled softly, keeping my shield up while focusing on the spell globe again. The new spell formula running across the globe was one that was familiar to me, and so while the spell globe formed the spell, I reached out with my Mana and disrupted the spell.

Mana Bolt Counter Spell Cast
Synchronicity: 89%

I received three points as the Mana Bolt fizzled out, its spell container disrupted by my injection of Mana. Counter-spelling came in many forms, but the one I had been taught was simple—the use of my Mana injected into the forming spell container, splicing my spell formula amendment to it. Of course, counter-spelling was complicated. You couldn't throw random "numbers" at another spell formula, hoping they would stick. You had to actually know which portion you were targeting with your splice. On top of that, each spell had gaps within their formula, areas where you could slide in your own Mana and spell formula. Miss those areas, and even if you knew what you wanted to adjust, you would still fail.

Counter-spelling basically required you to understand the spell formula being used and also be extremely quick at casting, since you were, in many ways, casting both the spell itself and the spell injector.

At first, I racked up points fast, counter-spelling everything the globe threw at me. The initial stages were simple—spells like Gust, Burn, Light, and the like were used in a combative form. Buckets of acid, sparks of electricity, and even waves of conjured water scrolled through the globe and were disrupted. I had to give it to the Mage Council—the spell globe was actually a good training tool. The wide variety of spell containers, delays in spell formation, and alteration in Mana channeling all required me to be inventive in my counters. But good tool or not, if this was the level of difficulty, this would be a cakewalk.

Ten minutes later, I was feeling the strain. My total score crossed the sixty-point range and my Mana dropped below half. From a slow and steady stroll, the spell formula had sped up, rolling past faster than the noob zone chat window on launch day. I'd stopped being able to read the spell itself and instead resorted to guessing. Which had obvious results.

"Head's up!" I twisted at the hips and slammed the decahedron of platinum into the air with my staff.

The force applied to the end of my staff was enough to numb both hands and nearly tear the staff out of my hands entirely. Thankfully, it was still considered a win. My count went up by another point and the spell globe burped, another spell forming.

"Foolish," Nicholas muttered to Muhammad.

Sadly, I couldn't disagree. I stopped trying to counter-spell, my latest attempt a definite failure, and instead focused on defense. That meant I'd have to deal with a lot more spells, but better that than failure. To begin, I reconstructed my Force Shield, shrinking its size so that it only covered my body. Next, I curved the wall so that I wasn't taking attacks straight-on. Not a moment too soon either, as the spell finished and a series of spinning air daggers flew toward me.

An academic portion of my mind noted that the air daggers weren't contained once they were released, but instead they used a series of three points to make themselves. First, the point of origin, the second about halfway toward me, and the third very close to where I stood. The last two target points adjusted the air pressure and direction of airflow, guiding the air daggers that had been formed at the first target point.

The shield took the individual attacks with aplomb, the air daggers bouncing off with the sound of a bad dubstep, making me smirk. But already the next spell was forming and I was reading its data.

Holding the Force Shield was easy, but considering I had another forty spells to go, I considered better, more interesting options. Because each moment I held the Shield, my Mana dropped. As I grasped the content of the next spell, I dismissed the Shield and jumped straight into the air, using a quick cast of Gust to elevate me even higher. A second later, the ground burst into verdant greenery, grasping vines searching for me. I let loose a second burst of the spell, keeping me in the air while flattening the already dying vines.

And not once did I shift my gaze from the spell globe as another spell scrolled past. Only to be joined by a second scrolling formula.

"Two!" I growled.

But I raised my staff, invoking the pre-made shield in the spell to deal with the first spell formula. All the while trying to grasp what the second spell formula was. It seemed they were intent on ramping up the difficulty.

***

Five spells. None of them were particularly complex—Force Spears, Mana Bolt, Freezing Rain, and the like—but each of them was enough to knock me out. Five spells scrolled past at a clip, forming from the globe and targeted at me.

All around me, the ground had been torn up, baked, and frozen. If not for the spelled enchantments around the perimeter, the entire riding stable would have been destroyed already. The acrid scent of materials materialized then dismissed lingered, traces of acid, ozone, and burnt soil assaulting my senses. Each breath I took made my chest heave, my Mana levels barely above "Henry is conscious" levels.

Five spells. I began triple casting again, the first the counter-spell container, then splitting the container to hold the counter-spells for each of the injections I was using to break two of the five spells. In my hand, my staff glowed, helping to draw Mana into my spells, while the Force Shield blocked off the remainder attacks.

As the strain of managing multiple spells increased my headache, I gestured with my hand, snapping it forward. A flicker of information showed the low Synchronicity rates—barely in their forties—but I ignored them, even as the lack of proper casting drained more Mana. Rather, I focused on the three spells that were aimed at me.

Frost Spear, Wind Drill, and Metal Missiles all slammed into my Force Shield. I angled the shield to take the Spear on the corner, allowing it to glance off sideways and strike the enchanted protections behind. The Missiles were like raindrops striking my shield, plentiful and annoying but not dangerous in and of themselves. The Wind Drill curved at the last second, taking my shield straight-on. I growled, trying to reinforce the spell only for the increased force in the spinning Drill to shatter it. I threw myself backward, attempting to dodge the attack, but I could only watch as the Wind Drill neared my chest, ready to punch through.

Just before it could strike, Mohammad waved and the Drill dispersed, sending a blast of air that ruffled my hair even as I landed on the ground. A sharp pain radiated from my tailbone and I groaned, making a mental note to look into enchanted underwear again. As I struggled to my feet with the aid of my staff, I surreptitiously rubbed my bottom while glancing at the scoreboard. For the first time in a while, I had time to really look at it.

117.

"Har. Beat it." I sniggered and slowly limped over to the testers.

Five spells might be my limit, it seemed. I absently eyed the experience notifications I'd received. The spell globe really was a great training tool, one that had pushed my comprehension and analysis of spells to a level I'd never had to get to.

"So do I get a nifty top hat or something?" I flashed the trio of examiners and Caleb a smile, only to find them staring at me in silence.

Chapter 12

"So what do apprentices get?" I repeated, waiting for the trio to speak.

The Mage Council examiners regarded me as if I were a bug that had crawled out of a movie theater seat, replete with stale popcorn and spilled soda. It was not the gaze of congratulations, which was rather interesting considering I should have passed.

"You were right," Mohammad said to Caleb.

"I told you." Caleb hocked a thumb toward me. "Though it seems that Mage Tsien has been holding back on me a little."

"By… thirty points, I would say." Nicholas sniffed. "It does not bode well for us trusting the warlock."

"Mage," I grumbled while rubbing my bum. I kept my head down though, since the one thing I really didn't want them to grasp was how I'd soft-balled the entire test. I could have continued counter-spelling longer than I did, and I definitely could have continued to deal with the spells. While my Mana shortage was real—hard to hide that fact—how fast I was losing it and how fast I could regenerate it was something I was trying to hide still. After being tricked once, I wasn't going to be dumb enough to reveal all my cards.

"Not if we don't say so," Nicholas said, glaring at me. He looked at my staff for a second, considering the piece of wood in my hand, before he turned to the others. "Your judgment?"

Patricia glanced at the spell globe then at me once more and nodded. "He has passed every test we have set. He is at the apprentice level at the least. A full Mage of the sixth circle."

I blinked, knowing there were seven circles, with those in the inner circles—the lower numbers—the most powerful. Caleb was considered part of the second circle these days. In that sense, I'd skipped the entire Apprentice level—or seventh circle—to become a journeyman. But it'd be at least one more circle before I could be considered a full member. In their view.

"Perhaps, but we are judging more than his academic ability," Nicholas said. "He lacks discipline and the right mindset. His work is sloppy, if prone to brilliance. Though, I would venture, much of the latter is due to his jinn. Otherwise, he is middling at best."

I narrowed my eyes but turned to Mohammad, who had started speaking. "Brilliance that we could harness. The theories he expounded upon in his essay are interesting. Both Beckett's Theorem of Fundamental Formulas and Obibje Principle of Sevens were quite illuminating. I do not believe the combination Mr. Tsien recommended would work as well as he thought, but perhaps if we combined the Ozmas Principle—"

"Enough. No one wants to hear you prattle. Are you for or against his inclusion in our ranks?" Nicholas snapped.

"Well, he has passed our tests. I think, in that sense, we should at the least let him know our conditions," Mohammad said.

Patricia nodded firmly, making me frown as Caleb stepped forward to speak.

"What conditions?" I said suspiciously.

"I told you the Council would have requirements of you. If we are to acknowledge you as one of us, if we are protect you, certain matters must be agreed on." Caleb took a breath and forged on. "You'll need to swear a binding oath to be loyal to the Council. And that, on your death, you would hand over the ring."

"And no more hiding of your secrets." Nicholas crossed his arms. "You will share everything that your jinn teaches you."

"A binding oath?" My eyes narrowed. "I'm assuming you're talking a blood oath?"

"No. A soul oath," Caleb said.

I hissed, and even Patricia looked uncomfortable. I wasn't surprised she was uncomfortable considering what a soul oath actually consisted of. Like its name, it bound me by my soul—the center of my being—rather than my body. Those oaths were nearly impossible to break, and when they were broken, they left the oathbreaker a shattered creature. Monsters were created when soul oaths broken, because the mind didn't break—just the things that made us human.

"You can't seriously think I'll agree to that," I said.

"If you desire our help, you will." Nicholas said, stopping Caleb when he tried to say something else. "You have little choice here."

"Pretty sure no is still valid."

Nicholas snorted, his gaze flicking to my ring then my face. "You could not even stand five spells. If I wanted to take that ring—"

"You'd fail." I shook my head and turned, walking to the car. I paused when a thought struck, my eyes narrowing as I turned around. "You are going to drive me back, right?"

"Henry, you need to consider your position more carefully," Caleb said, concern in his voice. "This might not be what you want. What I wanted. But the Council has made it clear that they want more from you."

My fist clenched as I looked at the all-too-smug Nicholas and the prideful Mohammad before turning to the conflicted Patricia. They thought they had me in a corner. That I had no choice but to accede to their demands. And truth be told, they were right. Lily's protection might stop over-Leveled assholes like these guys from attacking me, but it did nothing to stop them from sending waves of appropriately Leveled assholes. And unlike a game, I wouldn't gain much experience from protecting myself from them, because my Levels were tied to my ability to both physically manage and understand the magic that was input in my body.

Angry or not, I was in a corner. They were right. But… "I already did. I'm not taking a soul oath. No way, no how."

"Then they'll kill you," Caleb said.

"So be it," I said. "No one's immortal, eh?"

"Bold words. But know that if you walk away now, when we speak again, your deal will be even worse," Nicholas almost snarled.

"Don't worry. I won't be."

"Foolish child…"

I didn't bother answering and walked out, deciding to stop being childish and arguing. I stalked forward until I reached the edge of the enchantment, which had yet to turn off. For a moment, I waited to see if they'd turn it off, and when they didn't, I pushed my staff against the enchantment. My eyes narrowed as the enchantments on the staff flared to life, pulling at the shielding wall. Information about the enchantment flowed into my mind via the analyzing runes in the staff. My eyes narrowed as I searched for the gaps, then when the next pulse from the shield cycled through, I inserted an adjustment.

A moment later, the enchantment opened up, splitting aside for me to walk out. Behind me, I heard a few indrawn breaths, but I refused to look back. If they'd been willing to bargain, to help out, perhaps we could have come up with something. Instead, they'd decided to hold my feet over the fire and see how much I'd squirm. Well, bugger that.

Alexa looked up when I came over, her eyes narrowing when she took in my distressed demeanor. She spun her spear around, watching the riding stable. There was no need to say anything, not with how things had gone.

When five minutes came and went and Caleb didn't come out, I groaned softly and fished out my phone.

"Looks like we're taking a carshare back," I said, glancing at Alexa's spear. "They won't attack us. Can't."

"Fine," Alexa said, opening the sedan's back door and fishing out her duffel. She looked at me and flashed a grin. "Shotgun."

"Hey! You can't do that until the car's here," I said, having finished booking our ride back.

"Nope. Called it."

"That's—aargh!" I threw up my hands and waved down the driveway. "Let's go wait on the main road."

Together, we walked out. I couldn't say for sure what Alexa was thinking, but for myself, I was debating how on earth we were going to survive.

***

"To sum up—the government has pulled back a couple of blocks. The Druids and the other pagans have left. So will the Mage Council. The Templars and the rest of the Orders are going to leave now that the Council has made their position known. And none of the other quieter guardians, those who want the ring, are going to stick around, not without the big boys in play," Lily said, ticking off on her fingers. We were back in the living room, after I'd explained what had happened with the Mage Council and my decision. "That sound about right?"

"Yeah. I doubt they're going to leave entirely, just in case I manage to level…" I turned my attention to Lily. "Can we do that?"

"Do what?" Lily said, raising an eyebrow.

"Can we raise my level? Hit 100, like, in a week or something and release me from the spell?" Even as I finished speaking, I realized how bad an idea that was. Exactly what did I intend to do even if I did get a higher level? It wasn't as if that higher level, artificially inflated or not, would do anything but release the wish.

"A bit. Not all the levels, but we could flood you with more experience," Lily said. "I'm not sure why…"

Alexa pointed at me. "We should get you to train. Properly."

"Properly?" I said, blinking.

Alexa nodded. "No more random silly quests, no more hunting for the best clothing or carving silly sticks. You train and level and increase how much Mana you can wield."

"Training montage?" I said with a slight smirk, only to get smacked on the arm by Alexa.

"Idiot. This isn't funny." Alexa said, shaking her head. "But we should also talk about leaving."

"Our lease isn't up," I objected immediately, thinking about my poor damage deposit. Our damage deposit. Huh. I wondered if the Templars would want their share back?

"We're talking about getting killed, Henry. Focus," Alexa snapped, and I sighed.

I pointed at the wards we had. "But the house is warded."

"You know those won't last forever. If they really wanted us dead, they could breach the wards," Alexa said. "Staying here, we're just a target. If they all leave…"

I nodded, looking at my hands. She's correct that there really isn't a better option than leaving. If we can run and hide—*if* being the operative word—we had a chance of lasting. Lasting long enough to… to what?

"Henry?" Lily said, cocking her head.

"How did your other owners manage to not get killed?" I said, frowning.

"Well, first, they generally hid my presence," Lily said. "And then, well, most didn't ask for magic. Money—when wished for properly—was easy enough to offer them. Power was harder, but it could be arranged. You have no idea how many political marriages I managed to arrange. But for the ones who wanted or needed magic, I was more of a research assistant, you know?

"Then, well, they became the most powerful Mage in their surroundings. And with the way news and rumors got distorted, no one was going to travel for weeks or months to check out a bad rumor. Or fight someone who could be more powerful than them just for the chance of getting an artifact that was better than the one they had already. Maybe."

I sighed, rubbing my face. "So you're saying air transportation and phone lines are killing me."

"Sort of? It's not as if a lot of my owners weren't killed because they had me," Lily said. "My last couple of owners before you never let anyone know of my presence. They hid my power and barely used me as more than a research assistant. So we're in new territory here."

"Yay," I said desultorily. "I always wanted to break new ground."

Alexa snorted, then poked me in the shoulder. "It doesn't matter. We just have to get you strong enough that you can fight them off."

"What? You mean the entire world?" I said.

"Or you could look for someone who's strong enough to do it already," Lily offered.

"Like?"

"Well… ummm… Mer's stuck. Hecate… well. You aren't the right sex. Abe's sleeping somewhere. The Eight won't talk to you. Umm…."

I didn't know who Lily was speaking about, but what she was saying was clear enough. None of the people Lily knew who could have protected us were going to. Which meant I would have to do it myself.

"Well, if we're going to go, we should figure out how. And where." Alexa flashed me a half-smile.

I sighed. "You have a plan, don't you?"

Before Alexa could say anything, we were rudely interrupted. The screech of a tire-burning turn was the only notice we received before a truck barreled toward us. My eyes widened as I stared at the incoming vehicle, watched as it struck the windows and living room's outer wall. Watched as my wards, never meant to handle a vehicle driving straight at us, flared to life and tried to keep the vehicle out.

And failed.

Chapter 13

The wards bled most of the momentum from the vehicle. Force Columns, generated initially as Force Spikes, reared from the floor, meant to block or injure those who came through the windows. It had been easier to enchant the entire wall with the same ward form rather than pick out just the walls. They hit the truck's undercarriage as they grew, throwing it upward and tearing up the shaft and other mechanical bits.

Rather than come all the way in and smash us into pieces, the truck stalled, two-thirds of its body in our residence, the last third held off the ground by the spike columns. I stared at the shattered front window and saw no one there. Gasoline tanks on the truck tumbled and creaked, dented and broken in the initial charge, but not exploding. Perhaps it was the other defensive portions of the ward or perhaps it was the Force Spikes, but whatever had been meant to set the gasoline on fire didn't go off. Yet I smelled the spilled gasoline, heard it dribbling to the ground as my ears recovered from the cacophony of sound that the truck had created when it slammed into our building.

"Shit. We're under attack!" I snarled, turning to Alexa. Only to see that my friend was only partially responsive, coming to her senses as a gash down one side of her head spilled blood. "Oh gods. Alexa!"

I looked at Lily only to see her untouched by dust cloud or injury, but staring in shock. Not at the truck, but the shattered monitor on her laptop. Rather than waste time on her, I cast around for something, anything. And saw the rolled up enchanting circle, the portable habitat I'd been working on.

I snatched it from its place and threw it on the table before picking up Alexa with a heave and stepping into the circle. It hummed for a second as I shoved my Mana into the runes, powering them. As the walls of the habitat flickered to life, the gas tanks on the truck finally exploded. If not for the flash of magic I felt just before the tanks went off, I would have thought the explosion had something to do with the sparking electricity or the broken truck itself.

The world went red and orange, flames and pieces of the truck itself striking the Force Walls. But they held, having been reinforced for just such an occurrence. Well, this and more. Mana sucked out of my body, flooding down the runes, taking whatever I had recovered and a little more before the world flashed white again.

Just before we left, I caught a glimpse of Lily, untouched in the remnants of our home, looking forlorn and lost. Seated amidst flame and smoke as our home, our place of residence and relaxation, was destroyed.

And then we were gone.

***

Our forms blurred, transported through a parallel dimension, pulled apart and shifted before we were returned to harsh reality and the anchor point I had created, returned to the mark I'd set. I lurched forward, the motion that was not motion throwing off my sense of balance. I tumbled forward, holding onto Alexa, and only managed to twist enough to not drop her onto the ground.

As I pushed myself upward, Alexa weakly struggled out of my arms to fall onto her butt next to me. Pushing aside her hands, I shoved at the cut on her head, pushing it together while casting Heal. Thankfully, this spell was one I had grown so used to that I no longer needed to use a physical component to cast.

A few minutes later, Alexa pushed me aside and scrubbed at her face. She cleaned off the sticky blood that had congealed from the heat that had managed to touch us even through the barriers. While Alexa was busy cleaning herself off, I took stock of our surroundings. I touched a ward and sent my

Mana into it, reinforcing the wards that had automatically gone up when we'd teleported in. Among other things, it was meant to hide our aura signatures and Lily's signature too. It wouldn't hold forever, but it would give me time to work on the next step.

Before I could get to that, Alexa spoke up. "Where are we?"

"Uh... well. Storage depot. About two miles from the house. I needed a place to test out teleportation wards, and I used to keep this for my, well, other business and forgot about it." I gestured at the variety of suitcases, storage chests, and random pieces of furniture I'd collected and never managed to sell. Or in some cases, kept because I felt I'd make more later.

Admittedly, after I got my magic, I'd forgotten about my rainy day stash. I'd only remembered the storage shack because I had been considering a place for my teleportation experiments. And, I'd admit, I'd spent a little more time building the wards around here due to a quest that Lily have given me.

Which reminded me that I needed to make sure Lily's signature and mine stayed hidden. That meant a moving enchantment ward. The easiest way to do that was to inscribe the enchanted ward on something easy to carry. Luckily, among the other things I kept here were small wooden blocks and scribing tools. In short order, I had a workplace set up.

"Alexa, can you find some string? I'm thinking necklaces," I asked before turning to the blocks.

It took a few minutes for me to recall the wards I'd considered but never created. Once more, I considered why I hadn't, why I had been willing to believe that my 'allies' would stick beside me. And cursed myself for the foolishness. Too late for regrets though. It was time to get to work, time to complete things I'd considered but not put into place.

Thirty minutes later, I had a pair of amulets. The first one suppressed and changed Alexa's aura—that had taken me less than five minutes to create. The second warded amulet took the rest of the time, what with my stronger aura and Lily's. I'd mentally planned a few ways of doing this. At first, I'd considered creating two wards—one for Lily's ring and one for myself. However, the math on that didn't work. Even the ambient aura from the ring meant that I would have to carry around a much larger, more powerful aura ward.

To fix the issue, I'd decided on something a little more creative. First, I subsumed the aura from the ring into mine. That made my aura much stronger while changing it. Once I had changed my aura, I needed to reduce its output. Of course, one of the aspects was that my aura was now so powerful, it was impossible to keep it suppressed on a daily basis. Instead, I altered it in stages by first compressing the ambient aura down to reduce the radius. I needed to do that multiple times until I stopped being a beacon. The result was that my compressed aura made me seem even more powerful than I was, but it required someone to be close to me to feel it.

At least, that was the theory. I gripped the amulet, slid it over my head, and drew a deep breath before activating the amulet. I felt a cold wind run across my body, making me shiver, then felt the wind brush over me again and again, each time compressing my aura further and further. I felt the way my ward worked for what seemed to be hours but was only long minutes before my aura stabilized.

"What did you do?" Alexa said when I refocused on her.

"I concentrated my aura and hid the ring underneath it," I explained. "What does it feel like?"

Alexa regarded me with her head cocked before she answered. "Like I'm standing in the clear on a hot sunny day, feeling the sun beating down on me. Like a warm wind is blowing across my skin, but it's not really a wind."

"Huh. Almost poetic."

Alexa sniffed, then looked around before she asked softly, "Lily?"

"She's fine." I laughed bitterly. "An explosion would do nothing to her. She's already back in the ring, but we can't have her out."

"Why?"

"Her aura, when she's out. It'd tear through these wards," I said, gesturing about. "I'm going to have to inlay some proper wards and craft some suppression material to keep her hidden."

Alexa nodded then made a face. "I'm sorry. I didn't think they'd act so fast."

"Not your fault. You warned me. Not to rely on them. Not to keep putting things off. I just… I didn't want to believe they'd give up on me, on us, that easily."

Alexa flashed a sad smile, and I couldn't help but remember that she had been discarded. Perhaps I should have listened to her. Too late. Too damn late.

And now here we were, hunkered in a storage space, hoping the artifacts I'd created would work. Would be enough. But even now, I felt the strain placed on the wood around my neck, the way it had already begun to crumble. It wouldn't give away immediately, but eventually. Eventually…

"Now what?" Alexa said.

I closed my eyes before opening them again. "Let's grab what's useful here. Then we should get moving. I'll cast a dispersal spell, try to hide our exit. But we should get moving across water and fast. Out of this city preferably."

Alexa nodded. "I've got a place. And some funds set aside. We'll just need to make a quick stop."

By this point, I was too tired to be surprised by her words. In the end, all I felt was gratitude that at least one of us had planned for this. Planned to be betrayed.

***

"A bowling alley?" I said, raising an eyebrow at Alexa.

Once we left the storage center, we'd wandered around for a few hours, taking a ferry ride across the bay then back again, muddying our trail. It wasn't perfect, but it was better than nothing. After that, Alexa had taken the lead, first to a co-working space where we chilled for a few hours in a rented office before we finally arrived at the bowling alley as it opened.

"This way," Alexa said, leading me straight to the storage lockers.

I twigged onto the concept fast enough and followed, casting glances around to make sure we weren't watched. Unsurprisingly, the staff—made up of horny and bored teenagers—had little care for us.

Alexa pulled a large duffel bag from the storage locker and changed out her jacket for one that was within before she pushed the duffel at me. I frowned, opening it, before my jaw dropped.

"Where'd you get that?" I said.

"Took it," Alexa said.

Within the now-open bag was a casting wand, a smaller version of the staff I'd been forced to leave behind. I blinked, staring at the wand, and remembered how I'd tossed it aside due to my dissatisfaction with the placement of the wards and then couldn't find it. I'd lost nearly an hour searching the house for it before finally giving up, figuring I'd find it hidden beneath a couch cushion or stuck underneath my bed. Or on top of the bookcase, because that made *sense* when I put it there. But now, here it was.

I picked up the wand, frowning in consternation as I noticed numerous flaws. I'd made this nearly half a year ago, and I'd grown in ability and skill since then. Enough so that the mistakes I'd made were clearly evident with even a simple perusal. My fingers itched to fix them, but I pushed it aside and slipped the wand into my jacket. Not that I needed it, but like my staff, the wand could take over casting aspects—just not as many my staff.

I also took a bundle of cash, sliding it into my jacket after peeling off a few bills for my wallet. I didn't ask how Alexa had managed to squirrel away this much. It really wasn't my business. I was just grateful that she had done so. What was surprising was the set of fake IDs within, all in a Ziploc bag.

"Fake IDs?" I said, raising an eyebrow.

"Yes. Change them out quickly. We should leave the city when we can," Alexa replied.

"About that... how?" I said. "I don't think public transportation is smart, and it's not as if we can get a rideshare. Not without our phones."

"Got it sorted," Alexa said. "Relax."

I frowned but took her word for it, taking the proffered baseball cap and sliding it onto my head. Well, she was the expert in this. My expertise with disguise mostly consisted of pixels, rooftops, and killing the guards who found you sneaking by.

***

Three hours later, we were seated in the luxurious comfort of polyester cushions, colored a dirty grey and green, a black plastic divider between us and a LCD screen to entertain us in front. Cold air blew from overhead, doing little to drown out the loud grey-haired retirees making new friends and speaking of the next "attraction" they were going to see.

I muttered to Alexa, "A tour bus? Your great plan is a tour bus filled with retirees?"

"Yes," Alexa said, looking all kinds of smug. "Public transportation, but not really. The windows are all shaded, so there's no way for people to see inside. Tours like these run every day of the week, going to multiple locations. And unless they're doing full checks of the bus, even traffic stops won't matter."

I had to admit, the woman was right. Most traffic stops would never board a bus, especially not on any of the major highways. The kind of delay that would create would only happen in the worst-case scenarios, and I didn't think our opponents had that kind of influence.

Which meant…

"I'm assuming we're not going to stay for the whole tour?" I said.

"No. We'll change out three cities out, but for tonight…" She waved around the bus. "We'll sleep through the night here and be out of the city."

"As if I could sleep," I said, which made Alexa smile slightly.

"Well, I can. So if you're going to stay awake…"

I gestured, to which the blonde smiled and rolled up her jacket to rest her head against the window. In moments, the ex-Initiate was asleep, dead to the world, though I knew she would wake fully alert if necessary. I envied her ability sometimes.

"Might as well get to work," I muttered and fished in my bag for the crafting material. Nothing special, but with only the equipment I was wearing, I needed more tools. The carving knife and blocks of wood would get me that.

Our attackers might have driven us out of my house and nearly killed us, but that nearly would cost them. I might not know who had attacked us or why, but it didn't matter. We'd survived, and so long as we lived, we could get stronger. We could get better.

As the bus finally pulled away from the curb, its passengers fully loaded, I promised myself that I'd be back. Back to my home. Returned not in ignominious defeat but in triumph. One day.

I'd be back.

Chapter 14

"Are you ready?" Alexa asked as she stood over me.

I gave the ex-Initiate a quick nod, touching Lily's ring and sending a mental reassurance to the jinn. Four months later and we had yet to summon her. There were a dozen excuses—from needing the right materials, to prioritizing new aura blockers, to not locating a quiet enough place to do it—but in the end, it meant we had left the jinn in the ring.

I had to admit, I missed the game-addicted jinn, late-night Smash Bros duels and conversations over meals. Occasionally, when I finished a quest, she'd slipped a sentence or two into the quest notifications, but it wasn't the same. I missed my friend. But at least this way, the pair of us had a better chance of hiding.

"You know, I liked this place," I said, looking around at the small house we had rented.

We'd found the advertisement in a gas station, pasted in the window, and moved in. Once a wedding present, before the enterprising couple realized that the small house lifestyle wasn't for them, now the simple single-story, container-turned-house sat in their backyard, filled by transients like us. The rent was cheap, the amenities barebones, but it had been nice.

"It was a change from the flop-houses," Alexa said, making a face.

I flashed her a wry smile, knowing that the pretty ex-blonde had had it worse in those locations. She'd dyed her hair soon after we left the city, going for boring black, and touched up her roots every few days. But bad dye jobs and baggy clothing did little to hide her beauty.

"But we can't stay. You know that."

"I know. The dice said eleven days, so eleven it is," I said.

Rather than fall into any recognizable pattern, we'd chosen to stay where we could, when we could, based off dice rolls. We limited ourselves to a maximum of twelve days in any one location. Even our next destination was a roll of the dice, public transportation and small towns our go-to choices.

Hefting the backpack, I slid it on. We closed the door, left the key in the mailbox, and headed out into cold autumn weather. Luckily, we'd been trending south for the most part, staying in warmer climates by roll of dice and choice. We'd debated long and hard about moving into another big city or sticking to small towns before we decided to leave it to chance. Our enemies were varied and numerous, and there were no good choices.

Big cities had teeming masses of people, enough that we could get lost in the anonymity of the populace. On top of that, big cities had a wide variety of cash-only jobs, the kinds that we survived on these days. In a pinch, we could mug and steal from the local drug dealer or pimp, taking their illicit gains for our own before departing town. Of course, we'd only done that twice. While criminals might not make police reports, they were prone to gossip. And guns that don't fire, sudden disorientations and fatigue, and a highly-skilled female martial artist beating the crap out of them with a pair of sticks were the kind of rumors we didn't want spreading.

For all those advantages, big cities had higher concentrations of supernaturals, increasing the odds of randomly running into someone dangerous. On top of that, big cities were the centerpiece of our surveillance state. There were few areas we could go in a major city without having our faces recorded. And my new mustache, a ball cap, and a pair of contact lenses was a poor disguise, even if it was supplemented by magic.

Small towns, on the other hand, substituted technological busybodies with human irritants. The number of inquisitive neighbors we met—especially those who were surprised by our mixed-race relations in certain smaller towns—was staggering. It had gotten so bad that I'd used glamour spells to alter my race at times, just to avoid the questions.

On top of that, smaller towns and out-of-town cottages offered little in terms of employment or other amenities. With our resources extremely tight, we couldn't afford to stay in such places long before we had to move on, looking for work where we could. And rather annoyingly, smaller towns also often had their local guardians—pagan magicians, shamans, or local supernaturals. Even if they didn't desire to be involved in the politics of the greater supernatural community, we only needed a single one of them to put together the clues and report us.

"Do you think we've managed to lose them?" I said, cocking my head toward Alexa.

The town before, we'd been attacked. A group of journeyman Mages, bearing the symbols of the Mage Council—though probably not directly commanded to—had located us. We'd left their corpses and a destroyed neighborhood behind, stealing their belongings and funds before driving for two days straight.

"Maybe," Alexa said, weariness in her voice.

I saw the bags under her eyes, the tension in her shoulders, and I winced. She walked to the junker we'd picked up, dropped her bag in the back, and got in even as I hurried to catch up. I knew how tired she was, how little sleep she took each night. The duty, the burden of our safety had fallen on her, for I was focused on the only way out we had.

Studying. And leveling.

It would be fitting to say I had grown in strength by leaps and bounds. I was now Level 76. A significant increase in strength. But it had been four months, and at this rate of increase, to meet the standards of even a single Third Circle Mage, I would need another half decade. A decade minimum to be where we needed to be for battle.

As I looked at the strained face of my friend, the bags under her eyes, then looked at my hands, I wondered. Could we last that long?

***

We were taking a small country road, driving carefully because small and underused also meant badly maintained. We were doing just under forty miles an hour after taking a turn, green vegetation from fenced-in fields all around us, some farmer's crop swaying in the wind, when the man stepped into the middle of the road. I jerked up against my seat belt as Alexa braked, instincts overriding caution as we screeched to a stop a bare foot away from hitting him. The car fish-tailed slightly as Alexa tried to dodge him at the same time.

Turning my head sideways, I regarded the man standing in the center of the road, hands on a small cane. He was dressed in a simple green cotton jacket, sleeves rolled up on tanned skin, light brown hair close-cropped. When he smiled, the wrinkles around his eyes deepened, showcasing the lack of chemical injections to his face and his advanced-sixtyish age. My eyes narrowed when Lily flashed a Status notification.

Julian Barber (Level 218)
HP: 3100/3100
MP: 0/0

None of that told me who he was, but the lack of Mana signature, the lack of magic was a relief. His level, on the other hand, wasn't, and I had to wonder how he was that high-leveled and still not a Mage. The ridiculous hit points was a clue of course. A very pointed one.

"Mage Tsien. Ms. Dumough," Barber called, tapping the cane on the ground. "Do not flee. It will not help. I am here to speak only."

Alexa growled, backing the car a bit and straightening it out. She never took her eyes off Barber as she angled the vehicle to go around him, all the while trusting me to safeguard us. When she was finally happy, she reached down beside her seat and picked up the pistol, aiming it at Barber while keeping it hidden. Only then did I roll down the window.

"Talk," Alexa said.

Now that Alexa had her attention on him fully, I cast a quick Detection spell, a variation on the Scry & Observe spell that I had known so long ago. This one was a Detect Life spell whose gain was set to just a little higher than a squirrel. As the spell washed out, details flickered through my mind. A couple of crows and Barber were the only ones present in the five-hundred-yard radius the spell gave good data on. Outside of that, returned data broke down, but even there, the area around us was relatively clear of major life-forms.

"I have a message for you." The cane rose, making the pair of us tense. But it was not an attack, just a pointer. "The Mage, that is."

"What's the message?" Alexa said. Softer, her eyes never moving from Barber. "I've heard of him. He's a famous tracker. Lycanthrope."

I swore and almost missed what Barber said next.

"You have until the new year. If you do not return to the city by then, they will kill your mother. And one more for every month you continue to hide."

I shuddered, his words making me break out into a sweat. My family... my sister... What? How? For a time, my mind went blank, unable to process the threat so casually delivered.

"You can't!" Alexa said angrily. "They're not part of this. Not of our world. They're mundanes! The law—"

"Tradition can be broken. Will be broken." Barber made a face. "I am sorry. I am just one of many messengers. What they are doing, I do not agree with. But if you did not receive this message, they would have carried out their threats anyway. Those who want you dead are not the kind to offer clemency or extensions."

"Why end of the year?" I croaked, my mind latching onto the portion that had surprised me.

"A compromise. You have done well, hiding. There was some concern you would dodge all the messengers."

I grunted, my mind casting back to my mother, my sister. To those I'd left behind. I'd forgotten about them, forgotten they'd be vulnerable too. I should have thought of it, should have known. Should have...

"Is that all?" Alexa said, glaring at Barber.

When he stepped away from the car and nodded, Alexa floored the vehicle, taking us away from him. No longer caring about potholes or sudden cows, she took us away. All while I considered my failure.

***

We didn't stop for hours. We crossed half the state and ended up in another broken-down motel, paying in cash for a pair of beds that I cast Cleanse on the moment I finished setting up our protective wards. In the meantime, Alexa verified that the room wasn't bugged before snatching the keys and doing another check on the car. Not that she hadn't done that hours ago, but we were somewhat paranoid. Half an hour later, we'd done all we could to ensure that we weren't tracked and were seated across from one another on worn, if now clean, beds as an old cathode ray television played in the background.

"I have to go back." I broke the silence, facing the truth head-on. Stating what I knew had to be said, even though I knew it was the wrong choice. The expected choice.

"I know."

"You shouldn't try to convince me—" I paused as my brain caught up with me. "You're not going to argue with me?"

Alexa let out a bark of laughter that cut-off. "No. They are threatening your family. I would be disappointed if you chose not to go."

"Even if it might be a bluff?"

"Can you risk it being a bluff?" Alexa asked. When she saw the look on my face, she continued. "That is why it is such an effective threat."

"I should have..." I drew a deep breath, settling my emotions even as I pushed aside the need to explain, to make excuses. It was too late to tell the truth. To warn my family. To do something different. Yet I could not help but feel the gnawing guilt in my stomach, the pain from putting people I loved in danger. But I could not have given up Lily either. Not to be used, abused, for ages.

"It isn't your fault," Alexa said softly. "You never had a good choice."

"But maybe I could have trusted them. They asked. Begged me to trust them." I turned away and wiped my eyes. "Now they might die."

"They won't," Alexa said firmly. "We'll go back and we'll make sure they're safe."

"We?"

"You're not getting rid of me that easily," Alexa said.

"I can't ask you to do this."

"Who's asking?"

I found myself smiling in gratitude. "So. What? We go back now?"

"No. Not yet."

"But..."

"They're not going to harm them. He gave you the deadline for a reason," Alexa said, her eyes narrowing. "We have two months. Let's not rush it."

My stomach twisted, first with fear then with anger. "You can't be sure they won't act before then."

"And you can't be sure they won't hurt your family if you don't give them Lily," Alexa snapped. "There's only one ring, remember? What if you went there and they fought over the ring? What if the group that didn't get it wanted to take it out on your family? Or they tried to make you give it to them first by taking your family first?" When I had no answer, Alexa continued. "You don't know what the status of your family is. Are they captured? Are they just watched? I assume they're watching them, but what if I'm wrong? We don't even know who 'them' is. Not really."

"But it was the..." I fell silent. I had no idea who was threatening my family. I assumed it was the Mage Council, because... I wasn't even sure why. Because they were the ones I thought had been following me? But they weren't the ones who'd launched the first attack. After all, they had a way in back then. I'd just assumed. This entire thing was really getting to me.

"Exactly. They didn't even give you a specific time or place. Just the city. So what does that tell you?" Alexa said, her voice quieter now, no longer as forceful as I'd calmed down.

"I'm... not sure."

"Neither am I. But I think we should find out, don't you?" When I reluctantly nodded, Alexa smiled at me. "Tomorrow, we'll split up."

"Huh?"

"You can't find out what's going on. And it's obvious that together, we're targets. So we'll split up. You train and Level. I'll find out what's going on in the city."

"You?" I let my eyes rake over the statuesque woman. "Alexa, you're… ummm…"

"Less noticeable than a Mage with his magic aura? Trained in espionage? With knowledge and contacts in the supernatural world—especially in the city—over and above yours? And most importantly, not the most wanted man on Earth?" Alexa said.

"But you're known."

"I'll avoid our enemies. But the man on the street? The ones we've helped? They won't care. They won't even know. It's not as if the organizations are going to announce that they're hunting you. Not exactly the kind of news they want to spread around. Bad for their reputations in some cases. Dangerous in others," Alexa said.

Acting against me exposed organizations that might not want me to survive long enough to become a power to their enemies. It was one of the reasons the Mage Council had been willing to watch over me—a way to act against their enemies without expending significant resources. If the Council wasn't acting against me directly, nor the Orders, Alexa was safer. At the very least, she wasn't the final target. And we did need that information.

Still…

"Why are you doing this?" I said, tilting my head sideways as I regarded the ex-Initiate. "This, this is a lot more than what a friend can be expected to do."

"Friend… I guess so." Alexa offered me a half-smile. "But I don't think you're just a friend. You're family. And if I've learnt anything, family means giving everything."

"Without hope or expectation of anything in return." My lips twisted into another wry smile before I decided to admit it. It was the least I could do. "I think of you as family too. You and Lily."

Alexa flashed me a smile, then leaned forward as she explained her plan. I'd be surprised that she had one, but after so many years and hours of driving, I wasn't. If anything, sometimes I wondered if Lily should have gone to Alexa. Certainly she was better at planning and figuring things out than I was. All I had was a little knowledge from my gaming days.

Pushing aside guilt and my need to control things, I focused. Because my feelings didn't matter here, and more importantly, it wasn't just my life on the line anymore. Not even just Alexa's. Now it was about my entire family, and I would not fail them. No matter what.

Chapter 15

Twelve hours later, I was standing in the basement of a rented farmhouse. The farmhouse was one of those incongruities of the modern age—a building that had once housed the farmer and his family, now abandoned as pieces of a once-proud farm had been sold off in dribs and drabs until nothing more than a large field was available. Unsuited for a working farm now, it functioned as a country retreat for rich yuppies and the occasional tourist. Like me.

Of course, the homeowner had been surprised when I turned up alone, carrying nothing more than a single backpack, to take the entire location for myself. But once I handed him the month's rent up front in cash, questions had disappeared.

Once I was settled in, I had to clear out the basement and set up multiple repeating wards. I kept at it, layering ward after ward till I was fairly certain that between the wards and the ambient interference from a nearby ley line, I should be safe.

My hand hovered over my ring as I stood in the middle of the enchanted circle, my wards glowing, the entire basement lit by a quartet of fluorescent bulbs. If I was wrong, I'd be setting a flare off for everyone and their hellhounds to find me. But if I didn't…

Tired of my own hesitation, I rubbed the ring, sending a thought beckoning Lily out. At first there was nothing, and then… there was nothing. Frowning, I stared at my ring, wondering if I had broken it. Her. Then I discarded the thought for being silly.

"You're risking a lot," Lily spoke up and made me jump.

I turned toward her. Seated to the side of me, legs crossed, Lily tilted her head as she regarded my form.

"I had to."

"Your family."

"You heard?" I sighed. "Of course you heard. You're always around."

"I'm sorry. I wish… I wish we had thought of that."

"Covered them with the wish or something?" I said, grimacing. I should have thought of that. I should have… "Can I wish them away?"

"Your family?" Lily raised an eyebrow. "It's doable, but—"

"No, not them. My enemies. Can I wish them dead?" I said, anger heating my voice.

"All of them?" Lily's voice grew quieter.

"Yes!"

"And how'd you define enemy?"

"Those threatening my family. Those threatening Alexa. And me," I said.

"The entire organization?" Lily asked softly.

"Yes!"

"All of those organizations?"

"*Yes*!"

"Is that your wish? Your final wish? Master." Lily's voice grew cold, distant, and officious. It was enough to make me pause, to stare at her.

"Nooo…" I whispered, closing my eyes. "No. I'm not going to ask you to kill hundreds—"

"Thousands."

"Thousands for my-my peace of mind." I sighed and carefully stepped out of the containment circle, then sat on a dusty chair. I coughed a little, clearing my throat, and cast a grasping hand to float over a bottle of water. After taking a swig, I looked back at Lily, my lips twisting in a wry smile. "Sorry about that."

"For almost making me become a mass murderer again?" Lily said.

"Again?"

Lily looked sad, a hand fiddling with a stray lock of hair. "Dark history, remember?"

I nodded. For all that she had played fair with me, with the ring, if she had been given that kind of order before, she'd have no choice. Never mind whatever else she might have done before her imprisonment. "Yeah. Sorry. Could you have done it?"

Lily paused, cocking her head. Her eyes grew distant, weighing the lives and deaths of thousands before she shrugged. "Eventually. If you managed to stay alive and hidden long enough. But probably not."

"I'm not sure if I'm relived or sad about that," I said.

Lily let out a choked laugh before she fell silent, staring at me.

Eventually, I grew uncomfortable enough to ask, "What?"

"You've changed. Grown more serious."

"Being chased around the country has a tendency to do that," I said.

"Also, you're the one who summoned me. Did you have something in mind?"

"I need to Level up," I said. "I need to increase my strength. I need to learn, to get better."

"You intend to fight them?" Lily said, frowning.

"Not exactly. I think, I think I need to be a distraction. For Alexa to get my family out. And then while they're chasing me and the ring, then I'll need to escape too."

"Another portable shelter?"

"No. They'll be ready for that." I drew a deep breath before letting it out, resolve growing stronger in my voice. "I need to hurt them. Make them think twice about angering me. I need to be a credible threat."

"In two months?" Lily raised an arched eyebrow.

"Yeah." I knew how crazy that sounded. How impossible that request was. I didn't need the jinn to say it.

And thankfully, she didn't. The jinn just nodded before cracking her head to the side. "Then let's get to work."

***

How do you raise Levels fast? As any gamer knows, you grind. In my case, since my Levels were tied into my magical understanding and my body's ability to channel magic, I spent hours casting spells. Making adjustments in the spell formulas, pushing my understanding and abilities to the maximum. I cast spells while upside down, while blindfolded, without moving my hands, with only oral components or even without that. Spells were formed and created, mixed and matched with reckless abandon.

Again and again, the shielding spells I created—and recreated—in the basement were put to the test as my headlong rush toward enlightenment had explosive consequences. I burnt my eyebrows off twice, my hair four times before I gave up and shaved it tight. I picked up myriad scars on my hands, the Mana channels in my fingers and palms burnt and scarred from spell blowback. Late into the night, I trained, falling asleep on the table only to wake from the throbbing pain as my exhausted Mana channels protested the abuse. Only for me to start again.

Not that I didn't take care to not over-exhaust myself. I took expeditions, Quests that Lily offered as she stretched the boundaries of the ring to the maximum. A dryad's healing sap, taken from her tree after helping her with a logging problem from the local forestry company, put into a bath helped to fix some of the burgeoning problems. A local group of giant beavers needed their dam reinforced, the natural enchantments around the dam no longer sufficient to stop queries from the locals. A Chupacabra infestation killed off.

Those were the easier quests. Other, more dangerous ones saw me stumbling home, bleeding from wounds, my clothing and armor shredded. Victorious while fighting the monsters in the dark. Wendigos. Wraiths. Other darker, unspeakable creatures that lurked at the edges of civilization, waiting for the foolish, the unwary. Normally they'd be impossible to find without help, without significant time invested. But I had a cheat—I had a friend who could find them and give me their locations. And she let me throw myself at them, all in a bid to let me learn. Learn new and painful ways to stay alive.

But monsters were not all that I hunted. In two cases, I ambushed hunting parties, individuals searching for me. I ended their lives before they could get too close, before they could locate me. It was dangerous, going hours away in different directions to attack them, to leave trails. But it was necessary. For my training. For my safety.

Days passed, days of sweat and pain. It ended a month and a half later when my burner phone, kept turned off but for five minutes a day, beeped with a waiting message.

Meet in 5. Purple Green—Z

It was in code, a simple one that we'd agreed on. Three locations, each given a color. The time was in days—not five days as the number mentioned, but seven. Add two to the number offered. And the name was a simple transliteration, a shift of the alphabet. Z meant A—Alexa. But Z also meant she was doing this unencumbered, unthreatened.

A tension that I had not known that I carried released, the knowledge that my friend was fine relieving a little bit of my worry. But I sobered up soon after, knowing that the hard part was coming next. The bad part.

"Is it time?" Lily said from her corner.

I looked at where my friend sat patiently. Trapped in a circle, forced to stay there lest she let the world know where she was. Lest she bring their wrath upon us. More than what had been brought at least. One and a half months, and she had never voiced a single complaint. Not a request for a cell phone to play a game on, not a single whine about how bored she was. Every moment, every time we spoke, she had helped as best she could, pushing the boundaries of the enchantment, of the rules set upon her. Disregarding the pain to help. To help me.

"Yes," I said.

Steps took me over, and I stared at Lily, the jinn who had brought both wonder and terror to my life. Who had supported me while I threw myself into danger, all the while shackled to me and my life. I drew a deep breath, then let it out, trying to find the words.

"You don't have to say it. I'm ready. While you were out questing, before this"—Lily gestured around the dank basement—"I was downloading and copying all the games I could get hold of. They're all in my ring. All the books, all the games. Quite a few replicas of the various game machines too. If you fail... I'll be fine."

I ducked my head then, memory of the devil's deal we made pushing against my soul, my guilt. If I failed—when I failed and died—Lily would be forced to an eternity of solitude. Trapped by the ring, trapped forever by her own power.

"It's fine. The ring itself is failing. Another ten thousand years, I'm sure I'll be able to break free," Lily said with false cheer.

After so long, even I knew she was being optimistic. The greatest failure point in her ring was the material itself, but even that would take tens of thousands of years to break down. After all, the enchantment took a portion of her strength to bolster the durability of the ring.

"I-I wasn't thinking that," I said. Lily made a mocking hurt face and I felt my lips twitch. "Stop it. This is serious."

"Deadly serious."

I stared at the jinn incredulously before breaking into laughter, shaking my head. "Gods. You're impossible."

"Yup. That's why I'm stuck in here."

That kept me laughing until even Lily broke down and joined me. Together, we laughed until I had to wipe the tears away.

"Thank you. I think I needed that," I said.

"Almost as much as you need getting laid."

"Ugh. Don't remind me," I said and tugged at my jeans. Living with two beautiful women, neither of which I was sleeping with, had been hard. Especially when my social life had become non-existent. Hell, even when I was penniless and a hardcore gamer, I'd gotten better action. "And stop distracting me. I was trying to say thank you. And sorry."

"You don't have to." Lily placed a hand over her heart, looking me in the eyes. "This. This has been the best time of my life."

"Not a high bar, with the masters you've had before."

"No. Not just while I've been enslaved. In my life." Lily intoned those words with assurance. "You treated me like—like a friend. You let me stay out. You let me play games. You didn't push me when I had problems with going out. And then did, when I needed it. You listened to me and laughed with me. You and Alexa, you've offered me…" I waited for her to finish, but she did not. Instead, she flashed me a smile. "Thank you."

"No, I should—I'm talking to air." I sighed as the jinn disappeared, having gone back to her ring. There was no warning, no flash of light. One second she was there, the next she was gone. Except she wasn't really gone. I touched the ring again, twisting it on my finger. "I still think I owe you. And if I survive, we'll go find some of those augmented reality places and play them as much as you want."

I could almost swear I heard a squeal of excitement rise from the ring. Smiling, I turned away and began the process of packing up. Time to get ready to go.

***

Three hours later—one of which consisted of cleaning up the various enchantments and the other two of hiking into town—I was footsore and tired, waiting at the bus depot for the next cross-country coach. Traveling by coach into the city was neither glamorous nor smart, which was why our meeting point was not in the city itself. Still, the bus was convenient and cheap—and considering I had just spent the vast majority of my liquid funds, the last was highly important.

The bus stop was shaded from the midday sun and open to the elements otherwise. That left me shivering as winter winds blew through the single-road town. Magic could have solved the problem, but I was too close to my goals to break discipline. No more magic, not till the city. I couldn't afford to let them know, not now.

"Nice bag." A teenager on his skateboard kicked it up, marveling at my duffel. It had been purchased from an army surplus store, at first an ugly camo green, but now bedecked with gold and red thread. The gold shimmered slightly as it caught rays of light and the kid's attention. "Love the style, man. Peace and war."

"Thanks." I looked down, spotting the hippie peace symbol that had caught the kid's attention before shrugging. "You know what they say."

"What?"

"Hope for peace, prepare for war."

"Deeeep." The teenager nodded and let the board down, waving goodbye as he kicked off. "Later!"

Thankfully the kid hadn't queried about why the thread was glowing and shimmering. Residual magic from the enchanted objects within was bleeding off, too much magic in too close a place. The runic designs could barely suppress the magical signature, so the physical signs were a trade-off I had to make. If I'd had more time, if I'd had better materials…

If, if, if.

But I had no more time for ifs. At least, not for those in the past. The future, the potential ifs, those I had time for. Those I had planned for. With the many, many enchanted objects I'd made. And *if* I had the opportunity, maybe I'd be able to really show them what it meant to anger a gamer.

Chapter 16

"If I survive this, I'm never staying in another dingy motel," I said when Alexa walked in seven days later.

It had taken me two days to make it to our meeting spot, after which I'd ended up staying in a motel room, finishing up the last of my preparations. Most of that consisted of repeatedly making the same enchantments I had made before, carving new wards and enchantments into whatever materials I could get my hands on. Getting ready.

"They do have a certain disreputable character to them," Alexa said, wrinkling her nose. "Did you know, when I asked about the key you left for me, the receptionist winked at me. As if I was… I was…"

"Doing something illicit?"

"Yes!"

"Well, we kind of are…"

"Not like that!" Alexa said, looking scandalized. "I would never. Especially with you!"

"I'm hurt," I said, clutching my chest.

Alexa smacked the top of my head and I laughed. I stopped the moment she dropped a thick file folder on the bed.

"My family?" I said.

"Alive. Unharmed. And untouched. They don't seem to know what's going on, though they are worried about you."

I breathed a sigh of relief, grateful for all that she had said. But… "Worried?"

"Yes. They've even lodged a missing person's report."

"Shit." I breathed deeply and shook my head. Surely that wasn't as bad as I thought. Getting rid of a missing person's report should be simple. I was an adult. I could disappear for no good reason. After my house burned down…

"Hundred hells' worth of shit."

"Just about." Alexa said. "Good thing you changed your hairstyle. You don't look at all like the photo they have of you on the missing person's report. It's, like, six years out of date. Also, I like the spikes."

I ran a hand across my hair, feeling the spikey and now blond-tipped hair. It was a little eye-catching, but not much. Add a pair of glasses that I didn't need and bulky shirts and it was an easy change of appearance. As for the photo… six years? Had I not stayed for a photo, not taken one with my family for that long? In an age of selfies and mobile phones, of Facebook and Instagram, how had they not had a better photograph?

"Henry?" Alexa said, drawing my attention as she opened the file. "Are you with me?"

"Yes. Go on," I said.

"Okay. Here's what I found…"

***

Debriefing took hours. Not just because there was so much information to get through, but because I had questions. So many questions. I did my best to keep them on track, but questions about how she'd gotten all this information, what she'd had to do to get it abounded. Something in the way Alexa spoke, the way she held herself, the lines under her eyes and the pain in them told me I might not like the answers. And so I didn't ask, even if I wanted to.

"All right. So, to sum up. We need to get my family out in two days—Saturday—because that's when all my family will be in one place. They'll be watching more than ever, but you're hoping I can pull at least some of their people off. Because otherwise, there's too many," I said, my eyes narrowing. "That sum up that portion?"

"Yes."

"As for threats we're facing, we've got…" I took a deep breath and exhaled threadily. "The Dark Council. A small faction of the fey. At least four different Knightly Orders. Two different mundane hunter organizations. A naiad bounty hunting group. And a group of Oni gangsters."

"Those are the credible threats. There are more, but those are the ones you have to worry about. I want you to memorize their pictures and details." Alexa tapped the pile of files she'd drawn from her bag as we'd been talking. I'd glimpsed the details, but she was right. Knowing what they looked like would help. "Now, what were you up to?"

I found myself grinning, pulling up the duffel bag and plopping it onto the bed. Then I pushed against the bundle of Mana that made up my Level stats and made it visible to Alexa. "Why don't you check it out yourself?"

Class: Mage

Level 79 (11% Experience)

Known Spells: Elemental Control (4 Base, Force), Mana Control, Shaped Control, Forced Healing, Heal, Wards, Link, Track, Wards, Greater Glamour & Illusion, Lesser Summoning, Empower, Lesser Divination, Cleanse, Runic Script, Elemental Resistances.

"This is rather different." Alexa frowned as she looked over my adjusted spell list. "You're missing a lot."

"We decided to clean things up," I said. "Once I'd progressed my Elemental Control, I didn't really need a slot for Iceball, Fireball, Airball, or Earthball and then another one for each type of dart, spear, cone, or whatever else I decided to come up with. Part of my training was learning to deconstruct spells so that I'm just shaping the elements to make it what I need."

"Makes sense. Doesn't tell me what you can do though."

"Pretty much everything you've seen me do, except bigger. I can link two different elements together now, so I can generate a Firestorm or create a Freezing Fog without relying on the spell formula's Lily put in my head. Magma's a bit out of my wheelhouse and Lily refuses to teach me that one," I said, pouting a little. "But my biggest improvement is in my actual skill set. Here…"

Another mental prod and a new piece of data appeared.

Magical Skill Set
*Mana Flow: 7/10 ***
Mana to Energy Conversion: 6/10
Spell Container: 8/10
Spatial Location: 6/10
Spatial Movement: 6/10
Energy Manipulation: 6/10
Biological Manipulation: 4/10
Matter Manipulation: 7/10
Summoning: 2/10
Duration: 7/10
Rituals: 2/10
Multi-Casting: 6/10
Enchanting: 8/10

"Your spell container and enchanting abilities are really up there, aren't they?" Alexa said.

"Yup. Have to be. They feed into one another. Got to control the inscribed runes when I'm enchanting, so that's been progressing along with the matter manipulation. Same with multi-casting, though I've hit a wall there,"

I said. "When I'm enchanting, I can handle up to eight different flows. But once I start moving and fighting, I drop down to about four. Five at a push."

"Five spells?" Alexa's eyebrow rose in surprise.

"Five flows. Three to four spells, depending on how complicated the spells are and if I'm using a pre-generated one or not," I clarified.

"Oh. Right." Alexa fell silent, and I basked in her good regard, knowing that my month and half of struggle and pain had resulted in great improvements. When I stayed silent, Alexa frowned. "And the asterisk?"

"What asterisk?"

"That one!"

I frowned and looked closer, then blinked. "That wasn't there... *Lily!*" Of course the jinn didn't answer me. Couldn't. I glared at my ring instead until a tap on my thigh made me look at Alexa. "It's... nothing. Just a little reminder."

"About?"

"I had to raise my Levels. So I kind of—"

"Damaged some of your Mana channels and your body?" Alexa finished for me, flicking her gaze to my scarred hands.

"If you knew, why'd you ask?" I crossed my arms, hiding my hands belatedly.

"I wanted to see if you'd tell me."

"Gah! You're as bad as my mum!" I said. Then paused, realizing what I'd said.

We both sobered, the reminder making me sigh.

"I'm looking forward to meeting her," Alexa offered into the silence.

A thought struck me. I raised a finger, then lowered it slowly.

"What?" Alexa said.

"Nothing."

"Henry..."

"Ugh. She just might want to know who you are. It's not like we, you know, introduced you or Lily," I said. "And well, she knows of you. And might, you know, think you're my girlfriend. Or something." The last was squeaked out.

"Or something?"

"Well… we have been staying together. In the same house. And my mum's wanting me to… well, you know how old people are. Parents…" I coughed, flushing red.

Alexa blushed too when she caught on, smacking me on the thigh before turning aside. After a moment, when the blush had reduced, she turned back to me. "That… might be better."

"What!?!"

"I need them to come with me. Without question," Alexa pointed out. "Them thinking we're… together might make it easier."

"Right. Right. And we can just tell them otherwise. Later," I said, running a hand through crusty hair with a grimace. "That'll be fine."

"You don't sound convincing."

"That's because it's my parents," I whined.

Alexa gave me a half-smile and I shook my head, pushing it aside. Not the time for that.

"So, wanna see my toys?" I pointed at the duffel while hefting my smaller backpack too.

"Yes!" Alexa said, almost bouncing in eagerness. There was a flash of avarice in her eyes, but more wonder. Even after all this time, the ex-Initiate still found some wonder in our lives. I wished I could mirror that right now, but…

"All right. So first, my vest." I pulled out the simple buckled-on vest that I'd mashed together from a vest and a bunch of leather cords and pouches.

"Ugly."

"I never said I was a seamstress. Or fashionista," I retorted but had to admit, the brown and green leather straps and pouches clashed with the black base of the vest. In each of the pouches was an easily accessible wooden sphere a little smaller than a baseball. "Each pouch is linked to a pouch in the duffel. I've got more copies of each of these enchanted spheres in there. So all I need to do is pull one out." I demonstrated by pulling the sphere. "Arm it and toss, and while I'm doing that…"

"It fills up!" Alexa's jaw dropped. "That's amazing. You've got an automatic replicator. But how far…?"

"About a mile. I've got multiple smaller bags with the same kind of enchantment in the duffel too, with smaller ranges. So I can basically drop the smaller bags around beforehand, giving me multiple caches to run to—but with shorter range—or I run around a central area, pulling from the duffel as necessary," I said. "Gives me options."

"What do the spheres do?"

"Basically, they're magical grenades." I pointed at each of the four pouches in turn. "Fire. Ice. Wind and earth—dust storm basically—and force sphere."

"Force sphere?"

"This one takes a little more work, but I can either make it a defensive ward—though it holds me still—or a giant wrecking ball to throw at people. There's a weird interaction between speed and size. Seems like it keeps the same momentum even when the force sphere activates, so if you throw it hard enough, it's like a wrecking ball. I have a couple for you that are pre-charged."

Alexa grinned. "That's pretty good. How many do you have?"

"For myself? About a half dozen of each type. I've also got six wands," I said, pulling out the bundle of sticks and pointing at the holsters. "Same thing, but they're attached to this bag. They don't fire more than a half-dozen overcharged attacks before they're done, but they've all got their own charges, so it won't use my Mana."

"You're planning on a long fight."

"Yup. Got a couple of enchanted masks too, pre-set glamours and illusions." I drew a breath and let it out. "I can provide the distraction. But even if you get out…"

"You're worried they'll still be caught?"

"Yeah."

"Don't worry," Alexa said. "I worked something out."

"What?"

Alexa didn't answer me. My eyes narrowed, then I realized why she didn't want to tell me. If I didn't know, it couldn't be plucked from my mind. They couldn't be used to hurt me, make me give up the ring. Though if I was already captured, would they really care about any of my friends or family?

Ah hell. Better to be safe than sorry.

"I've got a few more things." I opened the duffel and showed her the tools I'd made. An assortment of pre-set wards, enchanted blocking wards, a couple of balls of grease, a couple of invisibility potions, and even one short-term gliding potion. All tools to help me evade and hurt others when needed.

In the end, when the show-and-tell was done, we regarded one another over the pieces of my enchanted gear, a choking amount of tension appearing. Knowing what was coming. And yet unable to avoid it.

"Alexa…"

"Thank me after."

"I—"

"After," Alexa said with finality and stood. "Now, get reading. I'll get us food."

I watched as the former blonde, now bottled redhead, walked out, and I sighed. If I had another wish…

But that was the thing about magic. It might be magical, but it was no miracle. It couldn't fix most things. It was a tool. A versatile tool, but just another tool.

Chapter 17

On the designated day, sneaking into the city took me an hour. It mostly consisted of paying the exorbitant fees to take a taxi from the motel to Faircreek in the southwest. There, the abandoned city docks and the crumbling warehouses made for an urban maze of derelict buildings and low population numbers. Of course, depressed business district or not, it wasn't empty. Which was why I made sure to drop off and hide my duffel in an empty building before making my way to talk to an old friend.

"Wizard. Haven't seen you in a bit." Andy, the green-skinned ganger orc that ran these streets—or at least, a portion of them—greeted me with a toothy smile. "Surprised to see you here. You running another quest?"

"No," I said, shaking my head. "I don't know what you've heard—"

"Heard enough. Didn't want to believe it, but you're really in trouble, aren't you?" Andy said, deep-set eyes crinkling. "You know I'd love to help you but—"

"No need." I knew what he was going to say and also knew what he could offer. The enemies I'd made outclassed my friends by far. "But they are going to come for me. If you can get word out to get off the streets…"

"You going to fight here? In my neighborhood?" This time, there was no friendliness in Andy's voice. He reared up, glaring at me. "What the hell, wizard? Why bring your shit to us?"

"It's not on purpose. I just need—"

"Bullshit. You're choosing our place. That's very much on purpose!"

"I need a place with fewer people!" I snapped. "Or do you want me to do this in the middle of downtown?"

"Sounds great to me. Better than bringing more shit onto us." Andy pointed at me. "I thought you cared, man. But you wizards are just like the rest. Once you need to, you're just out to shit on us."

"That's not true!" I growled.

But a part of me, a nagging part, pointed out that he might have a point. I could have chosen another neighborhood. I hadn't even really considered any place else, done any research. Had I chosen a place like this because it was easier? Or was it the best choice? Even if it was the best and reduced the amount of damage to the most number of people, did heaping trouble on those who had the least make it worse?

"Get the hell out of here, wizard. And don't show your face again," Andy said, shoving my shoulder.

I took the push and backed off, wanting to explain but realizing nothing I could say would ever justify what I intended to do.

As I backed away, Andy let off one last invective. "Every person hurt by this, it's blood on your hands."

Rather than reply, I retreated. Andy barked orders to his subordinates, people who glared at me. I hurried off, turning the corner before casting a glamour to hide my face. In short order, I was another person. I still had a lot of work to do, including scattering my other pouches around the suburb. There was no guarantee that Andy wasn't being watched, not with him being one of my few friends, but thus far, Alexa hadn't found them to be keeping an eye on him. That was why I'd risked meeting him.

As I headed away, I glanced sideways, calling forth the Quest Lily had created for me.

Quest Received: Survive for Four Hours
You have been challenged to reenter the city and make yourself available to your opponents. Failure to do so will see the death of your family. As bait, you will need to survive for four hours while Alexa brings your family to safety.
Reward: The safety of your family
Failure: Your death.

Bonus Objective 1: Each additional hour of survival ensures the increased level of safety for your family

Bonus Objective 2: Escape from your pursuers after achieving your first objective

Over the next hour and a half, I moved around the business district, breaking into abandoned warehouses and sneaking into backrooms, leaving my enchanted storage bags in those locations. Of course, just to mess things up, I also cast illusion spells on random pieces of equipment. Plastic bags, a garbage can full of rotten food, and a large pile of fecal matter were among the presents I left for my trackers.

Along the way, I dropped a number of my pre-made enchanted wards, each set to release a single burst of energy. I mostly tuned them so that they triggered when met by an aura with a high enough concentration, ensuring that your random supernatural would not likely trigger them. They were my early warning system. When they went off, I had to smile grimly from the rooftop where I'd been resting.

"Guess it's time?" I said, closing my eyes. I tapped the ring. "Lily, you might as well pop out."

"You sure?" Lily said as she appeared beside me, clad in her hoodie and slacks. She pivoted, taking in our surroundings then looking at the sky, taking in the salt-encrusted fresh air that blew in from the docks a few blocks away. She looked down, spotting the runic circle I'd drawn, and shook her head slightly. "You know they'll pick me out."

"Yeah. Can't have you following me, but I thought I'd say bye one last time," I said. "Can't stay too long, but… thank you."

"Good luck, Henry."

I flashed Lily a grin before hurrying down the stairs, leaving Lily and the trap behind. For a time, her signal and the ring's would seem the same. Which would lead my enemies right to her. Of course, once I hit the bottom of the stairs, I scattered a pouchful of pepper and cayenne peppers into the air, making sure to keep a Gust spell around my body to ensure that none of it touched me. Once I'd moved away from the pepper, I inverted the spell, keeping my scent locked to my body. It made moving a little harder, but was easier than trying to mimic an entirely new scent via an illusion spell. In the open air, I was forced to redirect the gust upward, shifting my scent into a column into the air and dispersing it high above so that it would be impossible to track me that way.

Head down, ball cap on, I trotted toward my next rally point. I didn't look back, knowing there was nothing to see. Fifteen minutes later, as I lounged behind a dumpster, the ripple of my ritual circle being broken washed over the entire suburb. The emotional resonance of anger and pain was carried on the spell remnants, making me grin. The ritual circle I'd formed had liquefied the concrete then hardened it, basically dropping anyone on the roof half into the roof before reforming around them. It wouldn't kill. Probably not even maim, if they were smart about releasing themselves. But it would scare them and hurt them.

I tilted my head, letting the Gust spell I was holding around me disappear. Turning to the side, I eyed the explosive ward I'd scribed into the wall, a ward that was integrated into a simple script—"I prepared Explosive Runes this morning."

They'd wanted me in the city. So there I was. And now, I would teach them why having me there was a bad idea. Though I was careful to keep my remote attacks to harassing attacks rather than lethal ones. I wasn't about to leave the equivalent of magical land mines for kids to walk over.

***

I was trotting up the stairs of a mostly empty office building, headed for the roof to get to the next building over, when I heard doors open beneath me. In the corner of my eyes, I noted how the timer was reading just about three hours after the start of this entire thing. The noise from below wasn't uncommon—the building wasn't entirely abandoned—but unusual enough that I poked my head over the railing. Only to see a large red, tusked face looking back at me.

"He's here!" the Oni shouted before he reached down his side.

I jerked backward and hugged the side of the wall as I ran up. A resounding boom made my ears ache and concrete chips rained down around me as the idiot opened fire. He couldn't even see me! "Asshole."

I panted as I ran up the stairs, pulling a fire sphere from my vest. I made it to the rooftop access and yanked open the door while hearing the trump of footsteps following me. Another blast, this one making my ears ache again, sent more chips scattering around me and making me nearly drop the sphere. I gripped it tighter, sending a surge of Mana into the sphere to activate it, and tossed it over the railing. It fell and I ducked out, twisting around the doorway. Flames exploded, channeled by the stairwell column into a chimney of heat and smoke. I heard screams from within the stairwell as a gust of fire heated my skin and toasted the tips of my escaped hair.

A part of me felt guilty, knowing that the creatures I'd hurt—maybe killed—were sapients. Living, thinking creatures. Then again, the asses had shot at me immediately, never even taking a moment to check that there wasn't anyone else there.

...

Fuck. I hadn't either.

I turned toward the staircase, taking a half-step to it, and got caught by surprise when the door slammed open. An oni, similar to the one that had shot at me but bigger, nearing seven feet tall, ducked out. The monster had to twist to get through the door, so wide that it couldn't make its way through normally. He saw me and grabbed my jacket and jerked me close.

I flailed for a second, one hand impacting against his face to try to push away. Another hand flicked and twisted, forming a shield just above the oni's hip—perfectly placed to jerk the creature to a stop as it swung its fist up toward me. The oni jerked to a stop, confused by the sudden jarring motion, even as I finished casting my second spell and sent darts of Mana and fire straight into the monster's eyes.

Eyes were small, fast-moving targets that were hard to hit. Not surprisingly, the Oni flinched as the bright light and the Mana flew toward its face, meaning that my attack left bloody, singed furrows across its visage. Eyes clenched shut in automatic reaction, the oni threw me aside. I didn't fly far though, being that I had been thrown into the rooftop access wall and bounced off the edge before landing on the concrete.

Only the impact-resistant wards in my jacket saved me from broken bones. Instead, it spread what impact it didn't absorb across my body, leaving me winded and in pain but functioning. As I rolled over, I adjusted the location and size of my Force Wall, placing it a foot above me. Just in time too, as the oni's fist crashed into my hasty shield. I felt myself pressed into the floor, the Force Shield cracking as the built-up momentum from the muscular demon nearly shattered my defense. Before he could throw another attack, I adjusted the Force Shield again.

This time around, I kept it formed as I sent it forward. Rising from the ground, it hit the oni in the chest and lower body and kept rising, even as I twisted the spell formula once more to alter its shape. From Force Wall to a

630

giant cradle, holding the oni around its body as the spell rose, it pushed my opponent farther away from me. There was a moment of surprise before he grabbed the edges of my spell and applied his overly muscled arms to it. In seconds, the already compromised spell shattered.

A little too late. In mid-air, the oni broke my spell and fell, but by this time, momentum and his position sent it off the edge of the roof to his death.

I couldn't help but grin grimly, hobbling to the side of the office building that had been my initial objective. A hand went into a pocket and another pouch of pepper, cayenne pepper, and durian-scented candles were dumped behind me. I left the durian-scented candles burning with a gesture as I retreated to the next building's rooftop, hopping down the six-foot drop and landing with a grunt.

With all the commotion, I was sure the rest of my opponents were on their way. I had to retreat far enough that my presence was harder to locate. I kept moving even as I reformed my wind spell to keep my scent contained. I ran along the warehouse roof to the edge of where it met the next street over, then a simple glide and levitation spell combined allowed me to jump across the street while I wrapped myself in a fourth illusion spell, hiding my presence.

When I landed on the other side of the street, I crouched on the rooftop and pulled out another sphere, adjusting the activation portion of the enchantment to target any supernaturally strong aura that came within range and wasn't mine. I hoped that no one would be wandering the rooftop before daylight rose again, but it was a risk I had to take.

As I rose, halfway to my feet, I froze when I sensed other auras. Strong, powerful, supernatural auras. My lips curled up in a snarl even as I noted that my enemies weren't bothering to hide their auras. Foolish and cocky. As I scuttled away, I rebuked myself. There was no guarantee that the auras I sensed were the only ones in play.

In fact... I grew more careful, scanning the rooftops for potential dangers. If it was me, I'd use both. Hidden and visible hunters—the first to catch me unaware and the second to make me overly confident. I reminded myself that it was best to stay cautious. That this was our first encounter and it was just a start.

***

For all my mental wariness, the next group caught me by chance twenty minutes later. I was hiding behind a dumpster, only my scent-erasing spell in play. I trusted my position and the aura-dampening enchantments woven into my jacket to keep me hidden. I was waiting, counting off the seconds as the mobile electric scooter running naiads zipped away, intent on the magic explosion two streets away. An explosion that I knew was from someone tampering with one of my enchanted packages.

I was so intent on listening and counting, I hadn't noticed the Order knights, their all-too-mortal auras bypassing my wariness. I didn't notice them till the first crossbow bolt took me in the shoulder, the blessed and faith-enchanted bolt cutting through my protective jacket and twisting me around. The second bolt, targeted at my head, missed by inches as I spun about, leaving the bolt thrumming beside my face. Even as the pair of Order knights dropped their crossbows and drew pistols, I was reaching for a sphere.

Fast as I was cross-drawing the sphere, they were faster. I ignored the loud bark of their pistols, watching the bullets glance off the defensive shield that had formed around me as the backup enchantments woven into my jacket came into play. A secondary spell enchantment formed a Force Wall the moment it was pierced. It drew upon the blood I'd spilled to power it, giving it a brief but powerful surge of strength.

An underhanded toss sent the ball skittering under my shield even as the pair of Order knights took turns firing at me while splitting apart. The moment they caught sight of the sphere, they took defensive action. One twisted his hand, raising it sideways as a glowing shield came up to protect him. The other skirted backward into the cover of a dumpster. As my sphere exploded, as the pain from my shoulder made itself known, I pulled open a potion and chugged it.

A blizzard appeared in the alleyway, one that coated the area with slick ice and dropped the temperature to about -40. It bypassed silly things like faith-based shields. Admittedly, it was not the sphere I'd meant to grab, but it worked well enough. The pair of Knights came out of hiding to level their guns at me. I flashed them a smile around the edges of the sports bottle that contained my potion, then I felt the spell kick in.

Unlike my previous translocation spell, this one dropped me into the earth, displacing my body about twelve feet down. I held my breath at the last second as I dropped before I began the slow—and entirely too painful—process of swimming away. The only good news was that the bolt in my shoulder was left behind, the foreign faith enchantments on the bolt hampering my potion's ability to grip it. Unlike my bag and the rest of my equipment, it didn't have my aura engrained into it through use and magic—and while the addition of my blood might normally have dragged it along, the faith enchantments rejected the sublimation of the bolt. That meant I didn't have to try to pull it out.

It did, however, mean that I had an open wound pumping blood into the earth that surrounded me as I swam away. On top of that, I had a limited amount of time in the earth. Not due to the potion's stability—though that was, admittedly, a concern—but due to my inability to breathe. I had just about a minute before my need to add oxygen to my lungs. If I swallowed earth, it would still be in my chest when I popped back out. That would be somewhat fatal.

As I swam away, searching for an appropriately sized and distant basement, I cast a healing spell on my shoulder. It wouldn't fix my shoulder, but it would, at the least, stop the gushing blood.

***

It could be worse. I muttered that to myself constantly as I wrapped myself in glamour and illusion, the scent of my now-healed-but-still-bloody shoulder contained into small balls of concentrated air. I sent those gusting off, contained until they reached their designated locations where they would break down. If I couldn't hide my scent, then I'd overlay it all across the neighborhood to confuse the scent.

Unfortunately, business districts, especially those that used to hold a bunch of warehouses, weren't particularly known for their small, twisting streets. That meant that I had to make my way down the street in open view. As I scurried along, a cold sweat that dripped down my back made me shiver—even more so when the group of Red Caps turned the corner. One of them was leaning down, sniffing the pavement as he tried to locate me. The others scanned the street, searching for me. One even held up an old monocle. I knew the enchantment in that monocle, knew it searched for telltale portions of magic.

Dangerous, but I'd taken that into account in my own spells. Still, I had never tested the spell against another, so I felt my breathing hitch as the Red Cap looked directly at me. He paused, staring at me, at what he saw through his monocle.

"What is it?" one of the other Red Caps asked.

"Distortion."

"The Mage?" One of the Red Caps reached into his jacket, pulling out a stone throwing axe.

I felt my breath freeze.

"Not sure. Might just be another trick of his. Or one of the other hunters. Or an ambient change."

"You could be clearer!"

"This isn't science." The Red Cap growled. "It's not moving."

"I'm going to throw my axe." The Red Cap hefted the axe, making a passing car swerve slightly as the driver noted the weapon. That drew the Red Cap's attention.

The car sped up, the female driver ashen with fear.

"Careful. We don't want the damn mundanes here," the monocle-user snarled.

Before he could continue, he shifted, following a flash of darkness, a moving shadow. I tracked the motion too, but with the monocle user no longer looking at me, I reinforced my spell warding, adjusting it, and took four quick steps forward.

By the time the monocle-user looked back, I was away from my original position and hurrying down the street. "Huh."

"What?"

"It's gone."

"So?" The axe-wielder grimaced but slid his axe back into the harness under his jacket, hiding it from casual sight again.

The Red Cap group kept moving, passing on the opposite side of the road. I made myself stop, watching them pass by but doing my best not to look at them directly for fear that they'd somehow sense my attention. Only when they had passed did I scurry forward, though as I turned the corner, I thought I saw the shadow on the second floor shift again.

I frowned, tempted to check it out, but then I felt the impingement of more auras coming down the street and I groaned. Time to move. I took off as my shoulder continued to ache. Maybe drawing everyone to one business district had been a bad idea.

Perhaps I had overestimated my ability to deal with my hunters. But it really didn't matter. I had a job to do, and my friend, my family were counting on me to keep them busy. I needed to keep going for as long as I could, give Alexa time to get them to safety, to get out of the house. Everything else, from my concerns to weird shades, did not matter.

Chapter 18

I dropped through the hole in the floor, landing in a crouch, and groaned as pain shot up my knees, through my aching bum and sore back, and into my shoulder. I gritted my teeth and stood, flicking a hand upward as I drew on my Mana again. A single, clear Force Spike formed in the middle of the hole. I concentrated, making sure that it was as clear as I could make it, then I staggered over to the door, barely casting a glance at the dilapidated hotel room with its single double bed and broken dresser.

Above, my pursuers crashed through the door and set off the ice spike sphere and the air sphere. One coated the air with dust and dirt, and the second sent shards of ice forming from the floor. I heard a shriek of pain, cut off as they stumbled forward. But I stumbled out the door and headed for the staircase, hoping to lose them.

I couldn't even tell who was after me this time. The naiads? More of the orders? Not the fey. I'd killed a pair of their sidhe warriors as I was entering the building, and I didn't think they had too many pursuing me. If my pursuers weren't so intent on fighting one another—settling old scores in the chaos—they would have caught me already. As it was, my counter had switched over from a countdown to a positive number, three minutes and up. I'd passed my quest, just barely.

Ever since they caught up with me, I'd been running. Every trick in the book I had, and some that I'd come up with at the last moment, had been pulled out. I'd stood and fought, killed and butchered. Splayed their blood across a rusty playground, leaving corpses scattered by wind blades, and then hidden among the destruction to double-back. I'd drawn my pursuers into narrow alleyways and released traps to web them close. I'd burnt the trapped dhampirs. From the pursuing oni, I'd run and hid, allowing lycanthropes to smell the blood I'd planted on them, and let age-old rivalry take its turn.

And none of it mattered. I'd barely gotten more than ten minutes of rest. Constant wear had me down to four spheres. My Mana reserves, carefully husbanded, were less than a quarter full. The hotel had not been what I'd wanted to hide, but it wasn't as if I'd had a choice. When the demon dogs howled, you ran—and those sidhe had used their black hounds to push me here.

And now, I was ducking between floors, trying to find a way out that didn't lead to another fight. But there was none. Around the corner, I stumbled, only to find a tall, gangly troll staring at me. Behind him, in the shadows, a trio of creatures stood.

"You guys made it," I said wheezily. I leaned against the wall, trying to catch my breath. The scream from behind me as one of my pursuers impaled themselves on my present barely elicited a twitch.

"You have run far. But you must know how this ends." The troll's voice was urbane, civilized. A big difference from the big, big fangs in its mouth.

I shifted a few steps away from the corner, putting myself closer to the troll, figuring I didn't want to get yanked back.

"I want to know why you're talking…" I said, cocking my head. I kept my hand low by my side as I formed a flame spear, building the container, position, and targeting options first.

"Because we have a question."

"Shoot." I inhaled further, then added, "Not literally."

"Do you have your final wish?"

I froze, some incidents clicking into place. And then…

"Take him."

I didn't see it coming. Shades came through the walls and yanked me back, smashing the back of my head into the wall. The first blow sent stars through my eyes and made my spell matrix fall apart. The second blow brought darkness even as the roaring troll and the screams of my pursuers mingled.

***

I didn't expect to wake up. After all, they were meant to kill me. End me, the ring goes away and the threat of Lily being used as a weapon was gone permanently. Waking up was a nice surprise in that sense, though the throbbing pain in my head reduced my level of gratitude.

If I was a hardened soldier, a spy, or one of those whisky-swilling detectives, I would have contained the groan. I would have tricked my captors about my state of consciousness and found a way to turn the tables. But I wasn't.

"Do not attempt to use your magic," a voice warned. A familiar British voice accompanied by the smell of formaldehyde. "The bracers we have layered on your hands will bring pain from the Mana you form."

"Don't think I could even if I wanted to," I said, prying my eyes open. I groaned as pricks of light slammed into my head, forcing my eyes closed again. I stayed lying on the floor, letting the cold of the concrete seep into my aching head. "I think I'll just stay here."

"Unfortunately, that will not be possible. Now that you are awake, you will need to speak to the Council." So saying, Bronislav picked me up.

The smell of rot and preserving liquids intensified while he hauled me to my feet. I could barely find my feet before he pushed me, mostly pulling me forward rather than letting me walk. The motion made my stomach lurch, and only discipline kept me from throwing up.

"Good. Do not throw up. I do not care to launder my clothing again," Bronislav said. "The Council still has not increased my laundry budget. Even if they have increased their… activities."

"I… thought you guys were good guys," I whispered, not liking the implications of his words. As he dragged me along, the new skin along my shoulder ripped open and a slow trickle of blood wet my jacket.

"We try. But the Nun'Yunu'Wi's dietary requirements are much stricter," Bronislav said. "We do what we can with my connections. But so many people want open casket funerals that acquiring bodies—especially those that fit requirements—can be difficult. And the butchering…"

"I don't really want to know," I whispered. "Just. Can you guys not eat me?"

He was silent.

"Fuck," I said.

In short order, I was brought to an all-too-familiar location. This time around, I was not left to stand but dumped onto a chair—an old school medieval-looking torture chair with restraining straps for arms and head. In short order, I was trussed up, though as I ran my fingers along the edge of the vinyl armrest, I realized something.

"This is a bondage chair!" I said. I mean, sure, it was great for restraining but I swear, if they hadn't cleaned it off properly, I was going to complain.

My shock and sudden exclamation threw my careful control of my stomach into turmoil and I found myself lurching forward, only to be brought up against the strap holding my head still as I tried to vomit. Dry heaving, some of the refuse bubbled up my mouth and spilled down my lips before rushing back down, throwing me into another paroxysm of coughing and spitting.

"Free him. Let him vomit. Then clean him," the Chair barked.

Bronislav was quick to follow his orders, releasing me to throw up then cleaning me up. The Nun'Yunu'Wi hissed and snapped his cane toward me, making my shirt burn off, along with the rest of the vomit. It cleansed me, though it scorched my skin too and left me screaming and thrashing, sending me into another paroxysm. Rather than wait for me to finish, another wave of magic flowed into me. This time around, I felt my head healing, my thoughts clearing. Surprisingly, the wound in my back and the blood that had escaped was not healed.

"I told you you should heal him. Mages are fragile," the troll growled.

"We should have just killed him," the Chair snapped. "We agreed to that. If the others learn—"

"They will not. Not even the Council can pierce my defenses," the Nun'Yunu'Wi said, laughing a little derisively at the vampire. "You worry too much."

"And you risk too much."

"For the jinn, this risk is nothing," the Nun'Yunu'Wi said.

"Enough. Let us get this over with," the troll said. "Many saw our fight. Some might suspect."

"Very well. Wizard." When the Nun'Yunu'Wi saw that it had my attention, it pointed at my finger. "Use your wish and release yourself from your previous wish."

"Or what?" I snorted at the trio. They couldn't hurt me. Not directly. Even now, Lily protected me. Protected me from—

A crowbar came down on my arm with full force, cracking the bones. I screamed, thrashing about but unable to move much. Bronislav looked back at his masters after the strike, stopped only by a raised hand.

"Your wish protects you from us. But we have many of the appropriate 'Level.'"

"Fuck."

"Yes." The Nun'Yunu'Wi leaned forward. "Save yourself some pain. I can heal you if you grow too damaged and you will repeat the pain. Again and again, till we get what we want. Why bother?"

"What—what do you want with Lily?" I said, doing my best to ignore the pain in my arm and the blood that ran down my back in fresh waves. Ignore the way I could tell even my normal Mana regeneration was being disrupted by the enchanted bracers. Ignore the welling feeling of helplessness.

"It is not your concern."

A nod and another strike. Except this time around, **Bronislav** hit me twice, cracking an upper arm and a rib before he was called off.

Once I was coherent again, when the waves of pain had subsided, I looked at the Nun'Yunu'Wi. "What does the Council want? You do know the ring goes to one person only?"

My words made Roland shift, but the Nun'Yunu'Wi laughed. "Did you think to sow discord among us?"

A gesture and pain came. This time, four strikes. Not all of them broke bones, but the pain was so great, it took me long minutes before I could focus again.

"Half-measures. Let me cut him up. Once I eat his foot in front of him, they always break," the troll was arguing with the Nun'Yunu'Wi.

"You know why cutting him will not work, Vallen," the Nun'Yunu'Wi snapped.

"Oh, yes. You and your fear of blood." Roland laughed, shaking its head. "How pitiful, to fear something so great."

"As if fearing sunlight was any better—"

"My lords," Bronislav spoke up, bringing the attention of the group back to me.

"Don't worry about me. I'll… wait," I said, trying for a smile and failing. The pain continued to radiate, the pulses of agony taking away my ability to plan. If not for the last while of training, I probably would not have been able to even speak that much.

"Make the wish."

I paused, considering. Make the wish. A wish. I could make a wish. Easy. Wish them gone. Wish them dead. Wish myself free even. Wish myself free…

"Okay," I said, looking up. "I wish—"

Before I could finish, the Nun'Yunu'Wi gestured and Roland cracked me across the face, shattering my jaw. I screamed, the strike throwing me back against the chair and nearly tipping it over. Pain, so much pain. And then, blessed darkness once again.

***

The next few hours were memorable, but not for the right reasons. The beating continued, interspersed with healing spells. It took about three tries before I realized that the son of a bitch was reading my mind—or a close facsimile of that—so that every time I tried to use the wish for anything other than what they wanted, I got smacked around. And while Lily might guess at my desires, until I voiced it out loud, she couldn't make it true.

I was no semi-mute hero, no tough-as-nails private eye or trained soldier. When I got tortured, I felt the pain and scream just like anyone else. If not for the last few weeks of training, I wouldn't have lasted even ten minutes. If not for Lily's notification, I'd have broken in twenty.

Active Quest: Last Till Help Arrives

Help is on the way. But it's taking time to get organized. You will need to hold out from the torture and refuse to make the wish until help arrives.

Requirement: -0:01:38

Reward: Rescue Attempt

Failure: Your Death. Loss of the Ring. Potential Armageddon.

It was those words I woke up to each time I was struck. That clock dominated my view and focused me whenever they struck me, when I felt the shattering of another bone. It was what I clung to when the pain of healing swept over me and my jaw and shattered pieces of my body stitched themselves back together.

There was only so much that magical healing could do. Only so much battering a body could take before even magic lost its effectiveness. Each time they broke something, each time my body bruised and blood vessels broke, pieces were left untreated, unfinished. Shards of bone lay amidst healed flesh, hurting and grating with each movement, each pulse of blood. My nose, shattered so many times that I made boxers look handsome, wheezed with each breath. My jaw, cracked again and again, was distorted. And my mind…

Multiple concussions in short order meant I was thinking feebly, barely able to focus on a single thought. It was perhaps because of that that the Nun'Yunu'Wi could not read my mind any longer. When I could not focus on my own thoughts, how could another?

"Make the wish!" the Nun'Yunu'Wi insisted.

"Urgh… I…" I leaned over, my head freed from its strap after the fourth? fifth? beating to spit and throw up. I coughed and coughed again, throat both dry and wet with congealed blood.

My hesitation made Bronislav glare at me.

"Enough," Roland said. "He is barely coherent. You need to let him recover."

"I have healed him," the Nun'Yunu'Wi snapped.

"Repeatedly. The human body cannot take such abuse," Roland said.

"Oh, it can take more. Much more—"

"Screaming insanity is not the result we need. He must be coherent to say what we want him to say," Roland said. "Give him a few minutes. If he is unwilling to continue, you can continue the beating."

The Nun'Yunu'Wi stroked his hand in thought before he nodded. "Yes. A respite will make the agony afterward more pronounced."

"How much longer?" the troll, wandering back with a haunch of meat, asked, glancing at my broken form as he flopped onto his oversized seat.

While they waited for me to recover and I played broken—not that that was a particularly difficult act—Bronislav picked up a new cloth and wiped me down. He had been doing that repeatedly, keeping me clear of blood from the occasional bone that popped out, the accidentally bit tongue or split lip. For all the brutality Bronislav had inflicted upon me, his touch was soft, gentle as he cleaned me. It was… nice. Comforting. I found myself leaning into his hands, seeking warmth. Comfort. It had been hours, hours of abuse and pain and now…

"He is tougher than I expected," the troll said, glancing at me. "But I still think you should cut off a limb or two. Maybe the one in between—"

"We agreed that this is mine," the Nun'Yunu'Wi said.

"I thought it would take an hour at most. Sooner or later…"

In the corner of my eye, I saw the clock counting down. Changing.

0:0:44

0:0:43

A flicker and the timer changed again.

0:0:11

"What? They can look all they want. But our people have shown that they do not know where we are. Or what we do," the Nun'Yunu'Wi said. "There is no way for them to find us. My wards are—"

The Nun'Yunu'Wi never finished his words as he lurched backward as if he had been struck. Which, in a sense, he had been. His wards, the enchantments that protected this room from scrying and other forms of assault, crumpled like a beer can in a frat boy's hand. A moment later, a portal opened, one that brought the light of day to the room, flooding it. Even before the portal had finished opening, a spear flew through the gap and slammed into the troll, pinning it to the wall. White fire—the flames of faith-based magic—burned around the wound and along the haft of the spear.

Roland screeched and threw himself away from the sunlight, bringing a jacket-filled hand up to his face as the vampire fled to the farthest corner of the room. Bronislav's eyes widened, hesitating over who to protect, and was rewarded for his hesitation by a blast of force magic that carried him back.

Congratulations! Quest Completed.
Reward: Rescue Attempt!

First to emerge from the Portal was Alexa wielding a pair of wands I had gifted her. She kept them leveled at Bronislav, sending the Frankenstein spinning away as he burnt and was smacked around by the fire and force magic. The moment she reached me though, she dropped the spent wands to work on my bindings.

Behind Alexa was Caleb, staff leveled at the Nun'Yunu'Wi as spell after spell formed and fired. It was a blitz of light and energy, Mana forming along spell formulas at a speed that was impossible to track. Even as distracted as I was, I couldn't help but note that Caleb was going with low-level spells instead of something more powerful.

"God, I'm so sorry, Henry! We tried to get here, but finding everyone…" Alexa said to me as she struggled to free me from the chair.

Everyone, to my surprise, included a tiny Pixie. Ela walked from the Portal too, her focus not on the others but the vampire. Instead of directly fighting him, she hurried around the portal with a bunch of mirrors, redirecting sunlight to trap Roland in his corner.

"It's fine," I said, touching my clouded head. I wheezed as I tried to breathe properly, then I looked at my ring. "Lily…"

The jinn popped into space right next to me, offering me a half-smile. "Hi, Henry. You got to go."

New Quest: Escape!
Your friends have arrived. Now it's time to go.
Time Limit: 00:02:11
Rewards: Freedom. Live for another day.
Failure: More enemies.

Rather than answer her, with both hands free and Alexa working on my feet, I turned to where Bronislav was picking himself off the floor. He'd looked better for sure, the majority of his shirt and jacket burnt off, exposed skin blackened and the stitching around his body torn. One entire flap of skin along his chest had slipped off, exposing blackened internal organs and copper wiring. But for all that damage, Bronislav was moving, dragging a lame foot over to us, the hated crowbar in hand.

I focused on the bar, then on Bronislav's grinning, savage face. And then... and then, my mind blanked. I only came to when I felt Alexa shoving against my shoulder, screaming into my face.

"*Enough, Henry! Enough!*" Alexa's voice was hoarse.

I blinked, and the break in my concentration saw the channeled Mana from my fingers die off. A smell assaulted my nose—not the piss and vomit, the blood that I had spilled, but the burnt smell of fat and skin, of crisped flesh. As Alexa retracted herself from in front of me, I saw the cause.

A burnt husk, a charred corpse. Skin turned to ashes, fat bubbling and organs shriveled, bones and metal wiring glowing. Beside it, the puddled remnants of the crowbar.

"Did I do that?" I said wonderingly.

"We got to go!" Ela screamed, already perched next to the Portal.

Lily was beside me, echoing Ela's words, a big flashing quest marker. I flinched, instinct making me grab and pull Alexa down beside me as my brain caught up with the answer.

Quest Failed: Escape!
Penalty: More Enemies!!!

The door leading to the room blew in. Reinforced wards, already weakened by our entry, were blasted apart. Ela, caught by the blast, was thrown through the opening she had been standing beside. The Portal flickered and slammed shut, the ritual holding it open disrupted on the other side. Caleb, caught by surprise, turned from his attack for a second—only to find the Nun'Yunu'Wi gone by the time he turned back.

As the wind and shattered remnants of the spell blew through all of us but for the jinn, it also destroyed and overturned the numerous mirrors El had laid out. Not that it mattered now that the portal was closed. Hugging Alexa, I rolled with the explosion, feeling barely healed old wounds and new ones bleeding.

Still, I was able to turn aside enough to see the doorway. To note the black hounds charging through only to be torn apart by the freed vampire. The pair of sidhe that strolled in, a pair of assault rifles to their shoulders, searched the room with precise motions, one of them targeting the troll that had finally freed himself and the other bringing its gun to bear on me. It fired immediately, only to have its bullets stopped.

Sidhe Lord (Level 184)

Out of Level attack blocked.

He snarled, stepping aside as he switched targets. "Knights. It's your turn!"

"We're coming, pagan monstrosity."

A quartet of mortal knights came rushing through the door. They had no guns, instead wielding melee weapons, the various sheaths where they carried additional magazines already empty. There was a story there, but one I had no time to learn. Not when Alexa shoved me off and stood, snatching her short spear from the floor and facing the quartet.

"Henry!" Lily called to me, and even through the chaos, I heard the jinn. Through all this, she stood. Untouched. Untouchable. Bullets flew and curved around her. Magic broke against an invisible ward, leaving her and her clothing unstained. "There's more coming."

I closed my eyes, my brain still muddled. The never-ending fire of assault weapons in an enclosed room beat upon my ears, against my chest like the tiny fists of a puppy. The smell of death and decay pervaded the room, my skin and muscles on fire from the repeated attacks. And in their corner, Caleb and the Nun'Yunu'Wi dueled, their magic pressing against that sense too.

It was too much. Too much.

My friends were trying to rescue me. My family. People who had given up time and safety. And I'd failed them, failed to get out when we should have. We were trapped. And I had nothing...

"Kill him. Before he makes a wish."

A spear, thrown at close range, was barely deflected by Alexa. It cut along my arm, tearing open a wound that I did not notice. Alexa, seeing me overwhelmed, fell back and pulled a sphere. She let it drop, and a small dome formed around me. A protective spell, one of Caleb's. Too complicated, wasteful. But still more powerful than anything I could do.

But there was something strange there. Something... I cocked my head as I realized that somehow, I'd heard those words. In all the noise. I'd heard...

Even through the glow of the protective ward, I spotted the jinn. Lily offered me a half-smile.

A wish. Simple.

"I wish..."

What?

I didn't know.

If I knew, I'd have made the wish before. To ask them gone? For what? Another day, another painful few hours. My enemies wanted me dead and would take it out on me and my friends if I wished their deaths. Their destruction. I had no time to come up with anything perfect, anything smart. No time to game the system, to figure out the right wording, the right way to do this. No time...

A wish. A single wish to make everything right. To fix... everything.

It was impossible. It always had been. That was why I'd never made the wish. How could a single wish fix anything? A single action? It can't. Nothing can.

Because the ills of the world, of existence were greater than any single action, any person.

All you can do was hope. And trust. That those around you would do the best they could.

"That you had my wish to use as you see fit, Lily."

A single wish. And trust. That was all there was. That was all there ever was.

Chapter 19

The moment the wish was made, silence spread across the entire battlefield of the room. It was not some weird movie effect, one of those unlikely silences that enveloped a battlefield because the director wanted to showcase an important moment. Lily flexed and suddenly, no one could move. A fraction of a second later, combatants were pulled apart, bullets moving through mid-air fell to the floor with a tinkle of falling rain, and Mana that had been gathering stilled.

"Well. That's enough of that," Lily said, straightening. When the troll tried something, she flicked a hand and squashed it against the wall, where it leaked blood. "Hush. All of you. This is my moment. And I won't have it spoiled."

"Lily?" I said, standing as I looked at the jinn, who seemed so different now.

Lily turned to look at me, no longer looking like a cute but somewhat scared gamer girl but an imperious queen. She was even taller than me now. As I glanced down, I realized why. The jinn was levitating, adding a couple of inches to her height. A snap of her fingers and the hoodie disappeared, as well as the slacks, and a regal gold-and-green gown appeared along with glittering jewelry.

"Much better. You really were slow. But you managed to do it," Lily said, looking at me.

"How—how are you able to do this?" I said, looking at the still-frozen fighters. At Alexa, who was taking the intermission in fighting to bandage her thigh. "You shouldn't be able to do this. The rules—"

"Are made by me. I just bent them," Lily said.

In answer, another notification appeared.

Hidden Quest Completed: Give the Jinn a Wish
Rewards: ???

"What? That's not how that works. You always indicated what the quest rewards are!" I protested.

"Not always. Sometimes rewards are hidden if you haven't completed the prerequisites," Lily snapped at me. For a second, I saw my friend in the imperious supernatural queen, then she was back as she turned toward one of the sidhe that was rubbing at an amulet. "Stop that. It will not work, but it is annoying."

The sidhe stopped, a resigned look in its eyes. "What do you intend to do, jinn?"

"Do? Hmmm… so much. So very much. But I should finish my wish. Then I'll deal with you." Lily turned to me and gestured.

The ring on my finger flew from my hand—taking a little bit of skin with it, such was the force of its movement. The ring hovered next to Lily, glowing before her. Another gesture and the glow expanded, resolving into runic script, the packed-together spell formulas becoming legible as she kept expanding the script. It took up the entire room, and we still had to squint to make out even a portion of the script itself. Considering a single rune could be considered a sentence, the complexity of the enchantment packed into the ring made my head hurt.

"Incredible," Caleb breathed, his eyes flicking as he took in what he could.

"Are you freeing yourself, lady of fire and smoke?" the Nun'Yunu'Wi said, bowing deep from its waist. "It was only what I wanted to do. To free such a magnificent lady."

"Do you know, it's been tried before?" Lily said. "Wishing me free? It was one of the first things my followers tried." There was silence as Lily flicked a finger and a section of the spell formula was highlighted. "But they were smart.

That is one of many things that cannot be wished for. Doing so forces me to end their lives."

The Nun'Yunu'Wi froze at her words while the Knights relaxed a little, the hard tension in their bodies disappearing. Relaxed, because the threat that was the jinn was gone—supposedly. Or at least, her being freed. Though I wondered if they considered—or cared—that their lives might be entirely forfeit at this point.

"What are you going to do?" I said as I hobbled over to Alexa and bent, taking hold of the end of the bandage that she'd been struggling to get wrapped properly.

The ex-Initiate flashed me a smile while I took over, and she found a healing potion in her jacket liner to chug. I focused on the bandage, noting how the blood still leaked. I didn't want to look at Lily, at the person I thought had been my friend. And who now looked or talked nothing like her. Who, I dreaded, might have tricked me.

"Mmmm… I cannot wish myself free. I cannot wish the stone apart. And my powers are still contained by this ring," Lily said, tapping her lips. "It's… annoying. Simple solutions have been blocked off for a long time. But I've had thousands of years to think about it. To test theories. To have other ring bearers try out other options." Lily let the silence grow. "To learn."

For two such innocuous words, they sent a shiver down all our backs.

Lily turned, looking around. Her gaze was distant, as if she was seeing things that I couldn't. "Well. I guess I should sort this out first. Give you your reward."

There was something in her voice that made my eyes widen.

"Stop!" Caleb shouted, lurching forward a half-inch before the spells holding him froze him.

I did not understand what he was screaming about, could not. Until I felt pain all over, all at once. Pain that came not just from my body but from my soul. I screamed, and then my body came apart.

***

I came back to my senses, still screaming, in a clearing, a lookout above the city. I was in the same position, hands splayed as if they were wrapping another person's leg. My chest heaved as I ran out of air, and I drew another breath to scream again. Only to find that I wasn't hurting. Not at all.

"Wha…?" I looked around at the slow-setting sun. At the white, fluffy clouds and the peaceful blue of the sky. The green of the grass, all the greener now after hours of harsh white light in a grey, concrete basement. Smells—normal, human, natural smells. And to my Mana Sense, the deep, deep upwelling of power coming from beneath me as multiple ley lines crossed over one another.

"There. That should do it," Lily said beside me.

I blinked, looking at the jinn. "Lily?"

"Sorry. I'm stretching the rules, but I need to make this wish soon," Lily said. "I've healed you. Your friends are back where they are meant to be. If this fails… well. You should run."

I nodded, knowing she was right. We'd had plans for if we had survived. If the ring was… well. Where was the ring? And then I saw it—around her finger.

"Time to try again," Lily said, raising the hand with the ring on it. The jinn stared at the ring, her voice far away as she contemplated things I could not hope to envision. "The problem with enchantments, no matter how powerful, no matter how smart their creators were, is that they are static. And.

"I.

"Am.

"Not."

Light. A soundless thunder, one that shook my chest and newly healed ear drums. That stole my breath and sent my Mana Senses abuzz. I felt it, the war between her and the ring. Her strength, pitched directly at the ring, changing it. Altering it. Flexing the spell and the enchantment.

I could not tell what it was she did, though I knew she was trying to twist the enchantment itself. Perhaps she was trying to break it, because I felt the strain that what Lily was doing was bringing to reality itself. I felt the power that she drew from the ley lines to assault the ring with, and I felt how it made my senses hurt, how the Mana conduits in my body expanded and soaked up the energy.

Rather than risk being burnt out, knowing I could do little, I retreated. Back and back again, even as Lily lit a beacon to anyone in the world that something momentous, something world-changing was happening.

No surprise that others came. A stray breeze, and a man with an eyepatch on a horse was there. A rumble of earth, and a stone rose. A stone that had hints of someone, something trapped within. The earth rippled, and from a crack that smelled of brimstone, a horned, goat-footed creature walked. Clouds gathered and formed more faces, some with long whiskers and wrinkled brows, another pudgy, long-lobed, and laughing. More. So many more gathered.

Just a single presence was enough to overload my senses. I could not stare at any one of them, could not hear them. Their presence was like a thousand pounds on my chest, forcing me to gasp as I tried to breathe. Tried… and failed.

Then it was gone. A delicate hand was on my shoulder, pushing away the presences. I turned and saw a fair lady clad in white robes who floated on a lotus blossom to place a hand on my shoulder. The smile on her face was kind and gentle, a promise of safety and mercy.

"Thank—thank you," I said once I could breathe again.

"No thanks is required." But as polite as she was, as nice as she was, I could tell her attention was not on me.

So I turned back to the show.

Not a single personage, not a single player moved to interfere. Where Lily stood fighting her battle, none took part. She struggled against the binding that held her still alone. Pitting thousands of years of knowledge against the spell, pitting everything she had against it. Altering rune by rune. Forcing a change. And all the while, the ring glowed and power welled.

For hours she stood there, power welling, the center of attention. Hours where, to mortal eyes, nothing changed. And yet we stood in silent vigil. The sun set, the moon rose, and still she stood.

And then, as suddenly as it had started, the Mana swell disappeared — as did Lily. One moment, she was there, standing by herself, then she was gone. The sudden change made me lurch forward as if a rug had been pulled out from underneath me.

A simultaneous exhalation of relieved tension rose from those around. A few of the personages looked at one another. Some glared. Others grouped up, chatting. Most just disappeared, including the lady who had saved me. I was not surprised. She had much to do. And what she did, she did not do for gratitude.

I stood there. Ringless. Alone. As I reached out to that bundle of power where my character sheet and my party interface was, I found it gone. Empty.

Truly alone then.

Epilogue

"I said no, Caleb." I cradled the phone to my head, while I attempted to juggle the call, my keys, and takeout as I stood before the door to my apartment. My new apartment, one that I'd found after spending over a month looking for.

The door was yanked open, revealing Alexa. She limped back to couch. "Is that Caleb? Tell him no. And I hope you bought extra egg rolls!"

"See? Even Alexa says no. I'm not joining the Council, no matter what they say." I listened to Caleb as I kicked the door closed and walked to the kitchen to drop off the food. "I don't really have that much to show them anyway. Lily left me with the spells she'd given me, but that was it. I don't have any more lost arts to offer." I listened a little more, nodding to his words and rolling my eyes as I sat the takeout boxes down on the kitchen counter. "Yeah, I'll see you Saturday for game night. Byyyye!"

Heaving a sigh of relief, I made sure the call was killed then stuffed the phone back in my front pocket. In short order, I had a pair of heaping plates of food that I carried over to Alexa.

"Think they believe you?" Alexa asked.

"Of course not. But without the ring, I'm just a little more powerful Mage. Not worth actually fighting for." I shrugged and handed Alexa her plate. "So long as I avoid the guys who are still holding a little grudge over who I killed, I should be good. Thankfully, they were all low-Level guys like me."

We ate for a bit, contemplating the fallout right after the fight. There'd been quite a few glares and shouted recriminations, but considering the fact that an all powerful jinn was loose, people had better things to do than throw accusations around. There were defences to raise, people to warn. In the chaos, we'd managed to sneak away.

"Do you miss it?" Alexa asked, raising an eyebrow.

"What? My powers?" I shook my head. "It was fun, playing the game. Making my life a game. But the consequences…" I recalled my family, the shell-shocked look on their faces when I met them. The screaming and tantrums. My father refusing to speak with me because of the way I'd put them all in danger. And my friends – injured, outcast, lost. "I think I like my games virtual."

Alexa gave me a half-smile, a trace of sadness settling around us as we remembered our friend.

"How's the leg?" I asked to change the topic. A few days ago, we'd been running another assignment, taking on a risky hunt for an escaped min-hydra pet. Not only had we been required to find it, we had to return it unharmed. Which meant Alexa had to get close – resulting in the bite. Unfortunately, hydra venom wasn't something you wanted a healing potion on.

"Better. The venom is mostly gone," Alexa said. "Another day and we could probably use a healing potion to fix this."

"Good, good." I nodded.

"You just want me to get back to earning my share."

"Well, we do have a few debts…"

Patching our lives together after the incident meant that we'd had to explain a "gas explosion" in our apartment as well as replace all our belongings. Not surprisingly, our renter's insurance hadn't paid out—what with us disappearing for months after the explosion. If not for some minor tweaking by a few friends, we would be in even worse trouble with the authorities.

As it was, we were just scorned and in debt.

"You okay, Henry?" Alexa said, eyes narrowing.

"I'm fine. Why?"

"You bought enough for three." Alexa pointed at the kitchen.

I turned, staring at the takeout. "No, that's for… after."

"Uh huh," Alexa said.

Thankfully she decided not to pursue the matter. Not as if we hadn't had this talk before. In strained silence, we focused on dinner. It was part habit – buying enough for three – and part… hope? Wish? It was a fool's hope.

***

Starlight twinkled as it entered our window, playing across the coffee table. In her bedroom, Alexa slept, thanks to the drugs for the pain from the wound that refused to heal fully. I sat in the living room, a hand caressing the gaming laptop. The one I'd bought a week ago and I'd never even cracked open.

"Stupid. It's just a game…" I swore at myself, fed up, and finally cracked it open. I tapped the power button and sat back, watching the computer boot up. Watched it get ready.

A feeling of dread, of fear washed over me. And even as it asked me to input a password, I reached forward to slam it shut.

"Hey! I was playing that."

"No, you're not. I don't even have any games downloaded," I retorted automatically. And then froze.

Slowly, I turned sideways to see a familiar figure seated beside me. A figure in a hoodie and jeans, brown hair escaping around the raised hood. A mocking half-smile on her face and a familiar ring on her hand.

"Hey, Henry. Long time no see."

###

The End

Author's Note

Ending this series was a bittersweet experience. I kind of knew this as going to happen, ever since I wrote the first book. Many of the events changed on me, the timing and the format, but the ending – with Lily being freed was always going to happen.

This is my first series that I've ever written 'The End' for. First series to put to bed, to set aside. Are there stories still in this universe? Yes. But, this is a good place to let Henry, Lily and Alexa stay. At least for a while.

I learnt a lot writing this series. A Gamer's Wish first released in March 2018. It's been nearly two years since then, and it's been a learning experience as I have written and developed more. Henry's story came from a single question – what happens when a gamer gets a magic ring and wishes for magic? Some characters, well, they made themselves known with a spearpoint and just refused to leave. Others faded away off, their part played. But the series and the characters will live on.

Really, I'm not sure what else to say but I hope you enjoyed the series. It was fun writing and one day, if enough people ask for it, I might write a sequel.

In the meantime, I have other series including my A Thousand Li (my cultivation xianxia series), the Adventures on Brad (a more traditional LitRPG fantasy) and the System Apocalypse (a post-apocalyptic scifi-fantasy LitRPG). Book one of each series follow:

- A Thousand Li (a cultivation series inspired by Chinese wuxia and xianxia novels)
  https://readerlinks.com/l/729231

- A Healer's Gift (Book 1 of the Adventures on Brad)
https://readerlinks.com/l/729327
- Life in the North (An Apocalyptic LitRPG)
https://readerlinks.com/l/729295

For more great information about LitRPG series, check out the Facebook groups:

- Gamelit Society
https://www.facebook.com/groups/LitRPGsociety/

- LitRPG Books
https://www.facebook.com/groups/LitRPG.books/

About the Author

Tao Wong is an avid fantasy and sci-fi reader who spends his time working and writing in the North of Canada. He's spent way too many years doing martial arts of many forms and having broken himself too often, now spends his time writing about fantasy worlds.

If you'd like to support him directly, Tao now has a Patreon page where previews of all his new books can be found!
https://www.patreon.com/taowong

For updates on the series and the author's other books (and special one-shot stories), please visit his website: http://www.mylifemytao.com

Subscribers to Tao's mailing list will receive exclusive access to short stories in the Thousand Li and System Apocalypse universes:
https://www.subscribepage.com/taowong

Or visit his Facebook Page:
https://www.facebook.com/taowongauthor/

About the Publisher

Starlit Publishing is wholly owned and operated by Tao Wong. It is a science fiction and fantasy publisher focused on the LitRPG & cultivation genres. Their focus is on promoting new, upcoming authors in the genre whose writing challenges the existing stereotypes while giving a rip-roaring good read.

For more information on Starlit Publishing, visit their website: https://www.starlitpublishing.com/

You can also join Starlit Publishing's mailing list to learn of new, exciting authors and book releases.
https://starlitpublishing.com/newsletter-signup/